A shadow crossed her, then something fell on her from above.

Her sword flew from her hand as a Wolf's weight flung her back, and she sprawled, helpless, under the creature's hot reeking body. She twisted. The Wolf's teeth missed her throat by a fraction, snapping the air by her cheek. Ozkar went down on his haunches under their weight.

Still in the saddle, Wynter felt the Wolf's hind claws rake her belly as he tried to gut her. Her many layers of clothes saved her from immediate evisceration, but her jacket fell open with a gasp of torn fabric and she knew that the next raking pass of his feet would expose her guts to the air. She fumbled for her knife with one hand and shoved frantically with the other, trying to push him off. He reared back, half-wolf, half-man, and glared down at her with his not-quite-human eyes.

Praise for
The Poison Throne

"Atmospheric, complex, and intense…"

—*Publishers Weekly (Starred Review)*

"A spectacular fantasy by a prolific, creative and multi-talented artist and author." —*The Anglo Celt*

By Celine Kiernan

The Moorehawke Trilogy
The Poison Throne
The Crowded Shadows
The Rebel Prince

The Rebel Prince

Book 3 of
The Moorehawke Trilogy

CELINE KIERNAN

www.orbitbooks.net

Orbit
Hachette Book Group
237 Park Avenue, New York, NY 10017
www.HachetteBookGroup.com

First North American Edition: October 2010
First published in Ireland in 2010 by The O'Brien Press Ltd.
12 Terenure Road East, Rathgar, Dublin 6, Ireland

Orbit is an imprint of Hachette Book Group, Inc. The Orbit name and
logo are trademarks of Little, Brown Book Group Limited.

Library of Congress Control Number: 2010932992

10 9 8 7 6 5 4 3 2 1

Printed in the United States of America

For Mam and Dad, I love you.
To Noel, Emmet and Grace, always and with all my heart.
To Angela Oelke (Moore) and Ellen "Sam" Samberg
who have been my unfailingly honest friends
and supporters from beginning to end.

Contents

The Rebel Prince

The Scarlet Ford

When Wynter was five, her father dressed her in a little red coat, put her on the back of his horse, and took her on a picnic. Wynter remembered the drowsy movement of the horse beneath her, and leaning back into the warm support of her father as they travelled the forest paths. She remembered his strong arms encompassing her as he held the reins, the scent of woodshavings and resin from his clothes. She remembered the light coming through the foliage, and how it had moved across her hands, so small on the big leather pommel of Lorcan's saddle.

Lorcan's friend, Jonathon, had been with them, and his sons, Razi and Alberon. All of them were happy, and laughing, which was something they seemed to do quite often back then. Just two friends and their beloved children out for a jaunt on a warm autumn day, getting the best of the good weather before winter finally tightened its grip. Looking back on it, Wynter knew there must have been some kind of military presence with them, but she had no recollection of soldiers or any kind of guards. Perhaps she was so used to the presence of soldiers around her father's good friend that she no longer noticed them. She never thought of Jonathon as "the King" back then. She recalled only thinking of him as Jon, that big, golden-headed man, so quick to lose his temper but just as quick to show affection. He had been best friend to her own father, and father to her two best friends, those brothers of her heart: the dark, serious, protective Razi, and the grinningly impulsive, loving Alberon.

Razi had kept trotting on ahead, his brown face all alight at the unexpected freedom of the day. Alberon was for the first time astride his own horse, and Wynter remembered watching with amused envy as he urged the little creature on, attempting to keep pace with his older half-brother. She recalled him calling anxiously across the sun-dappled air, "Razi! Razi! Don't leave me!" and Razi's smile as he turned back to wait.

They had stopped at a ford, and the men had stripped to their underthings and run into the shallow water, whooping and splashing and laughing at the cold. Wynter had hopped from foot to foot on the edge of the water, watching as Alberon threw himself into his father's arms. Jon had flung him high into the sunshine, Albi's small face luminous with sun-glitter and joy.

A warm presence by her side, and she had looked up into Razi's smiling face.

"Come on, darling." He had offered his hand. "It's only cold for a moment." He led her carefully into the stream, her hand held tight in his, then her father had waded over and hoisted them, one under each water-chilled arm, and carried them out into the bright water to teach them how to swim.

Almost eleven years later, Wynter Moorehawke sat on the warm, smooth-pebbled beach of a similar ford and listened to the furtive rustling of the surrounding forest. Half her mind was on the unintelligible conversation of the Merron warriors who sat on the rocks to her right, the other half on the forest shadows and all the lurking possibilities they might contain.

Down by the water's edge, the now twenty-year-old Razi crouched on his haunches and frowned out across the shallow water. For a blissful moment it seemed as though he might actually relax and sit down, but Wynter knew that he was unlikely to stay still for long. Sure enough, the dark young man almost immediately ran his hands through his hair, sighed in frustration, and rose, once again, to his feet.

Do not start pacing, thought Wynter, but Razi, of course, did just that.

His lanky silhouette stalked out of sight at the corner of her eye, then stalked right back in again, just as quick, and Wynter had to turn her head so that she wouldn't be driven mad by his ceaseless prowling. Since Embla's death, a deep and angry river of impatience ran very close to Razi's surface, and it manifested itself in constant, irritating motion. Wynter felt genuine sympathy for Razi's loss, but just at that moment, the crunch, crunch, crunch of his footsteps on the pebble shore was grating on her already stretched nerves. She tightened her jaw against the urge to snap at him.

An irritated sigh drifted across from the group of warriors. "Tabiyb," rumbled Úlfnaor, "sit down before I take back of my sword to your head." Razi glowered and the black-haired Merron leader frowned. "*Sit*," he ordered. "You wear me out." Razi sat, and Úlfnaor nodded in approval. "They be back soon," he said. "You take this time to rest."

The big man sounded calm, but even as he spoke, his dark eyes roamed the far bank with restless anxiety. His warriors sat tensely around him, the three women sharpening their swords, the three men staring at the trees on the other side of the ford. They had set out that morning expecting to make contact with Alberon and to engage him in diplomatic talks, so men and women alike were magnificently dressed in the pale green embroidered tunics and britches of the Merron formal costume, their arms and hands and necks heavy with silver tribal jewellery. But the day had grown old with no contact from the Rebel Prince, and evening was fast approaching. Wynter was beginning to fear that they had been misled.

She met the eye of the Merron healer, Hallvor. The sinewy woman smiled reassuringly, but Wynter could see the tension in her face. Úlfnaor's two giant warhounds were snuffling about at the water's edge. They looked up as Hallvor rose to her feet. She sheathed her sword as she made her way to the shore, and the dogs wagged their tails, hoping for action. But Hallvor just laid a callused hand on each of their wiry heads and stood watching the trees on the other side. She murmured unhappily in Merron. Úlfnaor answered in soothing tones.

Wynter wished that Christopher was here, and not just because she wanted him to translate. She frowned across the water, willing him to return. Behind her, the gravel crunched as Razi began to move about once again. His long shadow fell across Wynter and he hunkered by her side, his elbows on his knees, his eyes on the far bank.

"I do not think we will be lucky here either," he said quietly.

Wynter nodded. Since early morning, the Merron had been making their way along this river, stopping at prearranged rendezvous points, waiting for Alberon's men to show up and guide them to the rebel camp. This was the fourth such designated meeting place and it, like all the others, had proved deserted. They had been waiting for well over an hour now, but still Úlfnaor was loath to move on. Apparently if this rendezvous proved a wash-out, there was only one remaining point at which they could hope to meet their guides. If that, too, proved deserted, then the Merron's diplomatic mission would be a failure. The Northern warriors would have to return to their homeland with their duty unfulfilled, and Razi, Wynter and Christopher would be no closer to finding Alberon's camp than they had been almost three weeks previously.

"Chris and Sól have been away too long," murmured Wynter.

Razi just sighed and rubbed his face. He did not bother to reply. He'd heard enough of this from her, but Wynter didn't care. She was prickly with anxiety. There were less than four hours of daylight left, and she wanted Christopher where she could see him. She wanted him by her side, not out in the woods where the Loups-Garous might be prowling and where the King's men were still actively hunting the rebels.

"Úlfnaor should never have allowed Chris and Sól out there alone," she said. "Reconnoitre be damned! Truth be told, I think he let them go just to shut the two of them up and give them something to do."

Razi huffed in agreement. Christopher was an incorrigibly reckless fellow at the best of times, and as for Sólmundr—since the loss of his beloved Ashkr, the Merron warrior seemed possessed of a dangerous, unquenchable kind of restlessness. He and Christopher seemed to spark each other off, and both were champing at the bit, longing for action. They had set off into the forest with far too much enthusiasm and far too little caution for Wynter's liking. She wished they would come back. Even with Sólmundr's warhound, Boro, by their side, she feared her two friends were horribly vulnerable out there.

Wynter was opening her mouth to say so, when down by the river's edge, Hallvor and the warhounds suddenly came to attention. Frowning, the healer took a step forward, her eyes on the trees. The warhounds growled, and Hallvor gestured sharply to quiet them.

Razi and Wynter rose to their feet. On the rocks, the other Merron stood up, swords in hand.

"*Cad é, a Hallvor?*" asked Úlfnaor.

Hallvor shushed him, her attention fixed ahead. Then she pointed into the trees.

"Coinín," she said. "*Agus é ag rith.*"

It was Christopher, running soundless and very fast through the trees, his long, black hair flying behind him, his slim arms and legs pumping. He burst into the sunlight and crossed the shallow ford in a glitter of splashing footsteps. Boro and Sólmundr came racing after.

"Quick!" hissed Christopher. "Someone's coming, and they ain't no diplomatic party!"

The Merron spun for their horses, but Sólmundr called them back. He ran straight up the rocks and flung himself on the weapons pile, snatching up his longbow and arrows. His companions swerved to join him and he began hissing breathless explanations as they loaded up.

Christopher's grey eyes met Wynter's as he slid to a halt at her side.

"No time to run," he said. "Make a stand! They're right behind us."

She drew her sword. "How many?"

"Have I time to load the matchlock?" asked Razi.

Christopher shook his head to both questions. "No idea how many, don't even think they know we're here. But they're heading straight for us and they're in a damned big hurry. No time for the gun, Razi. Just draw your swords, the two of you, and stay behind the archers."

Sólmundr shouted, and Christopher spun just in time to catch the crossbow which the warrior had flung to him. Christopher's quiver of black bolts came sailing after, and Wynter caught it one-handed while Christopher pulled the lever to draw his bow. She handed him a bolt. He loaded the bow as he spun to face the ford and Wynter stepped to his side, her sword in hand.

Sólmundr shook his sandy hair from his eyes and drew his longbow, sighting on the trees. The Merron spread out along the beach, their longbows at the ready, their warhounds standing in disciplined silence at their sides. The wood and leather of the longbows creaked as the warriors put just enough tension on the strings to keep the arrows in place, not yet expending their energies on a full draw. The buzzing quiet of the autumn evening settled around them as they waited.

Christopher nestled the crossbow into the hollow of his shoulder. He settled his stance. "Here they come," he whispered. Wynter could hear them now, coming up fast. So different to Christopher's earlier silent approach, this was the noise of someone smashing heedlessly through the heavy forest. It was the sound of someone panicked, someone desperate. The Merron pulled their longbows to full draw and levelled their aim.

The man who crashed through the trees didn't register them. He came staggering from the shade into the sunlight and splashed halfway across the bright water without even noticing the row of imposing warriors standing on the far bank, tracking him with their arrows. His head was down, his arms wrapped around his belly, and all his energies seemed taken with simply putting one foot in front of the other.

"Hold!" cried Wynter. "You hold now!"

The man spun in response to her voice and staggered to a halt. Once his forward momentum deserted him, he seemed to lose his ability to stand and he immediately dropped to his knees and collapsed face first into the shallow river. The water around him instantly turned red.

There was a moment of stunned silence as the company watched the man's blood swirl and spread and trail away in dark ribbons from his body. Then Razi threw his sword aside with a clatter and waded into mid stream to roll the man onto his back.

Wynter had assumed the poor fellow to be unconscious, but as soon as Razi lifted his face from the water the man took a gasping breath and clutched Razi's coat with a bloody fist.

"Help me," he rasped. "Help me..." His half-opened eyes were on the Merron, who had switched their aim back to the trees and were dividing their attention between the newcomer and whoever might appear in pursuit of him.

Razi began to heave the fellow up and Wynter ran to help him. Christopher splashed out after her. Without dropping his guard, he circled around in front of her and Razi, his crossbow aimed at the far bank.

"Get yourselves behind the archers," he ordered roughly.

"Cavalry... cavalry..." moaned the wounded man as they dragged him to shore. "Escape... the Prince."

Razi met Wynter's eyes across the top of the man's head as they laid him on the warm stones of the beach. "You are a member of the King's cavalry?" he murmured, turning the man over, and opening his jacket to check his injuries. Wynter winced at the sight of a pulsing wound in the poor fellow's side. She had to look away from the mess of exposed bone and bulging organs.

"I will fetch your medical bag," she said.

But Razi shook his head, his face grim, and Wynter knew there was nothing that could be done.

Razi leant close. "You are a member of the cavalry?" he repeated gently.

"Yes...no...not...they're after me. Oh *Jesu*, help me..."
The man began trying to crawl away, his bloody hands scrabbling on the smooth stones, his face twisted in pain. Blood
pumped in horrible quantities from his wound and pooled on
the rocks around him.

"Shhh," said Wynter, laying her hand on his face. "Lie easy...
lie easy, friend." The man stilled, and rested his head on the
stones with a moan. "Who pursues you?" she asked.

"The cavalry...the cavalry...the King's men..."

Wynter glanced at Razi. *The King's men.*

"You work for my brother," said Razi softly.

The man looked up into Razi's dark face for the first time,
and his eyes widened in fear. "Oh God help me," he whispered.
"You're the Arab." He moaned and closed his eyes. "Oh, I am
lost."

"My father's men pursue you?" asked Razi. "You seek the
safety of the rebel camp?"

"The Lord Razi is hoping to meet his brother at the rebel
camp," whispered Wynter. "He wishes to reconcile him to the
King. We can take you to safety, if you will but show us the way
to the Prince." But the man just turned his face into the stones,
convinced now that he was amongst enemies, determined to
speak no more.

"Razi," said Christopher, glancing back at his friend. "The
Merron cannot allow the King's men to take them."

Sólmundr and Úlfnaor looked over their shoulders at Razi.
The rest of the Merron, unable to understand this conversation,
kept aim on the trees, but their eyes flicked anxiously between
their leaders and the dark-skinned man they'd sworn to
protect.

"*Razi*," insisted Christopher, "if your father's men arrive, we *must* fire on them! Else you are condemning these people to death—and your mission is failed."

Razi shook his head and would not lift his eyes from the wounded man.

Wynter laid a hand on his arm. She looked up into Christopher's pained face.

"The King's men will kill us, lass," said Christopher. "We must fight them or die; there ain't no way around it."

"Others is coming!" cried Sólmundr, and Wynter leapt to her feet at the sounds of riders approaching fast through the trees. She weighed her sword in her hand and stepped to Christopher's side again, her heart hammering with anger and with fear. Dear God, had it truly come to this? Must she now face loyal soldiers of the crown and kill them or die?

The Merron ordered their dogs to heel, and once again pulled their longbows to full draw. A flash of sun on metal showed through the shifting leaves of the forest as dark shapes advanced upon them. Úlfnaor, his huge arms quivering with the strain, held his aim and murmured softly to his warriors. He was obviously telling them, "Wait . . . wait . . ."

Wynter crouched low. She brought her sword up. She had made up her mind that she would not die here. She would *not* die!

Christopher looked back at Razi, wanting his permission to fire.

Razi bowed his head, his eyes squeezed shut. Then he snatched his sword, rose to his feet and stood ready at Christopher's side. Christopher took aim just as the King's soldiers burst through the trees.

There were only two of them, and they entered the ford with an almost childlike abandon. Wynter knew that she would never forget the looks on their faces when, expecting nothing more than a wounded soldier fleeing on foot, they suddenly found themselves confronted with a row of hard-faced archers.

There was just a brief moment of suspension, the smallest fraction of time, then the youngest soldier grabbed for his sword. Christopher's crossbow bolt took him between his eyes and carried him backwards from his horse. All other sound was buried in the heavy *twock* of longbows, and the hiss and thud of Merron arrows seeking and finding their target. The soldiers' limp bodies tumbled to the water with mighty splashes. Their blood washed downstream just as the rebel soldier's had done.

Wynter's sword-arm dropped to her side and she watched the King's men die.

The magnificent cavalry horses staggered under a second hail of missiles. They fell, and their blood mingled with that of their riders, eddying out into the clear water to flood the river with scarlet. The stain rapidly filled the ford, swirling and flowing, and stretching its arms outwards until it lapped in bright, sun-dappled wavelets on the shore and coloured the heedless stones at Wynter's feet.

Behind her, Razi turned from this spectacle of death, and knelt, once again, by the rebel soldier's side. Wynter watched as he closed the poor fellow's lifeless eyes. For the briefest of moments Christopher stayed at Wynter's side, his arm a sympathetic warmth around her waist. Then he splashed out into the scarlet ford and began to help the Merron harvest their fallen arrows.

The Rebel Camp Alone

It was very late in the evening, the forest shadows already deepening to gloom, when Christopher pulled his mare to a halt on the path ahead, blocking Wynter's way. He cursed softly under his breath. Alarmed, Wynter urged her own horse up the narrow space between them, and reined in at Christopher's side. She peered through the foliage to see what had disturbed him. Around them, the air filled with the snort of horses and the irritated jangle of tack as the rest of the Merron riders came to a stop. There were mutterings and low exclamations of concern.

Leaning forward to get a better view, Wynter felt her heart sink. Only six or so feet ahead, the trees ended abruptly, and the safety of their cover gave way to a wide patch of rocky ground—a break of perhaps twenty yards between this section of dense forest and the next. The open ground stretched away on either side, a long spine of rock cleaving the forest in two for as far as she could see from her limited perspective.

"Oh Christopher, this is not good."

Christopher nodded in agreement. "We'll be vulnerable as babes if we cross here."

Wynter glanced to the head of the travel party where Razi had prime position next to Úlfnaor and Sól. All three were gazing out across the gap with similar expressions of concern.

"I not like it," said Sólmundr quietly. "It feel bad. We should to go around."

Úlfnaor exchanged a look with Razi, who curtly shook his head. "I say we cross."

The Aoire nodded. "Then we cross," he said. "Wari, Coinín, Soma and Frangok will to watch our back while we pass over. Then follow when all is well." At Sólmundr's disapproving look, Úlfnaor sighed. "Time grow short, Sól. We not risk changing our route. We trust judgement of Tabiyb. We cross *here*."

Sólmundr glowered at Razi, who kept his eyes ahead, his face devoid of expression as he waited. After a moment, Sólmundr grunted his reluctant assent. Commands were given in Merron, and the guarding party drew their bows.

Wynter met Christopher's eyes as he loaded his crossbow.

"I'm warning you, lass," he said solemnly. "If we get to the other side with no holes in us, I'm stealing seven Protector Lady Moorehawke kisses."

He looked so sure of himself, so gravely confident and alive, that Wynter had to reach across the gap between their horses and take a fistful of his tunic. Smiling slightly, he let her pull him close, and she pressed her lips to his, hard and fierce and protective. They stayed together at the kiss's ending, their foreheads touching, their eyes half-closed.

"You stay safe," she whispered.

"If I do, you'll owe me six more of those."

She smiled. "Come across in one piece, Freeman, and I may just grant you more than kisses."

His cheeks dimpled as his own smile grew. "So many promises to keep," he murmured.

They kissed again, the horses shifting beneath them. Then Wynter drew away, covered her face, and, without looking back, pulled into formation with the advance party as they urged their horses into the glare of the late evening sun.

Glad to be free of the claustrophobic forest, the warhounds bounded ahead of their masters, their tongues lolling, their great tails lashing the air with joy. The Merron kept their eyes on them. When, halfway across the clearing, the enormous creatures abruptly stopped their happy exploring and froze, Úlfnaor immediately lifted his arm, and the advance party brought their mounts to a wary halt.

The warhounds lowered their heads, their attention focused on the forest ahead. Suddenly Boro howled and leapt forward, barking wildly at the trees. The other hounds followed suit.

Spooked by the dog's violent barking, Wynter's horse threw his head and tried to turn back. Wynter sat down hard in the saddle.

"Hold easy, Ozkar!" she hissed.

Out of sight in the trees ahead, another horse whickered in fear, and Wynter scanned the shadows, searching for the riders she now knew were hidden there.

At Úlfnaor's command, the warhounds came reluctantly to stand by the horses, where they milled in place, still barking. The noise was deafening.

"*Ciúnas!*" yelled Sólmundr, and the dogs instantly ceased their baying. Whining, they paced before their masters, their eyes fixed on the dark trees.

The forest ahead remained silent, the shadows impenetrable to Wynter's sun-blasted eyes. All around her, the Merron sat in tense expectation. She had no doubt that at that very moment, hidden in the trees behind her, Christopher was drawing the lever on his crossbow. She resisted the urge to look back over her shoulder and tried not to imagine the whine of arrows flying through the air, nor the dull thud of them hitting home. She forced the memory of blood-laden water and dead bodies from her mind, and inhaled the breeze for the telltale scent of slow-match. There was none. Good. At least no one in the trees was aiming a cannon at them. That was some small mercy.

To her right, Razi ducked his head and discreetly pulled his scarf higher on his face. Wynter blessed the glaring sunshine that had caused them all to tug their hats low, and the swarms of flies that made covering their faces seem less furtive. When Razi again straightened in his saddle, she was pleased to see that the combination of hat shadow and scarf made it impossible to distinguish his dark skin. In his borrowed green cloak and with his remarkable height, her friend looked just like any other Merron warrior. Wynter hoped that her own lack of stature would not be too obvious.

A whistle cut the air, and Wynter's heart leapt as she recognised the signal Alberon's allies used to identify each other. Úlfnaor whistled the correct reply. There was a moment's silence from the trees, then a cultured voice called out in Southlandast.

"So far?"

The first part of Alberon's password! Could they finally have reached their goal?

Úlfnaor called out the reply. "And not yet there?"

A rider detached himself from the shadows of the forest and brought his nervous horse to a halt by the huge boulder that edged the top of the path. He dipped his hat against the sunshine and squinted at the prowling dogs. The man wore no uniform, but his tack and weaponry were military issue and he rode a cavalry horse, which he handled well, despite it being white-eyed and skittish in the presence of the hounds. Wynter had no doubt that he was an officer of Jonathon's army. She regarded him coolly from under the brim of her hat. An officer of Jonathon's army, out of uniform and siding with Alberon against the King. How was she meant to feel about that?

The words *treacherous cur* sprang readily to mind, but then Wynter thought of the dead soldiers at the river. Their blood mingling in the water, their loyalties split on either side of the royal divide. Each had been as certain as the others of where their duty lay. Each was as irretrievably dead. She forced her animosity down. *Let us see what explanations this evening brings*, she thought.

Úlfnaor threw back his hat, allowing his long dark hair to fall across his shoulders. He shrugged back his cloak, revealing his tribal bracelets. Sólmundr drew his horse to his leader's side and he too threw back his hat, shook loose his sandy hair, and bared his arms. For a terrible moment, Wynter thought that all the Merron would follow suit. But Hallvor and the red-headed brothers kept their faces covered and their hats on. Razi's differences remained hidden.

Úlfnaor called out in his broken Hadrish. "I Úlfnaor, *Aoire an Domhain*, diplomatic envoy for Royal Princess, Marguerite Shirken of Northlands. I bring paper destined for Royal Prince, Alberon Kingsson. I seek safe passage to his camp."

The officer tore his attention from the bristling warhounds and regarded Úlfnaor closely. Then his gaze moved from rider to rider on the trail before him. Wynter stiffened as his eyes came to Razi, but the officer paid no more heed to her friend than to any of the others, and when it came to her turn, he passed over Wynter without pause. He turned once more to Úlfnaor, and addressed him in excellent Hadrish.

"You have men in the trees," he observed.

"As does you," said Úlfnaor.

The officer huffed. "Quite the travel party for a common messenger," he said.

There was a moment's silence from Úlfnaor. When he next spoke, his voice was laden with warning. "I *diplomatic envoy*," he said. "I *High Lord* of the Merron Peoples, entrusted by Royal Princess of Northland's peoples for to aid in her negotiations."

Wynter eyed the officer carefully. Unless Alberon was running an intolerably sloppy camp, this man would have detailed instructions as to the treatment of each visitor: his attitude to Úlfnaor should be a calculatedly accurate reflection of the Prince's.

"Do forgive me," he murmured dryly. "No offence meant."

Wynter did not like his tone. Úlfnaor regarded him coldly and did not reply.

The officer gestured over his shoulder, and another horseman emerged from the trees. "My lieutenant will accompany you to camp. By order of his Royal Highness Prince Alberon, you are granted safe passage. You may call your hidden guard to your side."

Úlfnaor did no more than incline his head, and instantly the path behind Wynter came alive with the thud of hooves and the jangle of tack as the others emerged from hiding. She felt a rider draw close to her left side, their horse snorting and shaking its head. She glanced sideways. It was Christopher, his face covered, his eyes fixed on the trees.

At a nod from his superior, the lieutenant wheeled his horse about and the travel party followed as he led the way into the forest.

It took a moment for her eyes to adjust to the gloom, and when they did, Wynter was startled to find that they were surrounded by soldiers. Fifteen or twenty well-armed horsemen flanked the path, watching in silence as the Merron guided their horses through their ranks.

When the travellers had passed, half the soldiers turned their mounts to face the clearing. The other half began to follow the Merron, silently shadowing their progress through the trees. Wynter took careful note of their positions and weaponry, then she focused her attention to keeping track of the route.

They travelled upwards, the ground steepening sharply, the forest thickening so that the Merron found themselves strung out in vulnerable single file. The soldiers guarding them were nothing but stealthy shadows in the gloom; the man leading them, silent and removed. Light fell in heavy pillars through the trees and Wynter noticed that it kept changing direction: first slanting in from the right, it would seem to swing around slowly to the left, then gradually back to the right again. *We are being led in circles*, she thought. She looked behind her, taking in the depth of the shadows, the impenetrable nature of the forest. They would never find their way back through this. Not without a guide.

Christopher was riding behind her. He was slouched casually in his saddle, apparently paying little heed to his surroundings. But, just as Wynter was about to face front again, she saw him reach to his left and break a passing branch. It was a barely perceptible movement, but it left the branch hanging at an angle, pointed back the way they had come. Christopher met her startled gaze, and his eyes creased into an unmistakably sly grin.

Eyes wide, Wynter turned forwards in the saddle. A few moments later, Sólmundr kicked out his left leg, and his boot scored a mark into the bark of a nearby tree. Up ahead, Hallvor ducked under an overhang. As she pushed it out of her way, the end of the branch got bent in two somehow; the broken piece happened to point back in the direction they had come.

After a calculated moment, Wynter glanced back once more at Christopher. He winked at her. Wynter grinned and turned to face front. These people would have no trouble finding their way home, whether Alberon wanted them to or not.

They cleared the trees suddenly and were confronted with a sturdy earthworks barricade. A squad of men stared down at them from atop its walls, crossbows at the ready, and the party found themselves neatly caught between these guards and the silent body of horsemen who had accompanied them through the trees.

Without a word, Alberon's lieutenant trotted past the sentry point and disappeared into the camp beyond. The Merron were left to jostle for position in the cramped space, the guards eyeing them with impassive curiosity. Wynter pushed Ozkar through the crowd and brought him neck to neck with Razi's mare.

Razi was staring through the gap in the barricade, and Wynter peered past him, trying to get a good look at Alberon's camp. It seemed exceedingly well situated. Occupying a rising slope, a stream at its foot, a shaley cliff at its back, it was not only easily defended, it was also a position that could be easily fled, should the need arise.

"Clever man," murmured Razi.

Wynter nodded in agreement. Clever man indeed. Albi had chosen well.

She glanced at the soldiers on the barricade. They seemed well fed and highly disciplined; not at all what one would expect from a ragged band of rebels fleeing the King's wrath. It would appear that her childhood friend had grown into an excellent leader.

Turning her attention back to the camp, Wynter found what she was looking for on the high ground furthest from the gates: a square tent, bigger than the rest and set apart from the others, its only ornamentation the royal pennant that flew from its centre pole. She stared at it, as if her will alone could make Alberon appear from its canvas depths.

The lieutenant returned and drew his horse into the gap. "You must disarm," he said to Úlfnaor. "Tell your people to fix all their weapons to their saddles. You shall be permitted to ride through the camp, but once at the royal quarters, you must dismount."

At Úlfnaor's nod, Sólmundr translated this and the Merron began to disarm. Christopher and Wynter drew their horses to either side of Razi, shielding him as best they could from the soldiers' view, and they too began divesting themselves of their weapons.

"I hope they do not take it in mind to search us," murmured Christopher, lashing his katar to his saddlebag. "I doubt our brown lad here will pass muster as a pale lord of the North."

"Aye," agreed Wynter, watching the lieutenant.

At any minute she expected him to order that they uncover their faces and spread their arms for a search. But once the Merron had safely secured their weaponry, the lieutenant simply wheeled his horse around and led the way into the camp.

Wynter turned to Razi in astonishment, and he looked at her across the top of his scarf, his brown eyes wide. They were to be let through? Just like that?

The Merron began to make their slow and stately progress through the gap in the earthworks, but Razi and Wynter continued to hesitate. The only contact they'd had with Alberon since this whole thing began was the assassins that he had apparently sent to end Razi's life. What kind of reception could either of them expect here, and what would he be like, this boy they had both loved, now a man they knew nothing of?

Christopher drew his horse close. He looked at Razi. "Well, come on then," he said dryly. "It's a mite late to turn back now."

Razi let out a breath, long and slow. Then he straightened his shoulders, pulled his hat low to hide his face further, and urged his horse though the barricades and into his brother's camp.

Alberon

They were led straight through the heart of the camp, heading for the large tent which was almost certainly Alberon's quarters. Wynter regarded her surroundings with wary admiration. This was no slow moving royal entourage, top-heavy with luxuries and cumbersome with staff. This was a lightweight, cleverly ordered military encampment. It had an air of disciplined flexibility to it, and she was sure that the entire settlement could be packed up and spirited away within an hour. There was a feeling of solid authority here, and Wynter had to admit she was impressed.

To the left of the main thoroughfare—surrounded by soldiers' tents and right under the watchful eye of the royal quarters—was a line of civilian shelters. Wynter saw the brightly coloured domes of the Haunardii *yurts*; she saw tents painted with Combermen icons, and a pale blue pavilion tent decorated with unicorns and other Midlander fripperies. She eyed these quarters with heightened unease. Haun, Midlander and Combermen. Representatives of the kingdom's three greatest adversaries, come here to negotiate with Alberon behind his father's back. It was difficult to believe there was any good explanation for that.

The Merron travelled through the camp in stately formation, Úlfnaor and Sólmundr taking the lead. The two High Lords kept their heads and their arms bare, as was the Merron tradition, but in defence to Razi, the rest of the People kept their faces covered, their cloaks loosely hiding their rich clothes. Their sturdy Merron horses stepped as lightly as any trained Arabian, their giant warhounds trotting alongside with courtly discipline and disdain. Wynter did not think that any royal entourage could have looked more majestic.

News of their arrival trickled through the camp, and amongst the military tents, soldiers paused in their work to stare. Men ducked from doors, people ran around corners to get a look. In the civilian quarters, two Combermen stood in the shade of their awning, watching the newcomers with suspicion. As the Merron drew near, one of the Combermen glowered at the pagan symbols painted on their horses, crossed himself and spat.

There were no Haun to be seen, and their quarters seemed lifeless, the bright felt shelters heavy and motionless in the evening light.

Something caught Wynter's eye, a dark figure moving through the military tents. She leaned discreetly back to get a better view, then startled at the unexpected sight of a Midlander priest wending his way through the camp, a bowl in his hands. He cut a path between the tents and came out onto the thoroughfare ahead of the Merron party. He did not seem to notice the new arrivals, and Wynter saw him duck his cowled head at the low door of the blue pavilion tent and pass inside. She shuddered. As part of his diplomatic duties, Wynter's father had been forced to spend no small amount of time in the Midlander court. It had left Wynter with some horrible memories of Midlander priests and their all too eager role in the inquisitions there.

She glanced at Razi, regally astride his gleaming black mare, his attention on the silently waiting royal quarters. Soldiers were crowding the edge of the road now, unwittingly closing in on him.

Unconsciously, Wynter's hand dropped to the empty belt on her hip.

At her side, Christopher chuckled. "I keep reaching too," he murmured. Up ahead of them, they saw Wari's sword hand creep to his own hip, then jerk back as he remembered his empty scabbard. "We look so sure of ourselves," said Christopher, "when we're naught but ducks walking on ice."

They were led to the base of the incline that led to the royal quarters, and the lieutenant signalled for them to halt. There was a moment of breathless anticipation, the Merron staring upwards, the jangle of tack and the breathy sighs of the horses the only sounds. At the top of the slope, the white canvas of the royal tent snapped and shivered in the faint breeze, an empty map table and chairs crouched darkly beneath the awning.

Voices filtered down to them, the words indecipherable in the quiet evening air. Then the insect netting on the main entrance was pulled aside and two Haun ducked out. They paused as they left the shelter of the awning, pulling their brightly coloured hats down to shade their eyes. The youngest gazed out across the tops of the trees as if deep in thought, but his companion glanced down the hill. At the sight of the Merron, his hand froze on the brim of his hat. He murmured something, and the younger man looked down. He stared for a long time, his flat, honey-coloured face expressionless, his narrow black eyes unreadable. Then he tugged his hat lower, said something to the older Haun and led the way down the hill.

The older man swept by with ostentatious disinterest. But the young man slowed as he approached, his eyes on the impressive Northern horses and Razi's wonderful mare. Wynter smiled knowingly. The Haun were famously avaricious when it came to horses. Razi would do well to sleep with his reins in his hand tonight.

As he passed her by, the young Haunardii glanced briefly into Wynter's masked face, then walked on. Wynter swivelled in her saddle to keep him in sight. *So that is a Haun*, she thought. *How strange they look up close.*

"Lass...? *Lass!*" Christopher kicked her lightly to get her attention and she spun in the saddle, startled. "Is that him?" he whispered, looking uphill.

A boy of about ten stood in the door of the royal tent—small, skinny, fine brown hair, obviously a servant. "Oh, Christopher," she hissed, her heart hammering. "Have some sense! Does that look like a royal prince?"

At a nod from the boy, the lieutenant dropped from his horse, jogged up the hill, and disappeared into the tent. The Merron sat in silence, waiting. A few moments later, the lieutenant reappeared. He trotted back down and stood squinting up at Úlfnaor, his hand shading his eyes.

"His Royal Highness thanks you for your duty," he said. "You may give me the papers."

Wynter's heart dropped. Úlfnaor sat for a moment, his face a raw canvas of shock. Then his eyes hardened and he sat straighter, his expression cold. He said nothing.

The lieutenant went blandly on. "You have my permission to rest your people and your horses while you await your reply. There will certainly be food available, should you be short of supplies."

He held his hand out for the papers, no trace of deference in his face. Wynter knew for certain then that he was acting on Alberon's orders, and that this was a calculated snub against the

Merron leader. She wondered if this was an indication of Albi's attitude to Úlfnaor himself, or was it supposed to reflect his feelings for Marguerite Shirken, whom Úlfnaor represented?

Úlfnaor remained coldly silent. Sólmundr, however, abruptly clucked his own horse forward, forcing the lieutenant back until he was a respectful distance from the Merron leader. Then Sól drew his mare to a halt and sat looking down on the lieutenant with all the scorn an eagle might show an ant.

"This my High Lord and Shepherd, Úlfnaor, *Aoire an Domhain*," he said softly. "He come bearing papers from Royal Princess Marguerite Shirken of Northlands. He come with permission granted to negotiate with Royal Prince Alberon of Southlands, on behalf of Princess and also on behalf of all the Merron Peoples. You may to announce him to your master as a leader of state and member of royal line of Merron Peoples. Then *you* have *my* permission for to escort us into Royal Prince Alberon's presence."

The lieutenant faltered for a moment, and Wynter saw him calculating his options. She felt sorry for the man, caught between the Merron's fierce nobility and his master's orders. But when the lieutenant turned to scan the party of coldly staring Merron, this sympathy did not prevent Wynter from straightening like the rest of them and glowering at him with all the haughty disdain she could muster. The lieutenant turned on his heel and took the long walk back to Alberon's tent.

Once the soldier had disappeared from sight, Úlfnaor turned to look Razi in the eye. The question was plain in his face: *if this goes the way we thought it would, shall I do as we discussed?* Razi nodded, and Úlfnaor turned front as the lieutenant made yet another appearance. There was someone with him, and Wynter's heart bumped when she recognised who it was. Oliver! Dear God, it was Oliver. Razi's hands tightened on the pommel of his saddle, and Wynter saw him lean forward slightly, as the man they had called "uncle" began making his way down the slope towards them.

It was five years since Wynter had last seen Oliver, but he was much as she remembered him. He was shorter than King Jonathon, his dark hair fine and straight, but he had the same vivid blue eyes as his royal cousin, the same athletic build. He was thin now, though, his face older than it should be, his eyes strained. Wynter watched as Oliver approached the waiting Merron, and she remembered with sadness all this man's great kindness, all his sly sense of fun. They had been such fast friends, Oliver, Jonathon and her father. He had been such a loyal subject. What had happened to cause him to plot in secret against his King, and to welcome Jonathon's enemies to his table?

Oliver came to stand by Sólmundr's horse, and Wynter felt cold determination close over her heart and seal off her fond memories. "Uncle" or not, this man was now a traitor to Jonathon's throne. He had knowingly acted against the King, and he had enticed the King's heir to do the same. At the very least, he had a lot of explaining to do.

"You refuse to hand over the royal papers?" Oliver asked, his Hadrish flawless, his cultured voice cold.

Sólmundr began to reply, but Úlfnaor raised his hand to silence him. The warrior bowed to his leader and drew his horse back into formation.

"I feel certain in my heart that there has been mistake in carrying my introduction to the Royal Prince," said Úlfnaor quietly. "I certain of this, because if Royal Prince knew that I am diplomatic envoy for Royal Princess, come with full permission also to negotiate for my Peoples, he would have greet me with honour and treat me with respect, as one head of state to another, with the grace

and nobility worthy of man destined to be king of his peoples."
Oliver pursed his lips at this, and Úlfnaor knowingly held his eyes.
"And so," he continued. "I allow my second again to introduce me,
knowing that, this time, there will be no more mistake."

Sólmundr once again clucked his horse forward. He once
again made his introductions, and the Merron once again
waited. This time, Oliver bowed and the lieutenant smoothly
followed his lead.

"Lord Úlfnaor," said Oliver, still bent at the waist. "Forgive
me. We had been told to expect a simple messenger, not a diplomatic representative. I fear we are ill-prepared. Had the Royal
Prince understood..."

"It not matter. I forgive. We go on."

Oliver straightened. "Unfortunately, his Royal Highness is
very busy. He begs that you forgive him this, asks that you hand
over the papers and says that he will speak with you as soon as
time allows."

Wynter briefly closed her eyes and shook her head. So, that
was how it was to be. After all he had done to get here, after
everything he been forced to sacrifice, it was quite clear that
Úlfnaor was never destined to get his audience. He would never
have the chance to negotiate on behalf of his people. He was to
be a messenger in all but name, and Shirken would laugh behind
her sleeve to the very end.

There was a long, empty silence, during which time Úlfnaor
sat heavy in his saddle, and Sól stared blindly out at the trees.

"I will come to royal tent," said Úlfnaor at last. "I will hand
papers myself, as is my duty. Then you will show my party to our
quarters and I will await the Prince's pleasure."

Oliver blinked in surprise. He had been expecting wounded
pride perhaps, had been anticipating an argument. He went to

speak, seemed to think better of it, nodded and gestured that the Merron should dismount and follow him up the hill.

Christopher fell into place at Wynter's side and they strode forward to flank Razi as the party trudged through the last of the daylight to Alberon's silently waiting tent. At the royal quarters, Úlfnaor and Sól went forward with the papers. The rest of the Merron closed ranks around Razi, shielding him from sight and obscuring Wynter's view of the tent. She heard Oliver's voice as he announced the Merron lords.

"Your Royal Highness, I present Lord Úlfnaor, Aoire of the Merron People, emissary from her Royal Highness Princess Marguerite of the Northlands."

This was greeted with silence, during which Wynter imagined Alberon stepping into the sunlight, Úlfnaor and Sól kneeling in the dust, Úlfnaor holding out the package of letters. She imagined Alberon reaching forward and taking it. She tried to picture him as something more than the boy she'd known. In her mind, she tried to form him into a man. But nothing came to her, nothing but a clear image of him as she had last seen him, a ten-year-old boy standing in a doorway, the bright sun in his hair, his hand raised in farewell—her final sight of him as she had ridden away from the palace. She waited for his voice, wondering if she'd know it. He did not speak.

Instead Oliver said, "His Highness thanks you."

At Wynter's side, Razi held his breath, waiting. She resisted the urge to take his hand. The wall of cloaked and masked Merron were blocking their view, and Wynter felt closed in by them. She could not breathe. She longed to push them all aside and pull the scarf from her face. She longed to shout, *Albi! It's us! It's Wyn and Razi! We are here!* She glanced at Christopher, standing to Razi's left. His hands were clenched.

Úlfnaor's voice rang out suddenly, his tone urgent, as though Alberon had begun to turn and the Merron leader wished to prevent him leaving. "Your Royal Highness! I have other package for you. It also my duty to deliver into your hands."

There was a pause, as if the Prince was taking his time turning back. A surprisingly deep voice said, "Another package?"

Razi took off his hat and scarf. He let the Merron cloak drop from his shoulders. He lifted his head. The Merron parted ranks, and the brothers were finally revealed to each other.

Alberon stood with his hand shading his eyes, puzzled. It took him a moment to comprehend, then he stepped forward, his face opening in surprise. His hand dropped to his side. His full lips curved into a smile. He whispered, "Razi."

Wynter gazed at him in wonder, and the world narrowed to just that moment, to just him. Alberon. She hardly registered Oliver bellowing for the guards, barely felt the Merron close in again to protect Razi. The clatter of the approaching soldiers was just a faint echo on the air.

Alberon. Alberon was here.

He is so tall, she thought in amazement. And indeed he was, tall as Razi, and strongly built, the bounding athleticism of their father evident in his broad shoulders and solid body. His previously curling hair was shorn to a choppy red-blond thatch, his pale eyebrows stark against his sun-browned skin. But his eyes were still the same, his vivid blue eyes under those sleepy lids. Still Albi. Still him.

Wynter felt a smile begin on her lips, but even as she went to step forward, Alberon's face closed up, his brows drew down, and his court mask slipped smoothly into place. No longer the lost brother, no longer the childhood friend, it was a prince who now stood before her, and the expression on his face brought

Wynter to a standstill. As Alberon lowered his chin and eyed Razi across the dust-laden air, Wynter felt a cold certainty that it was not a brother he saw, but a potential rival and a suspected adversary in his recent struggle with the King.

The sound of the advancing soldiers slammed into Wynter's consciousness. The Merron jostled close as they crowded around Razi. The warhounds began barking, and Úlfnaor yelled at them, "*Tarraingígí siar!*" Someone amongst the advancing soldiers shouted, "Shoot those damned dogs!"

Without taking his eyes from his half-brother, Alberon lifted his hand and cried, "*Enough!*" At his voice, the soldiers came to a jangling halt.

In the relative silence, the warhounds' growls were very obvious. Sól murmured, "*Tóg go bog é*," and the big dogs stilled. The late evening air filled with the shuffling of feet and the murmuring of anxious men. There was a dangerous edge to the sound, the nervous anticipation of battle. When Razi cleared his throat and stepped from the protective circle of the Merron, Wynter physically had to prevent herself from pulling him back.

He walked into the open and spread his arms to show that he was unarmed.

"Your Royal Highness," he called, "the Lord Razi begs permission to come forward and address you."

Wynter regarded Alberon tensely. This was a calculated beginning on Razi's part. It established both Razi's recognition of Alberon as rightful heir to the throne, and Razi's acceptance of himself as nothing more than a lord. With these few simple words, Alberon, and more importantly, Alberon's men, had been assured that Razi had no pretensions to the throne.

Alberon nodded coolly, and Razi walked forward to kneel in the dust at his brother's feet.

Wynter shifted her weight. Beside her, Christopher stood in lethal stillness, his grey eyes fierce within the shadows of his scarf. Razi's instructions, should Alberon simply decide to strike his head from his shoulders, were for the two of them to hide amongst the Merron, then slink quietly away. When Razi had told them this, Wynter and Christopher had eyed each other and mutually held their peace. Neither of them had any intention of slinking quietly away.

"Your Royal Highness," said Razi, "I come to you in the name of his Majesty, the Good King Jonathon, and offer my service as envoy and ambassador, should your Royal Highness so choose to make use of me."

Here we have it, thought Wynter, her heart pounding. *Here it is.*

Razi had just made it known that he had come in the name of the King. He had just knelt, unarmed and defenceless, at Alberon's feet, and told him that he would not aid him in his opposition of the crown. Wynter held her breath. Alberon now had two choices: he could take this opportunity to open dialogue with his father, or he could strike the head from his half-brother and thereby rid himself of the only other successor to Jonathon's throne.

Alberon spoke without looking up from his brother's bowed head. "Clear the tent," he said, addressing Oliver in Southlandast.

Oliver faltered. "Your Highness, I don't think..."

"Oliver. Clear the tent."

Reluctantly, Oliver disappeared into the royal quarters, almost immediately reappearing with the servant boy, a secretary and a royal guardsman in tow.

Alberon jerked his head at the staff, and they retreated to join the waiting soldiers. "Come in," he said, and without waiting for Razi to rise, turned on his heel and disappeared inside.

Oliver strode quickly after him.

Stunned, Razi remained on his knees for a moment. Then he got uncertainly to his feet and followed Oliver inside. Wynter glanced at Christopher. Just as the shadows of the interior swallowed their friend, the two of them dashed across the sun-baked ground and ran in the door before any of the guards could stop them.

Wynter slid into dimness, startling Razi and Alberon. The brothers leapt apart. Alberon, swiping tears from his eyes, drew his sword and pushed himself ahead of the unarmed Razi. The interior of the tent was filled with shadows as bellowing men rushed the door. Christopher spun to face them and Oliver leapt at him, a knife in his hand.

Razi pulled the knight back, yelling, "No, Oliver! Stop! Albi, it is Wynter! It is Wyn!"

Wynter ripped her scarf aside, and Alberon, his sword poised to strike her, jerked to a halt, staring in disbelief. "Wyn!" he cried.

Soldiers shoved their way into the tent, snarling in anger, weapons raised. They advanced on Christopher, and Alberon waved them away, all his attention on Wynter.

"It is fine," he said. "You lot can go…"

The soldiers hesitated, eyeing Christopher who glared dangerously at them, his fists raised. Alberon finally tore his eyes from Wynter, took in his men's posturing, and yelled in sudden anger.

"Oh, get *out*! *Out* for Christssake, you useless chards! They could have killed me twice over if they had wished! Get out!" The men retreated in shame, and Alberon immediately turned back to Wynter, his face transformed with joy. "*Wyn!*" he yelled, slamming his sword into his scabbard. "Look at you!"

To Wynter's shock, he took her face between his hands and stooped to kiss her. First on the mouth, then on the forehead, then on both cheeks, each kiss harder than the last. Then he grabbed her around the waist and spun her until she was breathless.

"Look at you!" he shouted. "Look at you! My little sister! Still no taller than a thumb, but all grown up nonetheless!"

He dropped her suddenly, and turned once more to his brother. Wynter staggered, and Christopher came forward, steadying her with his hand on her back. She blinked, dazed, and watched in numb disbelief as Alberon grabbed Razi's face, looked him in the eyes, laughed again and pulled him into a fierce hug.

"He sent you! I knew he would! I knew it! I knew the stubborn old bull wouldn't hold out long once you'd come home! I knew you'd make him listen!" He grabbed the back of Razi's head, knotting his fingers in his brother's curls. "Oh, but it was a cruel ruse," he said, his voice suddenly hoarse. "For him to make me think you were dead. That was too cruel, Razi. It was too cruel…" Razi's face creased up at that, and he squeezed his brother tight. "It was too cruel," whispered Alberon, and that was the last he said for a while, words being too much for any of them.

His Royal Highness

Oliver's sword came down to tap Christopher's hand. "You would do well to unhand the lady," he said softly, and he pressed the flat of his sword against Christopher's arm until he had pushed the young man's hand from Wynter's waist.

Christopher stepped back, arms spread, and Oliver gestured with his sword that he should back away from Wynter. Christopher looked at her, uncertain. She saw the surprise in his eyes when she didn't immediately defend him, and her heart dropped.

On the trail it had been so easy to forget their differences. They had been just Christopher and Iseult, and for what had felt like the longest time, that had been all that mattered. There had never been time to discuss this return to court life, and Wynter had always assumed that Christopher would simply adapt to it. In a sudden rush of panic and regret, she realised that they had left far too many things unsaid, and now it was too late. She stared at him, her face a cool mask, the memory of their last kiss still ghosted upon her lips, and she prayed that Christopher would play along until they had time to talk things through. But Christopher's clear grey eyes hardened, his chin lowered, and Wynter's heart squeezed in alarm as she realised that he was going to say something both of them would regret.

Alberon's dry laugh saved them. Wiping his eyes, he looked

Christopher up and down in tolerant amusement and addressed Oliver in Southlandast.

"Go easy on him, Sir Knight," he said. "These fellows have not the sense of propriety one might desire. The poor savage probably thinks he's gaining favour by protecting Razi's woman— forgive my crudeness, Wyn."

"Alberon..." warned Razi.

"Oliver, why don't you take him out to those others," continued Alberon. "Get them something to gnaw on and somewhere to squat down until I am ready to deal with them."

"Alberon..." said Wynter quietly.

"Actually," interrupted Christopher, uncovering his face, "this savage would prefer to stay, until the Lord Razi tells him otherwise."

There was a moment of strained silence as Alberon registered the fact that Christopher spoke perfect Southlandast.

"Freeman Christopher Garron is my second, your Highness," said Razi. "My bodyguard. As well as a very good friend."

"A friend," said Alberon. The Prince regarded Christopher coolly, his clothes, his bracelets. His eyes faltered on Christopher's horribly mutilated hands, then rose smoothly to Christopher's face. "Your Southlandast is excellent, Freeman Garron."

"Thank you, your Highness," said Christopher flatly.

Bow, thought Wynter. *Bow, damn it.* But, of course, he didn't.

"Do the others speak Southlandast?" asked Alberon. "It seems underhanded to conceal the fact if they do. I had expected to deal with the Princess's messengers via Garmain; 'twas a surprise to find these folk speak only Hadrish, and so poorly at that. Though, perhaps...?" He looked uncertainly at Christopher, doubt evident in his expression. "Perhaps you are their translator?"

Christopher glared, that dangerous pride rising in his face. "I have no doubt that the Merron lords speak Garmain with every fluency," he said. "They chose to speak Hadrish out of deference to the Lord Razi. He speaks neither Garmain nor the Merron tongue, and the Merron would consider it below their dignity as noblemen to indulge in a conversation that one of their party could not understand."

If Alberon felt the sting of that he did not let it show. "I see," he said. He glanced back at Razi, spent a brief moment in contemplation, then turned to Oliver. "Go out now and thank the Merron leader for his duty to my brother. Tell him that I am pleased. Find accommodation for him and for his entourage... make it *good* accommodation."

Oliver hesitated. He glanced at Christopher, then murmured, "There *are* no accommodations, your Highness."

Alberon sighed. "Just double up the men somehow. Commandeer some tents. I want those people settled by nightfall, Oliver. I have no desire to set them above their station, but if they are to stay, I want them where I can see them. You, Freeman, go with Sir Oliver. Keep an eye on your people; report back to him if there is discontent."

Christopher stiffened. "I ain't no spy," he hissed.

"Christopher," Razi's quiet voice drew everyone's attention to him, "it would probably be wise that you help the Merron get settled." Christopher held his eyes. "The Protector Lady and I will be safe," said Razi, smiling gently. "Thank you, friend."

Christopher flicked a glance at Wynter, and she nodded to let him know that she would be fine. She tried to soften her face, tried to smile and seem warmly grateful like Razi, but she had the horrible feeling that she looked as though she were haughtily dismissing a servant. Christopher compressed his mouth, staring at her. Then he gave Alberon one last suspicious glare, bowed stiffly and stalked out the door. Wynter did not turn her head to watch him exit the tent.

Oliver loitered unhappily, his eyes hopping from brother to brother.

"Shoo!" said Alberon with a smile. "Out! I shall write you a full report by morning."

Oliver gave him a tight-jawed look, bowed and left, leaving Wynter, Razi and Alberon alone.

The three of them stood still for a moment as the light within the tent flickered and danced with the movement of the men outside. Dust filtered through the open door, hazing the air as the soldiers retreated. Two long shadows fell against the canvas as Alberon's personal guard took position at the awning. It grew quiet.

The little boy servant came and peeped in at the door. Alberon smiled at him.

"Small ale, Anthony, please. Some cheese and . . . is there bread?"

The boy nodded, and Alberon waved him away. They listened to him scamper off, then Alberon turned to his family. "How shall we do this?" he asked softly. "So many things . . ." He looked to Razi. "I should like to finish my negotiations, Razi. Before we go back. I had always planned to bring it to him, a *fait accompli*, and there is still much to do. Though all is nearly ready."

Razi stood with his back to a small dark-wood folding table. He reached behind him and placed his fingertips on the scarred surface, as if to anchor himself. "The King did not send me," he admitted. Alberon's face immediately lost its warmth. Razi pressed on. "Father has told me nothing of you, nor of what you have done. I have come in secret, without his permission, in the hope that I may reconcile you to each other . . . before this goes beyond repair."

Alberon shook his head in what Wynter could only interpret as grim disapproval. "Well," he said. "Well, well. So, you play the politician even with me, do you, brother? I had hoped you would leave such games behind you in the Moroccos. I had hoped that *you* at least would talk to me as a man—straight and true."

"I play no games, Alberon. I merely—"

"You merely opened your mouth to me, and your first sentence was a lie," interrupted Alberon. Razi went to object and his brother lifted his hand to silence him. "No," he said. "No more now. I understand that you have spent years speaking from two sides of your mouth, Razi, and our father owes you much for it. But you will break that habit now, understand? You are here with *me* now. You are on *my* side. There is no more need for two faces. We go forward from here together, as men, honestly and without falsehood."

Razi frowned unhappily and clamped his lips shut, as if biting back a reply.

"Good man," whispered Alberon, his face softening. "Good man. We will all do so much better with just a little less guile." He slid a half-smile at Wynter. "Speaking of which, what brought you to drag our poor little sister along? Thought I might need my socks darned, did you?"

"Alberon," snapped Wynter, "what *exactly* are you doing here?"

Alberon grinned. "My!" he cried. "How very direct of you, little sister. How decidedly uncourtly. You have no idea how much that refreshes me. Perhaps your stay with Marguerite has taught you something of candour? Perhaps she has shown you what it can truly mean to be a ruler?"

"Only if being a ruler means bludgeoning your people into submission and burning all dissenters at the stake."

"Sometimes that is what it takes, Protector Lady. I have come to understand that a real leader needs to know when to leave the pretty words aside and hammer his opposition into line. 'If you are not with me, you are against me', correct?" Alberon nodded to himself. "Correct," he said.

Seemingly carried away with the force of his thoughts, he began to pace, his head down, his expression intent. "Until recently, I was not certain that my father truly knew what this kind of strength meant...but now!" Alberon smiled in admiration. "*Mortuus in vita! That* was a kingly act. I would not have thought him capable of it—to disinherit his only legitimate heir. Of course, he would be better simply to have had me killed— but, as ever, he continues to turn his face from the final stroke. I'm telling you if *I* were a king and *my* son stood against me, there would not be a tree left standing 'till his charred corpse and the corpses of all his supporters had been dragged down the mountain and strung up along the Port Road."

Wynter met Razi's eye as Alberon strode up and down between them. The expression on her friend's dark face was a mirror image of the confusion in her heart. Was Alberon actually *berating* his father for not yet having killed him?

"Your death, though," said Alberon, pointing at Razi. "A sly trick, but genius nonetheless! What better ruse to break me than the contrived slaughter of my brother? If anything would bring me down, that would! The old man knows me, Razi, I'll give him that. Damn near broke my will."

"But that was no *ruse*!" cried Wynter. "Albi, that was poor Shuqayr! It was *Shuqayr*! And Simon de Rochelle and all his men! Those murders were real, Albi. They really did those awful things! And they did them thinking that Shuqayr was Razi! Oh, Albi! The things they did to that poor man. If you only knew."

"Shuqayr?" Alberon came to a sympathetic halt. "That tall Arab boy you knocked about with? The apothecary's boy? I am sorry, Razi. Truly. He seemed a good fellow."

Razi said nothing. Just stood with his back to the little table, staring at his brother, his face closed up like a book.

"They did it because they thought Razi wanted your throne, Albi," said Wynter. "They did such terrible things to that poor—"

"Oh, aye," interrupted Alberon. "Aye—that would be it." He crossed to the door of the tent, and Shuqayr's terrible death seemed to slip into the background for him as he looked down into the camp. "My people would do anything to protect me," he murmured, his eyes roaming the neat tents, now pink-tinted in the failing light of evening. "I have much support from court, as you can tell. Though they are yet to know the nature of my misunderstanding with Father, they are utterly determined to keep *you* from power." He looked at Razi over his shoulder. "Not that I ever doubted you, brother. Though God knows, the gossips have you leaping across banquet tables and shoving weeping guards aside in your haste to get to my throne. I know it has never been in your nature to strive for such power. You are not a man destined to be a king. Do not take insult from that. I do not mean it as such. We cannot all be kingly men." He turned back to surveying his camp thoughtfully. "Indeed, where would we be if that were the case? Incessantly battering each other over the head while our kingdom went to ruin."

He smiled, his eyes slipping to Wynter. "You are ever the sly hand though, bringing our sister with you. No doubt you thought her presence would soften my resolve? I'm sorry, Wyn, but I'm afraid you must resign yourself to camp rations and a hard pallet for a while longer. I await my last representatives—the curs are days late—and I shall not be leaving 'till my work is done."

Wynter bristled at that. God knows she was used to court men assuming she was naught more than a bit of fluff to dandle or protect, but after all she'd been through, to hear this attitude coming from Alberon was just too hard to take.

"I came here of my own volition, Alberon Kingsson," she said stiffly. "It was only by chance fortune that Razi and I met up. I risked all to get here. I abandoned my poor father on his deathbed to come seeking you."

At the mention of Lorcan, Alberon's face fell. He blushed, opened his mouth to speak, but could find nothing to say. Wynter realised with a sudden flare of anger that her father had utterly slipped his mind, and all her courtly restraint flew out the window. Alberon stepped towards her, and she flung her hand up, halting him in his tracks.

"Alberon!" she cried. "What are you *doing*? You have the kingdom in an uproar! You have your father crazed with anger and fear. Those supporters you are so proud of? They are lying dead in streams and ditches on this very mountain! They are swinging in cages all along the Port Road! And those who *are* free have dedicated themselves to *trying to kill your brother*!"

Alberon stepped back, his eyes wide, and Wynter advanced, jabbing her finger at him like a common scold. "Everything our fathers have worked for is about to fall apart, Alberon! And you, goddamn you, *you* are at the very heart of this turmoil. Do not stand there, *your Highness*, and talk to me of kings and kingly acts, when you seem wilfully determined to uproot all the good our fathers have done, and turn this kingdom to the same pit of carrion in which the rest of the Europes currently wallow!"

She came to a halt, painfully close to tears, and for want of words, punched Alberon on the chest.

"Wynter..." he said gently. "Wyn..."

He went to take her hand, and she tugged it from his grip. Stepping back, she impatiently swatted the tears from her face. Why had she cried? Now he would think her an incorrigible girl, and would feel obliged to comfort her. The conversation would be hopelessly diverted.

"Wyn," he said again, "you must know that I have no desire to undo our fathers' work." She looked up at him in surprise. "Everything I do is for the betterment of this kingdom. Surely you cannot doubt that? My only desire is to build upon the foundations that our fathers have laid. It is simply a case of... Wyn, there are some things you simply do not yet know."

"Then educate us," said Razi quietly. "Please, your Highness. Help us to understand."

Alberon turned to look at him, his face sad. "Razi," he said, "must you still play the courtier?" At Razi's lack of comprehension, Alberon sighed. "Call me *brother*, for Christ's sake. At least while we are alone."

Razi looked uncertain. His eyes slid to the shadows of the guards standing just outside Alberon's tent, and Alberon followed his gaze, frowning.

Just then, a small voice piped up, and Alberon's servant announced himself at the door. Alberon smiled fondly in the direction of the boy's voice.

"Good chap, Anthony," he called. "Set up at the map table, there's the boy, then come fetch the pillow from my bed, that the Protector Lady may have some comfort."

The little lad squeaked, "Aye, your Highness," and Alberon turned to Razi again.

"Come, Razi," he said softly. "Let us eat our supper outside, shall we? We can sit side by side in the sunset, you and I: the heir and his loyal brother talking peaceably together for all my men to see and marvel at. What say you? Do you feel up to the fresh air?"

There was a moment of wordless communication between the two men, then Razi nodded. Alberon grinned. "Good man," he whispered.

"And you, Protector Lady?" He bowed with a courtly flourish and offered Wynter his arm. "Would you do me the honour of adorning my table?" She hesitated, unwilling to be made little of. "I promise," he said, sparkling a sly smile. "I shall leave no question unanswered."

Wynter took his arm. "In that case, your Highness," she said, "I shall be pleased to oblige."

Supper

"Anthony! Did you take this from the men?"

"And risk thee clapping me in irons? Indeed I did not, your Highness. They gave it up to thee as a gift."

Alberon leaned over the little pot of stewed meat and inhaled gratefully. "Who caught it?" he asked.

"Who dost thou think?"

"Surely not?" laughed Alberon, turning to grin at the little servant who was busy plumping a threadbare pillow into the crook of the chair he had reserved for Wynter. "Not the Italians again?"

"Aye. Again. There's none can beat them."

"Good Christ," said Alberon. "There'll not be a boar left alive by the time we head home. Where are they?"

"Loitering at the base of the hill this last twenty minutes, pretending to haul wood and hoping for a word of praise."

Alberon strode across to the head of the slope. The boy patted the cushion and glanced shyly at Wynter. "Protector Lady," he said, "I have made it all comfortable for thee."

His bashful courtliness and use of formal speech had Wynter unconsciously smoothing out non-existent skirts and nodding in gracious thanks as she took her place at the table. In his beautifully tailored scarlet long-coat and freshly polished boots, Razi looked far more the part, and the wee servant waited with tense anxiety as the Lord Razi surveyed the rock-hard cheese, tiny portions of unleavened bread and scoopful of boiled meat that were being served for dinner.

"There's onions in the stew, my Lord," he said hopefully.

Razi gazed at him for a moment, then turned to Alberon, who was watching two men drag a wood-cart around the base of the hill. "You set a generous table, your Highness," called Razi. "I am most grateful for your hospitality."

Alberon glanced wryly at him, but the young servant drew himself up with surprised delight. He enthusiastically lifted the jug of small ale. "May I pour thy drink, my Lord?"

Razi eyed the rather thick looking concoction, and Wynter hid a smile at his strained expression. "You may," he murmured and the little lad poured with careful ceremony.

"Thank you," smiled Wynter, as her own cup was filled. She took a sip, and eyed Alberon who was standing, hands on hips, watching the two men. His face was grave as he took in their ostentatiously slow progress.

"Did all the men get a little meat, Anthony?"

"Pickets and all, Highness. All equal."

"You are certain? None was left out?"

"No one left out, your Highness. 'Twas two full grown boar, plenty to go around."

"And the guests?"

"All but them newcomers, your Highness. They having arrived after ration-up."

"Very well," whispered Alberon. Then he stepped forward and lifted his arms.

"Eduardo and Phillip di Oliva!" he yelled. "Is no boar safe from your spears?" The two men at the base of the hill grinned and paused to shade their eyes. "If it's true that a soldier walks

farther on a full belly, then you two have, once again, length-
ened our stride!"

Alberon's strong voice carried far across the sleepy camp and,
at once, an answering cheer rang back from the darkening tents.
He cut an impressive figure, gilded in evening light, his strong
arms raised over his head, his pale hair rimmed with the last of
the dying sun. Razi and Wynter watched carefully as his men
gathered in the purple shadows of the thoroughfare and gazed
up at their prince, smiling.

"The Italians have filled our cook pots, once again!" he called.
"What say you, men? Once we are safe returned to my father's
palace, and settled again within the arms of our families, do you
think perhaps, that two swarthy brothers might find themselves
granted licence to hunt and provender for my father's kitchen?"

There was a roar of approval, and several good-humoured cat-
calls from the gathered men. The two Italians at the base of the
hill pucked each other and grinned in delight. Alberon nodded
to them, smiling, and they bowed.

"Now shift that wood, you laggards! Or I'll have ye tarred."

More laughter, and the camp quieted as the men returned to
their dinners and their work. In the civilian quarters, smoke was
drifting from the roof holes of the Haun shelters. The Combermen were seated in the shadows of their awning, their figures
intermittently outlined in the dim glow from their pipes. The
Merron were busy settling themselves down. Wynter discreetly
craned her neck, trying to catch a glimpse of Christopher, but all
she could see was Wari, crouched outside the main door of their
borrowed tent, blowing a fire to flame. Alberon stood for a
moment, his eyes on the blue Midlander pavilion. He shifted his
gaze to the Merron tent, then he sighed. Tiredly, he ran his hand
across his forehead and turned to smile at his guards.

"You may go eat now," he said. "I shall not need you again till morning."

The men's eyes slid warily to Razi, and Alberon chuckled.

"Charles," he said and one of the men snapped to attention. "You may fetch the Lord Razi his weapons, also those of the Protector Lady. They shall be my protection for tonight." The men's eyes widened in ill-concealed alarm and Alberon chuckled again. "Go," he said, and the soldiers reluctantly obeyed, glancing over their shoulders all the while, their disquiet obvious on their faces. Alberon watched them retreat down the hill.

"Your men love you," said Razi softly.

"They have risked all for me, and for my father's kingdom. They are men of gold."

Alberon watched as his soldiers approached the civilian quarters, then he crossed to sit at the table. Wynter thought he seemed spent suddenly, all his sparkle gone.

"Light the candles, will you, Anthony?" he sighed. "And have someone bring wood for the brazier. I do not want the Protector Lady to get cold." He glanced up when the boy hesitated. "There are no more candles?" he asked.

"I can look for some, your Highness, but..."

"Never mind. Go on now, get that fire built, good lad. It will give us light enough, along with the heat...oh, Anthony?"

"Aye, your Highness?"

"Make certain that Sir Oliver eats tonight."

"Aye, your Highness."

The boy left them, and there was silence between the friends as they watched Alberon's guards clatter up the hill with Razi and Wynter's weapons.

"That chop-fingered savage didn't want to give 'em up," muttered one of the soldiers, handing over the weapons. "He's a right difficult cur, that 'un."

Wynter leant out and saw Christopher standing at the base of the hill, a pale spectre in the rapidly falling twilight. She discreetly lifted her hand. *All is well.* He stood for a moment, watching her, then he padded away into the shadows. Wynter tried to follow his progress, hoping to see him return to the safety of the Merron tents, but he was lost almost as soon as he turned from her. When she faced back to the table, Alberon was watching her closely.

"You seem well in with the Merron," he said.

Wynter found herself momentarily lost for words, certain that any attempt to define her relationship with the Merron would betray her feelings for Christopher. Alberon frowned at her silent discomfort. He glanced down at the shadows where Christopher had been standing.

"I . . . I would not say we are *well in* with them," ventured Wynter, bringing Alberon's thoughtful frown back to her.

Razi huffed. "The Merron have been useful, that is all. We crossed paths on our journey here. I treated one of their warriors and they gave us shelter."

Alberon dismissed his lingering men, and waited for them to leave before speaking again.

"You called that thief your friend," he said.

"Christopher is *not* a thief," corrected Wynter.

"Freeman Garron is not one of them," said Razi. "Do not make that mistake, Alberon."

Alberon regarded the two of them carefully, his eyes hopping from one fierce expression to another.

"So you have no allegiances to those people?" he said at last.

"None," said Razi firmly.

"That is good, brother. There is no place in our world for them."

Wynter's heart went cold at that, but if Alberon's harsh words chilled his brother, Razi certainly gave no sign of it. He simply shrugged his shoulders as if the Merron's fate were of no concern to him.

"When you addressed your men, you said '*my father's palace*'," murmured Wynter. Alberon nodded. "Are we to take it that you do not stand against the King?" she asked.

Alberon tutted, waving his hand dismissively, as if the answer to the question were too obvious to articulate.

"He believes that you do," said Razi.

Alberon rolled his eyes. "Father and I have disagreed," he said. "That is all."

"Disagreed?" said Wynter. "*Disagreed?* Is that what you call this? Alberon, the kingdom is rocked to its *core*!"

Alberon smiled in galling amusement at her and Razi laid his hand on hers, squeezing gently to silence her. His voice was carefully neutral when he said, "I must agree with our passionate sister, Alberon. This would seem a touch more than a *disagreement*. People are dying because of it."

Alberon lost his smile. "People have been dying these last five years, brother. Did you forget that?"

"Of course not," said Razi.

"Perhaps death is easily disregarded when you have not been the one wading through the blood of the fallen?"

"Alberon, I do not deny that the insurrection was bitter fought. I am simply pointing out that this current rift between you and our father is doing nothing to heal the kingdom's wounds."

"This kingdom has no hope if Father continues rejecting my

plans, Razi. He must be brought to see sense. He *must*! Or else all we have endured has been for naught. We may as well have lain down our arms as soon as those damned troublemakers set their faces against his reforms." Razi went to speak and Alberon threw up his hand in a now familiar gesture of dismissal. "You will help me convince him," he said. "You have always been the one with the words, Razi. You will make our father understand how sensible my ideas are. You will bring him to see reason. We cannot rule this kingdom as lambs, Razi! Not as lambs! We must do it as lions, or we shall not rule at all!"

"I cannot see that your father has ever been a lamb," murmured Wynter. "Not in any way that endangered his throne."

Alberon huffed bitterly as if to say, *what would you know of it.*

If Razi had anything to add to this he bit it down as Anthony returned and began setting a fire in the brazier. The three of them sat in silence as he did so, and Alberon took the opportunity to demolish his paltry meal, draining his cup of small ale and pouring himself another. "Eat," he ordered, pointing at Wynter's plate. "Don't waste what is so hard won."

Wynter made a grudging attempt to gnaw at the bread, but not even her great hunger could combat its hardness, and so she crumbled it in with her meat, hoping the juices would soften it.

Alberon's lips tightened as his brother neither ate nor drank, but simply fidgeted with his cup as he waited for the little servant boy to leave. "Have you gone religious on me in your time away?" he asked abruptly.

Razi looked up at him, startled, and then down at the cup. "No, I . . . it's just . . ."

Wynter frowned. "Small beer never did agree with him, Albi," she said. "Particularly unfiltered. Surely you remember?"

Alberon tutted with sudden impatience and snatched the cup from Razi's hand. "Bring the Lord Razi some water, Anthony," he said. He grimaced disapprovingly at Razi. "You'll not find any cold sherbets here, brother. Let alone a concubine to serve them up to you. You would do well to toughen up."

"Alberon!" cried Wynter.

Razi was silent and motionless for a moment, then he nodded his thanks as Anthony poured him some water. "I shall try to live up to your Highness's example," he said.

Alberon sighed. "Do not get surly now. I do not mean to be short with you. It simply galls me that you would turn your nose up to the same stuff as sustains my men. You are amongst warriors now, Razi, you must learn to win them over."

"Razi is no *court fop*, Alberon. Do not be so—"

Once again Razi placed his hand on Wynter's and squeezed gently to silence her. "How do you mean to strengthen our father's kingdom, Albi?"

Alberon grinned, his face transformed with sudden delight. "Ah, now we get to it!" he said, shoving back his plate and leaping to his feet. "Finish your meal," he called, heading for the door. "Let Anthony clear the table."

The tinder in the brazier caught flame and Anthony sat back as the fire roared abruptly to life. At the door to his tent, Alberon paused and looked over at Wynter, his face illuminated in the blaze, his eyes shining with grave delight. "I have a lovely surprise for you, Wyn," he said gently. "You will be so happy." He ducked inside and disappeared from view.

Wynter glared after him, angry at his unfathomable attitude towards his brother and thrown by his unpredictable changes of mood. Razi kept his hand on hers, his eyes on the dark rectangle of the door.

"My Lord?" Anthony hovered at Razi's elbow, waiting for his dishes. Razi did not seem to hear him, and Anthony glanced at Wynter. She smiled tightly, ate the few mouthfuls of bread and meat on her plate and nodded for him to clear her place.

"Razi," she murmured. "Eat your meal. Let the child finish his work."

Razi mechanically complied, and the young servant pottered off with the dishes, leaving the pitchers and cups behind. Wynter shrugged her cloak up around her neck and watched as his little figure disappeared into the dusk.

She waited until he was well out of earshot, then murmured tightly, "Alberon has no right to speak to you that way."

"He has spent years at war," said Razi, his lips barely moving. "He does not think that I can understand."

"I cannot tolerate it. If he persists—"

"Hush now, Wyn."

Razi was intensely focused on the door to Alberon's tent. Wynter turned her attention there too, tilting her head to catch any noise from within. There was nothing but silence. They waited. The fire popped and crackled as it took hold of the bigger logs, and Wynter found herself glad of the extra heat. The thin mountain air had grown rapidly colder with the loss of the sun.

Soon the weather will turn, she thought, *and there will be no hope of feeding even this small number of men. It is perfectly obvious that his supplies are already starting to fall low. Alberon must surely know that his time is running short.*

If Alberon *was* aware of this—and how could he not be?—it certainly didn't show in his demeanour. He seemed nothing but doggedly determined to succeed. Glancing at Razi's intent face, it occurred to Wynter that, despite his tiresome needling of his half-brother, much of Alberon's confidence was rooted in Razi's ability to sell his plan to their father.

She leaned in, meaning to make this point to Razi, but a low muttering from within the tent silenced her. Alberon's voice came, gentle and low though the canvas, and Wynter met Razi's eyes as they heard him say, "Come now, do not be ill-humoured. It is only outside, and I promise . . . you will be pleased."

Slowly, Razi sat upright, alarm clear in his face. There was someone else in there! Wynter remembered Alberon's sleeping area—half obscured by heavy netting, the neat bedding dressed in shadow—and she turned in her seat, her eyes wide. Alberon came to the door of his tent, his face glowing with that mischievous delight so familiar from their youth. Under his left arm, he had Marguerite's folder and two rolls of bulky parchment. In his right arm, a bundle of cloth.

"Clear the damned table," he laughed, struggling with his ill-balanced scrolls. Razi jumped up, shoved the pitchers and cups aside, and wiped the table clear of crumbs and grease. Alberon threw his papers carelessly on top. Then he gently hoisted the cloth bundle in both arms and, grinning, deposited it into Wynter's lap.

The bundle moved and Wynter had to prevent herself from leaping to her feet in alarm and dashing it from her. Her first thoughts were that in a fit of his old puckish devilment, Alberon had put a sack full of rats on her knee. But then the bundle sighed with a familiar, haughty impatience and Wynter stilled, her hands up, hardly daring to believe it. The cloth was shrugged aside and a grey-furred head emerged. Wynter's vision blurred with tears as huge, gold-green eyes blinked up at her.

"Coriolanus?" she whispered.

The cat gazed at her for a moment, frowning. Then he rolled his eyes. "Oh," he said wearily. " 'Tis but thee. *Pfffft*. For *this* He-Who-Is-Heir drags me from a warm nest."

"*Coriolanus!*" She grabbed the disgruntled creature under his scrawny shoulders and held him up to the light. He let out a small whine of genuine pain and Wynter saw with dismay how thin he was, how threadbare his once sleek fur had become.

"Unhand me, girl," he hissed, and she lowered him gently onto her lap. He lay panting for a moment, his heaving ribs horribly defined in the flaring light of the fire. Then he slid a glance to Wynter and grimaced. "Great Hunter," he gasped, "I had quite forgot what a grabbish little human thou were."

"Sorry," she whispered, smiling down at him, her hands poised. She could not believe he was still alive. She had returned from the North to find them all gone—all those sleek, self-possessed friends of her childhood—fallen victim to an inexplicable purge; killed on the murderous order of the King. But here he was, Cori, her favourite, the smoke-coloured companion of her happy youth.

He closed his eyes for a moment to gather himself, then sighed. "Thou mayst pet me," he said graciously. "If thou wishest. I should be quite happy to allow it."

"Thank you." Gently she ran her hand from his shoulders to his tail, just as he had always liked it.

"Mmmmmm," he purred.

Wynter gazed at Alberon, her eyes quite uncontrollably full of tears as her old cat-friend stretched and stiffly curled himself on her knee. *Thank you, Albi. Thank you so much.*

Alberon smiled and nodded, his own eyes very, very bright.

Coriolanus sighed again and settled his chin down against his chest. His spine was a well-defined serration beneath Wynter's palm, his poor body a thinly covered collection of bones. "Great Hunter, girl," he murmured, already almost asleep, "what hast thou been doing? Thou smellest most strongly of dog." And he drifted off, perfectly content, his rusty purr in warm harmony with the crackling of the fire.

Maps and Plans

"Is GreyMother here too, Albi?" asked Wynter, her voice low in deference to the sleeping cat.

Alberon shook his head sadly. He reached and scratched Coriolanus's head. "I tried to get her to come, but she preferred to take the last of the kittens and go into hiding. Cori had already fallen foul of the poison, and he was simply too weak to keep running. When I sent Oliver and his men ahead, I had them take the poor fellow with them. He has survived it all, poor thing, but as you see, he is not terribly well."

"Oh, Albi. Why? Why did the King do it?"

Alberon twitched a smile. "I was quite relentless in my hunt for his wonderful machine, Wyn. I simply would not back down."

Wynter traded a startled glance with Razi. Wonderful machine? That could only be a reference to her father's infamous *Bloody Machine*. Were they finally to learn what it was?

Alberon, still occupied in gently scratching the top of Coriolanus's head, went quietly on. "The cats know every inch of the palace, just like the ghosts. I'm afraid to say that I was constantly questioning the poor creatures. They told me nothing of use, but in the end, Father felt he had no choice but to do away with them. I suppose he found it preferable to poisoning *me*."

He looked up into her eyes. *Your fault!* thought Wynter. *All your fault!* But Alberon's smile was so sad, his big hand so gentle on Cori's fragile back that she couldn't bring herself to say it.

Razi, apparently lost in thought, was sprawled in his chair, idly flicking the curled edge of the bigger scroll with the tip of one finger. It was a perfectly casual gesture, but Wynter knew that he was trying to see what the parchment contained. Alberon sat back. The wry amusement in his face told Wynter that he knew exactly what his brother was up to.

"You *sent* Oliver ahead?" asked Razi softly. "That is an interesting slant to the tale." Alberon's expression hardened and Razi glanced up to meet his gaze. "Court gossip has it the other way around. It is said that *Oliver* is the one who plotted treason, and that you took his lead, following after him when Father condemned him for it."

The corner of Alberon's mouth twitched. "Oliver is a knight of the realm, brother, and I the heir to the throne. Who follows whom in that ranking?" Razi tilted his head in acceptance of this point, and Alberon went on. "I sent Oliver ahead to set up this camp and to prepare for my negotiations. He has risked everything for me. Risked his title, his lands, his life and those of his men. Because he believes in me—his Royal Prince—and in my plan for this kingdom's future. Do not mistake him, Razi; he is ever loyal to our father and to this kingdom, and he is ever faithful to his pledge as a knight. I shall hear no word said against the man."

"You had better be very vocal in defending him on your return home, then, your Highness. Otherwise you have condemned the poor man to slow death as a traitor to the crown."

"Oliver is a man who knows what it is to risk his life for the throne, Razi. He is a warrior born. Both he and I would *gladly* lay down our lives for this kingdom."

Wynter frowned at this, annoyed by the implication that Razi would not be willing do the same, but Razi himself did not change from his expression of careful detachment, and so Wynter kept her peace.

Alberon spread his hands in abrupt dismissal of the topic. "Do not fret yourself over it," he said, rising to his feet. "Those who stand with me here will never regret it. I shall make certain of that. Our father himself will one day bless their names, you wait and see. Now..." He took a scroll and spread it on the table. "Hold that side," he ordered, then slammed the pitcher and cups down on opposite corners to keep the parchment spread. "Look."

Razi spread his hand on the corner nearest him and looked coolly down at the scroll. Wynter hoisted the sleeping cat to her shoulder and shifted to get a good look. Coriolanus mewed softly in his sleep, but did not wake.

To Wynter's disappointment, it was not one of her father's intricate plans, but a wonderfully executed map of the Europes, detailed with mountains and rivers and political divisions. The delicate bays and peninsulas of the Moroccos' coastline embroidered the lower borders, while the scattered coastline of the Northland territories decorated the top. Beautiful little gold leaf castles represented the seats of power in the various European kingdoms, and a gold palace icon symbolised the Qassabah of the Sultan of the Moroccos in Algiers.

Wynter gazed at the ornately drawn white-topped mountains that ringed Jonathon's kingdom. She looked at the long, straight ribbon of the Port Road, stretching a remarkable one hundred and eighty-seven bandit-free, well-policed miles. Her gaze followed its natural progress out into the channel of peaceful blue wavelets that stretched between Marseilles and Algiers. The only pirate-free shipping lane in the entire Mediterranean Sea, made possible by the unprecedented combination of Moroccan and Southland fleets working together as one. Once again, Wynter marvelled at Jonathon's remarkable achievement in preserving this small, unusual land in the midst of the violence and hatred that currently ravaged the kingdoms surrounding it.

We have come very close to losing it, she thought sadly. *So very close. This small island of tolerance. This little flame of hope in the dark.*

She ran her finger across one of the many *Here Be Wolves* legends that dotted the tumultuous Gibraltars, and gazed at the long, dark border of the Haun territories, now once again gnawing at the fragile borders of Italy and the Venetian States. Wynter's heart squeezed with anxiety. It was all so unstable, all such a threat.

"Abdallah ash-Shiekh," said Alberon, leaning on the table and staring keenly at his brother.

Razi, who had been regarding the map with uncharacteristic wistfulness, glanced up in surprise. "The Sultan of the Moroccos?" he said. "What of him?"

"He is having problems."

Razi nodded uncertainly. "Some," he said. "Much the same types of trouble Father has been having. The large numbers of dispossessed Musulmen and Jews pouring in from the Northern Inquisitions have put a terrible burden on the Moroccan economy. They have nowhere to live, they have little to live on... they are angry. The persecutions that they have suffered in Europe have caused an upsurge in anti-Christian feeling which the Sultan is finding hard to argue against. It is a delicate situation. But Alberon, none of this is news to you, surely? I understand that communications here were very poor, but I diligently sent Father the most detailed reports, and on my return he seemed well aware—"

"Why did you not inform us of the attempts to depose him?"

Razi frowned, obviously searching his memory. "There have been no attempts to depose the Sultan."

"The *Corsairs*, Razi. The Slawi Corsairs in Fez and their allies amongst the radical imams. I have absolute *proof* that they are determined to take power! But because *you* did not mention it, our father chooses not to believe me!"

There was a long moment during which the brothers regarded each other in silence.

"Are you going to tell me that you did not know about it?" asked Alberon, his eyes still on Razi. "You who have spent the past five years at the heart of the Sultan's court?"

The implications of Alberon's words slowly dawned on Wynter. "Albi," she whispered. "You do not think Razi purposely withheld this information from your father?"

"Perhaps you underestimated how important the information was?" asked Alberon. "Is that it, brother? I must confess, I cannot see how one could come to such a conclusion—but, still, I am willing to accept that you might have?"

Wynter stared at her old friend, willing him not to make the accusation she knew was poised on his tongue. Her heart clenched when he spoke again.

"Or perhaps," he said, "you were *persuaded* to stay silent?"

"Alberon Kingsson," she hissed, "you ignorant *pup*."

Alberon did not so much as glance her way.

"Tell me, brother," he insisted, still leaning across the table, "I am most interested to hear your explanation. Knowing that the future of our kingdom depends on the support of the Sultan, why is it that you concealed this mortal weakness at the heart of the Moroccan court?"

"Someone has misled you," said Razi very quietly.

"I think not!" cried Alberon, slapping his hand down onto the map. "According to my sources, the Sultan's court is hopelessly divided, and it is only a matter of time before our father's most powerful ally is dragged from his throne and cast aside. Tell me I am wrong, Razi. Sit there now, and *dare* to tell me that I am wrong, when I have documents proving it, and a contingent of ambassadors on their way here, ready to attest it."

"You are *wrong*."

Alberon held Razi's gaze for a long, intense moment. Then his face softened and he reached across to pat his brother's hand. "All right," he whispered. "All right, brother. I believe you are honest. You have obviously been misled. But I believe you *fully believe* that which you have told our father."

Razi sat back, his face rigid, his eyes full.

"Alberon..." hissed Wynter, almost speechless with rage. "Alberon, I swear it to you...I swear it, I will kick your..."

Alberon reached across to squeeze her hand, and she tugged free with a snarl. He chuckled.

"Do not be angry, Wyn. Razi understands, don't you, brother? I had to be sure of his integrity. Here," he tapped his head, then slid his hand to his heart, "as well as here. Tell her, Razi. It is simply what men like us must do."

Razi averted his eyes. He coughed into his hand. "It is...it is simply the world we live in," he said hoarsely. "One can never be certain."

"Aye," breathed Alberon. "One must be certain." He shifted the beakers slightly and gazed down at the map of his father's kingdom. "And so," he said, "one must make strong that which one has discovered to be weak."

"There are no weaknesses in the Moroccan court, Alberon. I can assure you, Sultan Abdallah ash-Shiekh is as strong as ever. He has no—"

"Hush now," murmured Alberon, waving his hand. "You will see. Tomorrow, if my informants finally arrive, I shall be able to prove to you that you have been misled."

"I *assure* you, brother—"

Alberon looked up. "That's *enough* now," he snapped. "You have proved yourself to me; you do not need to *go on*."

Razi blinked. His jaw popped. Wynter saw him push some dark emotion down behind his eyes.

"The Northlands," said Alberon, tapping the huge expanse of land that comprised Shirken's kingdom, "and Princess Marguerite. She is the key." He turned to Wynter. "What is she like?" he asked.

"An unrelenting tyrant," she said tightly.

Alberon laughed. "I have no doubt you think so. But that is not what I meant. I meant what does she *look* like, sis? Paintings can only tell one so much, and one wonders, doesn't one, how such strength would manifest itself in a woman." He looked fondly at Wynter. "She would have something of your look, I imagine? A certain fierceness about the eyes? That keen watchfulness not usual in a woman?"

"I am nothing like her," hissed Wynter. "It appals me that you would suggest it."

Alberon grinned, amused at her ferocity. "Oh, don't be tiresome, Wyn. In her letters, Marguerite constantly reminds me of you, her directness of speech, her single-mindedness."

In her letters. Wynter exchanged a glance with Razi.

"You have been in regular correspondence with the Royal Princess?" asked Razi.

"For many months now."

"To what purpose?"

Alberon just smiled slyly and reached for Shirken's folder. There was a watchful silence from Razi as the Prince undid the ties on Marguerite's folder and quickly leafed through the sealed parchments.

In the silence that accompanied Alberon's examination of Marguerite's letters, Wynter was ashamed to find herself battling wounded feelings. She had to admit, she was stung beyond any political rage by Alberon's communication with Marguerite Shirken. Over the past five years, Alberon had never once replied to Wynter's many personal notes and letters, and she had assumed that they had been lost in the upheaval of the insurrection. But this seemed unlikely now, considering his apparently rich communion with the Northland's Princess. She cradled the sleeping cat and stroked his brittle shoulders. She told herself to grow up. So Alberon had not answered her letters. So what? She was no court moppet, willing to take offence at every perceived slight. Alberon had been a prince at war. He would have had no time for the frivolous scribblings of his lonely little sister. *He had bigger things to consider*, she thought.

She looked beyond the firelight. The camp was lost to darkness, the mountains surrounding them invisible in the night. *I know my place*, Lorcan's patient voice whispered in her memory. *I know my place.* Wynter had always thought she understood that, had always thought she knew exactly what it meant to put one's self second to matters of state. Now she was not sure. She was not certain she had the depths of selfless calm that had allowed her father to accept his lot in political life. Down below, the Merron camp fire winked at her like a knowing orange star. *We know what that's like*, it seemed to say. *We know how you feel.*

"For Christ's sake, sis! Wake up!"

Wynter came back to herself with a start. Razi and Alberon were staring, Razi concerned, Alberon impatient.

"Tell me of Gunther Shirken," Alberon demanded, as if for the third time. "I understand he is ill? His mind is unsound?"

"You are tired, Wyn," said Razi softly. "Would you like to lie down?"

Alberon regarded her curiously, as if seeing her for the first time. "*Are* you tired?" he asked. "Because…" He gestured to his tent, as if offering her the chance to retire.

She shook her head.

"It has been a terrible journey, Alberon," said Razi. "You have no idea. Wynter, perhaps you should consider—?"

"I am fine." Wynter drew herself up, cutting Razi short. "King Shirken is an old man, Albi, and my father always claimed that he had a skewed view of this world. But his health is good and he is in firm command of himself. He is in no way of unsound mind. Why do you ask?"

Razi rolled his eyes in defeat and gave up, switching his attention back to the conversation.

Alberon dived straight back to it. "Marguerite tells me that her father is more and more unbalanced," he said. "His legitimate purges have turned to persecutions. His renewed inquisitions are causing unrest. She tells me that the Northlands is on the brink of ruin."

Wynter hesitated, momentarily overcome with memories of the North. The awful inquisitions, the terrible mass executions. It took her a moment to push these images down. "Certainly, Shirken is a rabid cur," she said. "In truth, I cannot understand how he has survived this long without bringing his country to its knees. While we were there, my father did a tremendous amount of work healing old wounds, but he feared that it was a frail kind of stability. His great worry was that Shirken's tyranny would push his people into a civil war that would break the Northlands apart."

"Disastrous," murmured Razi.

Wynter and Alberon nodded in agreement. Shirken's kingdom was the Southland's strongest ally in the Europes, and the North's primary defence against the Haun. Without Shirken's stabilising influence, Jonathon's fragile northern border would be impossibly compromised.

Alberon tapped his fingers against Marguerite's sealed papers. "So Marguerite's fears are well founded, then, and her father's excesses are a cause for concern."

Wynter frowned. "It is not just the *King's* excesses, Albi. The Princess herself is an appalling tyrant. In our time there, she called for the most outrageous of purges, her motives often obscure and deep rooted in her hatred of any differences. You would not believe the things I've seen there. Simply...simply appalling things."

Once again Wynter paused. She shook her head, remembering the Northland's Princess in all her finery, her beautiful clothes, her famous pearls glowing from every tight coil of her hair. She had always looked so magnificent, but always there had been that terrible smell off her. Wynter knew it still—had smelled it only recently—the fat, scorched, oily stench of human beings burnt at the stake. She would never forget that smell, nor its enduring association with Marguerite Shirken.

"She is an evil person," she whispered. "I have never met anyone with a heart so black."

Alberon was very quiet for a moment. "I see," he said. "You...
you are certain of this, Wyn? Father told me that Lorcan kept
you very much apart from court life while you were there, a
commendable decision of course, considering your sex."

Wynter's voice was colder then she wished it when she said,
"One can see a lot from the background, Alberon. Sometimes
more than would be considered appropriate."

"You were very young though," he said, as though he himself
were years her senior. "It is possible that you have misread the
situation?"

"I grow weary of your implications that Razi and I are somehow incompetent and untrustworthy, your Highness."

Alberon grimaced apologetically. "Sorry," he said. "I have
grown too used to soldiers."

Wynter accepted his apology with a nod, though she was not
certain what he might have meant by it. Alberon ran his fingers
across Marguerite's personal seal.

"She has managed to conceal this aspect of her nature from
me," he mused. "Such guile. Nevertheless, such things could
perhaps be gently curbed as time went by. The influence of a
good man and all that." Wynter looked up sharply at him.
Alberon glanced at Razi. "You cannot deny her value as an ally,
brother."

"She has made moves towards an understanding?" asked
Razi.

"The strongest of such."

Wynter straightened, a horrible light beginning to dawn.
"Alberon," she said. "You cannot mean...?"

She turned to Razi, unable to articulate her despair.

He remained calm, leaning back in his chair, his hand on the
map, his eyes on his brother. His voice was soft and devoid of

emotion when he said, "Father would never conscience such a marriage, Albi."

Alberon smiled sadly, drummed his fingers, shrugged. "What must be done, will be done," he said. "He will see the sense of it eventually."

"Marguerite would never take on a husband!" cried Wynter. "She would never relinquish the power of her throne to a man and put herself into a position of secondary importance. That is something she has always made clear. She...she is misleading you, Alberon. You...and in any case, your father is right! He has always said that the Shirkens must be kept just *so*!" She thrust out her hand, palm out, in an imitation of Jonathon. "Their policies are too destructive, their rule of law too...just too damned *awful* to be so closely associated with! It's a trick! It's a terrible trick! She'll see you ruined!"

Coriolanus whined querulously and squirmed in her arms. "Calm thyself, cat-servant," he hissed. "I am quite horribly pinioned!"

"Marguerite is not about to trick me, Wynter," said Alberon. "She needs me too much. Nor is she about to hand over the power of her throne to me. She is fully determined to rule. But she has learned the lessons of the Irish Pirate Queen, who grew old with no heir and now sees her once united court squabbling over her succession. Marguerite is not about to make the same mistake." Alberon patted Shirken's letters. "We have drafted a treaty, and will be bound as much by it as by the marriage vow. Marguerite will rule her country, free of an influence from me, as I, eventually, shall rule mine. We do not have to meet but occasionally, to parley terms and the like. And in due course, I have no doubt we will breed an heir or two. But Marguerite and I intend our relationship to be that most courtly of things, Wynter—a political marriage."

Wynter gazed at him, stunned. On a political level this was sheer brilliance. A completely courtly, utterly calculated and unprecedented alliance: the rulers of two kingdoms, equal in power, joined by marriage. But that Alberon should even consider such an alliance with a tyrant such as Marguerite was dreadful beyond thinking. It was sickening. It made Wynter's skin crawl.

Alberon quirked a knowing eyebrow at her. "The Royal Princess Marguerite is her kingdom's only hope of survival, Wyn. If her father has become as unbalanced as she claims—"

"But Shirken is *not* unbalanced! He is no more mad than—"

"Stop now, Wyn. Stop. I have only *your* word against Marguerite's. The word of an outsider viewing things from the edge, versus that of someone at the *very heart* of the Northern court. In my position who would you listen to? You were three months travelling home. In that time do you not think it possible that Shirken may have slipped back into frenzy?"

Wynter frowned and sat back. Alberon nodded in approval. He reached over and patted her arm. "Come now, sis," he said, his tone soft again and gentle. "It's only a political thing. We all knew I would never marry for love." He ducked his head and smiled up at her. "Love is what mistresses are for," he whispered.

Wynter looked down at the hand Alberon had laid on her arm and all her rage sank under a weight of sorrow. Despite what Alberon thought, Wynter's outrage up until that moment *had* been a political one. Now the full implications of what he was planning sunk in and she truly understood the depths of personal sacrifice he was about to make. What Alberon said was true, they all knew it only too well: no royal could ever hope for a love match. Even so, marriage to Marguerite Shirken was very far from what Alberon could have expected for himself. The

King had always made nods towards engaging one of the Sultan's eldest daughters. It would have been a politically expedient match, and Wynter had no doubts that Jonathon would have a least *tried* for some soft and willing girl, intelligent and not at all a trial to the senses. The thoughts of Albi with that viper instead, "breeding heirs" as Albi put it, made Wynter shudder. She looked to Razi for support, but Razi was suddenly miles away. He was staring into the fire, his face indescribably sad, and Wynter knew he was remembering his own recent chance at a love match. Embla. That beautiful, gentle woman who had so willingly sacrificed it all to flames of a different kind.

Wynter squeezed her eyes shut.

A long silence ensued. When Wynter eventually looked up, she was surprised to find Razi staring at Alberon. The piercing expression on Razi's dark face brought Wynter slowly upright in her chair.

"You are very quiet, brother," said Alberon softly.

"You intend aiding Marguerite Shirken in overthrowing her father's throne."

"*Razi!*" Wynter gasped, disgusted that he would even think it. But Alberon only shook his head in bewildered admiration, and Wynter knew at once that Razi was right.

"Oh, Alberon," she moaned, "no."

"By God, Razi," said Alberon. "I have been depending on your bringing your words to my assistance—but I had forgot quite how incredible your mind is. What a statesman you must be. With you by my side I shall be so strong. You must—"

Razi slapped his hand down on the table. "You are *plotting* the *usurpation* of a *king.*"

"I am doing what is best for this kingdom."

"Alberon!" said Wynter. "Such an act undermines the very

fabric of what it means to be a ruler born! You cannot knock a king from his throne simply because you do not like his rule of law! Why, if we all thought thusly, there would be chaos!"

"Oh, come along, sis!" he cried, "you sound like an ignorant peasant. You cannot, surely, still be so naive? Most royal families are less than three generations old and you *know it*! Our own great-grandfather wrest this kingdom from William of Comber. Our historians now call it a legitimate reclamation of title, but let us for one moment admit it for what it actually was, shall we? Two men with big sticks pummelling each other over land—and the man with the biggest stick won. A king only remains a king for as long as he can outsmart, outrun or outfight his opponents, Wynter, and that is the bare and honest truth of it."

Wynter was speechless. To discover this unabashed cynicism in her royal friend was shocking. It was no less than treason even to express such beliefs—indeed, in some royal courts it was actual blasphemy! Yet she found herself unable to offer a reasonable argument against Alberon's unflinching candour.

He patted her hand and glanced sideways at Razi. "Don't ever tell Father I said that," he whispered.

"I think he might already suspect it for himself," said Razi.

Alberon nodded, apparently oblivious to the dry irony in his brother's voice. "Yes, yes indeed. He of all men would be so aware of it. I still find it impossible to bear. After all Father has done to improve the lot of this kingdom, that he should almost have been brought down by those who wish a return to the terrible ways of old."

"The elite of this land come from far simpler times, Alberon, and are not used to the loss of power and wealth that Father's vision foists upon them. It will always be difficult to convince men of power that the payment of fair wages is better than slavery and that all men have the right to equality under law. Father has always known that his reforms would be the cause of trouble with some."

"There is nothing the aristocracy fear more than a confident well-educated populus," murmured Wynter, quoting her own father's favourite saying. "Your father has only ruled for fifteen years, Albi. It will take time for him to win over those who still believe in the old ways."

"Win over . . . or root out," said Alberon darkly. "There can be no in-between."

"Which brings us neatly back to the point, Alberon. Our sister is right. The usurpation of one king weakens them all. I cannot condone your plans. Tyrant or not, *mad* or not, Shirken *must* be supported against sedition."

Alberon withdrew his hand from Wynter's and sat back. "Feel free to discuss the immorality of sedition all night, brother; it will not change the fact that Marguerite is determined to take the Northland's throne. She will attempt this with or without my support. Without my support she may fail, and if she fails, her kingdom will be ruined and the Europes will fall into disarray—where will our father's wonderful plans for the future lie then?" At his brother's silence, Alberon nodded tightly. "So, I am determined to ensure the rest of the Europes shall not suffer for Marguerite's actions—in fact, I hope to use this opportunity to improve the lot of many."

"What do you intend to do?" asked Wynter.

"The Haun are my primary concern here, sis. If Marguerite cannot take the throne by political means and must recourse to war, I fear that the Haun will take advantage and attempt an invasion while her armies are divided. And *that*," he said, rising grimly to his feet, "is where I intended to come in."

An Impossible Device

"So we have it," said Alberon, spreading his hands on the map. "Marguerite's kingdom stands poised on the brink of extreme turmoil. On her left hand, the Haun. On her right, the Midlander King Tamarand and his Comberman allies, an undoubted source of trouble when she takes power."

"Tamarand is King Shirken's cousin," said Wynter. "He could legitimately grab the Northlands throne, should Marguerite's lords go against her deposition of her father."

"Tamarand on the Northland's throne would not be a good thing," mused Alberon softly, his eyes on the map.

It would be a disaster, thought Wynter. Capricious, wilful and rabidly devoted to the Comberman sect, Alexander Tamarand was quite certainly Gunther Shirken's equal when it came to the violent repression of his people, but he did not have a fraction of Shirken's understanding of government. Should Tamarand take the Northland's throne, it would only be a matter of time before he would lose control of it. Both the Midlands and the Northlands would fall into chaos, and the gate would swing open for the Haun to saunter in and take what they pleased.

Wynter hugged Coriolanus closer, as if his skinny little body could warm her against the oncoming storm. He turned his head to rest his chin in the crook of her elbow, and scanned the map, his enormous eyes shining in the firelight. Wynter stroked him gently, her attention on Alberon. The Prince was staring down at his father's kingdom, his eyes bright with some inner calculations. Razi was watching him closely.

"Why have you not tried to work this out with the King?" she whispered. "Why do you assume you must do this alone and outside of his consent?"

Alberon smiled. "You expect me to tell him of Marguerite's planned usurpation of her father? He would go to Gunther instantly and Marguerite would be dead."

"And this would be a bad thing?" murmured Razi. "Only hours ago you were berating Father's lack of ruthlessness in dealing with your own...disagreements."

Alberon's lips curved into a tolerant smile, his eyes roving the Port Road. "Gunther Shirken is an unpredictable canker. I am convinced it is only a matter of time before he turns on us. Marguerite will be a much stronger ally to Father's throne—and I intend to see her take power whatever way she can. Of course, Father will never tolerate her insurrection, but once she is actually on the Northland's throne Father will be free to accept her as an ally without ever having supported her deposition of the former King—it will be very neat for him." He chuckled bitterly. "Very politic."

"If you do not trust your father's allies then you should discuss it with him, Albi."

"I tried, Wyn," said Alberon. "But thanks to your father and our brother, the King refuses to listen to me. Lorcan had him convinced of Shirken's strength and stability—regardless of Marguerite's many testimonies to the contrary. And Razi here has convinced him that our allies in the Moroccos are as strong as ever. So Father remains confident of them both. He is quite thoroughly blind to their vulnerabilities."

"That is because those vulnerabilities do not *exist*!" cried Razi. "The only threat here is Marguerite and you are *aiding her in her plans*!"

At this first open expression of Razi's anger, Alberon's face abruptly darkened and his mouth compressed with sudden impatience. "That is *your* opinion," he snapped.

"Who would know the facts better than I? Listen, Alberon, for the last five years Lorcan and I have fought to keep Father's alliances strong. We—"

"Fought?" cried Alberon. He slammed his hand down on the table, startling Wynter. "*Fought?* You have never fought a day in your *life*, Razi! What is battle to you? Nothing! Nothing but a *word*!"

"Albi," said Wynter, shocked at the unexpected rage in her friend's face.

"No, Wyn! No! This must be said!" Alberon leaned across the table and hissed directly into his brother's face. "Where were you, *brother*? When the dead were piling up and we were soaked in the blood of our own men? Where were you, when we were waking morning and night to screams and the smell of rotting flesh? Fighting, were you? *Fighting?* I think not!"

Razi opened his mouth to speak and Alberon slammed the table again, making the beakers jump. "I will not see that *again*!" he cried. "I will not wake to that *AGAIN*! All your words did not stop it, Razi! All your *talking* did not stop it! So do not sit there now, with your court speech and your court clothes and tell me that you have *fought*, because YOU HAVE NEVER FOUGHT!"

Coriolanus mewed in fear, and Wynter clutched him to her. "Albi," she whispered, "stop."

Alberon slammed his hands down again, small beer splattering darkly across the face of his map.

"*This* will WORK!" he screamed. "It will WORK!"

He grabbed desperately at the stained map, his eyes huge and rimmed with red, and for a moment Wynter thought he would tear it to pieces. Then, to her immense surprise, Razi reached across and gently covered Alberon's clenched fist with his hand.

"Alberon," he said, "I am sorry."

Alberon flinched and gazed down at Razi's dark hand as if uncertain of what it was.

Razi squeezed his fingers. "I am sorry," he said again. "Of course I can never understand what you have endured."

Alberon looked up into his brother's face and slowly sank into his chair, apparently dazed.

His shouting must have alarmed his soldiers, because men began running up the hill towards them, their armour clattering in the dark, their panicked voices calling out, "Your Highness! Your Highness!"

Wynter and Razi sat back and carefully lifted their hands into sight.

Alberon put shaking fingers to his forehead.

Suddenly Coriolanus dug his claws into Wynter's thigh. "*Wolf*..." he hissed, his attention on the approaching men.

Wynter followed his gaze and saw the green light of a Wolf's eyes reflecting in the dark. She went to yell a warning, then realised with a shock that it was Christopher running alongside the soldiers, his sword drawn, his eyes phosphorescent in the night. In her arms, Coriolanus gathered himself for a cat-yowl of warning, and Wynter grabbed him, slapping her hand over his mouth. She clamped down hard, and his warning cry was reduced to a muffled *mmmwwrraaaffff* against her palm.

She leant to whisper in his ear.

"That Wolf is my friend, Cori. I am begging you to *hush*."

Shocked, the cat met her eyes. Wynter stared at him, plead-
ing. He blinked. Slowly, she uncovered his mouth, and to her
relief, he kept his peace.

Soldiers rushed into the ring of firelight, swords drawn.

Christopher, Sól and Hallvor followed on their heels, their
weapons also at the ready.

Sólmundr called out to Razi. "Tabiyb! *Cad é?*" He made to
approach the table, and one of the soldiers shoved him away.

"Back yerself orf! Yeh heathen savage!"

Sólmundr pushed the guard contemptuously backwards, and
the other soldiers rounded on him with a roar. Christopher and
Hallvor leapt to his defence. There was pushing and scuffling.

Razi remained motionless, his hands held up where the guards
could see them.

"Your Highness," he murmured, "your men are upset."

Alberon blinked at him.

"Albi," insisted Wynter, "your *men*."

Alberon slowly turned to take in the scuffle behind him. His
face cleared somewhat, and he seemed to gain focus just as Oliver
ran into the light. The older man took one look at the Royal
Prince, seemed to understand the situation instantly, and swept
his attention to the soldiers.

"Stand back," he ordered. "Come on now, split up . . . *You!*"
He pointed his sword at the Merron. "You were told to keep your
damned weapons in your tent."

Angrily, Sól went to speak, but at Razi's warning look, Christopher intervened. He laid his scarred hand on the warrior's arm,
bowed slightly and addressed Oliver. Wynter's heart swelled
with pride at his smooth, courtly tone.

"We had thought there was trouble, sir," he said, "and only
came to assist. We regret if our actions seem ill-meant."

Christopher sheathed his sword. Taking his lead, Sól and Hall-vor sheathed theirs and drew themselves up into noble silence. The soldiers continued to jostle and push at the Merron, and Oliver roared at them to *stand down*. They pulled back with shuffling uncertainty, their eyes on their Prince.

"You are dismissed," said Alberon softly. "There is no trouble."

Christopher looked to Razi, who nodded. "Thank you, Free-man. The Prince is safe."

Christopher glanced at Wynter. She held his eyes, the cat clutched to her chest, her face carefully neutral. Christopher bowed to her, very slow and solemn. There was not a trace of his usual mocking amusement in the action.

"At your service," he murmured. Then he led the other Mer-ron back down the slope.

Wynter watched his slim back retreat into the darkness. Somewhere near the base of the hill, she saw a brief flash of twin phosphorescence as he turned to look at her, then he was gone.

Coriolanus whispered in her ear, "A touch more than just friends, methinks," he insinuated slyly. "Little wonder you smell of dog."

"Hush now," she said, and scratched his thin shoulders until he purred.

Oliver dismissed the men, then turned to regard his Prince. Alberon smiled wanly at him.

"I lost my temper again," he said. "But there's no damage done."

"You are tired, Highness. Even the strongest of warriors needs to sleep."

Alberon waved a dismissive hand. "Stop lecturing me, you old hypocrite, and get you to your own bed."

Oliver's eyes flicked to Razi. "The Prince works too hard," he blurted suddenly. "No man could possibly push himself harder!"

"Oliver," warned Alberon.

"If you only knew what we'd been through these five years, my Lord. If you had seen a fraction of the things the Prince has seen—"

"That is *enough*," said Alberon sharply.

Oliver snapped to rigid silence, and Alberon sighed and rubbed his forehead in weary exasperation. "Go to *bed*, Oliver," he groaned. "Go get some goddamned sleep."

Oliver turned to go. Alberon called after him as he descended into the camp. "Oliver, if Anthony is still awake—only if he is, mind you—ask him to find us a little tea, would you?"

Oliver nodded without looking back and strode away into the dark.

There was a small moment of silence. Coriolanus purred. The fire crackled. Alberon sat looking into its violent flames for a moment, his face tired.

"It has been a long five years," he said eventually. Razi and Wynter stayed carefully silent. He glanced over at them. "For us all, no doubt," he said. They nodded. Alberon looked at Razi, his blue eyes very bright in the dancing light. "I will not see those five years happen again, brother. I've had enough talk; it is useless unless one has an iron fist to back it up with."

Razi nodded. "Tell me about Lorcan's machine," he said.

Alberon spread the second parchment and the two men stood leaning over the plans, absorbed. Razi said something and pointed to a section of the drawing, but his words were lost on Wynter. She remained rooted to her chair, gazing at Lorcan's neat and distinctive handwriting, his wonderfully delicate drawings, his careful diagrams of the working parts. She had not expected this sudden rush of sorrow. It completely overwhelmed her.

Slowly, she reached and placed her finger on the parchment, lightly tracing the perfect, serrated curve of a cog wheel.

In her mind, she saw Lorcan. He was leaning over the plans for a water-carrying device, a quill behind his ear, his fingers stained with ink. His brows were drawn down in concentration, and his red hair tumbled all around him in the candlelight. He looked up, saw her, and smiled as he had always done. *Hello, baby girl*, he whispered. *Can't you sleep?*

Wynter pressed her palm to the warmth of the paper. *Dad.*

"Your eyes are leaking, cat-servant."

She put her free hand to her eyes and pressed hard.

"My fur is quite damp."

"Hush," she said.

"Wynter." Razi's voice, suddenly close by her.

He crouched at her side. "Wyn," he said softly.

She shook her head, her fingers still pressed to her eyes. Razi put his hand on her back, warm and comforting. At his sympathy, Wynter felt tears surge dangerously, the kind of tears that she knew would not stop once released. She shrugged his hand away and swiped her face.

"What is it, Albi?" she croaked. "It looks..." she cleared her throat. "It looks to be a matchlock? A gun of some type."

Razi rose to his feet beside her, placed his hand briefly on her hair, then leaned back over the plan. "It seems more like—well I am unsure what it seems like. A series of rotating matchlocks, perhaps? But if so, I cannot figure...where is the serpentine? I can see no spark-wheel, no flintlock. Albi, where are the damned flash-pans? It makes no sense."

He glanced up at Alberon, who was sitting back in his chair, looking keenly at him.

"Do you...?" Razi glanced downhill towards the Haun and Comber tents. The camp was dark and still, watch-fires flickering silently in the night. He leaned forward and whispered, "Do you hope to mislead those others? Convince them, somehow, that we have a weapon they do not?"

Alberon grinned. "Politician," he said teasingly.

"What is this, Albi?" Wynter pointed to several vertical rows of strange pictographs. "That is not my father's work."

"That, apparently, is the key to the entire thing," murmured Alberon. He ran his finger along the little symbols, starting at the bottom and working his way up each column from left to right. "I cannot read it myself, but Oliver can. He suspects it is the work of someone called 'Borchu'."

"Borchu," breathed Razi. He frowned, obviously trying to recall something.

"You knew this man?" asked Alberon curiously.

"Well," Razi searched his memory, then spread his hands in defeat. "I...I do not think so. Though I seem to recall Father using that name. I half remember looking up from under a table, once, while he and Grandfather roared at each other. Father was in a terrific temper. They both were. One of those terrible moments between them. I think that the name came up. Perhaps this Borchu fellow was Father's friend?"

"Oliver claims not. He claims to know nothing of the man, except that he worked with Lorcan and that it is likely that he wrote this formula. It matters not in any case. Oliver has translated it for me." He pressed his finger to the row of glyphs. "It is a chemical procedure."

"What does it do, Albi?" asked Wynter.

Alberon glanced fondly at her. He leaned in. "It changes *everything*," he whispered.

Alberon ducked from his tent, a small box in his hands. "You understand how matchlocks work, sis?" he asked, laying the box on the ground and hunkering down to undo the lid.

"You ram gunpowder, shot and wadding into the barrel, you fill the flash-pan with flashpowder. You touch a burning slow-match to the pan; the flashpowder ignites the gunpowder and, BANG!" Wynter clapped her hands, making Coriolanus jerk. "The explosion sends the shot flying into your enemy... hopefully killing him before he has a chance to ram his sword in you."

Alberon laughed. "Very concise," he said. "Look at this." He held up a finger-length tube of what looked to be sturdy paper. "What do you suppose it is?" Wynter shook her head. Alberon turned to Razi. "Brother? What think you?"

Razi's eyes dropped to the parchment. "Hmm," he said thoughtfully. "Would it be...?" He squinted, and craned his neck, obviously reading from the plans. "A...waxed paper tube filled with powder and a ball of shot?"

Alberon laughed again. "It and forty-seven of its perfect little brothers are placed into the loading device detailed there." He pointed to the relevant section of drawing. "Then they are all rammed at once into the circlet of musket barrels. See that circle of blades on the loading device? There, see? Attached to the lever that swivels it? The paper cartridges are sliced open just before the ram shoves them in, they are reduced to powder, ball and wadding, just like any everyday matchlock..."

"Except that you load forty-eight at once, in double quick time," mused Razi.

"Faster even than that, brother...and see? The entire system of forty-eight barrels comes away at once, and can be cleaned and reloaded whilst a fresh one takes its place. It provides an almost continuous rate of fire."

"Utterly deadly," murmured Wynter. "Imagine a row of these atop a palace wall."

"Well said, Wyn!" cried Alberon. "Twelve men to each gun, that is all it takes! Twelve men and they do the work of hundreds of archers. It is incredible...not only that but, unlike our cumbersome cannonry, this entire device dismantles down to its smallest parts and is easily transported over the most inaccessible terrain! Consider its potential!"

"But it is impossible, Albi," said Razi. "An impossible flight of fancy, for surely it cannot fire?"

Alberon smiled up into his brother's regretful face. "Behold," he said softly, and drew another object from the box.

At the sight of it, Coriolanus tensed. "I shall retire," he said, shrugging from Wynter's arms and dropping stiffly to the ground. Her heart wrung to see how awkwardly he landed. She noticed that he gave Alberon a wide berth on his way back to the tent.

"I shall only demonstrate it once, Cori," whispered Alberon as the cat skirted around him. "I know you do not like the noise."

"*Pffffft!* Do not trouble yourself on account of *me*, Prince-and-Heir-to-the-Throne. I am no milk-addled kit, frightened of thunder. Make all the noise you wish, I simply grow tired of your company." He slipped into the shadows of the tent and Wynter pulled her cloak tight around her, suddenly cold without the warm weight of him on her lap.

"Watch," said Alberon. He unfurled a little section of the object in his hands, and Wynter realised that it was a roll of heavy paper tape. The tape was very thick and dotted along its middle with a series of raised bumps. Alberon tore off a section, then carefully put the remaining roll and the paper shot-cartridge back in the box and closed the lid.

"Watch this," he said, laying the piece of torn tape against a flat stone. He took out his belt-knife, grinned up at Razi, then struck the paper with the metal handle of the knife.

There was an enormous BANG and a flash of harsh light. Razi yelled and Wynter leapt in shock, shielding her eyes. Down amongst the tents, the warhounds howled, but their panicked barking was nothing but a faint noise through the high singing in Wynter's ears. She blinked against the light-scars on her eyes and heard Alberon laugh, a muffled sound. He spoke, and his words came clearer as her ears began to recover.

"...should have warned you," he yelled merrily, "but there's no preparing one for the shock."

You enjoyed that, she thought, squinting at him. *You imp!*

Razi was staggering forward, staring at the now blackened tape, Alberon nodding delightedly at him. "I hit a few at once, just for effect," he said, shouting over the ringing that still echoed in their ears. "But you get the picture, don't you, brother?"

Razi squatted, and placed his fingers on the scorched paper. "Good God," he yelled. "How? You used no fire...what then? A spark?"

"No fire, brother! No slow-match. No flint. No spark-wheel. No flash-pan. Just those ingenious paper cartridges, a little metal hammer poised over a brass lip...and these." He held up the tattered section of tape, grinning wildly, his eyes aglow.

"Welcome to a whole new world," he yelled.

Scones and Tea

Frantic footsteps ran towards them, accompanied by the clatter of metal. Anthony rushed from the dark, a steaming kettle held out before him, his little face bright with anticipation. He slid to an excited halt, saw the fragment of blackened tape and lost his smile. He stamped his foot, all his solemn courtliness lost in childish disappointment.

"Oh no!" he cried. "You did it without me *again*!"

Alberon laughed and got to his feet, brushing off his trousers.

"But you promised!" cried Anthony.

"Next time," said Alberon, ruffling Anthony's hair on his way back to the table. "Now, mind your manners, mankin, and pour the Protector Lady some tea...such as it is." He lowered himself into his chair and wearily began to fold the scrolls.

Wynter took them from him. "You're making a damned mess," she said softly, furling them and neatly securing the ribbon bindings.

Alberon smiled gratefully at her and slumped back. Razi drifted over, his attention on the blackened tape, which he was turning over and over in his hands. Anthony slammed the kettle down by the brazier, cleared the table and began sulkily washing out the beakers. Alberon regarded him with tired amusement.

"An explosive element, ignited by percussion," murmured

Razi, turning the tape again. "Unbelievable…" He sniffed it and touched it to his tongue, frowning thoughtfully at the taste.

"I believe the active ingredient is obtained by some foul exercise involving aqua fortis, some type of alcohol and—your favourite toy, Razi—mercury."

At the mention of mercury, Razi's eyes lit up and Wynter grinned fondly at him. She was instantly back in St James's fantastic laboratory, Razi's small, brown face alight with wonder as he demonstrated the magical liquid metal rolling in droplets around the bottom of a vial. "*See?*" he had lisped, holding the vial first to Wynter's, then to Albi's wide eyes, "*'tis water-metal, 'tis most amazing water-metal. See how it does flow?*"

"Mercury," breathed the now adult Razi, holding the tape up in awe, as if his beloved quicksilver might roll from it and drop into his lap.

"Excuse the intrusion, my Lord," said Anthony, laying the table with the freshly washed beakers. He carefully poured tea from the steaming kettle. "Mind now," he said, "'tis righteous hot."

Alberon took a grateful sip and his eyes widened in disbelief. "Anthony!" he gasped, "this is *fresh* tea!"

Anthony, not quite recovered from his childish pique, sniffed piously. "'Tis that," he said. Wynter smiled at the unspoken *not that you deserve it*, in his tone.

Alberon inhaled the steam and groaned with pleasure. "Oh, tea," he said. "Oh, blessed tea…where on earth did you get it? We haven't had fresh for nigh on a fortnight."

The little servant looked a touch uncomfortable. "I…" he said. He glanced downhill. "'Tis a gift," he said. "Along with these, your Highness." He took a little parcel from his apron and unfolded a square of cloth onto the table. It contained six sweet-scented griddle cakes, still gently steaming. Wynter recognised them as the distinctive Merron *scòn*.

"The chop-fingered fellow gave them to me," said Anthony. "He's down the bottom of the hill. Him on one side of the road, Sir Oliver on the other, both of them staring up at thee and nary a word passed between them."

Christopher, thought Wynter in alarm. She prayed that her friend had not been so foolish as to send a message with this gift. *Please do not say that they are for me!* she thought, willing the little servant to keep his mouth shut. Now was not the time to reveal the nature of her feelings for Christopher. Alberon's reaction would undoubtedly be stormy, and Wynter did not want tonight's delicate balance disrupted.

Alberon stared at the scòns, then across at Wynter. He frowned, and she swallowed hard.

He's guessed, she thought. *One look at my face was enough to give me away. Oh, curse you, Christopher Garron. Curse you and your damned pride. Let us simply screech our attachment from the rooftops, shall we? Dance the allemande together down the camp road? Announce our betrothal to the whole damned army.* She felt her cheeks flare red with embarrassment, and was instantly angry with Alberon for making her feel that way about Christopher, and with Christopher for attempting to force her hand.

The little servant leaned and murmured in Alberon's ear. "The Merron thief had me choose a cake at random, your Highness. I stood and watched him eat it. Stood with him for over three minutes to make sure he didn't push his fingers down his throat or any such thing. I am beyond certain that they are safe to eat."

"I see," said Alberon. He licked his lips, gazing at the scòns with an entirely different expression now he knew they were not poisoned, and Wynter realised with a searing pang of guilt that Alberon had no notion of their significance for her.

It had all been in her head. She sat rigidly expressionless, appalled by the fact that, when confronted with this warm and subtle gesture of affection, her first feelings towards Christopher had been of anger and of shame. She glanced at Razi who was smiling fondly at the little pile of cakes. Without putting down his precious tape, he took his beaker of tea and raised it in a silent gesture of thanks to the darkness at the base of the hill.

"Are you well, sis?" asked Alberon. "You have gone terribly pale."

"I am fine." She turned to look him in the eye. "Why has Marguerite chosen the Merron for her envoys, Alberon? The woman has nothing but contempt for them. Why would she trust them so?"

Alberon frowned at her. "Do not be dense, Wyn. Who better to convey her secret messages? What person in their right mind would suspect a bunch of God-cursed Merron pagans of carting Marguerite Shirken's papers for her? Besides," he said, taking a scòn, "even if they dared to spy, what harm could fellows like them do? Everyone knows the bloody savages can't read. Good Christ, these are good! What are they made of?"

"Chestnut flour," said Razi quickly. He kicked Wynter under the table, and she bit back her questions about the Merron.

Razi leaned forward and placed the strip of tape on the table between himself and Alberon. "The Haun and the Combermen," he said, "you plan to frighten them with this invention? In the hopes that they will let Marguerite be? If so, you may need to show them more than just a drawing and a flash of noisy light, brother. I suspect they would need to see the machine for themselves to truly understand its power. Do...do you have this weapon in your possession?"

Alberon chuckled. "If only I did," he said. "But Father has the one remaining machine. No, the Combermen have their own, very specific, reasons for being here. As for the Haun, they answered my call to parley in the smug belief that they hold a secret power over me; meanwhile they are *humouring* me, hoping to deepen the rift between Father and me. They have come here planning to gape at Lorcan's wonderful designs, feign alarm at their potential—then toddle off home to their leaders, all the while laughing up their sleeves at their own secret plot. They think they have settled an alliance in Algiers that will destroy the Sultan. But tomorrow—or however soon my damned envoys arrive from Fez—I intend to jerk the rug out from beneath the Haun's prettily slippered feet. Just wait and see."

Alberon smiled darkly at Razi. "They will soon be galloping home in genuine alarm. With their plans in tatters and the noise of my machine ringing in their ears. I shall strengthen the Sultan's court, set the Haun to fighting amongst themselves, and give Marguerite room to manoeuvre, all in one painless shuffle of the cards."

Razi waited, expecting Alberon to go on, but Alberon just continued to smile. "Wait and see," he repeated.

Wynter shivered and pulled her cloak tighter still. The fire blazed high in the brazier and the beaker of tea was warm in her hands, but she was cold to the very core of her, the kind of shivery bone chill that came with staying up too late after too hard a day. She was suddenly weary to her bones, the pillow behind her too comfortable.

Razi said something else, something to do with the poor supplies of mercury, but the chess-like intricacies of the men's conversation was beginning to scratch and blur on her and she no longer had the energy to follow it.

I shall miss out, she thought, *if I let them go on while I am in this state.*

"I am tired," she mumbled. "It is late."

"The moon is setting, believe it or not," sighed Alberon. "Poor Anthony, I have kept him up all night again."

There was silence from the little servant and Wynter leaned out to see that he had curled into a ball on the ground and was fast asleep by the fire. Poor thing. "He is very young, Albi, for you to have dragged him into this." She had spoken without thinking and immediately winced, expecting more of Alberon's unpredictable temper, but her friend just sighed.

"I know," he said. "I did not intend it, believe me. I took him from the palace to keep him safe from questioning, and left him with a charcoal-burner's family in the woods, ordered him to wait till I fetched him. Foolish pup followed me almost to the gates of the camp. Damn near got himself shot for his troubles." He looked at the child with undisguised regret. "Foolish pup," he repeated.

"His family would not take him?"

"I am not certain he has a family, Wyn. Truth be told, I know nothing of the child except his name, and that obviously he was in training to be a personal servant." At Razi and Wynter's enquiring look, Alberon sighed, as if he'd rather not go into it, then lowered his voice. "He is a member of the Truffaut household," he said. "All that remains of the Truffaut household, to be exact."

Razi groaned. They knew well the story of the Truffaut massacre; who could forget it? Wynter glanced at the poor little fellow. "I thought none had survived that slaughter," she whispered.

"Indeed," murmured Alberon. "By the time we got there, the insurrectionists and their Comber allies had already moved on. The damage was done...the Truffauts themselves were hanging from their famous apple trees, God rest them, and every man, woman and child of their household was dead and naked, piled in a heap at the main door, the mansion already naught but a blazing shell."

Alberon hesitated, as if seeing once more that terrible image. When next he spoke, his voice was very quiet. "We had already begun filling in the burial pit when I noticed him stir. I dug him out with my bare hands."

Wynter pressed her fingers to her mouth and shook her head in horror.

"I know, sis. Such a tiny movement. Had I not seen it..." Alberon cut the thought off with a grimace. "The blessing is that he recalls not a jot of it. He woke two days later, a merry, bustling little fellow, much as you find him today. He has never made mention of his life before we found him, and I must confess, I have not much desire to quiz him on the subject."

"Oh, Albi. The poor child."

"Aye. After that day I could no longer be kept from the field. Father said twelve was too young. But if six is old enough to be buried alive, twelve is old enough to fight." Alberon shrugged in a curiously detached way. "In any case, such is war. I'm afraid I have seen much worse since then." He heaved himself from his chair. "Anthony," he whispered, shaking the boy's shoulder, "come along. We are to bed. There's a good chap."

Anthony yawned. "Where shall we put the lady?" he asked sleepily. "I have not asked thee yet your... *thy* preference..." His voice trailed off and he sagged against Alberon who stroked his hair and gazed across at Wynter. He seemed beyond decisions suddenly, tired beyond words.

"I shall retire to Razi's tent," murmured Wynter, staring at the little child, her mind still filled with his story.

Alberon sighed. "I don't know, Wyn. I do not think that such a good idea. This is a camp of army men. They have army minds and army tongues in their heads. There have already been scurrilous associations alluded to in court. Whatever about your time on the trail, I do not think it wise to risk affirming the gossips by making poor Razi your chaperone here in camp."

"Good God," said Razi, jolted from his sad contemplation of the little boy, "you cannot *surely* think that Wynter and I...? That we...?"

Alberon winced in disgust. "Brother! Don't be foul! I'm simply trying to preserve what little reputation Wyn has left in court." He pushed himself to his feet, staggered, then nudged Anthony with his toe. "Up, little mankin."

Anthony climbed slowly to his feet.

"Listen, Razi," said Alberon. "If Wyn has any hopes at all of making a suitable match, we must be very careful to restore her character. Sleeping alone in the tent of the man already suspected of being her lover will do nothing for her future. She has already become..."

Alberon's voice went on, his intentions admirable, his words vile. With them, court life fell down on Wynter again with all its crushing weight of complexities, all its labyrinthine meanings, all its watchfulness. She stood silently listening, too swamped in tiredness to react, too filled with sorrow. She looked out into the night. It was blotted into nothing by the dancing firelight. She was too tired for this. She was too *tired*. She wanted Christopher. She wanted to stagger down the hill to him, to find him standing in the dark, to rest her head on his shoulder. She wanted him to chuckle and call her "lass." She wanted him to kiss her hair and not to give a damn.

Razi and Alberon were arguing over the wisdom of Wynter

sleeping the night in Alberon's tent. For some reason, Alberon did not see that as a compromise to her virtue at all. Razi, however, was insisting that were she to sleep in *his* tent she would at least not be alone in his company, as Christopher Garron would also be there. Alberon found this so ludicrous that he laughed loudly. Unheeded, Anthony swayed by the Prince's side, his eyes closing already.

"There are women," mumbled Wynter.

The men swivelled as one. "*What?*" they snapped, irritated that she should interrupt their debate.

"Women," she said, "amongst the Merron. Women. They can be my defence against scandal."

She began to stagger down the hill, heedless of the men's protests. Alberon was saying something about Merron women being as bad as the men. Razi was telling him to keep his voice down. Wynter passed from firelight into pitch dark. Stones gritted beneath her boots as she made her way blindly, not caring. Alberon said something about the blue tent and Razi said, "Tomorrow, damn it, Albi. Just leave it till tomorrow."

Wynter didn't care. Leave them to it.

It was cold, very cold, but the air felt pleasant on her tired face. She reached the base of the hill and someone stepped to her side, quiet as a cat. She smiled at the familiar, spicy scent of him.

"Hello, lass," he murmured.

"You waited."

"Did you doubt me?"

"Not for a moment."

His arms closed warm around her and she leaned in, her head finding his shoulder in the dark. "Let us to bed," she whispered.

"Alone?"

Wynter sighed. How lovely it would be, in the midst of all these complications, to find themselves alone. To simply take each other's hand and walk through the brooding maze of the tents and out into the forest; to lay their cloaks on a fragrant bed of pine, to undo the laces on each other's clothes and to press together, skin to skin in the dappled moonlight. It would be so good finally to allow themselves the gift of being together. It would be *so good*. It would be such a simple, such an honest joy.

The thought of it made Wynter squeeze her eyes shut and tighten her arms, pulling Christopher's slim body in against hers. He tightened his hold on her and they stood clenched together, their bodies so close, holding each other so tight that it felt as if their hearts were beating side by side with just the barest breadth of skin between.

I want you so badly, thought Wynter. *I want so badly to keep you. Please. Please. Can't I have this one thing? Just this one thing for my own?*

Her hair had fallen a little loose from its binding and, as he held her, Christopher ran his fingers through the stray locks at the nape of her neck. His touch sent delicious fire tingling down Wynter's body. It made her ache. He lowered his forehead to her shoulder. She touched her lips to his neck.

He groaned.

"We ain't doing ourselves any favours, lass."

"No," she whispered, "we are not."

"We need to let go, before neither of us has the strength."

"I know."

Still he held her, quiet and motionless, pressed close in the velvet dark, until finally she broke away and he took her hand. "Come on," he said hoarsely. "I will find us some company."

*   *   *

"Christopher?" she murmured, not certain if he was awake.
"Thank you for the scòns. They were delicious."

Christopher squeezed her waist in silent reply and Wynter
shifted her head against his shoulder, gazing out into the gloom
of the tent. Across the gentle rise and fall of his chest she could
just make out Frangok's back, and a tuft of Soma's pale hair.
Somewhere beyond that again, Hallvor snored softly.

At Christopher's whispered request, the three Merron women
had wordlessly risen from their beds, stumbled into Razi's tent,
flung their covers onto the ground and lain straight back down
again. Wynter suspected that they had barely even woken from
their sleep to do so. She was so painfully grateful to them that
she hardly knew how to express it. But, despite their presence
and despite her very great tiredness, she found it no easier to be
with Christopher without wanting to kiss him, without wanting
to touch him, and she lay tensely by his side, longing to run her
hand beneath his shirt, just to feel the warmth of his bare stomach beneath her palm.

Christopher lay on his back, Wynter's head on his shoulder,
her arm curled on his chest. He seemed perfectly happy just to
have her by his side, and was idly running his thumb across the
twisted woollen bracelet she wore around her wrist.

He spoke softly, his voice a gentle vibration beneath her cheek.
"What do you wish for, Protector Lady? When this is all over
and our lives are our own. What is it that will make you
happy?"

The answer to this unexpected question was so clear and sudden and complete that it almost brought tears. *A cottage shaded
by walnut trees*, she thought. *Beside a river filled with trout. A*

workshop, spicy with wood shavings and resin. Somewhere that I can make good things, strong enough to last a lifetime.

Christopher waited patiently for her reply, but Wynter did not answer. She might as well just say *why wish for the impossible*, and leave it at that. Her desire for Christopher faded slowly beneath the terrible knowledge that everything else she had hoped for was lost. In the softly breathing silence, she closed her hand around a fistful of Christopher's shirt and tried to figure what it might be that he would wish for. Wynter had an awful feeling that everything he had ever truly wanted had already been irretrievably stolen from him by Wolves. Still she turned her head and whispered, "What is it would make *you* happy, love?"

"Oh, you know," he said softly, "all the good things—a big shiny palace, solid gold servants, diamond studded concubines."

Wynter chuckled. That was so utterly *not* what he wanted. "You're a menace."

"Oh, aye," he murmured, "I am that."

There was a moment's silence, during which Christopher's scarred hand closed gently around Wynter's wrist. She felt him relaxing into sleep.

"Christopher," she whispered. "We should talk. There are things we should discuss about court life. Things that we—"

"No." Spoken softly, the gentlest of sounds.

"No?"

"I know all I need to know."

"Chris—"

"Protector Lady, I know all that I need to know."

She lay in uncertain silence for a moment, then went to speak once more.

Christopher tilted his head. His whisper caressed her cheek.

"Settle your head down, lass, and stop your fretting. Razi will be here soon."

Wynter settled her head back onto his shoulder. Frowning, she tightened her fingers in his and watched as their joined hands rose and fell with the easy motion of his chest. Eventually his steady breathing lulled her, her blood slowed to a peaceful rhythm, and she slept.

A Roar of Smoke

Wynter stood in the main thoroughfare of the camp and listened to the silence. The road was a humpbacked ribbon of moonlight stretching away to the deserted barricades. Behind her, Alberon's tent slept beneath the wide-eyed moon.

Why was it so quiet? Where were all the subtle noises of a night-time camp? Wynter listened in vain for the discreet tramp and murmur of the sentries, the snores, the sighs, the coughs of sleeping men. There was none of that—just a low creaking, like a heavy sack swinging idly from a pulley rope. She looked up and down the road, but could find no source for the sound.

Alberon's voice drifted from the tent above, his words clear, though softly spoken.

"You are on my side, brother?"

Wynter turned and looked up the hill, waiting for Razi's reply. None came. She knew Razi was standing up there, gazing at Alberon, his face as unreadable as a starless sky. She took a step forward, her intention to climb the hill, but that creaking noise distracted her again, and she glanced back over her shoulder.

For the first time she noticed the scaffolds that had been erected all through the camp. There were at least two for every tent, their criss-crossed timbers stark against the moonwashed brilliance of the sky. Men hung from them in sets of five, their lifeless bodies swaying in the gentle breeze. There were so many of them. How could they have escaped her attention before now? The thick ropes from which the men were suspended groaned against the wood of the scaffold bars, the source of that heavy creaking sound. Wynter blessed the shadows that hid the details; she had never been able to stomach the bloated spectacle of a hanged man's face.

So this is why the camp is so quiet, she thought. *I had best deliver this news to Alberon. I'm sure he'll want to know that his men are dead.*

A chill wind blew from nowhere, casting grit and dust into Wynter's face. She flung up her hands to save her eyes, gagging on the stench of gunpowder and rot. The ground vibrated beneath her feet, the familiar warning rhythm of an approaching horse, and a ghost rider broke from the dark of the trees. As he shot through the barricades and up the road towards her, Wynter recognised him as the soldier from the ford, the man who Razi could not save. He was barely clinging to his saddle, his transparent face creased with agony. He was shouting, his mouth opening and closing in silent desperation as he galloped through the camp.

He advanced at tremendous speed. Wynter had barely time to stagger back and he was upon her: horse and rider passing through her in a blast of icy cold. The gale from their passage howled within her, screaming in her ears, snatching the hair back from her forehead and temples, stealing the breath from her lungs. Her eyes were blinded with swirling milky light. The soldier's voice roared in her mind, *He will betray you! He will betray you! My Prince! It is a trap!*

Then he was gone, and Wynter fell to her knees in the dust, her hands clawed, her eyes staring, her heart clogged in her throat.

Razi bellowed, "NO," and Wynter turned just in time to see him fling himself between Alberon and the horse. Razi threw up his arms, turned his face away, and the messenger hit him full force.

Rider and horse exploded into cloud and dust, scattering the air with particles of light. Razi was flung into his brother's arms, his coat and his hair beaded in phosphorescence. As Alberon staggered under his brother's weight, Wynter saw his eyes lift to the barricades. His face fell, and Wynter spun once more to face the trees, seeking to find the source of his despair.

More riders were galloping from the forest. Their faces set, their crossbows drawn, they passed through the thick walls of the barricades, their eyes fixed on the Rebel Prince. Wynter recognised the two in front, knew them by the Merron arrows that still pierced their bodies and their blood-blackened horses. They led a charge of glowing, nebulous men—victims of God knew what distant battle—all intently following the two ahead. Wynter ran towards them, screaming, "NO! NO!" They advanced unheeding on a hurricane of dust and cold. As one, they raised their crossbows and fired. Instead of the *thwack* of arrows there came a belch of smoke from each bow, a roar as from a series of cannons. Trails of smoke shot outwards, passing over Wynter's head, ruffling her hair. She spun, following the smoke as it arced its deadly trail to the hill above her.

Alberon looked up, his face illuminated by the advancing light. Razi frowned and turned, too late to see. The missiles hit and the brothers were consumed in fire.

A warhound growled in the gloom, and Wynter snapped awake, listening. The dog growled softly again, but there was no urgency to it and no other noise except for the gentle breathing of the tent's sleeping occupants.

Christopher lay beside her, quietly dreaming. His arm was

heavy across Wynter's waist, his silver bracelets digging into her ribs. She burrowed against him, deep into the warmth of their shared bedding, and inhaled his lovely scent, trying to clear her head of the stench of gunpowder. Christopher murmured something and chuckled softly in his sleep. Wynter took his hand. The ragged ends of his woollen bracelet tickled her wrist. His slim body was warm against hers, a warm strength and a comfort to counteract the terrible chill of her dream.

Razi was asleep beside them, stretched out long and motionless, flat on his back. She watched carefully for the rise and fall of his chest—making sure that he was still alive. Gradually the horror of the dream began to fade.

The warhound growled softly again, his chain clinking. The hounds were tethered just outside the tents, dauntless guardians in the dark. Wynter shifted her head, trying to see them, but they were nothing but grey shades at the dim hollow of the door. Outside, the first robin trilled in anticipation of the day. He was a touch premature, as the sky had hardly begun to grey and the camp was lifeless and still.

Razi sighed. He dropped his arm from across his face and Wynter saw his eyes flash in the gloom. He was awake, staring at the ceiling.

"Wyn?" he whispered.

"Aye."

"He plans making some of Lorcan's machines and gifting them to the Midlander Reformists."

Wynter shot to her elbows. Damn it, the brothers had stayed up talking! She had assumed they would go directly to bed, but they must have continued their conversation long after she had stumbled off. She shook her head in grim frustration and cursed herself for having missed out.

"Midlanders!" she whispered. "The occupants of the blue tent, I assume?"

"Aye," breathed Razi, looking up at her. "In return for your father's weapons, the Midlanders have promised to keep Tamarand off Marguerite's back. While she is usurping her father's throne, they will use the machines against Tamarand, *their own King*. They hope to pummel him into signing the Reformer's Charter of Rights and so bring an end to his terrible inquisitions."

Wynter thought about that for a moment. She had to admit, it was quite a good plan. With Tamarand distracted by internal conflict, he would be unlikely to leap to Shirken's aid. It was possible that Marguerite could have her father dethroned and herself crowned before anything could be done about it.

"You know, if they carry this off, it is quite possible that the Midlander Reformists will succeed in ending Tamarand's tyranny. My father suspected that the reform had much secret support within Tamarand's court. His people are long weary of his madness."

Razi sighed and she barely made out the tired shake of his head in the darkness. He did not approve this toppling of yet another royal house.

"There are Combermen here too, Razi. What of them?"

"They are Comber liberals, sympathisers to the Midlander Reform. They come to pledge their support. Should the Midlander Reformists succeed, the Combermen have assured that there will be no reprisals from them."

"Have they the power to make such a promise? The sect is terribly strong in Comber, I find it unlikely that any liberal faction would have much foundation for..." A cold possibility occurred to her and she faltered in shock. "Oh, Razi, is Alberon offering *them* a machine too?"

Razi's silence told her that he suspected so.

Wynter did not like the vista this unfolded. Those mighty weapons, kept firmly in Southlander control, would be a terrific boon for Jonathan's frail little kingdom. But proliferated willy-nilly amongst the surrounding factions? It took all the advantages of sole possession from the Southlanders and put the kingdom right back into a position of inferior strength.

Razi shifted quietly beside her. "Wyn? Can you imagine those machines in the hands of the Combermen Sect or, God forbid, if Tamarand himself got his hands on one? And worse, can you imagine Marguerite Shirken and what *she* might do with them?"

"I am sure Alberon must have considered this," she whispered. "Why do we not—?"

Behind her, Christopher groaned and rolled onto his back. "Good Frith," he sighed. "What are you two yelling on about at this hour of the night?"

Wynter smiled down at him. He was barely awake. "Albi is convinced that King Shirken has lost his reason," she whispered.

"Wouldn't be surprised," mumbled Christopher sleepily. "The old bastard has always been cracked in his brainpan."

"Marguerite plans to overthrow her father," she whispered. "Albi plans to support her. He thinks she will be a stabilising force in the North."

Christopher lost his drowsy loose-limbed torpor and lay very still and quiet. "A stabilising force?" he said at last. "That ain't what *I'd* call her."

Razi sighed. "Alberon also plans supplying the Midlander Reformists with two of Lorcan's war machines, in order to help them force an end to Tamarand's inquisitions. In effect, he is plotting the usurpation of both of our father's strongest neighbours."

Christopher huffed dryly. "Does he plan on invading the Moroccos, too?" he whispered. "Just for the sport of it?"

"This is not funny," hissed Razi. "Alberon is bent on restructuring the kingdoms of Northern Europe. He will bring the entire delicate house of cards falling down around our ears."

"Well then," sighed Christopher, "we can all reshuffle, and start a new game."

Razi tutted, frustration evident in his quiet voice. "This is no joke, Christopher."

Christopher rose to his elbow and looked at Razi across Wynter's back. "Good job I ain't laughing, then, ain't it? Marguerite is a bloody-handed bitch, Razi, but she ain't no worse than her father. Alberon is simply trading one tyrant for another, what of it? And if he helps end a decade-long inquisition in the Midlands, I say, power to his hand."

Christopher glanced at the sleeping Merron, then leaned across Wynter to whisper quietly down at Razi. "You know what?" he whispered. "Leave him to it and let's you, me and Iseult take ourselves home to the Moroccos. This is all just the same old song with a different set of notes, Razi. That's all it will ever be. All your hard work, all the things you and Lorcan sacrificed, none of it has made one whit of difference in the end. You ain't ever going to *change* anything here, Razi; it ain't ever going to end! Ain't you tired of it? Don't you want some life? Don't you want some *joy*?" He glanced down at Wynter, then back to Razi, who remained silently motionless in the shadows. "Don't you want something better than this, Razi?" he asked softly. "Let's go find something better than this."

"I cannot," said Razi.

Christopher huffed and hung his head in aggravation.

Wynter ran her hand up his bare arm and he looked down at

her, his pale face floating above hers in the dark. She resisted the urge to push his hair from his forehead in case he felt she was making a child of him. "This is a delicate situation, love," she whispered. "There are bridges burnt between the King and his heir that only Razi can remake. Alberon has devised a wonderful plan to strengthen this kingdom, and Razi is his only means of persuading the King to listen. Without Razi's influence—"

"Wonderful plan?" said Razi. He huffed under his breath. "My father's kingdom is a miracle, Wynter. He has maintained its stability all this time, not by brute force, but by diplomacy and by care. The tyrants that surround us may continue to shred and tear at their own people, and their policies may be vile beyond conscience, but my father has maintained the most cordial of relationships with them all. They make use of his Port Road, they benefit from the safe shipping lanes that he has established via his relationship with the Sultan. And while they may sneer at his *ridiculous* laws and at his *scandalous* humanism, they *leave us be*—because Father has ensured that they all profit by his continued presence on the throne and because he has never *once* posed a military threat to them." Razi shook his head. "Alberon will toss all that aside," he said. "He will give it all up, in the futile belief that violence will end violence."

Razi paused. Wynter and Christopher waited in silence for him to continue. Wynter wished that she could see his face more clearly; she could get nothing from his soft, calm voice. "My father's kingdom is a miracle," he whispered again. "I have no intention of aiding my brother in its destruction."

Wynter lifted herself to her elbow, shocked at the implication of her friend's words. "Razi," she cried, "you cannot mean to betray him!"

"Betray him? Good God, Wynter! What would make you use such a word against me?"

"Without your support, Alberon is dead, Razi! He is *dead*! You can't be unaware of this!"

"What Alberon proposes will destroy our father, Wyn! It will destroy *everything*! I cannot let this happen. But I will not betray him. How can you even...? How can you even begun to have...?" Razi cried out in sudden desperate frustration and covered his face with his hands. He lay in total silence for a moment. Wynter was certain he had his teeth gritted, his eyes squeezed tight. Finally he pushed his hands back through his tangled shock of curls and took a deep breath. When next he spoke, his voice had dropped back to its calm, even tone.

"Once I have found a way out of this, and I have the bloody fool back home and settled down, I shall begin to dissuade him. Particularly in relation to this damned marriage—does he honestly believe that Marguerite Shirken will breed him anything but vipers? He may as well simply hand this kingdom over to her and her spawn." He paused again, Wynter staring down at him, her heart hammering in her chest. "Yes," he whispered to himself. "Once I get him home. Once I have him settled, then I shall begin to make everything clear to him. Slowly and carefully—"

"Razi!" interrupted Wynter. "Alberon is not some fractious baby to be dismissed to his bed with a beaker of warm milk! He is heir to the throne of this kingdom, and he is making decisions as such. Why must you dance around him so? Talk to the man! *Talk* to him! Give him the respect of sharing your opinion!"

Razi twisted to face her. He went to speak, but Christopher shushed him suddenly, his attention on the door. One of the warhounds had growled again, this time with intent. The three friends stilled, listening carefully.

The air had brightened, and they saw the misty shapes of the great hounds standing to attention outside the door. One of them trotted from sight, its long chain clinking gently. There was another low chorus of growls as the remaining dog shadows lowered their heads. They were all looking in the direction of the Midlander tent. Quietly taking their weapons, the friends pushed back their covers and crawled to the door. Behind them, the Merron women stirred.

Christopher crouched at the edge of the door and peered out. Wynter and Razi crept to his side, strapping on their swords. The Midlander quarters were dark and motionless in the morning gloom. From this position, Wynter could only see the back of the tent. There were soldiers surrounding it, their faces bored, their attitudes weary, as if they'd been standing guard all night.

Hallvor came to kneel behind Wynter, her eyes on the soldiers. The healer gestured the dogs to her side and they came reluctantly. She leaned to whisper in Christopher's ear. "*Cén fáth na saighdiúirí, a Choinín?*"

He shrugged and shook his head. "She wants to know what they're doing," he murmured, but before Razi could answer, a cultured Midlander accent rang out from the front of the tent.

It was a man, very affronted and annoyed. "What in the name of God are you doing?" he demanded. "Have you lost your reason? Let me pass!"

Oliver's voice drifted quietly across the air. "Get back inside, Presbyter, please."

"I must attend my lady's need! Tell your men—"

"Shut your *face*," said Oliver wearily. "Get inside, set on your damned arse, and await the Prince's pleasure."

Wynter met Razi's eye. "Let us go see," she suggested, and before Razi could speak, she ducked from the tent and out into the cold air.

Mary

Alberon was tramping down from his quarters as Wynter rounded the blue pavilion tent. He was swaddled in a thick, red cloak and his young face was tired, his brows drawn down. Now that she was outside and in the growing light, Wynter saw that Razi, too, was drawn-looking, his skin grey with fatigue. The brothers must have been up for most of the night, talking.

Wynter glanced behind her. The Merron women had emerged, their swords drawn. Christopher gestured them to stand down and the warriors slipped discreetly into the neighbouring tent where their male companions lay sleeping.

There were more soldiers guarding the entrance to the blue tent, and Oliver stood just outside the closed door, speaking quietly to a lieutenant. Wynter, Razi and Christopher came to a wary halt at the corner. At their appearance, the soldiers came to attention, eyeing them suspiciously, and Oliver turned to see what had alarmed his men. His eyes dropped to Christopher and Wynter's bared blades, then lifted meaningfully to Razi. Razi spread his hands in a gesture of non-interference, and the three friends sheathed their weapons. Oliver tightened his jaw in irritation, then turned his attention to the Prince who was just coming up the main thoroughfare.

"They up?" grunted Alberon. Oliver nodded. "You say anything to them?" Oliver shook his head. "Come on, then." The

Prince went to duck in at the door and Oliver stayed him with a hand on his arm.

"Highness," he murmured, "we can't just crowd in. She has no maid, no type of chaperone at all, other than that...that *fellow*. It's not seemly."

Alberon sighed impatiently. "Christssake, Oliver..." he began.

"Highness, it is not *seemly*. This is not some camp follower we're discussing here, a certain amount of propriety, surely, must be maintained, even in the roughest of situations, and for a woman in her—"

"Oh, *enough*," groaned Alberon, flinging up his hand. He looked around him in desperation and saw Wynter standing at the corner with Razi and Christopher. "Protector Lady," he called, gesturing her over. "And you, too, Lord Razi, please."

"Wait here please, Chris," said Razi softly. "Do not try to come any closer. And, Chris, when you have the chance, it would be best to leave your weapons back at the tent as my brother has ordered. Do your best to persuade the Merron to do the same."

Christopher nodded. Razi straightened his bed-crumpled shirt and crossed to his brother, Wynter following silently behind. She eyed the guards as she passed through their ranks. They were sneering at Christopher, and she had to push down her anger at the contempt in their faces.

Suddenly, Boro trotted from nowhere, and all the soldiers stiffened, their sneers wiped away at the sight of the giant hound wandering free from his chain. Wynter saw the barest trace of a dimple crease the corner of Christopher's mouth at the alarm in the soldier's faces.

"*Ná bac faoi, a chú,*" he murmured. "*Níl iontu ach amadáin.*"

Whatever he said, Boro must have agreed, because he flopped to the ground, laid his head on his paws and closed his eyes, dismissing the soldiers from his sight. Christopher slouched against the tent pole, the massive creature snoozing placidly at his feet. The soldiers turned their eyes front, and Wynter smirked in satisfaction at the colour in their cheeks.

She was startled by a hand closing on her arm and she turned to find Alberon frowning down at her. He flicked an irritated glance at Christopher and drew Wynter around so that she was between Razi and himself.

"What can we do for you, brother?" she said uncertainly. She found herself hemmed in with Razi, Alberon and Oliver on each side. Each of them was considerably taller than her and she had to look up into their faces like a child loomed over by adults. Unconsciously, she stepped back, and Razi, at least, had the self-possession to give her some room.

"I have need to speak to the woman in this tent," said Alberon tightly. "She's high-born and...and a little...delicate. Another female presence would do much for her peace of mind."

Wynter quelled an amused snort. The thought of herself, head to toe dusty and dressed in men's clothes, acting as a feminine buffer between a "delicate" female and her male companions was just too amusing. She managed to nod politely. "I shall do my best," she said. "Who is the poor flower?"

"The Lady Mary Phillipe D'Arden," said Alberon. "She—"

"Lady *Mary*?" said Wynter, startled into remembrance, the words out before she could stop them. "Isaac's Mary?"

"Good God," moaned Razi. "Wyn!"

Alberon clamped down on her arm and dragged her closer, his eyes wide. She choked back a cry and forced herself not to struggle as his strong fingers bit into her flesh.

"Alberon," she whispered, trying hard not to make a scene. "My arm."

"How do you know Isaac?"

Wynter hesitated, not certain how to explain her horrible interview with the poor tortured ghost, and how he had been so keen for Wynter to find the rebel camp and get a message to his "darling Mary." Her hesitance seemed to further enrage Alberon and his brutal grip on her arm tightened even further. Wyn couldn't help it; she winced and squirmed.

"Albi," she whispered, "stop!"

Razi's hand came between them. He grabbed Alberon's fingers and squeezed so hard that the tendons in his hand stood out like knotted ropes under his skin.

"Let. Her. Go," he said, staring into his brother's eyes.

Alberon released Wynter and she stepped back, her arm numb.

Razi maintained his grip on his brother for just a second longer than necessary, then released him. He slid a look at Oliver. "Sir Knight," he murmured. "Take your knife from my back or I shall break your arm."

Oliver looked to Alberon, who nodded his consent, and the knight slipped his little sleeve-knife back into its hidden scabbard.

Wynter glanced anxiously at Christopher. He was standing to attention just outside the awning, his hand on his belt-knife, his face uncertain. The guards around him were similarly poised, and Wynter realised that the entire confrontation had been so quick and so subtly enacted that the witnesses were not sure what had transpired.

"The Protector Lady is innocent of any plotting, your Highness," whispered Razi. "I told you nothing of her communion with Isaac because I want her *out of this*. Do you understand, Alberon? I want Wynter *out of this*. She's been through enough."

"You bloody fool!" snapped Alberon. "What was I to think, after you had told me she knew nothing of the man? How am I supposed to trust you if you insist on playing games? What else have you kept from me?"

Alberon was flushed with rage, Razi darkly intent, and they were hissing furiously at each other across the top of Wynter's head. She stood between them clutching her aching arm and looked up into their angry faces.

"Do not manhandle me again, your Highness," she said quietly. "I will not take kindly to it."

Alberon faltered. He blanched. His eyes fell to her arm. "Oh, sis," he whispered. "Did I hurt you?"

She turned to Razi. "And as for you, my Lord, perhaps we can dispense with the furtive politics? At least between the three of us, it would be refreshing not to stumble around each other's lies."

Razi's lips parted in shock and his cheeks flushed ever so slightly, whether from anger, or from shame, it was difficult to tell. The brothers lapsed into a suddenly self-conscious silence. Wynter glanced at Sir Oliver who was gazing blankly into space while his superiors settled their differences. Sometimes there was a lot to be said for courtliness. She turned once more to Alberon.

"So, your Highness," she said. "What is it you wish us to do?"

The interior of the Midlander tent was dim and stuffy, smelling of damp canvas and un-aired blankets. The two occupants did not show any concern at the group's abrupt entrance. The priest simply lifted his head to regard them, and the lady did not look up at all. They were occupied in prayer, the lady kneeling at a delicate looking prie-dieu, the priest standing behind her, his hands folded into his sleeves. Wynter regarded him cautiously as she ducked in the door. Within the frame of his dark cowl, his long, square-jawed face was as smooth and arch as a Comberman icon. He gave no discernible reaction to the unlikely combination of an Arab and a bare-headed woman at the Royal Prince's side.

The lady continued her prayers, her lips moving gently, her eyes closed. It was obvious that she had made an effort to maintain a level of courtly presentation, despite her reduced circumstance. Her once rich gown was travel-worn and frayed, but she had taken care to keep it clean, and it was well brushed and neat. Her dark hair was carefully coiled and pinned beneath her skullcap, two heavy rolls of it decently hiding her ears. Her hands were respectably covered to the tips, only her ring finger bared to show her status as a married woman. She was in every way a decent, God-fearing Midlander lady, and she was determined to be seen to finish her prayers no matter what was going on.

Alberon cleared his throat with quiet impatience, tapping his fingers against his thigh.

The lady continued to ignore him, her slender hands folded under her chin. She had a sweet enough face, a very acceptable court-face in fact—heart-shaped, her little mouth a soft undemanding pink, her eyelashes long and delicately shading her cheeks. Wynter was sure that she would have had her pick of suitors before making what must have been a good match.

What had brought her here, though? To this musty tent in the middle of nowhere, surrounded by soldiers, with nothing but a rope cot, a prie-dieu and a folding chair for furniture; no one but a stone-faced priest as chaperone.

Wynter hoped she would not be relegated too long into this

woman's company. On the whole, court women bored her terribly. The poor creatures' lives were so narrow, their view of the world so horribly constricted that Wynter could rarely find anything in common with them. She did not wish to spend her time here discussing frivolities while her menfolk pursued the hard realities of life.

"Lady Mary," prompted the priest.

The lady sighed, her lips tightened. She opened eyes of the darkest brown and looked straight ahead, staring at the canvas wall as if gathering something within her. She turned to look at Alberon. There was such weariness in her young face, such stony, hopeless pride, that Wynter could not help but feel sorry for her. Then the lady heaved herself to her feet and Wynter realised with horror that she was pregnant. Under her full skirts it was difficult to tell just how far gone she was, but a goodly seven months by the looks of it. Wynter looked back up into the lady's face, unable to hide her shock, and the lady made brief, expressionless eye contact before looking back to Alberon.

"Lady Mary," he said. "I would speak with you. To that end, I shall be happy to introduce the Protector Lady Wynter Moorehawke. She would be more than pleased to make your acquaintance, should you desire it."

Wynter curtseyed slightly. She watched the lady's expression, waiting for the usual Midlander distaste at her father's unique title. But to her surprise, the lady's face opened slightly, and she seemed to lose some of her reserve.

"*Protector* Lady?" she asked. Her musical accent gave the title a lovely poetry. "You are the great Lorcan Moorehawke's daughter?" Wynter nodded, pleased, and the lady smiled in welcome, clasping her hands at her breast in the formal gesture of delight.

Alberon formally introduced the Protector Lady Wynter

Moorehawke to the Lady Mary Phillipe D'Arden, and Wynter crossed to take the chaperone's proper place at the lady's left hand.

"Thank you, your Highness," said Mary, her gratitude genuine. "What a pleasure!"

Alberon regarded her with pursed lips. There was a laden silence where his reply should have been. Mary's eyes flicked uncertainly to Razi, then back. She glanced at Oliver. Both men were watching her with unreadable expressions.

Her face closed over again.

From this side of the tent, Wynter saw her companions anew, and the change in perspective was a little shocking. Razi's dark face was rough with stubble, his clothes dishevelled. His hair, unruly at the best of times, was an uncombed mess. Despite his courtly posture and his smooth manner, he looked unpredictable and wild. By his side, Alberon was hard-faced and speculative, his silence a deliberate act of hostility. Oliver stood at their backs, solid, deep-rooted and darkly ready. He gave the impression of a man waiting to strike.

All three were at least a head taller than the two women before them, all armed, all staring across the barely furnished tent from a position of absolute power. The priest, standing out of Wynter's line of sight, was an unknown quantity. Wynter felt a sudden, strange rush of protectiveness towards the woman by her side.

"Your Highness?" ventured Mary. "You wish something from me?"

Alberon jerked his chin at the folding chair. "Sit," he ordered.

Mary's hands tightened briefly into a sudden, anxious knot. Then she seemed to force herself to relax, and, smiling, she curtseyed in gracious welcome.

"Your Highness," she said. "How happy I am to receive you to my quarters. Please, allow me to make you comfortable."

She swept her hand to the rope cot, as if offering a golden couch strewn with velvet cushions. For a moment, this struck Wynter as a rather pathetic, peculiarly *female* thing to do, but then she saw the discomfort in the men's faces and she was filled with admiration. In the face of such courtly hospitality, how could any gentleman behave other than civilly?

Mary stood waiting, her arm out, her face politely expectant. It was a horribly shaky, desperately fragile form of self-defence, but Wynter thought it gave the Lady Mary a strange type of power, an undeniable dignity and an air of unbreakable self-worth.

Alberon fumed, his jaw working.

Oliver shifted his eyes to the wall.

Razi blinked. Then, to Wynter's great pride, he pushed his sword back on his hip and bowed. "You are kind, Lady Mary," he said, "and we are most obliged. Will you not also take a seat?"

Mary nodded graciously and settled herself into her little chair. Razi lowered himself onto the low bed with as much dignity as he could muster. It took him a moment to arrange his long legs, but he managed to do so in the end, without looking too much an awkward fool. He gazed blandly at his brother. Alberon glared, his lips tight.

"Protector Lady Wynter," murmured Mary, leaning back and looking up. Wynter, seeing her face properly for the first time, realised that she could hardly be more than nineteen or twenty. She bent to listen. "Would you like to sit, dear?" asked Mary. "I am afraid there are no more seats, but we can pull Jared's pallet from the corner there and you could use it as a cushion."

"No thank you, Lady Mary. I am perfectly happy to stand."

"You are certain? I am sure Jared would not mind."

Wynter could only assume that Jared was the silently lurking priest. Smiling, she shook her head and straightened once more. She found herself standing almost to attention, her hand resting casually on her sword. Quite apart from the fact that she had no desire to sit on Jared's possibly infested bedding, she felt the overwhelming urge to stand protectively at this woman's back and stare down the very men she had come in with. Alberon looked from her to Razi as if they had both quite spectacularly lost their minds.

"Won't you sit down, your Highness?" said Razi, patting the cot.

"You must be the Royal Prince Alberon's brother?" asked Mary, leaning forward and touching Razi lightly on his dirty sleeve. "I should not like to be forward, but I would be so pleased to make your acquaintance. Should we ever be introduced."

Wynter smiled. One would think oneself at a reception! *Should we ever be introduced*, indeed. She glanced to Alberon's still glowering face and leant to murmur into Mary's ear. "I have the honour of being a member of the Lord Razi's circle," she said. "As you and I are now acquainted, Lady Mary, I doubt anyone could take offence should I provide an introduction."

Mary smiled up at her, no trace of irony in her expression at all. "I should like that very much, Protector Lady. If you think you could arrange it."

"My Lord Razi," said Wynter formally, "would you allow me the pleasure of introducing the Lady Mary Phillipe D'Arden? She would be more than pleased to make your acquaintance, should you desire it."

The Lord Razi did not attempt to rise from his awkward seat, but he managed to contrive a little bow nonetheless. The Lady

Mary dipped her head and Wynter introduced her formally. Razi shook Mary's hand. Her cuff was terribly frayed, Razi's stained with soot.

"Pleased," he murmured.

"I shall take it from your presence here, my Lord, that my dear Isaac found you at last?"

Razi's big hand tightened in shock, and Mary's face showed momentary pain and fear before freezing into a strained calm. "Your *dear*...?" said Razi.

Mary remained motionless, her eyelids fluttering, convinced perhaps, that Razi was purposely inflicting pain, and unwilling to plead with him to stop.

"Razi," murmured Wynter.

"Your *dear* Isaac," said Alberon, drawing the lady's eyes, "betrayed my trust in him and, instead of opening dialogue with my father, as I ordered, abused his access to court in an attempt to *assassinate my brother.*"

Mary, still leaning forward, her arm stretched awkwardly between herself and Razi, shook her head mutely. Wynter said Razi's name again, and he realised that he was crushing Mary's hand. He released her and she withdrew with careful composure, discreetly opening and closing her fingers. He reached as if to check her hand, and she drew back.

"Isaac would never do that," she whispered. "Never."

"Your Highness's brother is mistaken," said the priest, his deep rumble surprising them all.

"Mistaken?" said Alberon, his tone dangerously low. "Mis...?" He strode abruptly around the cot and pushed Razi's head aside, jerking his shirt down from his right shoulder. Razi yelled in protest, and the Lady Mary gasped at the ugly, knotted scar that marred his brown flesh.

"Good *God*," cried Razi, shrugging his brother off and yanking his shirt back into place. "Albi!"

Alberon ignored him, all his attention on the priest. "Isaac threw a knife across a crowded room," he snarled. "He *threw a knife*."

The words "threw a knife" seemed to have some resonance for these people, and the priest deflated. He exchanged a stricken look with the lady. "Oh, Isaac," he said.

"Do not feign shock," said Alberon. "Nor you!" he snapped at Mary. "Courtly and all as he might have been, Isaac was no politician. He was just a damned soldier, and hopelessly infatuated with *you*, Lady! Do not sit there with your doe's eyes and tell me you had no idea of his plan to kill my brother!"

Mary shook her head, her bruised fingers held to her breast, her eyes glittering with tears. Wynter stood very still, her posture and expression an unconscious mirror of Oliver's who stood in position by the door, his hand on his sword, his face carefully neutral. She glanced sidelong at the priest. Like the Lady Mary, he seemed genuinely thrown.

"Isaac..." ventured the priest, "Isaac was very devout."

Whatever he meant by this was lost on Wynter, but Mary closed her eyes in dismay. "Oh, Jared," she said, "no."

"You imply, perhaps, that he could not bear the thought of a Musulman on the throne? Is that your thought, Presbyter?"

The priest gazed at Alberon mutely. His eyes flickered to Razi.

"Would you perhaps have encouraged these opinions?" hissed Alberon.

The priest's eyes widened and he stayed silent. Wynter wondered what it was that Alberon expected to hear from this man. A confession? In the priest's position, Wynter would have had her tongue drawn rather than implicate herself. On the other hand, did Alberon really think it likely that a Midlander priest and a devout Midlander soldier would be open to the idea of a Musulman heir to the Southland's throne? Did he really think it likely that they would have been anything but appalled at the thought? For the priest to deny such feelings would be patently ridiculous.

She stared at the priest's terrified face and wondered just how much or how little he had had to do with Isaac's fervent beliefs. She wondered if he would have been willing to compound them, had he known what a terrible death the poor man would face because of it.

"We did not discuss the Lord Razi," whispered the priest at last. "It never seemed likely that he would be put in your place. It was so far from possible that your father would have been so—"

The priest cut himself short, but everyone knew what he meant to say. *Stupid.* It was so far from possible that Jonathon would have been so *stupid.* Alberon looked the man up and down, and Wynter could see it in his face. Like her, Alberon was considering the possibility that Isaac had acted alone, on the spur of the moment, as a violent reaction to Razi's sudden and unexpected accession to heir.

Razi's deep voice drew her attention. He was staring at Mary. "His Royal Highness told me that Isaac was your squire, Lady Mary." His eyes flitted to Mary's swollen belly. "I had not understood..." he said softly.

The lady placed her hands on her stomach, as if to hide it, and drew herself up straighter in her chair. Wynter blushed for her. It must be terrible to have a man see one in that state. The poor woman should have been safely in her confinement by now— happily sequestered from sight, surrounded by her ladies and female relatives, knitting and sewing and preparing in joy for the arrival of her child—not stuck in this godforsaken backwoods, surrounded by rough men, with not even a beaker of fresh tea to give her comfort.

"This is my *late husband's* child, my Lord," she said. "Please do not stoop to sully my friendship with Isaac. I could not bear it." Her voice was cold, but it trembled and it was obvious that she was nearing the end of her self-control.

"I am so sorry," said Razi. He leaned forward and squeezed her hand in sympathy. It had the effect of undoing the poor woman's restraint somewhat and her eyes overflowed. She shook her head, extricated her hand from Razi's grip and pressed her fingers to her face until she got herself under control.

"He was simply my friend," she said. "He was my friend."

Razi glanced at the priest. "Presbyter, would you like to fetch the lady some tea? Or something to eat?"

The priest stared at him for a moment. He looked at Alberon, then Oliver, then his eyes went to the door. The sun had risen fully, and within the angular shade of the awning, the soldiers' shadows loomed tall. The priest shook his head, and Wynter felt a small spark of admiration for him. He would not leave his lady alone under these circumstances.

"Oliver?" said Razi. "Please arrange something for the lady."

Oliver remained unmoving, waiting for Alberon to give his orders. Razi sighed, and looked to Alberon. The Prince returned his look with a disapproving shake of his head and crossed to take a seat on the cot instead.

Razi gaped at him. "Albi!" he cried.

"I shall ask Freeman Garron if he would be so kind," murmured Wynter, heading for the door before the brothers could descend into a repeat of their recent irritation.

Soldiers glanced at her when she came to the door, then looked away.

She gestured Christopher to her and he came, Boro trailing in his wake. "Freeman," she said quietly, "the Lady Mary..." She paused in embarrassment, then leant to whisper in Christopher's ear, her cheeks burning even as she said the words. "The lady is quite heavy with child, Christopher, and though commendably restrained, I suspect suffering a good deal of mental distress. I wonder...do you suppose Hallvor might have something suitably soothing for her to drink? And perhaps something more substantial to eat than seems to be available to the camp?"

Christopher, his face close to her own, nodded. Their cheeks brushed for a moment as he pulled away. "I'll see what I can do, Protector Lady," he murmured, bowing.

She watched him leave, glanced again at the soldiers, and ducked back into the tent.

The priest was speaking rapidly to Razi. "I am sorry for what Isaac did to you, my Lord. I can understand the light that it must throw me into, but I can assure you, I have come here in all sincerity to finish my Lord D'Arden's work. I would do nothing to jeopardise it. Certainly, had I an inkling of how Isaac would act, I would have done my utmost to dissuade him. I hope..." He looked anxiously at Alberon. "I can only pray that this has not put an end to our negotiations?"

Alberon regarded him coolly.

"There...so many people are depending on...Phillipe himself gave his life for..." The priest stuttered to a hopeless silence. "You have reason to think me guilty?" he cried suddenly. "Isaac said something that would lead you believe it? It is lies!" He jarred to a halt again, frantic.

Innocent panic born of fear, mused Wynter, *or wretched guilt?*

She looked to Razi. He, too, was assessing the priest, his eyes narrowed. Under their combined scrutiny, the man looked as if he were about to cry with fear.

Finally Razi shook his head. "Isaac said nothing of you, priest. Only that Alberon was in negotiation with the Midlanders over the Bloody Machines." He paused, then pointedly switched his focus to Oliver. "Isaac *did* say that you had arranged his access to the palace, Sir Knight."

Oliver's face flared red and his spine stiffened. His eyes stayed firmly locked on the blank canvas of the far wall.

"Which you had done, of course," said Alberon. "On my orders."

Oliver's eyes flickered to Razi.

"Mind you," said Alberon. "None of *my* orders involved killing my brother."

Wynter's stomach went cold at that and she looked at Oliver anew. Both Alberon and Razi sat motionlessly regarding him, their faces blandly inquiring.

Oliver remained still and silent, his eyes front.

"Do you recall a man named Jusef Marcos, Sir Knight?" Razi's soft question elicited a stiff nod from Oliver. "He told me that the Prince sent him some orders. I suspect those orders came from you. Do you recall them?"

Oliver said nothing, just gazed straight ahead, his face immobile.

"Do you recall what orders you sent to Jusef Marcos, Sir Knight?" At Oliver's continued silence, Razi sighed. "Oliver," he said tiredly, "did you tell Jusef Marcos to kill the pretender to the throne?"

At last, Oliver looked at Razi. His mouth drew down. He nodded. Wynter gasped in shock, but Alberon and Razi's expressions did not change. Instead they remained seated side by side on the low cot, their elbows on their knees, their very different faces intent.

In stark contrast to their strange composure, it was all Wynter could do not to rip her knife from her scabbard and fling it at Oliver's face. "You goddamned *traitor*," she cried.

"How could I not?" he said, sadly. "The King would never leave himself without an heir. With my Lord Razi dead, Jon would have had no choice but to allow his Royal Highness to come home. With Razi dead, there can be no *mortuus*."

"And the attack on Simon's men?" asked Razi, his quiet voice hard, his jaw tight. "His murder, and that of my good friend Shuqyar ibn Jahm? Was that also your plan, dear uncle? Did you also order that? That I should be bound behind my horse? That I should be dragged until dead? That my head should be removed and kicked about and finally sent home to my father in a hessian sack? These too were your orders?"

Oliver shook his head. "Oh no, Razi," he whispered. "God, no. Not that."

Alberon was on his feet before anyone could register it. Moving with deadly silence, he strode to Oliver and punched him hard in the temple, felling him as sure as if he'd stabbed him in the head. Oliver dropped to his knees, his face creased in agony and despair.

The Lady Mary jumped in shock, but to her credit, she did not cry out.

Alberon stood over Oliver who knelt, dazed, at his feet. "Did I order it?" he hissed. Oliver blinked rapidly, his hands hovering as if he had started to shield his head, but forgotten to finish the action. "Did I *order* it?" repeated Alberon quietly, and he punched again, sending Oliver to the ground.

Wynter bit back a protest. Despite her rage, it was shocking to witness Alberon's violence, and frightening to see Oliver's silent lack of resistance to the younger man's attack.

Alberon leaned down to snarl quietly into the knight's ear. "Answer me, you cur! Did I *order my brother's death*?"

"No, your Highness," whispered Oliver, his eyes averted. "No." He kept his hands up, anticipating another blow.

Alberon slapped his face. "You seditious *mongrel*," he said. "You faithless goddamned *renegade*. How *dare you*?"

"Alberon," murmured Razi, "leave him." Alberon did not respond. "Your Highness," said Razi, "please, I beg you, leave him."

Alberon straightened, his fists clenched, and Oliver pushed himself slowly to his knees. He looked up at Razi, his face a picture of sad regret. "My Lord," he whispered. "What else could I have done?"

"Waited for your *damned orders*!" hissed Alberon.

His words registered on Wynter, and she realised with a sudden chill that it was Oliver's insubordination that had most angered the Prince. Shocked, she stared at Alberon's scarlet face. It was suddenly very clear to her that if Oliver paid the ultimate price for his actions, it would be due more to his disloyalty to Alberon than his attempts to end Razi's life.

Alberon continued to glower in silent rage, and it struck Wynter that, for all his usual bellowing and his obviously genuine anger, both he and Razi were going about this in a very quiet manner. She glanced to the shadows of the soldiers who were guarding the door. There had been no reaction from them. They seemed to have no idea what was happening within the canvas walls of the tent. Wynter straightened slowly, her heart tightening in understanding.

They mean to let him go, she thought. *Good Christ, after what he has done, they will let Oliver go!*

She looked to Razi in disbelief. He was watching Oliver.

"You should have trusted me," he said sadly. "You should have known I would never..." His voice trailed to nothing and the two men gazed at each other in silence, both knowing that Razi had had very little say in his accession.

Oliver shook his head in genuine regret. "I am sorry," he whispered.

"Do you not understand," asked Razi, "that I have no desire to usurp my brother? Do you not trust me to act with only his interests in mind? You do not have to protect him from me, Oliver."

Oliver regarded Razi with glittering eyes, and Wynter knew what he was thinking. All Razi's good intentions were as naught should the King remain set to put him on the throne. From any angle, Alberon's position was greatly strengthened by his brother's death, and Oliver could not in all conscience kneel at Razi's feet and offer his fealty if it meant Alberon's disinheritance.

"Sir Oliver," said Wynter. The man turned to her. "However it may seem, I assure you that the Lord Razi is his Royal Highness's only hope of returning to the throne. The lord has risked everything in coming here, just as you have risked everything in support of your Prince. I beg you understand this, Sir Knight, without the Lord Razi you are doomed; his Royal Highness is doomed. In fact, I sincerely believe that this kingdom is doomed, sir, unless the Lord Razi lives to complete his mission in reconciling the King and his heir."

The man that she had known as "uncle" looked up at her from where his beloved nephew had knocked him to the ground. This same man who had jogged around the parapets with Razi on his back, neighing like a horse and pretending to jump hurdles; who had cried as he carried Wynter back to the palace the day she'd fallen from that damned tree and broken her arm; who had swung Albi onto the back of his first horse and told him, "Ride boy! Don't be afraid! Just ride!" The very same man who had been her father's great friend, who was the King's cherished cousin—now spread his hands in apology for having ordered the death of her beloved Razi and shook his head.

"Protector Lady," he said, "I did what I had to do."

A shadow moved across canvas and the lieutenant made a perfunctory noise before pulling back the door flap. His face froze at the sight of Oliver, crouched at Alberon's feet, his face blotched and swelling from the Prince's blows, and he came to a terrified halt, not certain what to do. His eyes slid to the far wall, pretending not to see, and Oliver looked miserably across his shoulder at him.

"What is it?" growled Alberon.

The lieutenant, still frozen in place, his eyes focused on absolutely nothing said, "R-reporting as ordered, sir...uh...your Highness. The changing of the pickets has come and gone, and still no supplies, sir...Highness...sir."

"Sir Oliver will be with you in a moment. Go and await him outside."

The lieutenant dropped the door with unseemly haste, and Oliver gaped at Alberon, hardly daring to believe his ears.

"I should have you whipped to death, Oliver."

Oliver nodded, his eyes wide.

"I should hand you to my brother and allow him exact his vengeance upon you. Allow him drag *you* to your death, perhaps...play a little football with *your* head."

Oliver shook his head. "That was not me," he whispered. "I would never..."

"Get up," said Alberon. "Go tend to our men."

Oliver got stiffly to his feet. He turned to leave.

"Oliver," said Razi softly. The knight froze, his hand on the door. He looked reluctantly back.

"I understand you had no choice," said Razi. "It is simply the world we live in."

Oliver could not contain himself at that and he sobbed, his eyes overflowing. He shook his head. "I am so sorry," he whispered. "I'm so sorry."

"It is over," said Razi. "I have forgotten it. Go do your work." And he allowed Oliver to duck from the tent and walk away.

A Woman's Place

There was an uncertain silence after Oliver's departure. The Lady Mary and the priest remained very still, as if frightened to draw attention to themselves. Mary sat erect, her hands knotted in her lap, her eyes on Razi.

Wynter stared at Alberon. "You cannot mean to trust him?" she said.

Alberon tutted, and Razi sighed and rubbed his forehead with his hand. Wynter looked from one to the other in disbelief.

"He has proved himself disloyal!" she cried. "He has betrayed the King, he has acted behind your back and he has *tried to kill Razi*!"

Alberon snapped his attention to her. "In what way has he betrayed the King?" he said. Wynter dropped her outstretched hand. Alberon glared at her. "In what way has Sir Oliver betrayed the King, Protector Lady?"

"Albi," said Razi softly, "she did not..."

"No one in this camp has betrayed the King. I would charge you remember that! Bad enough these men have had to risk all to support me, without my very allies sullying their names!"

"Your Highness," said Razi again, "please. She did not mean it."

"He *ordered you dead*!" cried Wynter, unable to contain herself. "Are you *insane*?" She turned to Alberon. "He *ordered Razi dead*! Tell me that means something to you!"

"Wynter!" Razi's voice was sharp now and he slapped his hand on the cot. "That is enough!"

She clenched her hands, enraged beyond words, and Razi's face softened. "Keep your voice down," he said gently. She shook her head at him. They could not possibly plan to ignore this? It was not possible that they would.

"Oliver did what he felt he must to protect the Prince's position as heir," said Razi. "He felt he had no choice...I shall not condemn him for it." His eyes flickered to the Lady Mary, and he looked suddenly drained and lost. "We've all done terrible things in our time." He heaved himself to his feet. "What now, your Highness?"

Alberon gestured grimly to the priest. "I must discuss details with Jared, here." He looked his brother up and down. "Go shave your face and comb your hair, Razi; you look like hell. Wynter, you will tend the Lady Mary. I shall send breakfast." He was already ducking out the door as he spoke, his voice drifting off. Jared followed him.

Razi remained standing for a moment, his face blank with exhaustion. Then he shook himself. "Stay here, sis," he said. He smiled. "We'll be going home soon...Lady Mary? Is there anything I can do for you? Any comforts you might need?"

Mary just stared at him, her hands clasped at her stomach. Razi nodded, bowed and headed tiredly for the door. He was about to duck outside when Mary spoke out.

"What did you do to him?" she asked. Razi came to a halt, his hand tightening against the canvas wall of the tent. "Isaac," clarified the lady. "What did you do to him?"

Oh, no, thought Wynter. *Don't. Don't tell her.*

Razi turned his head only a little. She saw him hesitate. Then he turned to face the lady and looked her in the eye. Wynter felt Mary stiffen by her side, her small hands clenched.

"I had him tortured," said Razi.

Mary shook her head in horror.

"I had him tortured," said Razi again, his voice too loud. "It was vile." He held Mary's appalled eyes, as if to punish himself with the look in them. "He died," he said. Then he ducked outside and the tent flap fell into place.

Wynter stood behind the lady's chair, waiting for tears and searching her mind for suitable platitudes, but when Mary spoke, her voice was curiously steady and distant.

"Poor Isaac. I always suspected that he had feelings for me."

He called you "darling," thought Wynter. "My darling"...he said to tell you that he had stayed true. I do not think I shall ever tell you that. I think it might break your heart if you knew it.

"It was not for revenge that he was tortured, lady. You understand that? To have done that to another person...it is so far from what Razi is. I wish I could make you understand *how* far."

Mary remained silent. Wynter stared down at the lace cap settled neatly on her glossy black hair, overwhelmed with sympathy for her. "Lady?" she asked gently. "Do you think it likely that Isaac acted alone?"

Mary nodded. "I suspect so. Poor Isaac was unbendingly loyal to my husband, but he was no reformer. I'm afraid that your Lord Razi's dark skin would have been enough to appal the poor fellow...and the thought of a non-Christian on the throne!" The lady shook her head. "I can just imagine his outrage." She looked beseechingly at Wynter. "It is true that Isaac was no humanist, Protector Lady, but I hope that you can believe me when I tell you he was a good man."

Wynter nodded. "I understand," she said.

"The inquisition took Phillipe the very week that he had

planned to journey here. Jared knew I would not be safe and so he came for me and took me with him. Phillipe's fellows were meant to meet us on the trail. They never appeared, but Jared knows they are still active. They await news of this negotiation—so eager for change."

Mary paused, her thoughts running away with her.

"Do you think they will effect that change, lady?"

"Oh yes," breathed Mary. "Oh yes. With your Prince's machines they can do it. I have no doubt."

The Prince's machines.

"Lady?" asked Wynter, her mouth dry. "Will it be a change worth effecting?"

Mary looked up at her. "Protector Lady, *anything* would be better than the current situation. My husband's plans have robbed him of his life, and they have left me with nothing. I doubt that even one member of my family remains alive. But I still believe in the reform, Protector Lady. I must. For if you could only know what it is like there..." She shook her head. "A change must come," she whispered.

Wynter looked from the lady's dark, earnest eyes to the swell of her pregnancy, appalled at how little the poor woman had left. What on earth would become of her, now that Tamarand's purge had robbed her of all she was?

Mary ran her hand across her belly. "This only became apparent on the trail," she said softly. "Silly child." She tapped the fullness beneath her skirts. "What a time to come into this world."

At last, Mary's voice cracked, and Wynter came from behind her chair to sit on the cot, looking into her face. She took Mary's hand. The satin of the lady's gloves was soft, the grimy lace at her fingertips very fine.

"Isaac stayed behind, while Jared and I fled, and when poor

Phillipe was finally released from the inquisitors and set to burning in the executions square, Isaac threw a knife across the crowd
and risked his own life to end Phillipe's pain. It was only then
that he joined us. Brave Isaac. He made the endless journey here
so much easier to bear," she whispered. "He had a way of lightening any situation." Finally the tears came, slow and soundless,
rolling unheeded down Mary's pretty face. She glanced at Wynter. "My husband was very much older than me, Protector Lady.
Isaac was . . . he was a very *dear* friend."

"I am so sorry," whispered Wynter. She went to speak again,
then hesitated. She wanted to justify Razi's actions somehow, wanted to reveal his true nature to this seemingly gentle
person, but she did not know how.

"It is a burden to him," said Mary suddenly. Wynter frowned,
not understanding. Mary wiped her face with her lace-gloved
hand. "Your friend, the Lord Razi, he carries his deeds as a terrible burden."

She said it in sympathy, not judgement, and Wynter felt her
face crease up, tears threatening.

She nodded.

"Poor man," said Mary. "I suspect it sears him."

Their attention was drawn by the calling of men outside the
tent, and they looked over to see the soldiers moving away, no
longer needed now that the Midlanders had been proved loyal.

"And so we are left," sighed Mary, "while men shape the
world."

Wynter frowned, anxious to be out there, her hands opening
and closing in frustration. Mary eyed the sword at her hip and
her dusty men's clothing. "You are not a person used to this woman's waiting, Protector Lady. This isolation will madden you."

"It does not madden you, Lady Mary?"

Mary smiled. "What difference would it make if it did?" she said dryly.

A shadow crossed the tent and Wynter rose to her feet at the distinctive shape of Christopher and Boro coming to the door. "My friend is here," she said. "I suspect that he has brought food and some tea for you, if you should like?"

The lady brightened and Wynter hesitated. "He is Merron, lady."

Mary's expression fell and she seemed to shrink a little. She glanced to Christopher's shadow, obviously frightened.

"He is a good man, lady. He will not harm you."

Christopher's shadow came to a halt by the door. He cleared his throat and called softly through the canvas. "Lass?"

Wynter rolled her eyes. Just because the soldiers were gone did not mean he could be so lax, goddamn it.

Mary eyed Christopher's slim shadow, Boro's giant shape hulking threateningly by his side. The dog's breathing was disconcertingly loud as he snuffled along the door.

"One . . . one hears stories," said Mary faintly, "of Merron and what they do."

"Do not worry," said Wynter, opening the flap and letting Christopher in. Thankfully, Boro contented himself with peering in at the door and did not try and invade the lady's domain.

Hallvor stood a little distance away, clasping her elbows, her grave face watchful. Wynter lifted her chin in greeting, then ducked back inside, dropping the door in Boro's curious face. The big dog whined in aggravation and his huge shape plopped to the ground, a long, panting shadow barring the threshold.

"What's prickled our lad?" asked Christopher, nodding a perfunctory greeting at the Lady Mary. "He looks like a mule kicked him."

"Where is he?"

"He tried to wander off towards the river but the Merron ain't having none of it. Sól has grabbed him and sat him by the fire. He's planning on getting some tea and porridge in him. Razi ain't got a hope of declining."

He waited for an explanation, but Wynter just nodded gravely, avoiding his eyes.

"Alberon's big manly knight was sobbing his heart out behind the tents," he continued. "The soldiers near turned themselves inside out pretending not to notice."

"The Lord Razi and Sir Oliver had a misunderstanding," mumbled Wynter.

"Iseult!" he cried, almost spilling the tea with frustration. "Don't *do* that to me!"

Wynter glanced into his anxious face. Christopher's eyes were huge with desperate enquiry, but she could remember his rage the day they had found out about Shuqayr. She remembered the hard brightness in his eyes when he had said, "If it turns out that Alberon ordered his brother dragged to his death, and had a football made of his head, I will kill him. Whether Razi wants me to or not." Wynter was certain that he would feel the same about Oliver. Christopher would go for the man and, Razi or not, that would get him killed.

She took the steaming beakers from his hands. "They had a misunderstanding, Christopher. In the heat of the moment, Oliver said some horrible things. He instantly regretted it, but it hurt both of them. It is over now. They are reconciled, and it would do no good to rehash what was an unfortunately low exchange."

She felt Mary's eyes hop from one to the other of them, but she trusted that the woman was wise enough to hold her tongue. Christopher continued to scan her face.

"Let me introduce you to the Lady Mary," she said gently, and Christopher relented with a sigh.

Mary was regarding him with a nervous type of curiosity and surprise. Wynter was familiar with the Midlander idea of what a Merron would be. No doubt Mary had been expecting some looming great hulk of a creature, more hair than man, leering and making crude suggestions, battering people over the head left, right and centre. Christopher must have been quite a surprise: slim-built, small in stature and clean-shaven, he hardly conformed to the fables. Still, he lived up to the Merron reputation as uncouth when he crossed without invitation and crouched at Mary's feet, openly eyeing her pregnant belly.

"How far gone are you?" he asked.

Mary's eyes widened in shock and she flung a panicked look at Wynter. Wynter sighed in exasperation. *She's not a God-cursed brood mare, you fool.*

"Lady Mary Phillipe D'Arden," she said. "Please allow me to introduce, in so far as he will permit the nicety, my very good friend Freeman Christopher Garron. Forgive his manners; he's incorrigibly dubious."

Christopher grinned wryly, tickled at Wynter's use of their old private joke. He extended his hand. The Lady Mary automatically went to take it, then faltered at the sight of it. Christopher waited, and after a moment Mary tentatively closed her own, small hand around his horribly mutilated fingers.

"It's all right," he said softly. "You ain't about to hurt me."

The lady looked into his face, searching, then she tightened her grip and firmly shook his hand.

Christopher glanced around the tent, wrinkling his nose at the musty smell. "How long has it been since you were out and about?" he asked. At Mary's blushing silence he sighed. "This ain't exactly a cosy harem, is it, lady? Come on!" He leapt to his feet and extended his hand to help the lady up. " 'T'ain't good to sit about with a baby in your belly . . . all the waters head for the feet and you end up looking like an African Oliphant."

"Christopher!" moaned Wynter.

He ignored her. "Come on, lady," he said encouragingly. "There's women in the Merron group. Their *healer* is a woman. They'll be your entourage if you decide that you fancy a stroll."

Mary gazed up at him, uncertain, her hand hovering as if trying to make up her mind.

"They *are* admirable women," said Wynter, surprising herself with the depth of sincerity behind her words.

"Though incorrigibly dubious," confided Christopher solemnly.

Once free from the shadow of the awning, the lady closed her eyes, lifted her face to the sun and inhaled deeply. "Oh, my," she said, a look of almost painful pleasure on her face. "Oh, my goodness. Oh, how lovely." In the broad light, Wynter was shocked at how unhealthily pale she was, how dark the patches beneath her eyes.

Mary put her hands to her cheeks as if doubting the fresh air upon them. "Oh, my," she said again. Wynter's heart twisted for her. The poor woman must have been cooped up for an intolerable length of time.

Razi was sitting by the Merron fire, a beaker of tea languishing in his hands, his thoughts miles away. Sólmundr glanced up as they led Mary from her tent. He grinned approvingly at Christopher, who was carrying the lady's little folding chair. "It nice day for to eat outside," he rasped, and went back to turning sorrel cakes against the hot stones of the fire.

Soma and Frangok were making their way back from the river, dripping waterskins hanging ponderously from their shoulders. The men of camp were leering and whistling. The women ignored them, but Wynter took cold note. She would have a word with Alberon as soon as she could, and the same men would be dipping their heads and saying *ma'am* to the warriors before the day was out. Hallvor eyed Mary as she approached, her lips pursed in professional concern.

"Lady Mary," said Christopher, "this is the Merron healer. Her name is Hallvor an Fada, *iníon* Ingrid an Fada, *cneasaí*."

Christopher grinned at Mary's strained look. "You can just call her Hallvor," he said. "But I'm afraid that she ain't got any language but Merron and Garmain."

"Freeman Garron would be happy to translate for you," suggested Wynter. "But as luck has it, I speak tolerable Garmain. I can just as easily translate if you…"

"Thank you kindly, Protector Lady, but I can speak Garmain very well. I shall be glad to effect my own communications." Mary curtseyed to Hallvor. The healer nodded gravely, and they shook hands. The lady introduced herself in Garmain.

"It is my pleasure to meet you," replied Hallvor. "I am certain that your people have provided you with excellent shelter and care, but the Lady Iseult seems to think you might appreciate my aid, and so without meaning any insult to your protectors, I place my skills at your service."

Hallvor's flawless Garmain astounded Wynter. Until now she had never understood a word the healer had spoken. She was ashamed to admit it, but hearing Hallvor's familiar, smoke-husky voice communicating with such grace and skill elevated the healer in her eyes. It felt as though Wynter was seeing Hallvor properly for the very first time. She listened in wide-eyed silence as the healer introduced Mary to the other Merron. They all seemed to have similarly fluent if pleasantly accented Garmain. Sólmundr rose to his feet, his usual broken drawl transformed into a hoarse courtliness very reminiscent of Wynter's father's voice. Watching the warrior grin his gap-toothed grin and shake the lady's hand, Wynter found it deeply moving, and inexpressibly sad, to realise that all along she could have had the chance truly to understand these people, if only she had opened her mouth to talk.

Wari and Úlfnaor returned from tending the horses. The Lady Mary curtsied low to the kindly smiling Aoire, and without any further ceremony, she was included in the Merron breakfast.

Hallvor unfolded the lady's chair, and with a significant glance at Wynter, plopped it down beside Razi. He looked up, registered Mary's presence with a shock, and went to leap to his feet. Mary waved him down.

"Sit, sit," she said, getting herself settled. Once seated, she leant forward, as if to examine Razi more closely. "How are you?" she asked softly, gazing into his face.

Her concern seemed to undo him a little, and Razi winced and shook his head. *Oh don't*, his expression said, *please.*

Mary nodded in understanding. She thought for a moment. "I heard once," she said, "that you were studying to be a physician?"

Razi nodded tiredly.

"How interesting," said Mary. "I assume you know of Padua? It is my favourite city, you know. My family lived there for three years when I was a child."

Razi's face opened in surprise. Mary smiled, and soon they were involved in a soft discussion that made Wynter's heart ache with gratitude and fondness. Her eyes met Hallvor's. The healer winked in maternal conspiracy and turned back to her work.

"Lass," Christopher plucked at her sleeve and gestured her away from the fire. "Talk to me."

They rounded the corner and came to a halt in the passage between the Midlander tent and the large army supply tent beside it. The camp was fully awake now, men scurrying about, the air heavy with camp fire and dust. The sun was bright but brittle, and the shadows between the tents were cold. Wynter shivered, hugging her elbows and peering out at the soldiers coming and going on the main thoroughfare. Christopher handed her a warm sorrel cake and she ate it absently.

"Have some tea," he said.

She shook her head, sucking the bitter grit of the cake from her teeth and gazing up the hill to Alberon's tent. "I need to go talk to the Prince," she said. "Now is a good time, while Razi is distracted."

"What are you going to talk to him about?"

Christopher's tone of voice made her glance at him. His narrow face was hard and wary.

"I want to find out about my father's machines," she said. "I want to understand Albi's plans for them."

"Razi *told* you his plans for them. He *told* you that they won't work."

Wynter held Christopher's eye. There was a moment of silence between them.

"I want to make up my own mind about that," she said.

Christopher shook his head in sad disbelief. "Surely you ain't going to side against our lad?"

"Christopher." She put her hand on his forearm, but at the look on her face he twisted his arm and pulled it gently from her grip. "Chris, this has nothing to do with how I feel about Razi. This has to do with bigger things. Surely you can see that?"

He remained silent, his face set, and Wynter sighed. "The world is not simple, Christopher," she said, "and I am going to talk to the Prince." She went to move away and Christopher put his hand on her elbow. She paused, not looking at him.

"I'll walk with you," he said.

There was smoke coming from the ventilation holes at the top of the Haun yurts. The first in line was quiet and lifeless, just like yesterday, but Christopher murmured that there were at least three Haun in there. Wynter smiled wryly—he must have been sniffing about in the night, getting the lay of the land. Her heart once again swelled with warm pride; her man was the best kind of sly.

They walked slowly, side by side, their eyes on the Haun crouched outside the second yurt. One of them was the young man of the day before, and with him his companion and another older man. The two senior Haun were occupied with boiling something over the fire. The young man seemed in the process of changing his clothes. He had already removed his many layers of colourful jackets and vests, and as Christopher and Wynter came level with him he was just untying his undershirt. Wynter politely glanced away as he slipped free of the garment, but her eyes snapped immediately back at the sight of his scars. Christopher almost stopped walking in shock, but they both recovered themselves in time and simply slowed their pace, their eyes uncontrollably drawn to the young man's back as they passed by.

The scars were old, puckered and stretched with time. Their shapes had distorted as the young man's body had grown from what must have been a very small child at the time of his injury, to his present age of perhaps twenty or so. His stocky body was firm and closely muscled, as if he had worked hard all his life, but his strong back was marred with a row of ugly puncture wounds, starting just above the waist of his trousers at his left hip and continuing up to his right shoulder. Four in all, they were deep, evil-looking holes, as if a cruel giant had held him down as a child and neatly drilled his back with a sharpened stick.

The man put on his clean shirt, and as he tied the stays, his eyes lifted to meet those of Wynter. She immediately averted her gaze and passed on by.

"Good Frith," whispered Christopher, "how did he survive that?"

"Excuse me!"

The cultured voice stopped their progress, and they turned to find the young man advancing on them. He drew on a jacket as he came, his focus on Wynter, his black eyes and his broad-featured face politely unreadable. He looked Wynter up and down as he came to a halt, his attention particularly drawn to her hair. When he spoke, she was impressed by the smooth courtliness of his manner and his remarkable Southlandast, only very faintly tinged with an accent.

"Lady Green-eyes," he said, "I am struck by the colour of your hair. It is magnificent."

Wynter blushed. Christopher snorted softly in disgust.

The young man smiled and made a motion with his hand. "And those unique eyes," he said. "Like translucent jade. How unforgettable."

His face was as blandly polite as before, but there was something in this man's voice that Wynter did not like and she felt herself grow tense.

At her side, Christopher huffed. "Ain't you a poetic wee thing?" he said.

The Haun's eyes flickered his way, then back to Wynter. "Unique eyes," he repeated softly. "Even amongst your own kind, I would say. Defining."

Wynter's heart had begun to beat a little quicker, and she raised her chin, a suspicion growing.

"Am I to take it that you knew my father?" she asked. "Is this what you are implying?"

The man grinned suddenly and it reminded Wynter of the little orange cat that, a lifetime ago now, had led her through the passages at home. Like this man, its grin had been filled with hatred, and its disdain for her had been so deep that it had never even offered her its name.

"The Protector Lady Moorehawke," said the Haun. "Of course."

At her name, the older Haun suddenly rose to their feet, their faces wary, and their dark eyes hopped tensely between Wynter and the young man.

"How *is* your father?" he whispered, leaning in. "Nice and comfortable, I am sure. Lauded as the warrior who rid the Southlands of the Haun threat. What do they call him? A hero like himself must have some wonderfully descriptive name. Moorehawke the Great, perhaps? Moorehawke the Undefeated? What about Moorehawke the Bloody? What about Moorehawke the Butcherer of Children?"

Without thinking, Wynter slapped the man's face, and his head rocked sharply back. His friends rushed to his side, gabbling, and drew him away. He grinned as he went, his hand to his cheek, his eyes on Wynter. Christopher glowered after him, but Wynter turned away to hide her unexpected tears, trembling with shock and distress.

Next thing she knew, she was stumbling along, guided by Christopher's firm hand on her elbow. "But what did he mean?" she said. "What did he mean?" She went to turn back, but Christopher tightened his grip and kept her moving forwards, heading for the slope and Alberon's tent. After another moment of mindlessly following, Wynter dug her heels in and jerked to a halt.

"I must know!" she cried.

Christopher held tight to her elbow and pulled her close, staring into her eyes. "It was a war, Iseult," he whispered. "Things *happen* during a war. That lad was on the losing side. He ain't likely to write a sonnet lauding the winners' good character now, is he?"

"But he's talking about my *father*! It's not true! I can't believe it!"

"Lorcan was a *soldier*, lass! What did you think he did in battle? Throw buns at the enemy?"

"Why would a *child* have been in battle, Christopher?"

He frowned at her in sympathetic confusion and Wynter knew that he would never understand. Christopher came from a world where the inquisition threw babies onto their mother's execution pyres. He had been adopted by a race for whom the word *soldier* meant only death and torment and pain. He was looking at her now across the chasm of their differences and she had no doubt that he was thinking, *why would a child* not *have been in battle*?

"Iseult," he said gently, "whatever your questions may be, that man is not the one to give you your answers. He's too full of hate." Christopher smiled at her and pushed a stray lock of hair behind her ear. "You don't want to see your poor dad through that fellow's eyes, do you, lass?"

A cough behind them startled Wynter, and she realised with a jolt that she was standing in the main thoroughfare of the camp, gazing into Christopher's face as he murmured to her and stroked her hair. She stepped sharply backwards. The passing soldiers seemed to slide knowing glances at each other. The Combermen, lounging beneath their awning, seemed to eye her with leering contempt. At the head of the slope, Anthony was watching from the shadow of the Prince's tent.

Her face burning, Wynter turned to face the man who had coughed.

"Presbyter," she croaked, "how fare you?"

The priest was eyeing her with alarm. *Are you mad?* his face said. *Have you no sense?* His gaze flickered to the grip that Christopher had on Wynter's arm, then up to meet the young man's eyes. Christopher lifted his chin in defiance, and to Wynter's surprise, the priest's face filled with pained sympathy.

"Don't be an arrogant fool, boy," he whispered. "You have nothing to give her but despair."

At his gentle tone, Christopher's defiance seemed to melt from him and, frowning uncertainly, he let Wynter go. The priest nodded. Up above them, Anthony turned and disappeared into Alberon's tent.

"I must tend my Lady Mary," said the priest, and bowing, he left them.

"I . . ." said Wynter, staring after him. "I must go talk to the Prince." Christopher nodded and made to accompany her up the slope. Wynter stayed him with a hand on his arm. "I must talk to him alone, Christopher."

Christopher's cheeks flared red and he stepped back, his face stiff with embarrassment. "Of course," he said.

"He will not speak to me with you there," she explained softly.

He nodded, his eyes averted.

"Will you wait for me?"

He nodded again. His determined silence was what made up her mind. After all Christopher's quiet gestures of love—the sending of the scóns, the courtly bow, his gentle acceptance of her way of life—how could Wynter ever deny her feelings for him? How could she ever have considered denying them?

"Chris?"

He glanced at her. When she stretched up to kiss him, he drew back in alarm, his eyes darting to the hill. "Don't, lass," he said.

Wynter gripped his tunic at the chest and tugged him near. "You listen to me, Freeman Garron. I am telling you now, I *love* you."

Christopher shook his head, doubt and concern visible in his clear grey eyes. "You don't have to say that," he whispered.

"I *love* you," she insisted, her face very close to his. "To court I shall always be the Protector Lady Wynter Moorehawke. To Razi and Alberon I shall always be Wyn—Razi's baby, Albi's little sis. These things are what I am, Christopher, and I am proud of them. But I am also your Iseult. You are the only man to whom I shall ever be thus, and I shall never let that go. We shall find our place," she promised. "I'm not yet certain *how* we shall find it, or where it will be, but wherever it is, we shall be together, Christopher; and whatever we are doing, it will not involve me sitting in a tent waiting for my menfolk to change the world."

Christopher grinned at that, his wicked, lopsided grin, and, in clear view of the scandalised camp, Wynter kissed him, full and slow on the mouth. His hand found its way to her waist, and he made that delicious *mmmm* sound in his throat that always weakened her knees.

"Wait for me here?" she whispered.

He nodded, smiling, and with one last solemn kiss Wynter parted from him and made her way up the hill to Alberon's tent.

Machines and Machinations

Alberon was waiting grimly in the shelter of the awning. The sun was hard on his angry young face, and bright as fire in the pale spikes of his choppy hair. The breeze had risen and it snapped the awning over his head, shivering its way through the tent at his back and snatching at his red wool cloak. Wynter felt its early morning chill and wished for her own cloak. Her sword hung heavy at her waist. The slope reminded her of how weary she was.

"Your Highness," she said, coming to a halt in the cold sunshine. "May we talk?"

Alberon's eyes flickered briefly to Christopher, still standing at the foot of the hill, then back to Wynter. "Get in," he hissed, and she ducked past his guards into the dimness and relative warmth of his empty tent. Alberon strode after her.

The little servant peered around the door, his face red, his eyes wide. Wynter was certain that he had run, like a good little courtier, and told the Royal Prince that the Protector Lady was making love to an untitled savage right in the main street of the camp. She grimaced at him and his little face twisted in miserable embarrassment.

Alberon stood in the centre of the tent and glared. "What in God's name are you up to, Wynter?"

Wynter smiled gently. "Christopher Garron is not what I

came here to discuss, your Highness. Perhaps we can talk on that another time?"

"Whatever you believed you could get away with on the trail, Protector Lady, your conduct here lays the foundation for your very future. I already have my work cut out trying to restore your reputation, and I shall not have the court saying you've opened your legs for a God-cursed thief and a Merron savage!"

Alberon's unexpected crudeness took Wynter completely by surprise. She felt her face flare scarlet, and she was speechless for a moment with shock. "Alberon," she said eventually, "don't..."

"I'm no goddamn puritan, Wynter. But you cannot afford to dandle your scrap of rough pleasure on the highway for all to see."

Cold rage swelled to replace Wynter's embarrassment, and she lowered her chin, her face hardening. "I'll ask you to watch your tongue," she whispered. "No man has a right to speak to me in that fashion, not even a Royal Prince. Christopher Garron is my intended, Alberon. My dad loved him, I have no *doubt* he would have approved our match. *Razi* approves our match. Our attachment is a *fait accompli*, your Highness, and I am afraid that you have no say in the matter."

Alberon's eyes flew open in a sudden rush of horror and disbelief. "A match?" he cried. "For Godssake, Wyn, the man has nothing! He's a bloody *gypsy*! He will *ruin* you! Do you really want to spend the rest of your life living in a *ditch*?"

He clutched his head at the thought, and Wynter's anger was blown away with the understanding that Alberon was utterly terrified for her. She opened her mouth, and he threw his hand up to silence her.

"Don't," he cried. "Don't give me Lorcan's old shit about making your own way in the world! You are not a *child*, Wynter. You will be sixteen years old at the end of the month and you have *nothing*. Your father has raised you on delusions. He should have spent his time securing a future for you, instead of indulging those damn games of make-believe! Carpenter indeed! Who the hell is ever going to *hire* you? You are a *woman*. Even if you ever do secure work, can you see yourself climbing the scaffolds with your belly full of that vagabond's pups?"

The word *pups* was such an unfortunate choice that Wynter couldn't help but smile. *Cubs might be a touch more accurate*, she thought, but she refrained from articulating the comment. Bad enough that Alberon considered Christopher a gypsy. What colour would he turn if Wynter revealed the rather more dangerous aspects of her young man's nature?

"What are you *grinning* for?" cried Alberon.

She shrugged, her smile widening, and he ran his hands through his hair, staring at her in disbelief. Her smiling silence seemed to calm him down a little and he began to pace, his brow creased in thought.

"Anyone can make a mistake," he muttered. "Women have recovered from much worse. Mind you, usually women with far greater prospects than yours. Still, a sizeable dowry can be arranged..."

"Albi," she said.

"Of course you've no damned land. No annuity of your own. No God-cursed family connections. But you are not unattractive and you are still relatively young..."

"Albi."

"Your friendship with us might stand to you. If there is no issue from this dalliance and the men here can be persuaded to keep their mouths shut." He glared out the door. "*He* can be paid off..."

"God*damn* it, Alberon! That is *enough*!"

He came to a halt, staring belligerently at her, and she sighed.

"Albi," said Wynter gently. "I trust Christopher Garron. I love him. And he loves me. Would you deny me that, Albi? In this terrible bloody world, would you deny me *that*?"

The little servant was blatantly eavesdropping now, standing out in the open, his face rapt. They were better than a play, it seemed, and he had quite forgot himself in their dramatics. His round eyes brimmed with the tragic wonder of Wynter's speech and he clasped his hands at his chest.

"Oh," he whispered, "that's righteous lovely."

Alberon turned to him, and the little fellow froze like a rabbit under torchlight. "Boy?" grated Alberon. "Have you nothing to do with yourself other than act the old maid?"

The poor child stared with panic-stricken eyes, and Wynter took pity on him. "I should very much like some breakfast, Anthony. Would there be anything available to eat or drink?"

"Wouldst...wouldst like some gruel, Protector Lady? I can get thee—"

"You can get thee bloody OUT," yelled Alberon, swiping the air in mock threat. Anthony squeaked and fled, and Alberon strode in his wake, yelling after his retreating back. "Get some God-cursed tea while you're at it!"

There was a distant little, "*Aye, Highness.*"

Alberon stood at the head of the slope, glaring downwards. Wynter had no doubt that he was looking at Christopher, who undoubtedly was staring right back. She sighed and waited patiently while her brother had himself a good look at the man she had chosen as her own. She briefly considered introducing them properly and letting them talk, but there were many things she wanted to discuss with Alberon. Wynter did not think that it would be conducive to open conversation were the two men to commence the prowling that would be their inevitable reaction to each other. No. Introductions could wait.

"Well," murmured the Prince, "I suppose a marriage, no matter how ill-advised, is one solution to your hopelessly slandered reputation. Should the worst come to the worst, as it inevitably will with a fellow such as him, we can always wed you off again as a dowered widow."

"Alberon," she hissed.

He did not turn around.

"*Alberon!*" she insisted.

He tilted his head, which was as far as she suspected he would go towards looking her way.

"There will be no *widowhood* in my future, brother. No matter how much my husband sullies the landscape of your plans for me."

Alberon shrugged. "Court life is a danger to us all," he said. "Nothing lasts for ever."

"You had better make sure my *husband* lasts for ever, Alberon Kingsson. Crown Prince or not, you will play no courtly games with Christopher Garron's life. If he so much as stumbles and bruises his knees, I shall..."

Footsteps crunched up the dry slope and Wynter snapped to furious silence, certain that Oliver was about to beg access to the Prince. God curse him! Of all the damned times to interrupt. Right at that moment, Wynter did not think that she could face the knight without losing her now hopelessly tenuous self-control.

But it was only Alberon's lieutenant, and he came to attention with a smart salute, waiting for permission to approach. Alberon waved him at ease and gestured him to speak.

"Sir Oliver has taken watch with the pickets, your Highness. He sends word from the tree line."

"What news?" asked Alberon.

"No sign of the supplies, your Highness. It being two days now, and considering what the Lord Razi witnessed by the ford, Sir Oliver is of the belief that the provisioners might have been taken."

Alberon sighed. "It is more than possible. The valleys are crawling with the King's soldiers. If Sir Oliver is right, and those poor men *have* been taken, it will only be a matter of time before they crack and tell my father where we are... I'm afraid we may have to move again, Marcel, and soon."

The lieutenant nodded gravely and gazed out across the camp. "No need for the men to know it yet, though, Highness. " 'Twould only rattle them."

"Aye. In any case, we must await these last envoys. We certainly cannot up stakes till they are here. There is no sign of them, I suppose?"

Wynter saw the lieutenant's face crease in momentary distaste. "No, your Highness," he said coldly. "No sign."

Alberon sighed again and dismissed the man. He watched as the lieutenant walked away, then he drew his cloak around him and stood staring pensively out across the trees. His thoughts seemed utterly diverted from Christopher, and Wynter glowered at him—torn between needing to discuss the desperate politics of their situation and the desire to settle the subject of her future for once and for all.

At the back of the tent, something stirred and a thin whine drew Wynter's attention. With another grim look at the Prince, she crossed to see what it was. On the trunk that acted as Alberon's bedside table, Marguerite Shirken's papers rested, their seals as yet unbroken. Wynter glanced suspiciously at them, then she drew the insect netting aside and looked behind it for the source of the noise.

It was Coriolanus, hidden in his nest of blanket at the foot of the neat cot. The poor creature seemed in the grip of a bad dream, and he mewed hoarsely in his sleep, his little teeth flashing.

Wynter crouch by the bed. "Cori," she whispered, reaching to stroke him. "Cori...wake up."

The cat hissed and lashed out, and Wynter withdrew with a cry, her hand scored with four shallow gashes. She cursed vehemently. "Cori!" she snapped. "Wake up!"

His eyes flew open and he lay on his back, staring at her, his small white forepaws held to his bony chest. "Cat-servant," he rasped.

"You *scratched* me."

He looked at the blood she was sucking from the back of her hand and frowned, rolling to his side. "I...I was dreaming of my dear mother. The soldiers-who-kill had come again. I was too sick and my mother...my mother drew them away. But," he squeezed his beautiful eyes shut, "but in my dream they came again," he whispered. "Reaching."

"It was only me," said Wynter, moved by the poor creature's obvious distress. "I was only going to pet you."

"*Ahrrrrrr*," he huffed, flustered. "Humans. Always touching. Always grabbing!" He slid a look at her. "Though I am sure I can bring myself to tolerate it, if you must lift me."

Wynter gathered him to her, a fragile collection of brittle warmth, and cradled him like a baby. "Your mother still lives, you know," she whispered gently. "An orange cat told me so. GreyMother hides somewhere in the castle with the last of the kittens."

Coriolanus didn't react to this, except to rub his head against her caressing fingers and gaze into nothing. "A flame-coloured cat," he murmured, "with a heart full of hatred?"

"How did you know?"

"SimonSmoke's tenth daughter, the only flame-coloured cat of her litter. She has no human-given-name. She rages against you all now, brave thing. She and her litter-mates were the last of the palace-born. GreyMother carried them down into the woods, where they live like foxes." He sighed. "I am surprised she spoke even to you, cat-servant. She must have considered you instrumental."

"I think she did. She wanted Razi to learn about the Bloody Machine. I think she thought the discovery would undo the King."

Coriolanus huffed sleepily. "She was wrong. It is their suppression that has undone him." His eyes were growing heavy. "You have grown very like your father," he murmured. "With your fur and eyes, you would both have made handsome cats, had you not been unlucky enough to have been born otherwise."

"My father is dead, Cori."

The cat shrugged, drifting now back into sleep. "It will happen us all," he sighed.

"Cori?"

"Mmm?"

"Why is the King suppressing the machines?"

"Oh, human reasons, for human things...how is a sensible cat to understand?"

Alberon came and sat quietly on the cot. Wynter continued to stroke the sleeping cat and would not look up.

"You must think me unbearably hard," said Alberon.

She did not reply.

Alberon reached and touched Cori's head, just once, then withdrew his hand. "Thank you for the letters, Wyn. They meant so much to me all these years."

She glanced up at him in surprise. "You received them? You... you never replied."

He chuckled grimly. "What had I to write of? Blood and death and betrayal? The imminent destruction of Father's wonderful dream? You know I have no art with words, Wyn. I would not have been able to lie, and what would the truth have done for you? Your letters were always so happy, filled with such happy things. I couldn't bear to hurt that. I couldn't bear to let you know just how bad everything was."

Happy? Was Alberon serious? Wynter had poured her heart and soul into those letters. All those miserable years, how could Alberon have ever thought she was happy?

"What... What did I write of that was so happy?"

Alberon smiled, a genuine smile this time. "Oh you know— all your adventures! Your father's wonderful inventions. The way he smooth-talked all those vile Northlander toadies. Everything. I especially liked when you wrote down your memories of home. I used to love when the messengers came from the North. Those little pages of sunshine arriving in the middle... in the middle of what we had become. I would read them and think, '*This* is what we're struggling for. *This* is why we must prevail.' You have kept me going, Wyn. I read something of yours every day. Look!" He reached past her, shifted Marguerite's papers aside, lifted something. "See?" He handed it to her.

Wynter unfolded it with an unsteady hand, the parchment was creased and tattered, the stain from the wax seal still visible at the edge. It was one of her shorter notes and she remembered clearly the day she had written it. It had been a particularly hard day—the end of a long week of mass trials in the Shirkens' castle. They had burned the convicted in batches of ten. Wynter remembered writing this letter with shaking hands, her ears filled with screaming, her window filled with smoke. Until now, she had recalled only that awfulness, the actual contents of the letter had not been part of her memory. Her writing shocked her, how legible and steady it was.

My Dearest Brother,

How much I miss you! I was thinking today of the time we stole the cakes from the Moroccan ambassador's birthday feast. Do you recall? We were dressed up stiff as coffin mummies in our brocades, still you managed to pilfer seven jam tarts and an entire cinnamon cake. The stains they left on your pockets! You said cake always tasted better eaten beneath the table, and so we sat, surrounded by legs, stuffing our little faces while a discreet panic consumed the staff! Razi (of course) was the one to find us. I recall his brief grin as he peered beneath the cloth, then his voice—it was pure Razi—"Father, I am certain they are not here. I have searched every inch and there's naught below but Mama's little dog." Oh! I am laughing aloud now.

Tell me you recollect this!

Alberon's quiet voice brought her back to the tent and he took the letter, folding it and putting it away again. I have kept them all, you know. I have most of them back at the palace, in my trunk. Safe in my room."

Wynter felt her face fall at that—the palace had been stripped of every possible reminder of Alberon. She hardly imagined that his room had been left intact. He must have seen something of this in her expression because his eyes slipped from hers, and he cleared his throat.

"How is Razi?" he asked quietly.

"Oh, Albi, why do you not ask him *yourself*, instead of just telling him to comb his hair and shave his face as if nothing had happened. Why must you act the prince around him?"

"Oh, please! He has done nothing but act the politician since he got here! He'd talk knots into a string, that man! I feel like I am wrestling a God-cursed eel every time he opens his mouth!"

Wynter huffed. "That is just Razi, Alberon, he has never been any different."

"He was never thus with me."

You never before gave him reason to be, thought Wynter. But she did not articulate it. "He has only the best of intentions," she said. "You are his brother, Albi. He loves you dearly—you know this."

"I . . . I shall try harder to hold my patience." Alberon glanced at her. "He really approves this match of yours?" At her warning look, he spread his hands in defeat. "I suppose between us both we can afford to support you," he sighed. "You and your gypsy."

Wynter gritted her teeth against a reply.

"I am sorry about Lorcan, Wyn. I want you to know that. It must seem that I do not care, but I do. It is so difficult, these days, to react to things the way one should." Alberon's attention drifted to the door and he watched the insect netting blow in the breeze. "I am calm, or I am angry," he said softly. "There seems to be nothing in between."

"Why did our fathers suppress the machine, Albi?"

"I don't know!" he cried, animated once again by his frustration. "It makes no sense to me! Father simply dragged it into the light one moment, then pushed it back into the shadows the next. It was madness! We had already lost so many men! Things had come *so damn close*. Then to find that we had, all along, the ability to make these wonderful machines! That we actually had one to hand and had not used it until the very last moment? My God, Wynter!" he lowered his forehead onto his clenched fists, his face hidden. "My God, I was so angry I almost killed him."

"Don't say that."

"I'm only talking to you," he mumbled, "I'd never say it out loud."

"Well, it is a little late for caution in any case. The poor man thinks you mean to usurp him, Alberon. It has broken his heart."

He shook his head. "I can't let it go, Wyn. I simply *know* that this will work."

Wynter stroked the cat, and carefully considered her words. "I think that certain aspects of your plan have flaws. This marriage to Marguerite Shirken, for example."

He looked up at her from between his fists. "Are we about to trade insults over marriage partners, Wyn?"

She tightened her jaw and slid him another warning look. "As I was saying, your plan has flaws. I think you could do with sitting down with your *courtly* brother and discussing some of the finer details. But on the whole, Alberon, I agree with you. I think the production of more machines is this kingdom's great hope. I cannot understand our fathers' suppression of them."

Alberon lifted his head to gaze at her in wonder, and he looked so like her childhood memory of him that Wynter nearly cried. "Really?" he asked.

"Really," she whispered.

"And Razi?"

She dropped her eyes. "Razi can be persuaded. Later."

"Oh...I see."

He sighed, and there was a moment's thoughtful silence between them.

"That Haun," said Wynter, "I think he knew my father."

"The youngest one? Their linguist?" At her nod, Alberon pushed wearily to his feet and went to the door, looking down into the camp. The insect netting blew about him in the wind, and he looked like a red-clad ghost seen through mist. "He is a strange fellow. I think he might be mad. I suspect he was one of the Lost Hundred."

Wynter startled at that. The thought had not even occurred to her. "He would have been very young when the Haun were sent east," she said doubtfully.

"Aye. But, think about it, sis. His excellent Southlandast, his fine manners. He has a feel of the palace about him, don't you think?"

Wynter stroked the cat and thought about that. It certainly would explain a lot. The young Haun would have been perhaps six or so in the aftermath of the Haun Invasion, and so it would be possible that he could remember her father. Particularly if his family *were* among the Lost Hundred and connected in some way with the life of the palace. Of all the Haun sent east, it was those Southland-born nobles and business men—the so-called Hundred Lost Families—that had suffered the most. The young Haun's family would have lost everything when Jonathon's father expelled the Haunardii from the Southlands. No wonder he was so bitter. That kind of injustice would spread rage through generation after generation of the dispossessed.

Wynter's stomach went cold suddenly, and she looked over at Alberon, her eyes wide with unwanted inspiration. They had been told that the Lost Hundred had been sent back east. That their goods had been piled onto their well-bred backs, their weeping families loaded into carts, and their land and businesses redistributed amongst the Southlander aristocracy. But what if it were even colder than that? What if something else entirely had been done? Something that so ate at Lorcan and Jonathon's consciences that they could not bring themselves to articulate it—even to each other.

"Albi," she whispered, "did you see that man's back?"

Alberon did not seem to hear her. His attention was fixed on a point at the far end of the camp, and as Wynter spoke, he drew back the insect netting and frowned in concentration.

"What is it?" she said.

On her lap, Coriolanus tensed, and his claws exposed briefly in his sleep. "No . . ." he whined. "No."

In the camp the warhounds suddenly began to howl.

"What *is* it, Albi?" she said again, gently placing the cat into his nest and crossing to join the prince.

Alberon stepped outside. "A messenger from the pickets," he said. "My envoys must be here." He lifted his hand to the rider just arrived at the base of the slope, and the man nodded, wheeled his horse around and trotted back towards the barricades.

"We shall have to chain those damn hounds," mused Alberon.

Indeed, the warhounds were going mad. Wynter could hear them baying and howling down amongst the tents. At the base of the slope, Christopher was standing with his back to her, his attention focused on the far end of the camp, and something in his posture set Wynter on edge. He looked like a dog that has scented trouble. As she watched, he began to walk in the direction of the barricades. Then, without warning, he broke into a jog. Within moments, Christopher was running.

On the main thoroughfare, Sólmundr and Razi emerged from between the tents, their faces turned expectantly towards the barricades. They must have heard that there was a new arrival and had come to see. Christopher shot past them. Razi called after him, but Christopher ran by without looking his way. Sól and Razi began to follow, but the young man was already far ahead of them.

Dodging and weaving through the curious men now crowding the road, Christopher seemed utterly focused on getting to the gates. The frantic baying of the hounds urged him on, and Wynter followed his desperate progress with increasingly cold alarm.

"Alberon," she whispered, "who are your envoys?"

Alberon just watched the barricades, his face attentive.

Fez. He had said that they were coming from Fez. Wynter followed the Prince's gaze to the end of camp, and when the Loups-Garous rode their horses through the barricades she felt no surprise at all.

Again

At the sight of the Loups-Garous, Christopher came to a staggering halt, his knees bent, his arms spread as if to catch a thrown ball. He remained frozen like that, stricken, and Wynter was absolutely certain that he was going simply to stand there and allow the Wolves to advance upon him. She began to dash down the hill, scanning the road as she did, searching for Razi.

Behind her, Alberon called an order to one of his men. "Tell the Merron to secure those God-cursed hounds or I shall have them shot."

Shoving her way past a knot of soldiers at the base of the hill, Wynter caught sight of Razi. He was standing, open-mouthed, at the edge of the road. Sólmundr was shaking his arm and speaking impatiently, as if trying to get his attention. Wynter bit down the urge to scream Razi's name, and veered for him, dodging quickly through the soldiers and the rising dust. As she approached, Razi mumbled something to Sól. The warrior stepped back, shocked, then spun with a cry, frantically scanning the road. He spotted Christopher, still frozen in the Wolves' path, and began to run towards him.

But at that very moment—just as it seemed utterly certain that the Wolves would see him—Christopher jerked to sudden life. He crouched, reached for his katar, realised it was not at his hip, then turned and darted away between the tents. Sólmundr, still only halfway to his young friend, slammed to a halt and cut right, heading in the same direction as Christopher.

Wynter slid to Razi's side. At the same moment, Úlfnaor strode from between the tents. "Who is these men?" he asked, squinting at the Wolves. "They from the King?" Then he got a look at the wolf-skins draped across the horses' rumps, and his face went cold and dangerous.

Oliver was leading the Wolves into camp, his dappled mare skittish next to David Le Garou's big, dark stallion. As he urged the shying horse onto the thoroughfare, Wynter saw his eyes inadvertently settle on Razi. The knight's face creased up in misery and he averted his gaze.

The Wolves were magnificent, their horses beautiful, their clothes and weaponry very fine and rich. David Le Garou's attention was focused solely on Alberon's quarters. But his three seconds-in-command were ranked behind him—Gérard, Jean, Pierre—and their slanting eyes scanned the surrounding soldiers, looking for trouble. The two young Arabs followed close behind, calmly guiding their sturdy little horses in their masters' wake. The silver bells at their wrists and on their boots tinkled merrily, and Wynter felt a moment of blazing rage that the Wolves would bring them here, openly and without any attempt to hide the fact that they were slaves. Then it registered that the Wolves had only one of their three pack mules with them, and that the six dark-dressed shadow-riders that made up the rest of David Le Garou's pack were nowhere to be seen.

"Razi," she whispered, "where are the rest of them?"

Razi ignored her. His eyes were on the tents where Christopher had disappeared. For a moment it looked as though he would just keep standing there, staring. Then Úlfnaor went to speak again, and Razi turned, grabbing him by his shoulders, and hissed urgently into the big man's startled face.

"He's gone for his sword! He means to attack them. He means to attack them at last! We have to stop him!" He shoved the Aoire back and pushed his way past him, heading for the Merron quarters. Confused, Úlfnaor followed him.

Wynter found herself incapable of turning her back on the approaching Wolves, and instead of spinning and running, she backed slowly into the shadow-filled gap between the tents, her eyes on the brightness of road. The light tinkling of the slave-bells made itself known over the tramp of hooves and jangle of tack, and Wynter crouched slightly as the silhouette of a rider blotted the light. It was Oliver, there one moment, gone the next as he rode past the mouth of the alley. Then David Le Garou went by, his eyes ahead, his fine profile clear against the bright blue sky. The row of seconds came next, slowly crossing the bright space, their faces watchful. The dark-skinned Gérard was closest to her, his eyes scanning his surroundings. He turned his head, and before he could see her, Wynter broke from her trance and ran.

She caught up with Razi and Úlfnaor by the Midlander quarters. The air was frantic with the baying of hounds and there was shouting and scuffling coming from the direction of the Merron camp. Jared was herding Mary up the side of the supply tent. The lady was distraught and she flung herself on Razi, gripping his arm in fear.

"The dogs have turned savage!" she cried. "They have gone wild!"

Razi grabbed Úlfnaor, pushing him towards the noise. "Don't let him leave!" he yelled. "Take his weapons and don't let him leave the tents!" The big man shook his head, confusion in his face. "Christopher!" clarified Razi. "Don't let him get his weapons!"

Úlfnaor ran, and Razi turned on Mary, clutching her shoulders and glaring down into her frightened face. "Get to your tent!" he yelled. "Do not leave it!" He pushed Mary towards Jared. "Do not let her leave her tent!"

Jared, appalled at Razi's rough manner, put himself between the dark young man and the woman he was so violently shoving about. Mary still clung to Razi's arm, so that the priest was caught between them.

"What has happened?" snapped Jared, his face very close to Razi's.

"Loups-Garous."

The priest went still. Mary stared at Razi, her arm stretched around Jared, her fingers clutching Razi's sleeve. "An attack?" she whispered.

Razi shook his head. He pushed Mary gently away. "Stay in your tent," he urged. "Presbyter, I beg you, make sure she stays inside."

Jared nodded grimly and hustled Mary around to their quarters. She gazed back, wide-eyed, until they rounded the corner out of sight. Razi dashed towards the noise of the dogs and Wynter followed.

There was deafening chaos at the Merron tents. Thoar and Surtr were struggling with the huge warhounds, heaving on their collars, trying to keep them in place while the women finished hammering tent pegs into the ground to shorten their chains. The warhounds were snarling and baying, their jaws flecked with foam, wild with desperation to get away and find the Wolves.

The soldier Alberon had sent to secure the hounds was pressed against the canvas of the Merron tent. Úlfnaor was shoving him away, yelling in Merron and gesturing for him to go. Boro lunged for him suddenly, his eyes burning, and the soldier didn't need any further persuasion. He ran off, his duty done.

Christopher was just ducking from the Merron tent, his katar in his hand, his face set. Sólmundr ducked out after him, his sword also in hand. As he emerged from the tent, Sól shouted to Hallvor and flung her a sword. It sailed across the air between them, its long blade shivering slightly in the sun, and Hallvor rose smoothly to her feet, catching the weapon by its handle.

Sólmundr gestured that she follow.

Úlfnaor yelled something and Sól paused, shocked. "*Cad é?*" he said.

Christopher kept striding purposefully towards the road.

Razi yelled, "Stop him!" and Thoar and Surtr stepped into the young man's path. Christopher simply swerved and dodged gracefully past. The warriors glanced uncertainly at Úlfnaor. "Stop him," repeated Razi, and Úlfnaor nodded.

Surtr side-stepped and put his hand on Christopher's chest. "*Cosc ort nóiméad, a luch,*" he said.

Christopher came to a surprised halt. He blinked up at the red-headed warrior for a moment. Then looked around the ring of uncertain faces.

"Come on," he said, as if they'd forgotten what they were meant to be doing.

No one moved. Their eyes hopped from Christopher to Razi.

"Come *on!*" urged Christopher, gesturing impatiently that they should follow. Then he caught sight of Razi's hard face, and Wynter saw his certainty fall away into dismay. "Oh no, Razi," he whispered.

Razi would not look at him. "I am sorry," he said, "I need to know why they are here."

"NO!" Christopher launched himself forward and the red-headed brothers lurched in surprise, then leapt and caught him under his arms, stopping him in his tracks. "No, Razi!" he cried. "Not again! Not *again*."

Razi, his eyes down, pointed to the Merron tent, and the two huge men began to manhandle Christopher back towards the door. Christopher howled with despair and disbelief. "No!" he wailed again. "Noooooooo!"

Razi would not meet his eye and that seemed to enrage Christopher. More than anything, that seemed to tip him over the edge. He went mad then. Snarling and screaming in rage, he struggled against the two brothers so that they almost lost their footing and stumbled under his thrashing weight. He raised his katar, meaning to smash it down onto Surtr's head. Hallvor leapt forward and grabbed his upraised arms, twisting them so that he was forced to release the weapon. Christopher howled again and kicked out at her, his face vicious.

Wynter lurched to help him, but Razi jerked her violently back.

"Let him go!" she cried.

Christopher snarled at her, his face unrecognisable. The brothers dragged him to the tent, and as he was borne backwards into the dimness he released an animal howl. The door fell closed and, out of sight now, Christopher's inarticulate rage stormed on. Surtr and Thoar roared at him, trying to calm him down.

Furious, Wynter struggled free of Razi's grip and shoved him away. She ran for the door, determined that Christopher should be released.

"No, Wyn!" yelled Razi. "Wait! *WAIT!*"

Suddenly, the dogs stopped barking, and their abrupt stillness froze the humans in their tracks.

All sounds of the struggle within the tent had ceased.

Wynter clearly heard Thoar say, "Coinín?"

The hounds backed to the ends of their chains, whimpering, their tails between their legs. Boro whined in fear, his sharp ears swivelling to catch the sounds from within.

Sól took an uncertain step forward, then he and Razi simultaneously dashed for the door. Wynter went to follow, but Razi pushed ahead of her, literally shoving her aside and dodging under the flap before she could get past. Within the tent, Surtr screamed. There was a rending, splitting sound, and just as Wynter went to duck inside, the redheaded warrior flew past her, propelled backwards from the tent as if flung from a catapult.

The huge man flew ten or more feet before landing with a *whoomph* in the dust. His tunic was torn open, his belly scored with claw marks and scarlet with blood. He immediately tried to roll to his feet, his face creased with concern for his brother.

"THOAR!" he yelled, falling back in pain, "THOAR!"

Wynter ducked into the tent and was confronted with a frenzy of noise and movement. Sólmundr and Thoar had thrown themselves onto Christopher, trying to pin him down. Razi, in turn, had flung himself onto the warriors, trying to pull them away.

"No!" he shouted, "He does not mean it! Give him a moment."

Razi kicked Thoar away, at the same time heaving backwards on Sól. The three men tumbled back, propelled by a violent shove from Christopher.

"Give him a moment!" screamed Razi as Thoar went to draw his sword. "He doesn't mean it!"

Wynter went to run forward, but came to halt at the sight of

Christopher's terrible face. Utterly transformed, his eyes flashed yellow in the gloom, and he growled and snarled about him like a dog at bay. He was writhing in the shadows at the back of the tent, as if in battle with some unseen demon, his scarred fingers gouging deep claw marks into the earth.

"Christopher," she whispered.

He made no effort to attack, just remained where he was, struggling on the dirt floor, his body twisting around itself as he tried to overcome his rage. The noises coming from his distorted mouth were not human—they were anything but human—but Wynter understood fear when she heard it. She understood pain.

"Oh, Christopher," she whispered again, and knelt on the ground just out of his reach, her hand outstretched as if to comfort him. He continued to thrash and struggle, apparently unconscious of her presence. Razi crawled to her side, his face intent, but he, too, came to a halt just out of reach of his friend, and knelt there, doing nothing.

In the end, it was Sól who went to him. He crawled straight past Razi and Wynter, and without hesitation, rolled Christopher onto his back.

Christopher's yellow eyes widened at the contact, his lips pulled back. His distorted hands shot to Sólmundr's shoulders. The too-long fingers dug into Sól's flesh, and the warrior gasped in pain. Gritting his teeth, Sól grabbed Christopher's face in his hands and jerked the young man's head around, staring into Christopher's inhuman eyes.

"Coinín!" he cried. "*Is mé atá ann!* It's me! It's Sól!"

Christopher opened his mouth, those long, sharp teeth only inches from Sólmundr's throat. His fingers tightened brutally on Sól's shoulders and, to Wynter's horror, blood welled up beneath his fingertips.

Sólmundr's face tightened in agony but he did not pull away. Instead he shook Christopher's head between his hands and yelled, "You free man, Coinín! You *not* hurt me! You *know* who you are!"

Christopher's yellow eyes locked with Sólmundr's. His fingers abruptly relaxed their grip on the warrior's shoulders. His face softened in recognition. Then he was Christopher again, just Christopher; his scarred hands clutching the fabric of his friend's tunic, his fine, narrow face appalled and painted with despair.

"Oh no," he whispered. "Oh no!" He lifted his hand from Sólmundr's shoulder and stared at the blood that reddened his fingers. "Oh no!" he cried. "Iseult! *Iseult!*"

Wynter shook her head, her hands pressed to her mouth. She couldn't speak. Christopher struggled to sit, calling for her and groping blindly about him as if unable to focus his eyes or coordinate his body. Sólmundr drew the young man to him, stilling his frantic attempts to rise, holding him close.

"Iseult!" croaked Christopher.

"Iseult is good," murmured Sól shakily, patting Christopher's shoulder. "You not hurt her." He looked out through the door to where Thoar was helping Surtr to stand. Hallvor had joined them. Surtr gingerly pressed his fingers to the long, deep gashes on his bloodied stomach. "You not hurt her," whispered Sólmundr.

By Wynter's side, Razi rose slowly to his feet. Sól looked up at him. Razi met his eyes and the warrior's dazed confusion iced over to cold disapproval. Wynter did not look up into Razi's face. She could not take her eyes from Christopher.

Breathless and shaking, obviously in pain, her friend drew in his arms and legs and laid his head against Sólmundr's chest. He squinted up at Razi through the tangled mess of his hair, and, at the look on Razi's face, Christopher's expression filled with bitterness and despair.

"You will stay here," said Razi flatly.

"You promised me," said Christopher, "you promised…"

"You will stay *here*," commanded Razi. Úlfnaor's dark shadow filled the door, and Razi turned to him. "You will keep him here," he ordered. "That is my wish. As your Caora, that is my command."

Úlfnaor, his expression lost in shadow, bowed his head in obeisance. Christopher groaned.

"Stay here, Wyn," said Razi, "I mean it."

She turned her head, glaring up at him from the corner of her eye. He was nothing but a black shape against the light. He ducked out the door, and she saw him briefly in the sunlight, striding away between the tents. Then he was gone.

"He promised," rasped Christopher. "He said never again. He promised."

"Why the Wolves here, *a luch*?" asked Sól, searching Wynter's face. "What they have to offer the Prince?"

She shook her head. She glanced sideways at Christopher and the corners of his mouth turned down as he read her expression.

"Oh, no, lass," he whispered, "not you too."

"There must be a reason," she said.

"I'M SICK OF HIS REASONS," screamed Christopher suddenly, making Wynter jump. "I'M SICK OF THEM." He lurched in Sól's arms so that the warrior almost lost his grip. "I want them *dead*!" howled Christopher. "I want them *dead*! Like he promised! Like he said! I don't want this anymore! I *want them deaaaddd*!"

His howling became less than human again and Sól was no

longer cradling him, but holding him down. The warrior looked sadly to Úlfnaor, and the Aoire came forward to help restrain the young man as he battled the hatred within him.

Wynter backed slowly to the door, her eyes fixed on her thrashing friend. Sólmundr said something to Úlfnaor, and the big man put his hands on Christopher's shoulders, murmuring. Wynter thought he might be praying.

Wynter knew that Christopher was no longer a danger to these men. "*There ain't no pain,*" he had told Razi. "*Not when you do it on purpose. It feels good.*" And Wynter could see the pain in him. She could see him fighting to quell what he called his *dark power*. She had no doubt that this was a battle Christopher would win.

She knew she should stay with him. She knew she should be there for him when he emerged from this fight, weary and sore, and needing comfort. Still, she backed for the door.

Sólmundr met her eyes as she rose to her feet, and his eyes widened at the realisation that she was leaving.

"I need to know," she said.

Condemnation flared in the warrior's face, but Wynter held his gaze. After a moment Sól deflated and looked away. Having spent his life protecting the man he loved, only to then allow his people sacrifice him to their god, Sólmundr was in no position to point accusing fingers at those who put duty before love.

"I shall bring him his answers, Sól," she promised.

Sólmundr just shook his head and turned his attention back to Christopher, who thrashed and snarled and struggled beneath his restraining hands. The dogs had resumed their baying, and Wynter strode from the tent, pushed past Hallvor, and kept walking until the sounds of their howls were indistinguishable from those of the man she loved.

*   *   *

Once free from the accusing eyes of the Merron, Wynter paused. Standing in the dusty sunshine, she breathed deep and clenched her teeth and her hands as she tried to get herself under some control.

Razi was striding towards the foot of the slope, his eyes on Alberon's tent. He passed the knot of older Haun who were staring up the hill, murmuring anxiously amongst themselves. He passed the Wolves' beautiful horses and the slaves who tended them. He didn't so much as falter at the base of the hill, just strode purposefully upwards as if he had always expected this meeting, as if he had planned for it all his life.

Wynter lowered her chin and dashed after him, dodging the Haun and the horses and the patient slaves. Running to Razi's side, she fell into step with him, her eyes fixed ahead, her hand on her sword. He came to a halt and she strode on, not looking back.

"Wyn," he said flatly, "go back to him. I do not want you here."

"Don't bother, Razi," she snapped. "I'm not about to waste my time arguing with you." She kept walking, but Razi did not follow and she was forced to stop and look back at him.

His face was utterly hard. "You will not meet these men."

"Yes, I shall," she said. "I shall most *certainly* meet these men. I want very much to meet the men that stole his hands and enslaved his family. I want very *much* to look into the faces of the ones who hurt those poor girls at the inn. I want to know why it is they still wander about Algiers day after day without you baying for their blood, Razi. I want to know why it is that our brother has called them to his table. I will *not* sit on my arse like a good woman and let this go on without me. If Christopher is to be once again denied his vengeance, I shall be there to find out why."

"This is not the time for childish displays of defiance," he cried. "I have had the weight of these creatures hung around my neck since I was fourteen years old, Wynter. Christopher's life has been blighted by them for as long as he can recall. Do not step in now and act as though you understand a whit of what we feel."

Wynter didn't bother to reply. She simply stood with her hand on her sword, waiting for Razi to start up the slope again. Razi snarled and looked away. His eyes slipped to the tents behind which the hounds still voiced their frustration and rage.

"Do not expect me to go in there with my sword drawn," he warned quietly. "I doubt Alberon's plans will afford me the luxury. This world is not simple, Wynter. One cannot always have the blood one wants."

The dogs howled again, and Razi's furious mask slipped a little. He shook his head and squeezed his eyes shut.

"Oh, do not fret, brother," said Wynter coldly. "It is only the warhounds. Christopher is a good man, and strong. I have no doubt that he has already regained his self-control. I wager he has grown uncommonly good at suppressing his feelings. He has, after all, been associating with the likes of us for long enough."

Razi snapped his eyes to her, and Wynter stared flatly back at him.

"Fine," he said at last. "Fine! If you're coming, let us go." And he strode towards the waiting tent, Wynter by his side.

Le Garou

The guards around Alberon's tent eyed Razi and Wynter as they approached. Oliver was standing in the shadow of the awning, and he came quickly forwards, striding down the slope to head Razi off before he got anywhere near the wary soldiers.

Wynter expected Razi to shove his way past, but instead he halted, regarding the knight from under his brows.

"Do not do this, my Lord," warned Oliver quietly, "please."

Razi spoke just as quietly, his voice inaudible to the watching men. "Either let me past, or kill me, Oliver. Which will it be?"

Oliver regarded him closely and Razi held his gaze. "I shall get access, or die trying, Sir Knight. I ask you again, which will it be?"

Oliver's eyes fell to Wynter.

"I shall accompany the Lord Razi."

Oliver briefly squeezed his eyes shut, then he gestured the soldiers to give the lord and lady access. Wynter and Razi strode into the shade of the awning and straight through the door. Oliver stood for a moment in the sunshine, as if too weary to move, then he followed them in.

The map table and its four chairs had been brought inside. Alberon sat on one side of it, David Le Garou on the other. David's seconds-in-command lined the wall behind him, loose-limbed and ready, watching their leader's back. At Razi's entrance, they straightened as one, their slanting eyes filled with amused delight.

David Le Garou rose smoothly to his feet, all his teeth showing in a grin. His eyes dropped to Wynter, then back to Razi. "Al-Sayyid," he murmured. "What a pleasant surprise. I had heard that you were dead."

"Why are you here?" asked Razi.

David lifted his eyebrows and he turned to Alberon in feigned shock, as if expecting the Prince to reprimand his brother for his rudeness. There was a moment of heavy silence. Alberon drummed his fingers on the table. Once. A gesture of contained anger.

"I take it that you know each other," he said tightly.

Le Garou shrugged and spread his hands. "We have met, in passing. Now and again."

"You have done your best these past five years to destabilise my relations within the Moroccan court," said Razi. "You have done everything you can to use me to drive a wedge between the Sultan and my father. I ask again, why are you here?"

"The dealings at court were not my idea," tutted David. "That was my father, the great André Le Garou. It is he who tries to distance the Sultan from his old allies. I have no personal opinion on who rules the Moroccos. But we all must support our fathers, must we not? In word and in deed. One must do one's father's bidding... Still," the Wolf smiled slyly. "If my father has been a trouble to you, you have never seemed too discomforted, al-Sayyid. If he has offended you in speech or act, you have yet to let it show."

"Your father thought I would cry havoc, did he not?" said Razi. "He thought that my pride would drive me to act rashly. He hoped I would run riot with some bloody-handed vendetta and so damage my standing as a diplomat. No doubt he thought a half-breed boy-prince would never have had the self-control to let such an act go."

Le Garou shrugged. "If so, you proved him wrong. How proud that must make you feel."

Alberon looked warily from Le Garou to Razi, not understanding.

"What did you do?" he asked the Wolf.

Le Garou smiled again. "Oh," he said, "al-Sayyid thinks we damaged his property... some trifling act of vandalism for which he blames us. It is not unusual. The Loups-Garous tend to get blamed for such things. It's just the way the world is."

Wynter realised with a sudden jolt of horror that he was speaking of Christopher and of what had been done to him. It was abruptly, shockingly clear that Christopher's terrible mutilation, the theft of all that he was, had been done for no other reason than to get at Razi. It had been nothing more than a vicious jab at al-Sayyid. Christopher had been taken and broken like a stolen toy, all as a petty attempt to goad Razi into vengeance and ruin his reputation in the Sultan's court.

She stared at David Le Garou's slyly smiling face and understood at last the depths of Razi's restraint and of Christopher's patience. For nearly four years, her friends had suppressed their rage and their grief, all for the sake of this kingdom. Wynter wondered how often in those years Razi had told Christopher *soon, soon*, and how often he had needed to go back on his word?

The hounds outside the tent raised their voices once more, and Wynter struggled to quell the hatred that rose within her and the rage that threatened to cloud her vision.

"*Jesu*, Razi," sighed Alberon wearily. "Whatever these men

did, I shall be certain they make reparation for it, but now is not the time to settle old scores. Horse theft and broken trinkets will need to be put aside for the time being. We have bigger things to hand."

"Yes, al-Sayyid," said Le Garou, smirking at Razi. "Please do not fret. Though the Wolves have naught to do with your loss, I am certain we should have no trouble replacing your damaged goods. After all, though rare here, such things are ten a penny where we come from. I believe I may even have some with me, if I look in my baggage."

The Wolf called Jean snickered, and Alberon and Oliver looked sharply at him. Wynter saw a cold resolve harden in Alberon's face and it served to settle her nauseating rage. She knew that Alberon could not possibly have grasped the context of the Wolves' vile needling, but the look on the Prince's face told her that he would not tolerate their sly amusement at his brother's expense. Whatever Alberon's original thoughts towards Razi's inclusion in these talks, Wynter was certain the Wolves had just won their rival a place at the Prince's table.

Sure enough, Alberon patted the chair on his left. "Brother," he said, "come now, and take your place by me. As ever, I should benefit from your contribution to my affairs. Your insights are always so acute."

Le Garou lost his smile, and Razi rounded the table to sit at the Prince's left hand. He was darkly contained, his movements smooth and unhurried. When he had taken his seat, he folded his hands on the table and gazed blandly at Le Garou as if waiting for him to read from a menu, or serve up some tea. His calmness astounded Wynter; it reminded her of exactly what Razi was capable.

Oliver moved to stand at Alberon's back, his hands resting on the handle of his sword, consciously mirroring Le Garou's three watchful guards.

"Protector Lady," said Alberon, "you will attend?"

Wynter nodded stiffly, grateful that he had chosen to recognise her and not, as would have been his right, ignored her and shamed her into leaving of her own accord. She did not commit the horrible presumption of sitting at the treaty table, nor did she set herself up as Oliver's equal in guarding the Prince, but she crossed instead to take a seat on the relative obscurity of Alberon's cot.

The row of seconds followed her movement with bemused interest. Even before crossing the tent she had succeeded in forcing down her rage. By the time she took her seat, she felt almost nothing—so deeply had she buried her feelings. Her face cold, her hands steady, she settled herself on Alberon's cot, then stared at the leering Wolves until they looked away. Their expressions gave no doubt that they presumed her to be Razi's woman, and the idea of it entertained them no end.

"Pretty," murmured Gérard.

"But small," added Pierre, "scarcely more than a mouthful."

Wynter glanced at Razi and Alberon, expecting them to rage, but either they had not heard, or they refused to be needled by it. Pierre smirked to himself and licked his lips.

Were you at the tavern? thought Wynter suddenly. *Was it you?* She knew it was not. These higher ranking Wolves had not been involved in those terrible deeds at the Wherry Tavern. Still, looking at their faces, Wynter could not help but recall the feel of teeth and fur against her cheek, the clench of iron-strong arms around her body, the hot blast of a chuckle in her ear. Christopher had sacrificed himself to save her from them, but the landlord's daughters had not been so lucky. The face of the eldest girl

was a clear memory, bruised and swollen and white with shock
the next day, her little sister's broken body laid out before them
on the kitchen table. Wynter closed her hand on the hilt of her
sword. Her face betrayed nothing, but there was a sudden acid
pain in her belly, and she wondered if it was all her hidden anger
and fear, finally burning itself into the pit of her stomach.

There was a small movement beside her and she slid her eyes
left. Coriolanus cowered in his little nest, his beautiful eyes huge.
Wynter thought she had never seen a cat so close to tears. Forcing her fingers to release her weapon, Wynter reached and discreetly stroked his trembling back. It seemed to comfort Cori a
little, but it also centred Wynter and let her think.

David Le Garou pushed back the embroidered tails of his
moss green coat and resumed his seat. "Your Highness—" he
began.

"You have brought slaves to this camp," interrupted Razi.

"Oh, are we to speak of slaves?" asked Le Garou, raising his
eyebrows in fascination and folding his gloved hands on the
table top.

"They are forbid here."

Le Garou sighed patiently. "I remind you, slaves are only forbid to those residing in your father's kingdom, al-Sayyid. Travellers are allowed their property."

"Only if travelling the Port Road, and only after paying the
appropriate taxes. We are far from the Port Road here, David,
and I have yet to hear of Wolves paying taxes."

"I have dispensation." Le Garou looked pointedly to Alberon.

"I did not sanction the conveyance of human chattels," corrected Alberon.

Le Garou sat back, spreading his hands in mock defeat. "Then
I shall set them loose," he said. "Perhaps they'll be fortunate

enough to find work somewhere—or perhaps they can throw themselves on your charity, al-Sayyid? Your generosity being what it is."

Razi lowered his chin, his lip curled back to reply, but Alberon silenced them both with a raised hand.

"Enough!" he said sharply. "We have *business* to discuss and I shall not be distracted from it! Monsieur Le Garou, when you are resident here, I shall not tolerate the retention of slaves. Those whom you and your men cannot gainfully employ, you must free with ample purse to set them up in a trade. You understand?"

Le Garou shrugged. Wynter and Razi gaped at Alberon. *When you are resident here?* Could he be serious?

Alberon turned to Razi. "Lord Razi," he said firmly, "we shall stick to the subject that Le Garou and I have brought to this table. Your own agendas will fall aside."

Alberon turned back to Le Garou and went to speak, but almost immediately his lieutenant made himself known at the door, and the Prince hung his head in exasperation while Oliver went to take a message.

While waiting, David Le Garou smiled across the table at Razi, who still stared at Alberon in disbelief. "Those dogs sound a mite savage, my Lord," said the Wolf, tilting his head to the distant baying of the Merron hounds. "I hope they are well fettered."

Razi turned his head as if on rusty hinges, and Alberon looked at Le Garou from under his brows, irritated at the obvious resumption of verbal hostilities.

Le Garou just kept smiling at Razi. "Of course, there's naught more dangerous than an unchained cur," he murmured. "One would hope the owner of such an animal would be wise enough to keep him tethered."

At his back, the row of Wolves grinned and Razi regarded them with hatred.

Oliver came and whispered in Alberon's ear. The Prince's young face brightened into a wicked smile. "Oh, I have no doubt they do," he said. He glanced at Le Garou as if sharing a great jest. "The Haun have requested access to my presence."

David Le Garou chuckled. "Of course they have."

"Tell them no," said Alberon, and Oliver nodded and went to convey the message to the lieutenant.

"My arrival has thrown them," smiled Le Garou. "Poor things. They do rely so on my father's collusion in the Sultan's demise. They can only be alarmed at my unexpected communion with you." He sighed and ran his gloved hands across the table top, his eyes on Alberon. "Now," he murmured, "tell me my reward."

"The Lord Gascon De Bourg," said Alberon. "You recall him, Lord Razi? A foolish man. So foolish, indeed, that he sided with my father's enemies during the insurrection."

"This proved bad for his health?" asked the Wolf.

"Extremely."

"And his heirs? Can I presume that their father's foolishness prove bad for *their* health?"

"It proved fatal."

"As it should. No house should take arms against a king and live to think the better of it. Tell me, your Highness, this dead traitor to your father . . . he left a sizeable estate?"

"Large, rich, well established. It has vineyards, lake and pasture. Marvellous stock and well-managed tenantry. The King has planned to divide it between four of his supporters, and a fine living they all would have made of it too . . . I shall ensure it is given to you instead, Monsieur Le Garou, in its entirety. You and your men will be set for life."

Le Garou sighed again and closed his eyes. He rolled his head as if some unseen hand were kneading the tension from his shoulders. "An estate," he breathed. "At last."

Wynter shook her head. She watched Alberon closely. This must be some kind of trick. He was planning to fool the Wolves somehow; there could be no other explanation.

Alberon's eyes went hard. "Now, Monsieur," he asked flatly, "what do *you* offer *me*?"

Le Garou's face darkened with bitter satisfaction. "My father has denied me my due too long," he whispered. "He grins at me and calls me his best, but keeps me to heel like a common whelp while lesser sons get their title and are released. I grow weary of an old dog's suspicion. His lack of faith has made of me that which he feared all along." He tilted his head, his smile cold. "I will split the packs for you, Prince. I will draw my father's allies from him with the promise that they will join me in my new life. The ones who are left in his command will smell his weakness and tear him apart in their efforts to gain control." He jerked his head towards the camp. "Those Haun await confirmation that my father and his Corsair allies are ready to forge an alliance to topple the Sultan. They will be sore disappointed when I break the news of my father's change of heart."

"A change of heart which exists only in your imagination," murmured Alberon.

Le Garou grinned wide and Wynter clearly saw the Wolf behind the man. "I am my father's voice and claw, Prince. Why would they doubt me? The Haun are weak already. Spread thin by time and distance, this is a blow their leaders will not recover from. When they realise that the Loups-Garous are no longer on their side, their scheme for an invasion of the West will be destroyed. They too will rip themselves apart with recrimination and struggle. The Western Haun will be weakened beyond repair."

Razi huffed. "What use are Wolves and Corsairs to the Haun?" he murmured. "Why would they seek the support of ragtag pirates and rabid ungovernable scum like you?"

Le Garou glanced darkly at him from the corner of his eye. If looks could poison, Wynter was certain Razi would have dropped to the floor and writhed to his death in the dirt.

"The Haun would have much to be grateful for if the Corsairs and the Wolves pull the Sultan from his throne," snarled Le Garou. "When he is no longer in charge, this kingdom will no longer have an ally in the Moroccan court and the Haun need have no fear of reprisals when they ride in here and rape your land. They would be so very, very grateful to my father for this, al-Sayyid. So grateful. They have already offered to give what is left of this kingdom to those who helped them gain power. And my father and his allies will merrily divide it amongst them-selves. The Corsairs will receive the Southland ports and free reign over those damned shipping lanes of your father's. The Loups-Garous will gain dominion over the Port Road. And the Haun?" The Wolf grinned, too wide a grin, with too many teeth, and his eyes darkened until there was no colour left in them at all. "The Haun will simply let loose on the Europes, for sport, to see what they can get."

Wynter's hand tightened on Coriolanus's back and the cat shuddered and mewed softly in fear.

"But I can halt all that," said Le Garou. "With one or two words from me, it all falls down; the Moroccan throne will be safe, the Southlands will remain secure. All I ask in return is a home of my own."

"Lies," said Razi.

Le Garou slid his dark gaze to him again, and Alberon turned to regard his brother with open interest.

"The Corsairs have lost all their supporters," said Razi. "Thanks to the Sultan's reforms, even their old Slawi allies have turned against them. They are adrift at sea, portless, friendless outlaws, desperate for a haven. And the Wolves? You are as you always were: a loose alliance of disparate packs, some strong, some weak, too rabid ever to come together long enough to act as one."

Alberon frowned at Le Garou and Wynter could see that he was listening, really listening to Razi's words. Hope rose in her chest as she saw the Prince regard the Wolf with new eyes.

Razi went calmly on. "The Sultan's enemies have no strength, David, and you know it. Your father and his allies are naught but noisy, squabbling bandits and rabble trash. They have no hope of uniting a force strong enough to topple the Moroccan throne. You have come here with nothing but empty words, and have hoped to build an empire upon them. You will not succeed."

"Do you really expect the Prince to listen to you?" growled Le Garou. "You, who have set your arse on a velvet cushion this last five years while your little brother has hacked his way through your father's enemies?"

"No," warned Alberon, pointing a finger at the Wolf. "That is enough."

"*You?*" continued Le Garou, snarling at Razi despite Alberon's obvious disapproval. "How dare *you* accuse *me* of empty words, when all you ever *have* is words? You gelded calf!" he cried, slapping the table. "You ball-less *bint*! Do not force me to test you, al-Sayyid. I would tear your throat with a look!"

Alberon surged to his feet, and David sat back, suddenly aware that he had gone too far. Wynter was utterly certain, then, that Razi had won. Alberon's rage convinced her so. Then Razi made his terrible mistake, and two angry sentences brought the Prince's wrath swinging back around to fall on his brother.

"You will not use my brother's foolishness as a tool to further your own ends," said Razi to the Wolf. "I will not let you."

As soon as he had uttered them, Wynter could see that Razi wished the words unsaid. His eyes widened and he all but slapped his hand across his mouth. But the damage was done. Alberon's rage turned cold. Le Garou's uncertainty became a grin, and the battle was lost.

Empty Words

Alberon took his seat and did not look at his brother. "Tell the Haun to come up now, Sir Oliver; Monsieur Le Garou and I are ready to speak with them. Lord Razi, you may stay, or you may go. It makes no odds to me either way."

"Alberon..." whispered Razi.

But Alberon looked to David Le Garou and said, "How shall we handle this, monsieur? Do you prefer to speak, or shall I?" and that was it. Razi was out in the cold, watching from a distance as his brother went about his business.

The Haun came—eager, fawning and utterly thrown. Their linguist translated Le Garou's news with frozen shock, and the older men's subsequent efforts to cajole and deny flowed around Wynter as a stark contrast to Razi's broken silence. He simply sat through it all, his eyes on the table, his face weary. He seemed utterly spent.

At some stage, Coriolanus had crawled onto Wynter's lap and she cradled him with absent protectiveness as the Wolves leered sideways from the corners of their eyes. Oliver hovered in the background while Alberon put the panicked Haun in their place. The knight was as poised and imposing as ever, but he looked exhausted, and sometimes, despite his courtly detachment, Wynter caught him glancing at Razi or at Le Garou, his face naked with misery.

The Haun left at last, and Alberon rose to dismiss the Wolves. He grinned crookedly, reached across the table, and to Wynter's dismay, shook David Le Garou's gloved hand.

"So," he said, "we are done."

"Our bargain is sealed now, Prince?" asked Le Garou. "My pack will rest easy in your protection?"

Alberon's face hardened a little and he tightened his grip on the Wolf's hand. "Do not cross me, monsieur, and I shall endeavour not to cross you."

Le Garou smiled his sharp smile and held the Prince's eye. "I shall not cross you, Prince," he said. His eyes dropped briefly to Razi, as if dismissing a spot of dirt on the table, then he turned to his men. "Go direct the boys to set up our quarters."

They bowed. "Yes, Father," they said, and Wynter saw Le Garou soak up the title, closing his eyes to it, as to a lover's caress.

"Yes," he whispered. "Father. At last."

Alberon frowned in distaste at this, and Wynter saw him unconsciously rub his hand on his trousers. "Sir Oliver will direct your men as to where they can camp," he said. "And, Le Garou, your followers will behave around the Haun, you understand? There will be no triumphalism."

Le Garou bowed. "None at all." he promised, smooth as buttered oil.

Oliver led the Wolves from sight and Alberon stood in silence for a moment, listening to their retreating footsteps. Wynter held Coriolanus close, waiting for Alberon's anger. Waiting for the moment he would turn on Razi and let loose on him all the rage of a prince whose authority has been slighted. She actually jumped when Razi was the first to speak. He kept his voice very soft and did not look up at his brother.

"The Wolves have six riders in the forest," he said.

Alberon glanced coldly at him. "To what purpose?" he asked, crossing to retrieve Marguerite Shirken's papers and seating himself at his battered little writing table.

"Self-protection," said Razi.

Wynter waited while Alberon uncorked his inkwell and set up his quills. Perhaps there was a chance Razi could work his way back from this? If he was quiet and respectful and of use? Alberon untied the diplomatic folder, chose a letter and broke the seal. He scanned the document, then moved on to the next. "They are of danger to my men?" he asked.

Razi lifted his eyes to Wynter, and she gazed hopefully at him. "I doubt they are a threat," he said. "Not at the moment."

"Good," said Alberon, scanning another letter, his tone leaving no doubt that he was concentrating on things infinitely more important than his brother's opinion. Laying the document aside, he snapped the seals on the next. Sitting in the crossways slash of light cast by the door, the sun in his pale hair, his face hard with regal detachment, Wynter thought he had never looked more like his father. He had never looked more like a king.

"Alberon?" said Razi.

"I am busy now, brother. We shall talk later."

"Alberon, I should be grateful if the Loups-Garous were quartered as far from my tent as possible."

Alberon lowered the parchment and looked at Razi at last. "Your diplomacy only goes so far, is that it, brother? You cannot bring yourself to—"

"Albi," said Razi softly, "the damaged property the Wolves spoke of was my friend, Christopher. The vandalism to which they refer was the removal of his fingers."

Alberon's face opened in shock and he regarded Razi for a moment with pure and untainted sympathy. "*Jesu*, Razi," he breathed.

"He has borne my tolerance of them all these years, brother. Do not force him to endure their close proximity now, not when it is clear that his patience may never be rewarded."

Alberon dropped his eyes to Marguerite Shirken's letter. She had written in dark red ink, and the neat script put Wynter in mind of blood. Perfect little instances of blood, laid side by side in marshalled rows. The impossibly neat aftermath of a mass execution.

"Marcel!" shouted Alberon suddenly, his unexpected yell making Wynter jump again.

The lieutenant came to the door, and Alberon spoke without looking around. "Go now, and within the earshot of Le Garou, tell Sir Oliver that I have decided to spare those Wolves that are lurking in the forest. If Sir Oliver is lacking enough to look puzzled, tell him that the Prince has no further need to keep his knowledge of the Wolf spies secret."

"Aye, your Highness."

"Marcel."

"Aye, Highness."

"Make certain that the Wolves are quartered as far from the Lord Razi's tent as is physically possible."

Marcel flicked a curious glance at Razi, saluted and left.

Razi shut his eyes in gratitude. "Thank you," he whispered.

But Alberon had already turned back to his reading. He did not bother to dismiss his brother, just sat in busy silence until Razi got to his feet.

Wynter hoped she might be allowed stay, had resolved herself to gentle persuasion once Razi had left. But as soon as Razi moved to go, Alberon said, "I am busy, Protector Lady Moorehawke."

"Will you not spare me a little of your time, your Highness? There is surely..."

"Perhaps you can visit later," snapped Alberon, his eyes on the letter. "When I have time to spend on the nicer things."

Wynter glanced at Razi, who was waiting by the door. He gestured bleakly that she come along. Gently, she deposited a reluctant Cori at the foot of Alberon's bed and rose to leave.

She had only passed Alberon's table when he cursed low and furious and shot to his feet.

"He is not an envoy!" he cried, brandishing Shirken's letter. "That Merron snake! He is not an envoy! She says here that she has been forced to entrust her representatives to...see here," he indicated a section of text and read aloud, "*to the care of a man I am not certain I can trust. A churlish knave, one leader of the Merron, named Úlfnaor, Air...Aeeur...*curse it, I cannot pronounce that bloody name! In any case, listen to this... *I am most concerned by this man, but have been left with no choice and must hope that he does not live up to his people's reputation of treachery and deceit. I have...*Wait, where is the next? Yes, listen... *my envoys are a handsome pair, twin brother and sister, the most becoming of God's creatures. Certainly, my dear, when you behold them you shall not fail to know they were sent by me. They are blond as God's blessed sunlight and their demeanour is quite wonderfully courtly and refined—one can only pray to God's divine grace that these same manners will influence the savages with whom they are forced to travel. As it is, I fear it likely that this Merron cur will do away with them entirely and set himself up in their place...for no better reason than he will have the chance to act the lord and so be showered in trinkets on his arrival.*"

Alberon looked up from the paper and his face said it all.

"Which he DID!" he exclaimed. "He did! You saw him! Acting the nobleman! Good Christ! I shall have his goddamned pagan head for it! Listen to this... *My dear, these two envoys are most trusted and beloved of me. Should worst come to worst, I beg you take leave to avenge their mistreatment on my behalf. This mission has been a calculated gesture of faith from me to the Merron. I pray that they are sensible and accept my generous trust in them. Should they, once again, prove incapable of civilised behaviour, I shall be left with no option but to react. A sensible ruler, after all, can only stretch her tolerance so far.*"

Alberon stared at Wynter and Razi in disbelief. "I cannot believe it!" he said. "That he thought he could get away with it!" He started for the door, his face thunderous.

"Alberon," tried Wynter, her voice scratchy with shock. "Perhaps there... there may have been..." She jerked to a panicked silence.

Ashkr and Embla: it could only be them to whom Marguerite was referring. The beautiful, gentle and ultimately doomed pair, whom the Merron had cherished for their entire lives—then sacrificed in the most savage manner. Wynter closed her eyes at the memory. Every single thing she wanted to say seemed wrong. Shockingly, her strongest impulse was to shout "No! She lies! They did nothing!" But no matter how willingly Ashkr and Embla had gone to the grave, it did not negate the senselessness, nor the brutality of their passing, and Wynter could think of nothing to say that would not paint the Merron in an impossibly dark light.

She looked to Razi. His face was cold and set. As he lowered his chin and moved to let Alberon out the door, Wynter knew he was about to reveal the Merron's crime, and use the distraction to return to his brother's confidence. She could not bring herself to condemn him for it. After all, Embla had been his lover—no, more than that—she had been the woman he *loved*. Razi had every right to take his revenge. But looking up into his dark face, Wynter wished that it was not so. To her shame, she found herself wishing that somehow the Merron might walk free of the consequences of those horrible and pointless killings back in the forest.

For a brief moment Razi's cold eyes met hers. Wynter lifted her hands, she clasped them, *please.* Razi looked away. Her heart sank. But, just as it seemed certain that he would let Alberon stride past and summon his guard, Razi clenched his fist, squeezed his eyes shut, then put his hand out to stop the Prince in his tracks.

"I think I know the people to whom Marguerite refers," he sighed, "the brother and sister she speaks of in her letter."

Alberon's eyes widened in anger. "For God's sake, man!" he cried. "Why did you not—?"

Razi met his eye. "They were ill when I met them," he said. "The same disease for which I treated their leader's right-hand man. I attended them myself, but there was naught to be done for them."

Alberon deflated slightly, "Oh," he said.

"Úlfnaor attempts negotiation with you only because he was entreated to do so by the envoys themselves. Before they died, they bid him to take their place. He comes to you in the innocent belief that he has been granted right of parley."

"Oh," said Alberon again. He looked down at the papers in confusion.

Wynter stared ahead of her, afraid to look at Razi in case some twitch of expression or some tic of posture might give away her shock at his smoothly believable lies.

"Marguerite has misrepresented Úlfnaor to you," said Razi. "She portrays him as a savage and a brute, but I suspect that he is neither of those things. Try not to be offended by his manner. He behaves as a lord because to his people he *is* a lord. In his own way, Úlfnaor is a nobleman and I do not think that you have cause to distrust his intent."

This must have come perilously close to Razi offering his opinion, because Alberon seemed to remember that he was no longer accepting advice from his brother, and he dropped his eyes to the grip Razi had on his arm. Razi carefully removed his hand and Alberon simply stood in expressionless silence until Razi bowed, and turned to leave. Wynter followed stiffly on his heels. At the edge of the tent's shadow, just before they stepped out into the cold sunlight, Razi turned back once more.

"If you like, your Highness, you can send my word to Princess Marguerite. You can tell her that I can attest to the fact that her envoys were treated with all the care and devotion she could ever have hoped for. You can assure her that I was witness to this, and that they were tended to with great dedication and with much love, right up until the day they died."

Alberon did not move or reply, and after a moment Razi nodded and walked away. Alberon glanced at Wynter.

"What he says is true?"

She nodded dumbly, her neck stiff. Alberon looked down again at Shirken's paper, obviously confused at the differences between his brother's story and that of the Princess.

She makes a toy of you, thought Wynter. *She uses you to her own end*. But she said nothing, because sometimes the truth was easier to take when you were allowed see it for yourself. Alberon wandered back into his tent, and Wynter watched him return to his little writing table and sit. He spread Marguerite's letter on the table, smoothed her blood-red writing beneath his hand, and once again, he began to read.

Without a word, Wynter turned from him and followed Razi down the hill.

A String of Silver Lies

The Wolves had not yet moved from the foot of the hill, though Oliver, already mounted and obviously fuming, was doing his best to get them going. Razi did not falter as he neared the milling horses, but the Wolves' smirks and sly glances made it obvious that they had delayed moving off so that he would be forced to make his way past them.

Wynter was alarmed to see the female Merron warriors striding up the road towards them, their eyes fixed firmly on Razi. Led by Hallvor, the women had their shields in hand, and their weapons, though sheathed, were strapped around their waists. They were coming to protect their Caora. Wynter knew that such a show of strength would bode ill for them, and for Razi, so she lifted her hand to them, her face set in grim warning. *Stop where you are!* Hallvor saw her, and gestured the others to a halt. Wynter glared and jerked her chin to the tents, *get back*, and after a moment's hesitation, the warriors bowed and melted away.

David Le Garou pointedly ignored Razi, but when Jean stepped into Razi's path and bowed low, Wynter saw Le Garou smile to himself in sly amusement.

"Al-Sayyid!" cried Jean. "Where go you? Will you not stay with the Prince? Have you not more advice you can give him?"

Razi swerved past without answering.

Gérard chuckled as he swung himself into his saddle. "Don't be a whelp, Jean," he murmured.

Oliver's face darkened. "You are clogging up the thorough-fare," he snapped at David. "Tell your men to get going."

David just smiled at him, and took his time gathering his reins.

Gérard suddenly walked his horse backwards and Razi was forced to jerk to a halt as the huge animal blocked his path. "Oops," said Gérard childishly, but he made no move to pull his mount out of the way. Wynter came to Razi's side, staring up into the Wolf's dark, grinning face.

"It will be nice to be neighbours again," called David Le Garou. "One gets so used to the familiar. It feels empty when one does not see the same faces every day."

Razi clenched his hands and strode away through the choking dust. But Le Garou was not finished, and he wheeled around and kicked forwards until they were on level. Wynter, jogging beside her silent friend, glanced up. The Wolf was simply walking his horse along, matching Razi's pace. David's handsome face was serene, his eyes roaming the tents as if seeking a nice spot to picnic.

"Lovely," he sighed. "Simply perfect."

His men fell in behind him, and the whole entourage trotted slowly along beside Razi, their faces painted with glee. Razi just kept striding forwards, stubbornly refusing to duck in amongst the tents and out of Le Garou's range.

"Hmm," mused the Wolf, arching an eyebrow towards the now silent Merron quarters. "That mongrel has finally ceased his yapping. Perhaps the Prince has done the sensible thing and had him muzzled...certainly I should do the same, were I lumbered with such an undisciplined beast. They're simply too untrustworthy, these packless creatures. In fact, I believe I may go so far as to say—"

To Wynter's relief, Oliver chose that moment to urge his horse between David and Razi, cutting Le Garou off in mid sentence. The knight kept himself between them and glared across at the Wolf with every ounce of his courtly disdain. "You will break off *here*, Le Garou. *Now.* Or I shall be forced to make you sleep in the forest with the rest of your mangy curs."

Wynter lost sight of Le Garou's face as Oliver danced his own mount sideways, forcing the Wolf's big stallion to shy off.

"We shall talk later, Lord Razi," sang Le Garou, as he drew away, "when I have had my rest."

And to Wynter's surprise and relief, the Loups-Garous allowed themselves be herded away, veering towards the tents on the far side of the road, their pack mule and their slaves trotting placidly behind, the sound of bells following them. She watched them ride off, then she ran to catch up with Razi, who had simply kept on walking.

The Merron women were shadowing Razi through the tents, staying abreast of his progress, but keeping their distance. Up ahead, Wynter saw Jared standing at the corner of the supply tent, glowering at the retreating Loups-Garous. He had strapped a sword around his waist and his cowl was thrown back, revealing his tonsured head. Mary lurked behind him, her eyes hopping keenly between Razi and the Wolves. Wynter was fairly certain that Jared did not know the lady had emerged from the safety of her quarters.

Razi must have seen the priest, because he turned abruptly away from him, and cut between the nearest tents. Wynter dodged to keep up with his long-legged stride. The Merron women ducked from sight. Razi just kept walking, apparently with no destination in mind.

"Razi," said Wynter, jogging breathlessly at his side.

He shook his head.

"The Merron are this way," she said, pointing. "We must tell Úlfnaor. He must be warned...he must...he must know what to say...should Alberon call him. Razi!" she cried. "Please! I am running out of breath!"

Razi came to a sudden halt and pressed the heels of his hands to his eyes. Taken by surprise, Wynter slid to a stop, then slowly came back to his side.

"Razi?" she said.

"Am I never to have one single, honest feeling?" he whispered. "Am I never...will it always be one betrayal weighed against another?"

Wynter put her hand on his arm. "Come back to the Merron," she said softly. "Come sit and think and—"

"I cannot," he said, pressing his hands harder against his eyes. "I cannot face him. I simply...I cannot."

"My Lord," Mary's quiet voice made Wynter startle.

The lady came from between the tents, Jared trailing anxiously behind her. It was obvious that the priest wished her back in seclusion, and equally obvious that he was not having much luck persuading her to return.

At Mary's voice, Razi shook his head and groaned without looking up, but Mary crossed to him without hesitation. Wynter stood back. Mary took her place, reached up and gently took Razi's hands from his eyes.

"My Lord," she said again, her face gentle with concern.

"Four years, Mary," he whispered, taking both her hands and holding them between his own. "Four years I have held my tongue. And today, of all days, I allow myself to speak in anger. Mary, I have ruined everything."

He spoke to her as if she had every knowledge of what he was saying, as if she were someone he had confided to many, many times over the course of his complicated life. And the Lady Mary looked up into his desolate face with all the sympathy and understanding one would give a cherished friend.

She nodded. "Our lives are such, that words can lay the deadliest traps, *n'est-ce pas*? But you are the cleverest of men, my Lord. You will find a way."

Razi pressed Mary's hands to his chest and Wynter saw a flame of gratitude rise up behind his desperation. "Thank you, Mary," he said.

Wynter could not fathom it, this understanding between two people who had only just met. Where had it come from? But she was extremely moved by it, and she found herself wanting, more than anything, that right here and now, Mary would put her arms around Razi and squeeze him gently and tell him, *it will be all right.*

"Are the Loups-Garous a danger to us?" asked Jared.

"They are *Wolves*, Jared," sighed Mary. "They are hardly likely to invite us to tea." She glanced wryly at Razi. "Unless, of course, we are to be their entrée."

To Wynter's astonishment, Razi smiled. It was a broken smile, to be sure, but a smile nonetheless. Wynter might well have fallen in love with Mary then, so thankful did she feel towards this gentle, soft spoken, beautifully self-possessed little woman.

"Come now!" Mary released Razi's hands and smoothed the front of his shirt in a businesslike manner. "Come to my tent. I shall send Jared to beg some tea, and you will sit in blissful solitude and think for a while with no one to bother you. Oh, do not grimace so, Jared! What could even the most scurrilous mind construe from a woman in my bloated condition and a man of the lord's standing sharing an innocent pot of tea?"

"I will speak to Úlfnaor for you, Razi," offered Wynter. "If you like, you can take your ease for a while. Perhaps get some sleep? You can speak to Christopher later, I am sure that he..."

Razi shook his head. "Thank you, Wyn," he said, "but I must face up to this now. To leave it will only make it worse." He kissed Mary's hand. "Thank you eternally, sweet woman. I cannot fathom your kindness to me after... after what I have done. It shames me... I feel..."

Mary silenced him with her fingers on his lips. "We have been through enough, you and I. I shall not torment you with recriminations, when it is obvious that you already torment yourself. In the small time that I have known you, my Lord, I have witnessed much forgiveness in you, and forgiveness breeds forgiveness. The man you are shapes those around you."

Razi clutched Mary's fingers to his lips, his eyes glittering. Wynter felt certain he would come undone. But after a moment he simply drew a breath, nodded, kissed Mary's fingers once more and let her go.

"You have business to attend," said Mary, smoothing her skirts, "I am tired. I shall retire. Protector Lady, a pleasure." Wynter bobbed a curtsy, her heart full of gratitude. Mary nodded. "My Lord Razi." Razi bowed. "Feel free to call," she said, turning for her tent. "I am home most days between sunrise and sunset. You have no need to send a page; I shall receive you with no ceremony," and she made her way between the tents, Jared following ruefully in her wake.

When they returned to the Merron, the women had already rejoined the group and the warriors were standing in a huddle, murmuring grimly to each other. At the sight of Razi and Wynter, they fell silent and waited.

Sólmundr and Christopher were sitting by the fire, Christopher leaning against his friend, gazing darkly into the flames. Sól murmured and stood, his expression belligerent, and Christopher looked up. To Wynter's distress, his narrow face hardened, and without a word, he pushed awkwardly to his feet and made his way into the Merron tent, pulling the flap down behind him. She came to a halt, staring at the starkly closed door.

Úlfnaor bowed warily, and Razi tore his attention from the tent and bowed in return. "I must speak with you," he said.

Úlfnaor gestured to the fire and Razi took a place beside it. All the Merron except Sólmundr crouched and listened carefully as Razi began to explain the things that Marguerite Shirken had said in her papers. Wynter ignored everyone and picked her way around Úlfnaor's dogs, heading for the tent.

"He not want talk to you," said Sólmundr coldly.

Wynter just glanced at him and passed on by. With a grimace, the warrior went to join his companions by the fire, and Wynter ducked past the growling Boro and into the tent.

"I'm angry," said Christopher. "It ain't a good time to come calling."

His voice was hoarse and gravelly, barely recognisable as his own. He stood at the back of the tent, a slim darkness amongst the shadows, and Wynter couldn't help but feel a prickle of fear.

"I cannot see your face, Christopher," she said softly. "Will you come into the light?"

He laughed, the harsh, dry sound of a sneer articulated. "You're afraid of me," he said.

"Do you expect me not to be?"

There was silence, then he came forward so that his face was dimly visible in the interior gloom. His eyes were strange. His usual sly grace seemed wickedly transformed. It was as though the Christopher that Wynter knew—that loose-limbed, smiling blade—had become something dark and prowling; something horribly *ready*.

"Oh, Christopher," she whispered. "Don't."

"I can't *help it*," he hissed. "I've had *enough*."

Wynter spread her hands. She shook her head. Her eyes filled with tears.

"I know, love," she said. "I *know*. I'm sorry. I'm so sorry. It's not fair."

Christopher gaped at her, his mouth open. He seemed so astonished by her tears that Wynter would have laughed were she not suddenly occupied with sobbing into her sleeve.

"Don't . . . don't cry," he said.

"I'm sorry." It seemed to be the only thing she was capable of saying because it came out again, almost immediately. "I'm sorry."

He came and held her close, and she put her arms around him. His slim body was strung with tension, his muscles twitching in the aftermath of his battle to suppress the creature inside him; the creature that his hatred could make of him. Wynter clung to his tunic and looked up into his face. The eyes looking down on her were clear and grey again. As honest as sunlit water.

"I'm sorry," she said again, firmly and with a fierceness that overcame her tears. "I mean it. The Loups-Garous are monstrous, Christopher. I do not know how you have managed all these years in their proximity. I do not know how you have not gone mad."

He laughed, a strained thing, on the edge of crying. "I thought I had. When they arrived, I thought I'd lost myself. I nearly..." His eyes grew huge at the thought of what he had almost done. "I nearly killed Surtr."

"But you didn't," she said firmly, and he nodded.

"Aye," he whispered. "Aye. That's right. I didn't."

"What will—?"

She was cut short by the door being lifted aside. Sólmundr peered in. He seemed amazed to find them in each other's arms, then his weathered face softened into sad understanding. "You good?" he rasped.

They nodded.

"Tabiyb want to talk. This good with you, Coinín? You want that Tabiyb to come talk?"

Wynter felt the power surge within Christopher's body, a frightening, physical manifestation of his anger. He abruptly disengaged from her and retreated once again into the shadows.

"I can't," he growled.

Wynter turned to Sól, her heart battering the inside of her chest. "Let Razi in," she said.

Sól looked uncertain.

"Let him in, Sól. Christopher is not about to let the Wolves steal this friendship from him."

There was a long silence from the back of the tent. Then Christopher whispered, "Let him in, Sól. But you stay too."

The wiry man nodded, and ducked outside. Moments later he returned, shooing Razi into the tent and closing the door behind them. Sól remained by the wall, his face watchful, and Razi came forward, his eyes on Christopher.

"I'm sorry," he said.

"Let me kill them, then."

Razi winced. "Chris," he pleaded.

"Let me kill them. Let it be over."

"Chris, I can't."

"You can. Let me take my sword, let me take the Merron, let us go kill the Wolves. It is very, *very* simple, Razi. Do it now. Fulfil your promises. Let me kill the Wolves."

"I cannot," whispered Razi.

"WHY?"

"Alberon needs them for a while."

"*For a while*," hissed Christopher. "I've been hearing *for a while* for almost four years."

"I know, friend. I am—"

"Do not tell me you are sorry, Razi!"

Razi looked bleakly at him. He seemed to hesitate for a moment, as if uncertain, then he took something from his pocket and went to crouch by the Merron's neat piles of bedding. Wynter saw the dull gleam of silver in the dim light as he laid the object on the gritty curve of a rolled ground sheet.

"I had this made," he said, "back at the Merron camp. I wanted to give it to you, but I was not certain that it was tasteful. And then the situation . . . the situation became difficult."

He fell silent. He had no need to go on. They all knew how *difficult* things had become. He straightened the object with one finger, pushing it about until it was a perfect circle, glittering against the dark fabric. Wynter leant to see. Behind her, Christopher shifted but did not come forward.

It was a plaited leather necklace, secured with a beautifully wrought silver catch. Set onto silver mounts and strung onto the leather were four silver fangs and four amber stones, shaped like eyes. Wynter recognised them immediately as having belonged to the Loups-Garous the Merron had caught spying on their camp. She remembered Razi rooting furiously through the dead Wolves' belongings and understood, at last, what it was he had been seeking.

Razi carefully arranged the necklace, as if displaying it on a jeweller's board.

"I swear to you, Christopher," he said, "one day you shall have them all: twenty-four amber eyes, sixteen silver fangs, eight gold." He looked around at Christopher. "You shall wear them around your neck, and every day they will remind you that nothing has gone unpunished. I *swear* this to you."

"But not today," said Christopher. "That's what you're really saying. Not today."

Razi nodded. "Not today," he whispered. "I need to reconcile my father and my brother, Chris. I must find a way to combine their visions of the future and so make this kingdom whole. My brother needs David Le Garou in order that he may confound relations between the Packs and the Haun. Until this is done, we cannot act."

"Your brother's wrong. You said it yourself."

"But perhaps not about *this*. We just need to wait and—"

"I *have* waited! In *Algiers* I waited! Every passing year I told myself, *soon* will be the time! *Soon!* But it never came! And then you asked me to come here and, *God forgive me*, Razi, I said *yes*! I said *yes* and I left my girls there! Slaves to those vile creatures! I gave up on my *family* and I believed in this new life of yours. But *the Wolves are here*! Look at them! They're *here*! There *is* no new life! I want their blood, Razi! You promised me their BLOOD!"

On the word *blood*, Christopher's voice rose into a howl. It was a savage, elongated sound and Wynter couldn't help it, she took a frightened step back from it. The shadows surrounding her friend were suddenly too thick and Christopher was lost in them. Then he moved, a sly flicker of darkness, and she jumped.

"Coinín!" snapped Sólmundr.

Christopher stopped. There was a moment of silence. "I'm still here," he whispered. "I know who I am."

Sól nodded, and Wynter understood why Christopher had asked him to stay. The warrior gave Christopher a warning look and stepped back again.

"I will find a way, Christopher," promised Razi quietly. "Both to secure my father's kingdom *and* to finish this." He rose to his feet and held out the necklace. "I swear it."

Christopher came at last from the shadows. "You can swear all you like," he said, "but it wasn't *you* that got these. It was the Merron." He took the necklace from Razi's fingers, and he stared coldly into Razi's eyes until his friend ducked his head and left.

"Oh, Chris," said Wynter, "that was unfair."

Christopher did not look at her. He just stood with the necklace of silver teeth in his hand, his eyes on the door, his face hard.

"Tabiyb has saved us from Shirken's plan," said Sólmundr softly. "He tell lie to his brother, and so has saved us. I must admit, it surprise me that he not take his revenge. It make me think that he will to let Úlfnaor go. It make me think he will to let us all go, even after what we did."

"Aye," whispered Christopher. "Well . . . Razi ain't no hypocrite." He lifted the necklace, the silver teeth glittering between his scarred fingers. "But he ain't no Merron, either, is he, Sól?"

Wynter did not like the implications of this. "Christopher," she said, "you must not act."

Christopher looked at her, that stubborn razor of a look which she had always admired and which now sent a spear of icy panic through her heart.

"Chris," she said, "please, I beg of you, do not act."

"Don't worry, lass," he whispered. He gave her a smile, but it was a thin sliver of a thing, his lips stretched tight across his teeth, his eyes hard—and he did not give her his promise.

Trinkets and Honour

"What we do about them?"

"Nothing. Like Tabiyb say."

Sólmundr glanced at Razi and back again to Úlfnaor. "We just to roll and show our bellies, this is what you say?"

"No one is asking you to roll over for the Wolves," said Razi. "I'm simply asking for time, that's all." His eyes flickered to Christopher, but his friend, hard faced and silent, did not look up from his dinner. "Not everything can be solved with a sword to the back of the head, Sólmundr. Give me time to find a better way."

"When we get to talk to the Prince, then?" asked Sól. "When the Merron get to make our case for new life?" Neither Úlfnaor or Razi replied, and Sól shook his head in disgust. "So," he rasped, "we pissed on at home. We pissed on here. And now we must to lie down and let Wolves piss on us too."

"I told you, Sól. No one is asking you—"

Christopher stood abruptly, left the remains of his meal by the fire and strode away. There was a moment of silence, then Wari took Christopher's abandoned dinner and began eating it. Hallvor looked at him in amused disapproval and the big man shrugged blandly. After a decent moment, Soma helped herself to a morsel.

"This not what Embla and Ash give their lives for," hissed Sól getting to his feet. "That we be messengers for tyrants and bitches to Wolves. This not what we is. This not the Merron way." He flung his empty bowl to the ground, took Boro by his chain and stalked after Christopher.

Úlfnaor sighed and pressed his fingers to his temples. His warriors watched him from the corners of their eyes, and concentrated on their food. No questions were asked, and Úlfnaor made no effort to translate for them.

"It not right, Tabiyb," he said eventually, "that we let those cur wander about after what they do to Coinín. Even if he had not been one of the Tribe, it would be not right, but Coinín, he Sól's *son* now. He wear the bracelets of Bear Merron... it our duty and our honour to avenge him."

"Úlfnaor," grated Razi, "if you truly wish to attain this new life you keep asking for, you must be willing to try and live it."

The big man grew silent and thoughtful, and Razi flicked a glance to Wynter. She briefly met his eye but didn't speak. She had nothing to add to the conversation. Her mind was a numb void, her chest constricted with anger. Sighing, she slammed her bowl on the fire-stones; the food tasted like sawdust and ashes to her anyway. Frangok eyed the uneaten dinner and Wynter nudged the bowl towards her with her foot.

"Take it," she said. "I shall vomit if I have more."

Frangok's eyebrows shot up in surprise at Wynter's use of Garmain.

Wynter didn't acknowledge her, just drew up her knees and laid her head against her crossed arms, watching as Christopher came into view between a gap in the tents. He was striding furiously down the slope towards the river and the horse lines. Sólmundr quickly caught up with him. Boro wove about ahead of them, pulling at his chain and snuffling in excitement. The men fell into step, their heads down. Wynter followed their progress until they passed from view. She would not be foolish enough to intrude on them. Christopher had made it perfectly clear that he wanted to be left alone.

All through that long day, Wynter had been hoping that Alberon would send a message, if not to Razi, then at least to her, as a beginning to reconciliation with his brother. But there had been nothing. Now evening was coming on, and the rhythms of the camp were slowing, the smoke from the fires hanging sweet and hazy in the lowering light. It did not seem likely that a pardon would be granted today.

Wynter was distressed by this, but she could not in honesty say that she was surprised. One did not call a Crown Prince *foolish* at the negotiation table. At the very least, it would have wounded Alberon's pride to hear himself described in such terms, particularly when he had gone to such pains to confirm Razi's status as his right-hand man. Wynter squeezed her eyes shut. God help them, but it had been such a stupid, *stupid* thing to say. And then to compound it with *I shall not let you*! What an absolute and unmistakable assertion of superiority. What a disastrously contemptuous thing for a bastard son to say against his royal brother. In many a court, those words alone would have been enough to see the end of Razi.

"*Jesu,*" she whispered to herself. "What are we to do?"

There was a small scuffing of ground as someone sat down beside her. Wynter smelled cook-fire, and the lingering scent of bitter herbs. Hallvor's smoky voice, spoke low and private.

"*Luichín,* you speak Garmain. Why have you never told us of it?"

Wynter shrugged. She was in no mood for talk.

Hallvor looked across at Razi who was frowning in their direction, obviously trying to understand.

"Ah," she breathed, "your companions do not speak it. That is a commendable reason for you to have hidden this skill, *a chroí*. It is a terrible disrespect to speak above one's company." She smiled down at Wynter, her usual, grave smile, her dark eyes kind. "Still, I am glad I know this. So glad, that I think I shall now commit a terrible sin against manners and have a conversation with you."

Oh God, thought Wynter. *Go away. Please.* Her eyes drifted to the last place she'd seen Christopher and she pulled her knees in tighter against her chest.

Hallvor followed her gaze. "Don't fret, *luichín*. Your *crot-eile* will return to you. When a Wolf loves, he loves with everything he is. There is no stronger bond."

Wynter straightened. "There are many Wolves amongst the Merron?" she whispered.

Hallvor shrugged. "Some. Those who survive their childhood grow to good strong warriors, loyal and proud—not like those *caic* that call themselves *Loups-Garous* and are raised as naught but rabid cur."

"Those who survive their childhood?"

Hallvor shrugged again. "Not all are lucky enough to have someone like Aidan *an filid* Garron to raise them." She settled her arms across her own bent knees, looked thoughtfully down towards the river. "Wolf children can be very wild," she murmured. "You know, if he ever gives you trouble like today?" She tapped her temple. "Hit him *hard* in the head. They can't keep the Wolf-shape once they've been hit in the head."

"Hallvor! I would never hit Christopher in the head!"

"Never say never, girl. A man is a man—especially when he is a Wolf!" Hallvor slid a wry glance at her and Wynter was no longer sure if the woman was being serious or simply trying to cheer her up. Hallvor chuckled at her confusion. Her dark eyes switched from Wynter to Razi who was in desultory conversation with Úlfnaor. "I think it is a strange and wonderful thing," she said softly, "how Tabiyb and Coinín are brothers-of-the-heart. And you, with your pale skin and Tabiyb with his black, yet he sees you as his sister." She frowned. "I had thought it meant good things for us here. This great love between three such different people."

"If we can heal the rift between Razi and the Prince there is still hope," said Wynter.

Hallvor glanced at her and her wry smile told Wynter that she didn't hold out much hopes of reconciliation between the brothers. The healer squeezed Wynter's knee and made to rise to her feet. "Well," she sighed, "Ashkr and Embla made Tabiyb our Caora for some reason. If it was not to heal a rift, then it must have been for some other purpose. We shall have to see." This casual mention of the sacrificed dead froze Wynter's heart. On impulse she grabbed Hallvor's hand, halting her rise to her feet. *Have you no guilt?* she wanted to cry. *Do you feel no shame?*

Hallvor sank to her haunches, her face concerned. "What is it, *lucha*?" she said. "Have you more questions about your man? Do you fear for him?"

How can you do it? thought Wynter, still gripping the woman's hand, staring desperately into her face. *I want to know! I want to know how you can have killed like that, then just go on as normal!*

She went to ask, but Surtr's voice cut her off before she could speak.

"*Tá na Haun ag imeacht, a Aoire.*"

Wynter looked around. The red-haired warrior was standing at the corner, gesturing to the road. Úlfnaor rose to his feet. He thumped Razi on his shoulder. "Surtr say the Haun is leaving."

Razi shrugged listlessly and stayed where he was, but Wynter got to her feet and she and Hallvor went with the men to look.

Once Alberon had shown his hand and the Haun had realised that their plans were come to naught, they had immediately begun packing. It was quite obvious that they could not believe the Prince would be lenient with them, and were keen to leave before he changed his mind about sparing their lives. After all, to a Haun, the clearest form of message was often the poor envoy's severed head returned home in a box. Clearly these men did not trust that Alberon's methods of communication with their superiors would be anything less than blood-soaked. Wynter could not help but wonder what reception these men would receive at home. Her father had told her the Haun punishments for failure were often savage in the extreme. Being pressed to death under the corpse of your own horse was one she remembered most vividly.

As she rounded the corner of the tents, the elder Haun were already urging their horses down the road, their heavy laden little pack mares tottering along behind. Some of the camp had come out to watch them leave, but Wynter was impressed to note that only very few of Alberon's soldiers stood about staring at the fleeing men, and those who did line up to watch, confined their reactions to smirks and a few subdued whistles.

Alberon must have ordered them to behave. Wynter admired that. It showed unexpected refinement and diplomacy towards a confounded enemy.

The youngest Haun was last to get going, and he mounted his horse as if in a daze. He appeared stunned and distracted with confusion. It was apparent that he could not believe this sudden reversal of his hopes and plans. As he urged his mount to catch up on the others, Wynter stepped from between the tents and watched him with the strangest mixture of fear and regret. There was so much this man might be able to tell her about her father and his past; so much that she longed to know. At the same time, she felt almost glad she would never have the chance to ask those things of him.

The young man saw her, and to her surprise, he reined to a halt, staring at her. All at once, his bewildered confusion transformed to hatred. Wynter saw his face darken, saw his intentions rise clear in his eyes, and he abruptly burst into action. Kicking his horse to a gallop, he thundered towards her. As he advanced, his hand dropped to his side, and Wynter—fixed like a rabbit under an eagle's eye—stared in horror as he drew his sword.

Úlfnaor whispered, *"Frith an Domhain!"* then yelled, "STOP!" Running forward, he flung himself between Wynter and the charging horse as if his body alone could stop its wild-eyed advance. He was knocked aside. Behind Wynter, Hallvor spun and bellowed in Merron, undoubtedly calling for weapons.

Wynter stayed rooted in place. The young Haun's eyes were locked with hers. His bitter grin was mesmerising. On the road, someone yelled a warning, and even through her frozen shock, Wynter knew it was Oliver. Still she could not move. The Haun swung his sword over his head; his rage, the gleam of his weapon, his thundering horse, filled the world.

"Tell your father!" he screamed. "Tell your father!"

Tell him what? thought Wynter idiotically, gazing up at him.

The Haun stood in the stirrups, his grin widening. Wynter thought, *but I don't want to die.* Then he was gone, and she found herself blinking up at empty sky.

The Haun landed with a *thud* at her feet, a crossbow bolt sticking from his throat like a scarlet thorn. His horse veered away, passing Úlfnaor, who stood, dazed, in the middle of the road. The alley behind Wynter filled with noisy, shouting warriors. There was pushing and shoving as they streamed past to get to their Aoire. Soldiers filled the road.

In the thoroughfare the Haun that had fired the bolt lowered his bow and lifted his hands. "He die!" he shouted to Oliver. "I kill! He no hurt woman!"

Soldiers ran forward, their swords drawn. Across the road, the Wolves had come to see the show, and a high cackle of laughter signalled Jean's amusement at the sight of the young man, gurgling and twitching in a pool of his own blood.

"Is not quarrel!" shouted the older Haun as the soldiers crowded his horse.

Oliver was striding towards him, his face livid. "Protector Lady?" he shouted as he strode by.

Wynter lifted her hand, her attention on the young man at her feet. *I'm fine.*

"Is not quarrel!" repeated the Haun. "Borchu-xah dead! I kill! I kill!"

Borchu-xah, thought Wynter, dropping to her knees by the young man's side. *Is that your name?* His eyes rolled towards her. He jerked, dark blood pouring from his mouth and oozing from around the arrow in his throat. "Get Razi," she whispered to no one in particular. Then she yelled it, staring around for whoever would listen. "Get Razi!"

The Haun's arm spasmed outwards and Wynter realised that he was trying to get his sword. She grabbed his hands. "Stop it!" she cried. "Stop! You're dying! Can't you stop?" His eyes widened at that, and he clutched her hand. She saw his desire to kill fall away in terror as the truth of his predicament hit him.

"Borchu-xah?" she whispered. "Is that your name? Borchu-xah?"

He hissed a sound, but no words.

"Shhhh," Wynter wiped the dirt and blood from his mouth, and squeezed his hand tighter. "Shhhhh. My friend will help you."

The young man's eyes filled with tears and he stared desperately into Wynter's face. He did not want to die. Wynter could see that. He did not want to die. No matter what he had thought just moments before, no matter how determined he had been. This man wanted to live. "Be still," she whispered. "My friend will help you. Just hold tight to my hand and be still."

All the tension left his body at once and the terror left his face. Still clinging to Wynter's hand, his gaze slid past her and the young man looked up into the sky. His dark eyes overflowed. His lips parted, and he sighed, scarlet bubbles popping on his lips. He slipped away just as Razi dropped to his knees by his side.

"Good God," cried Razi, pressing his fingers to the young man's bloody neck. "What happened?"

"He tried to kill me," she whispered.

"What?" He jerked back from the Haun. "Why?"

"He knew my dad, Razi. I think he wanted revenge on my dad."

Across the road the Wolves were regarding them with delight. Jean whistled to get Razi's attention. "Hey," he called, "I'm no doctor, but I think he has something stuck in his throat!"

Razi gritted his teeth but did not reply. Wynter was ashamed by the tears that suddenly welled up and flowed down her face. She could not seem to release the dead man's hands.

"He knew my dad, Razi," she quavered again. "He wanted revenge on my dad. Why?"

Razi glanced behind her to where Oliver was in discussion with the Haun. "Come away now, darling," he said, his eyes scanning the road. "Come back to the Merron."

"No, listen, it wasn't those others. It was him. It was just *him*. He knew Dad, Razi. He knew him, I'm certain of it! And he hated him! He called him a butcherer of children! Why, Razi? Why? Tell me why anyone would call my father that?" Wynter's voice had risen beyond her control and she still clung to the young man's hands, her eyes blinded with tears. She felt on the dangerous edge of hysteria.

Across the road Jean called, "Give the girly a kiss, al-Sayyid! Kiss her all better!"

The Wolves chuckled. Oliver glared across at them, warning clear in his face, and Jean grinned at the knight, spreading his hands. "Only jesting," he laughed. "Lightening the mood is all!"

David Le Garou came up behind his men then, all dark grace and smiles. "Shut up, Jean," he said, and Jean instantly fell silent. "Need help, Sir Knight?" called Le Garou. "We can dispose of something for you, perhaps?"

Oliver curled his lip. Ignoring Le Garou, he strode across to crouch in the dust by Wynter's side. "Protector Lady," he said gently, "the Haun claim that it was their translator's lunacy that led him to attack. I have to admit, he struck me always as an unstable man. The Royal Prince was ever wary of him."

Wynter would not look the knight in his eye. Even in her present state, her anger with him was such that she could not even speak to him. He sighed. "Protector Lady," he persisted, "I will arrest these men and I will make certain that they pay the price for allowing this man advance upon you. I will endeavour to exact the full extent of whatever vengeance you wish, but I must tell you, the Royal Prince needs at least one of them to make it home. No matter what happens, I'm afraid that I shall have to allow at least one of them to leave here intact."

Wynter looked down into the Haun's dead face. She forced herself to release his hands. "Let them go," she whispered.

Oliver faltered, surprised.

"Let them go," she said again, not looking at him. "They were not involved."

"Wyn," said Razi softly, "they might have your answers. They may know the reason for this man's—"

"No." She shook her head. "No. I don't want to know. Just send them away."

"What answers, my Lord?" asked Oliver.

"Just send them *away*!" yelled Wynter. "Just send them *away*!"

Oliver shot to his feet and strode off. Wynter remained kneeling in the dust, shaking and unable to contain her tears.

Razi reached for her. "Get up now, Wyn," he said. "Come back to the tent."

She stayed on her knees. Eventually he put his hands on her shoulders and pulled her gently to her feet. On the hill, Alberon was standing in the shelter of his tent, watching from afar. Wynter stared desolately at him until Razi turned her on her heel and guided her away from the busy road. He led her up the alley.

"If you had been hurt," he whispered, "you know that Albi would be down here with a sword in his hand and those men would be dead."

Wynter shook her head.

"You *know* he must seem above it all, Wyn," insisted Razi. "You know he must seem as though every single event has been expected and planned for. This has been dealt with now, and for him it must seem to be over. He cannot be seen to be touched by it. But he will come see you later," he assured her. "When the time is suitable he will come, I promise he will."

No, he won't, she thought numbly. *He won't come. He won't come at all.*

"Have you no idea of that man's identity?" asked Razi, sitting her by the Merron fire and crouching by her side.

Wynter shook her head again. The world felt very detached from her and Wynter didn't mind that at all. She would be happy if the whole damned thing just sailed away entirely, just drifted off for ever; then perhaps she could have some peace.

Hallvor handed her a beaker of tea. Wynter held it without drinking until Razi took it and placed it on the fire-stones. "Would you like to lie down?" he asked, his concerned face floating before her. She did not answer.

The Merron made a noisy return from the road. Úlfnaor said, "They letting the Haun *go*!" disbelief clear in his voice. Razi stood and the two men exchanged words that had no meaning for Wynter.

Someone nudged her in the back. She shrugged them off. They nudged again and she turned, dully swatting them away. It was Boro, looming over her with anxious enquiry, filling her face with panting, musty breath.

Christopher came running up from the river. "Iseult!" He slid to a breathless halt on the opposite side of the fire, his eyes wide. "Lass!"

Wynter shoved Boro aside, elbowed her way past Razi, and ran to Christopher's arms. He clutched her to him with every ounce of his amazing strength and she buried her head in his chest, clinging silently to him as he fired questions across the top of her head. Sól ran up behind them. There were anxious exchanges in Merron as the two men learned what had happened.

Oliver's cultured voice broke through the incomprehensible babble. "My Lord Razi?" he said. "Is there anything I can do? Would the Protector Lady like to retire to solitude? I could ask if the Lady Mary would give her shelter in her tent."

Wynter raised her head to glare at him. He bowed uncertainly to her and she glowered in reply. She stepped free of Christopher's arms and wiped her eyes, her face hard.

"Who was he, Sir Knight?" asked Razi. "The Protector Lady thinks he knew her father. Is this possible?"

Oliver shook his head. "My Lord," he said wearily, "I did not even know the fellow's name. His companions treated him with great wariness. They seemed to distrust him entirely... I suspect because of his unhinged nature. He simply translated all that was said, and had no part in the negotiations. But always there was about him... I cannot explain, my Lord, always a sense of patient malice. It was as though, by just being here, he was exacting a vengeance long sought for."

"His name was Borchu-xah," said Wynter. "I'm certain of it."

"Borchu," whispered Oliver, and Wynter saw a moment of recognition cross his face.

"You know him!" she cried. "The name means something to you!"

Oliver sighed and seemed to shrug himself free of old memories. "I am sorry, Protector Lady, but Borchu is a common name amongst their kind. "'Tis like asking me would I know a John or a Michael. There were plenty of Borchus and Borchu-xahs running about the land before the late King sent them home."

"But he knew my father," she insisted. "I am certain of it. He knew my father and he hated him. Why?"

Oliver tilted his head with that old paternal sympathy, and Wynter fought the urge to slap his courtly face. "*All* the Haun hate your father, Protector Lady. He is famed for routing their invasion and ridding the kingdom of their threat. But it is unlikely that so young a man would have known Lorcan personally. Your father *did* have an acquaintance called Borchu, and this is what I recalled when you mentioned the name. Do you recall him, my Lord? The chap who worked with St James? It was the man the late King called *that yellow weasel.*"

"I do remember Grandfather using that vile sobriquet," frowned Razi, "and the fact that my father detested it."

"Aye," admitted Oliver, blushing. "Aye, that's right. The late King used delight in taunting the present King with it. I had forgot. But the yel…that fellow was already in his thirties back then and…" Oliver sighed again. He seemed to have run out of energy for the conversation, and it occurred to Wynter just how utterly weary he was. He looked as though he had not slept for days.

"Forgive me, Protector Lady," he said. "I am genuinely sorry, but if you had questions, you should have asked me to hold onto those men. If you pardon me for saying so, it is a little late to be asking them now. I cannot give you the answers you seek."

The sound of silver bells silenced everyone and an icy stillness settled over the Merron.

The Loups-Garous slaves were standing at the mouth of the alley, their posture regal, their faces knowing. They had empty waterskins draped across their shoulders and they looked at Razi in false innocence.

"Our masters bid us ask, is this the way to the river?"

Wynter frowned at the slaves in momentary confusion. Then she realised that their sleeves were rolled to the shoulder in imitation of the Merron, and that Christopher's stolen snake bracelets were gleaming against the hard brown muscles of their upper arms.

She jerked forwards, suddenly blind with rage, but Christopher, his eyes on the bracelets, looped his arm around her waist and held her in place. "No, lass," he murmured.

Seeing the bracelets, the Merron cried out and surged forwards as one.

"LEAVE THEM." Razi's roared command stilled all but Sólmundr, who shot around the fire, his intent clear on his face.

Úlfnaor stepped into the warrior's path, bringing him to a clench-fisted halt. "*Fan*, Sól," he said softly. "They only do their masters' bidding."

The slaves grinned, the brands on their faces puckering in amusement. "Oh, I see the river now," said one. "It is that way."

"Get out of my sight," hissed Razi. "And if you take this route again, I shall send you home to your masters in a hessian sack."

Smiling, the slaves picked their way through the glowering Merron and walked off with an insolent lack of haste. Úlfnaor watched them go, more pity than anger on his face.

"Do not feel badly for them, Aoire," said Christopher. "André Le Garou has convinced them that they will become like him, if they only prove themselves cruel enough and ruthless enough. I have yet to meet one of the Wolves' *boys* who does not believe in this lie. They are vicious and underhand, and they are undyingly loyal to the Wolves. They would slit your throat without a thought."

"Where did they get the second set of bracelets?" asked Wynter.

Christopher's hard veneer cracked, and despair showed in his eyes. "They are my father's," he said. "It is a favourite joke of David's, to parade them about like that."

Wynter groaned, squeezing his arm. "Oh, *no*, love," she said.

"Now they have two sets to taunt me with."

Hallvor glowered enquiringly at Sólmundr. She snapped a question, obviously demanding that he explain. Sólmundr gripped her by the elbow, turned her on her heel and walked her away between the tents.

"Úlfnaor," warned Wynter, her eyes on the departing warriors.

"Not worry," murmured Úlfnaor. "Hally, she talk him into sense."

Wynter was not so certain. Sólmundr was speaking furious and low, his sandy head close to Hallvor's, and the healer listened intently as they walked. Just before they turned the corner, Hallvor gasped and looked back at Christopher, her eyes wide, then Sól marched her from sight.

Razi and Oliver were watching the slaves walk off. The knight had his hand to his nose, as if to block a bad smell, and Razi was frowning in intense concentration.

"Oliver," he murmured, his voice miles away. "I must speak to my brother."

"It is not my place to command the Prince, my Lord."

"Oliver..."

"*He will not be dissuaded*," cried Oliver.

Wynter bristled at his raised voice, and Razi drew himself up.

Oliver pressed his fingers to his temples and squeezed his eyes shut for a moment. "*Jesu*," he whispered. Then he stepped closer, his voice low, gazing at Razi as if willing him to understand. "I am ever loyal to the King, my Lord. His Highness, the Royal Prince, is ever loyal, but you will not dissuade him from his course. You and your father, my Lord, you are brilliant men—brilliant—but you rely too much on the strength of the Moroccan court."

"Oliver," sighed Razi. "There is *no weakness* in Abdallah ash-Shiekh's court. This plot that David Le Garou has spoken of is doomed to failure. The Corsairs have nothing, they are already destroyed. The Sultan can deal with the Loups-Garous himself, and as for the Haun—"

"*We came this close to losing*," cried Oliver, his hands held up in despair. "*This close*. Don't you understand? You say there is no weakness in the Sultan's court. Well, that may be so *now*, but what about tomorrow? Or next year? What about when the Sultan dies? Abdallah ash-Shiekh loves your father, my Lord, and rightly so; your father is an extraordinary man. But what about the Sultan's successors and the successors of all those kings that Jon has so carefully feted? Will *they* love him? Will *they* tolerate him? Your father is a man who bows to no church, while all those others use religion like a whip to keep their people in line. He is a man who refuses to allow slavery, when slavery benefits the economy of all around him. We cannot always rely on the tolerance of these stronger men, my Lord! We cannot! We are small and vulnerable, and your father's beautiful view of the world makes us a thorn in the side of everyone but God!" He dropped his hands, his eyes full. "And I don't care what the priests told us when we were young, God lends no hand to the weak in this world, though he may love them in the next. In this world we must make ourselves strong, that we may battle the wicked and protect the good."

Oliver closed his eyes suddenly. His emotion was such that it moved even those who could not understand him, and the surrounding warriors stood in respectful silence while he gathered himself.

"I am faithful to your father, Razi," he continued softly. "I love him. But I am angry that he let things come so close. I will never understand why, having such a wonderful invention to hand, he did not draw out Lorcan's machine and end the insurrection sooner. Your brother was furious when he found out." Oliver smiled fondly. "God help us, but the Prince is a remarkable young man. If you could see him at the war table! From the moment your father let him partake in battle, Alberon exhibited such clarity of vision, such understanding of men. He amazes me. Your father calls him his *little Alexander*."

"But he does not need to go this far," whispered Razi. "He does not need to bring filth like David Le Garou to his table, nor ally himself so irretrievably to a canker like Marguerite Shirken."

Oliver looked briefly into Razi's eyes and away again. "I... perhaps... I don't know." He sighed deeply and ran his hand over his weary face. "I'm just a soldier, my Lord, these are things I do not understand. The Prince could well have done with your advice on them. But..." He shook his head and looked away into the rapidly gathering twilight. "I do not know what to do," he whispered.

Razi put his hand on his shoulder. "Help me talk to him, Oliver," he insisted softly. "That is all you need do. Help me talk to him, and I will make this work."

The Music of Memory

"Where are you going?" Christopher caught Wynter by the elbow, stopping her from following Oliver down the alley.

She flicked a glance to Razi. He had drawn Úlfnaor aside and was engaged in a low, secretive conversation. "I want to ask Oliver something," she whispered. "I will only be a moment."

"You ain't going on your own. I'll come with you."

"No, love," she said, laying her hand on his chest. "The Loups-Garous may still be out there and I do not want you to have to face them. I will be all right."

He frowned at her in irritated disbelief. "Are you *deranged*?" he snapped. "Come on."

He shooed her up the ally, and they made their way into the noise and waning sunshine of the thoroughfare. By the supply tent, there was a dark patch of ground where the young Haun had died. Already the sharp outline of his blood had been smudged by the passage of feet and the drifting of dust from the busy road. Scuff marks showed where the soldiers had dragged his body away. Wynter came to a halt, staring down at these fading signs of violence, and released a shaky sigh.

Christopher took her hand, his eyes on the bloodstain.

"Good Frith, lass," he breathed, "you came so close."

Wynter squeezed his fingers gently, then let go. "Come on," she said. They skirted the blood and hurried after Oliver who was just striding away from his lieutenant, on his way back to Alberon's tent.

"Sir Knight!"

He turned, surprise clear on his face. "Protector Lady."

"Sir Knight." She came to a halt before him, gazing up into his face. "You *will* do your best to open dialogue between the Prince and Lord Razi?"

He nodded. "Aye, Protector Lady. I shall."

"It is vital, sir. You understand? You must not play politics with this."

The knight stayed silent for a moment, reading her face, and Wynter knew that her suspicions had been right. Oliver was still in two minds as to Razi's usefulness to the Prince and was in no way certain that he would repair communications between the brothers. In an appeal to their history, Wynter softened the formality of her tone and lowered her voice.

"Listen to me, Oliver," she said. "I believe I understand why it is that our fathers wanted the machine forgotten. I suspect they used it before, to end the Haun invasion."

Oliver frowned. "With respect, Protector Lady. If that were the case, I should know of it, but I had never seen nor heard of these machines before Jon—"

"*Listen* to me, Oliver. I suspect they also used it..." Wynter hesitated. She looked back at the wide patch of darkness on the ground.

Oliver's eyes followed hers and he stared in confusion at the bloodstain. "Also used it for what?"

"Where were you when the Haun were defeated?" she whispered.

"I was up North. Jon sent me North to fetch his father home."

"And when the Lost Hundred were expelled?"

Oliver was silent for a moment. "I was still in the North, mopping up the last of the Combermen," he said slowly. "The late King left me there to help finish things up. I didn't get home until well after the Hundred were gone."

Wynter met his eye. He began to understand.

"Oh no, lady!" he said appalled. "The Hundred were just sent east. That is all. They were simply..."

His voice trailed away and they gazed at each other. Wynter could see memories falling into place for him, connections being made, things clarifying. His eyes grew wide in horrified comprehension. She reached behind her and took Christopher's hand. He held gently on. *I am here.*

Oliver went to speak and Wynter shook her head, willing him not to articulate what they were both thinking.

"Lorcan," he managed finally. "Lorcan was *destroyed* when I got home. I thought it was because of your poor mother...I must admit I got very impatient with him after a while. He lay in his bed for months. He spoke to no one. He was..." Oliver moaned in despair and guilt. "Sweet Christ," he whispered, "I was only fourteen. How was I to understand?"

"And the King?" asked Wynter. "Our present King. How was he?"

"My God," said Oliver, remembering, "my God."

"How was he?" she whispered again.

"I thought it was because of his *father*," cried Oliver. "Though they never got on, sometimes it happens that way, a son mourns for what he never had—I had thought he was grief-stricken on account of the late King's death."

"He was in a bad way?" asked Christopher softly.

"Jon was drunk for almost two months," said Oliver. He

glanced defensively at Christopher. "Not falling down, you understand, but just... he did not stop drinking for..." He trailed off and shook his head again. "My God."

"Neither the Lord Razi nor the Prince seem aware of this, Sir Oliver. I believe it may aid to reconciliation between all parties if these things were made clear."

"Might help them understand their dad a little better, all right," murmured Christopher.

"It will be a delicate business," said Wynter, "approaching sons with such a secret. Particularly one their father never wanted them to share. We will need to be very gentle."

Oliver looked at her kindly. "Wyn," he said, "Lorcan was a most wonderful man. Whatever the circumstances of this terrible... this terrible act. I should not like you to think that he—"

Wynter snapped a hand up, cutting him off. "I do not need *you* to defend my father, Sir Knight."

Oliver drew himself up and blinked to silence.

"You may talk to the Prince," she said harshly. "I shall talk to my Lord Razi. Between us we will get this done and that will be the end of it. We can all return to the palace, no more to speak of this, and life will simply continue on."

Oliver stepped back, his face set, and bowed. "I shall do my best, Protector Lady. Please God, by tonight the lord and the Prince will be in communication once again."

He turned away.

Christopher squeezed Wynter's hand and she shut her eyes. *Please, love*, she thought, *don't say anything*. She did not think she could bear him trying to defend her father. She did not think she could bear questions. To have to open her mouth and articulate all the terrible things she now suspected Lorcan of having done was beyond her power. But, to her great relief, Christopher did not speak. He just maintained a patient, waiting silence and Wynter loved him for it. She loved him more for every minute he was alive.

"Gérard was listening," he whispered.

She snapped her eyes open to see the dark-skinned Wolf step from the shadow of a tent and hurry to catch up with Oliver. He swerved around in front of the striding knight and bowed smoothly. Oliver kept walking and Gérard walked backwards, keeping pace.

"You aim to reconcile the Prince and the pretender, sir?" asked Gérard. "Would that be wise? I fear the Prince would be livid with you if he thought you sided with the upstart contender for his throne."

Oliver replied coldly, still striding forward, "If you value your teeth, you will remove yourself from my path."

Gérard stepped aside with exaggerated grace and allowed Oliver to sweep past him. He watched as the knight climbed the path and disappeared into Alberon's quarters, then the Wolf turned and smiled from under his eyes at Christopher.

"So your master still keeps you, does he, pup? You must have some wondrous skills to have stayed in favour so long, and you nothing but a cripple." Gérard licked his teeth and looked Christopher up and down in a way that made Wynter want to cut the eyes from his head. "Oh aye," said the Wolf. "I'd wager you have learned *many* a way to please. I've no doubt al-Sayyid rattles your bells whenever he chooses." Gerard chuckled. "I've always said there's no better music than that of slave bells, sounding out their rhythm in the dark." With that he tipped a gracious bow to Wynter and strolled away into the dying light.

"Scum," hissed Christopher. "*Scum!*"

Wynter took hold of his clenched fist. Her throat was so

tightly packed with rage that it took a moment before she could speak. "They are only words, love," she managed. "Just words."

Christopher tore his hand from hers, and spun to go. His angry face grew even darker at the sight of Jean blocking the path. Unaware of Wynter and Christopher, the big, broad-shouldered Wolf was crouched by the supply tent, face to face with Alberon's little servant, Anthony. As they watched, the Wolf leaned close and murmured into the child's ear. Jean's voice was inaudible to Wynter, but at his words the already frightened little boy turned white and his body went rigid with terror. Still whispering, Jean smiled and ran his fingers through the silky fineness of the boy's hair.

With a low sound of fury, Christopher darted forwards. But even as he and Wynter rushed towards him, Jean rose to his feet, pinched the child's cheek and wandered off in the direction of the Wolves' quarters. Anthony was left staring at nothing, his cauldron of water held stiffly before him, his little chest rising and falling in rapid, terrified breaths.

"What did he want?" snarled Christopher, dropping to his knees beside the child.

Anthony yelled in fright and jumped back, slopping water from the cauldron.

"What did he *want*?" shouted Christopher.

Wynter laid a restraining hand on Christopher's arm. "It is all right, Anthony," she murmured. "Freeman Garron does not mean you harm."

But the little servant took another step back, his eyes fixed on Christopher. His terror seemed only increased by the fury on the young man's face. Christopher did not even seem to notice the poor child's distress. "Tell me what he *wanted*!" he cried, grabbing Anthony by his narrow shoulders. "You have to *tell* me!"

Wynter tightened her grip on Christopher's arm and crouched down. "Anthony," she said.

It took him a moment to tear his gaze from her friend.

"It is all right," she said again. "You may go."

The boy fled, heedless of the water he was slopping over himself, running frantically for the hill and the safety of Alberon's tent. Christopher went to lurch to his feet, meaning to follow him, but Wynter pressed down on his arms, halting his rise. She looked into his dangerously tinted eyes.

"It is all right," she said firmly. "The boy is safe."

Christopher growled at her without any recognition, and she took his knotted fists in her hands, squeezing them tight.

"It is all right, Christopher," she repeated. "Come back now."

He frowned uncertainly. Blinked.

"Come back to me," she said. "I need you."

Christopher suddenly breathed deep. His eyes cleared as they stared into hers. His fists relaxed.

"Are you with me, love?" she whispered.

He nodded. Up on the hill, the little boy had made it to the Prince's tent. They watched him run into the protective shadow of the awning and disappear inside—a tiny figure barely large enough for the cauldron he carried. Wynter squeezed Christopher's scarred fingers one last time, and together they rose to their feet and made their way back to the Merron quarters.

Wynter told Razi about the young Haun's scars and her theory on the Bloody Machine. Razi was quiet for a very long time after.

In the silence, Wynter gazed down at her hands. To her surprise, they were clasping and unclasping as of their own accord. She clenched them tightly together, forcing them to be still, and squeezed hard so that her knuckles gleamed brightly in the firelight.

Sitting across from her, his face intent, Christopher waited for Razi to speak. On the other side of the fire, the Merron sat quietly. Though they were trying hard not to eavesdrop, they had been intrigued by Wynter's low, intense conversation and they kept glancing furtively across the flames, their curiosity impossible to hide.

"I shall have to see his body," whispered Razi at last.

Wynter nodded absently, watching as her filthy nails dug into the backs of her hands. It had been very easy, in the end, to say the words. It was such a simple sentence, after all, and so quickly over: *I think our fathers killed them all.* But when she had finally said it, she had felt a pain in her chest, a sharp, tearing sensation, and now she felt nothing.

She spread her hands, watching the firelight play across her grimy fingers. Her nails had left pale half-moon indents in her skin. Wynter regarded them with interest, then tried to fit her nails back into the exact position again, pressing hard. *Would it take a lot of pressure to break the skin?* she wondered. She dug her nails deep, frowning in concentration.

"Iseult!" snapped Christopher, and she glanced up at him, startled. "Stop that!" he hissed.

"I shall have to see his body," murmured Razi again. He scrubbed his hands on his trouser legs and nodded. "Yes. After all...those scars could have been from anything. You are not a doctor, darling. Perhaps the poor fellow had the smallpox. Perhaps he was mauled by a bear. Perhaps he..." He stopped talking, and his hands stilled. He looked up into the star-strewn sky. "Perhaps," he said desperately. Then he seemed to give in. "Oh God," he whispered.

Christopher looked down at Boro, his mouth unsteady. The

dog grinned at him and Christopher scratched between his ears. "Good boy," he whispered.

The night was very still, just the muffled sounds of the surrounding camp, the crackling fire, the snoring of the other warhounds. Sólmundr and Hallvor were sitting with the Merron, grave and withdrawn. After dinner, they had been caught hassling the Loups-Garous slaves down by the river. The soldiers had returned the two of them to their quarters in shame. Úlfnaor had been furious with them. He had made them apologise to David Le Garou, and forced them to fetch the Wolves' spilt water. They had been tense and silent ever since.

Music came drifting from somewhere deep within the camp, a guitar strummed low. Wynter glanced dully at Christopher. He too heard the music, and she saw his face soften at the sound. He shut his eyes, tilting his head to listen as gentle memories played across his face.

" 'Maidin Ór'," he whispered.

Across the fire, Úlfnaor smiled in recognition of the tune and murmured something in Merron. Hallvor glanced fondly at him. Surtr nodded in time with the music, tapping his fingers.

"*Go h-álainn*," he sighed.

Suddenly, Frangok asked a sharp question, and the Merron lost their warm good humour and straightened slowly, their expressions hard. Frangok snapped the question at Christopher. His face drew down in pained understanding, and he groaned, dropping his head into his hands.

"Oh," he breathed, "the scum."

"What is it?" mumbled Wynter.

Christopher shook his head.

"It 'Maidin Ór,' " snapped Sólmundr. "It Merron song! It *Merron*! Who teach it to *coimhthíoch*?"

"I did," whispered Christopher, "when I were a slave. I taught Pierre to play it on my father's guitar."

Sól sank back in shock. "But *why*, Coinín?" he cried. "It *Merron* song, we not ever—"

"Because I *liked it*!" hissed Christopher, glaring across at him. "I *liked* it, and I used play it, and he made me teach it to him! All right? Is that all right, Sól? Can you accept that?"

At Christopher's taut anger, Sólmundr softened instantly and held up his hands, his face gentle.

"Shhhh," he said. "Shhhhh, *a luch. Ná bac faoí*... it all right."

Christopher's face darkened and he bowed his head again. He dug his fingers into his hair and squeezed hard, as if trying to hold himself together.

"You not to worry, *luch*," rumbled Úlfnaor. "No one blame you. It not your fault that those *caic* steal everything they see."

The music continued to float gently around them and it was as if the entire camp had paused to listen, so quiet had the night become. Somewhere out there, the blond Wolf sat and played that lovely tune, and Wynter had no doubt that this terrible pained reaction was the very reason he had chosen it. She imagined him glancing up from the strings to look at David Le Garou, the knowledge of what he was doing clear in his grin, and she wondered if he was still playing Aidan Garron's guitar.

At that thought, anger blazed hot and clear and sharp within her, and she welcomed it. It felt good. It felt much better than her previous, muffling fog. Razi sat at her side, his hands clenched, his face dull, and Wynter glared at him.

"When shall we act?" she asked.

"Soon," he whispered. "Give me time."

"For *what*? The Haun have gone back to their leaders, bearing the message Alberon wished. What use have you for the Wolves now?"

Razi sighed and shut his eyes. "Please, Wyn," he said.

Christopher looked up from between his hands, his face hard. She met his eye, rage to rage. "Soon" was not enough.

The music ceased without warning, cutting off in mid chord, as if the guitar had been snatched from the player or dropped from his hand. It was so abrupt an ending that everyone sat frowning for a moment, waiting for it to start again. Christopher straightened, staring out into the quiet night. The silence stretched on, and the sounds of the camp filtered in to fill the void. Hallvor glanced at Sólmundr, sidelong, from the corner of her eye. Sólmundr studiously did not look her way.

With a warning growl, the warhounds stood up, and the Merron snapped to attention, following the hounds' gaze.

"Stand down your dogs," said a familiar voice. "I must speak to my brother."

Wynter and Razi got to their feet as Alberon stepped into the light. His face was drawn, his red cloak bundled around him as if for comfort. Oliver, just visible in the shadows at his back, eyed the assembly with caution, but Alberon only had eyes for his brother.

"Razi," he said hoarsely, "do you know?"

"Wyn told me," whispered Razi.

Alberon shook his head. He drew his cloak even tighter and stayed at the edge of the light. "*Jesu*," he whispered. "To have slaughtered them all. Even women, Razi...even little children. I cannot conceive of such a wicked act. It is no wonder Father struggled so hard to hide those machines."

With a whine, Boro trotted across to the Prince. The Merron straightened anxiously and Oliver tensed, but Alberon, ever a lover of dogs, just glanced down and fondled the hound's sharp ears. He seemed to lose himself for a moment in this innocent activity, then he took a deep breath.

"Razi," he said at last. "What are we going to do? How am I ever to bridge this rift?"

"We must talk," said Razi quietly.

Alberon glanced with uncertainty at the ring of attentive faces sitting around the fire.

"Not here," said Razi.

Alberon nodded. "Come on," he said and wearily gestured Razi to his side.

Wynter and Christopher went to follow, but Razi held his hand out to still them.

"Stay," he said.

They leapt to object and Razi snapped at them, "*Stay, goddammit.*"

Wynter drew herself up in frozen disbelief. He would deny her this? After all they had been through, he would leave her out in the cold? "Razi!" she cried.

But Razi strode past without another word, and she watched in useless rage as he followed his brother out into the dark.

"*Cad a rinne tú?*"

Christopher's incredulous whisper scratched the surface of a dream, so that one minute Wynter was gazing into her father's face—impossibly young and streaming with rain, as he screamed, "Stop them! For Christ's sake, Rory! Stop them!"—and then she was struggling awake, her hands clutching the empty blanket where Christopher should have been.

She lifted herself onto her elbow, looking all about her.

Christopher was at the door of the tent, a black shadow dimly outlined against the faint glow of the dying camp fire. Someone was with him, just a dark shape at first, until he spoke and Wynter recognised Sólmundr's distinctive throaty rasp. The warrior murmured something low in Merron, and Christopher exclaimed in shock.

Sól clapped a hand to his friend's mouth. "Shhhhhhh, *a luch*," he said. "Shhhh."

Wynter made out Christopher's nod and Sólmundr carefully removed his hand from his mouth. She peered around the tent; it was empty but for her. Razi must not yet have returned. She reached for her tunic.

After Razi had left, the women had discreetly retired to the Merron quarters, leaving Christopher and herself alone. Wynter had thought nothing of it, and she had simply stalked into her tent and lain down, taut as a bowstring, her head filled with anger. But then Christopher had lain down beside her, put his arms around her and pulled her gently to him, and she had instantly come undone. Before she knew it, she had been sobbing into his chest, great shuddering lungfuls of breath, long gasping sighs, too grief-stricken to stop, too overcome to speak.

"It ain't what Lorcan was, lass," he had murmured. "It ain't what he was. You know that. He were a lovely man." She had shaken her head, bawling silently against the fabric of his shirt. "Maybe it was the King that done it," he said. "Maybe it was the King's dad. You ain't ever to know, lass, because the King ain't ever likely to tell you, is he?" She had clung tighter, drawing him in, wanting him close, and he had stroked her hair. "Lorcan was never anything but good to you," he whispered, rocking her gently. "Ain't that all you need to know? He was never anything but good to you."

She had tumbled into sleep like that, weeping inconsolably,

with Christopher holding her close. Now her nose and eyes burned with the aftermath of it, and the bed was cold because Christopher had left her to go whisper at the door. She pushed back the covers and dragged her cloak around her, shivering at the intrusion of night air. Good Christ, it was damnably cold.

"Chris," she whispered, jerking on her boots and getting to her feet. "What in God's name are you two doing?" Christopher didn't answer, and she went to the door, suddenly nervous. The small space in front of the Merron tents was empty. Christopher was gone.

The Merron Way

Ulfnaor's hounds had run to the end of their chains and were peering up the alley between the tents, their postures curious. Wynter ran past them, strapping her sword in place, and came to a halt in the shadows, peeping out into the moon-washed thoroughfare. The camp was utterly silent and empty of life, but Wynter knew that there would be patrols, and the guards around Alberon's tent would see any movement on the road if they were looking that way at the time. A shadow caught her eye, a fleeting impression of movement at the far edge of the road. She saw Boro outlined briefly against the moonlit side of a tent. He took a corner and trotted from view.

Oh, curse you, she thought. *You fools.* She glanced anxiously at the royal tent, then ran across the too-bright road. Crouching low as if that might save her from detection, she hurried along the narrow belt of shadow beneath the awnings and turned into the alley after Boro and the two infuriating men he was no doubt accompanying.

Alberon had certainly fulfilled his promise to quarter the Wolves far from Razi's tent. In fact, as Wynter trailed the two men through the seemingly interminable rat's nest of the camp, she found herself wondering if he had quartered the damn creatures on the moon. She moved as quickly as she could, all the time praying that she did not trip on one of the many guy ropes or boxes of supplies that lurked slyly in the black shadows. The last thing she needed was to bring the canvas crashing down onto a squad of sleeping men.

She was picking her way, stork-like, through a particularly dense configuration of guy ropes when a sound brought her to a listening halt. It was Sólmundr, speaking softly and chuckling. Wynter crept to the edge of the shadows and peered out. She was at the outer fringes of the camp, the army tents standing with their backs in a row, the Wolves' quarters separated from them by the open space of their cooking area. Behind that, the ground sloped down to horse lines, the river, the brooding barricades and trees.

Sólmundr was wandering around the Wolves' camp, his sword in his hand, Boro at his side. Christopher was standing by the almost dead camp fire, a slim, black shape in the moonlight. He was looking down at the sprawled body of a Loups-Garous slave. The young man was crumpled and motionless, a bowl of spilt food on the ground by his out-flung hand. Wynter stepped from the shadows, stunned. At the door of the Wolves' tent Sól hissed something and both Wynter and Christopher looked up as the warrior stepped across the slumped body of the second slave and disappeared inside.

Christopher stooped, grabbed the nearest slave by the ankles and dragged him into the shadows of the awning. He left him there, bundled against the motionless form of his companion, and followed Sól into the tent. Wynter quietly made her way to the door. Slipping into the shadows beneath the awning, she crouched and laid her hand on the chest of the nearest slave. He was breathing gently, his companion the same. Wynter rose to her feet, peering into the tent.

There was darkness within. Then the quiet striking of a flint.

A fire-basin flared to life, illuminating Sól who was crouched intently over it. He glanced up at Christopher and moved aside as if presenting a gift. The light from the basin filled the gloom and the interior of the tent was revealed.

The Loups-Garous were scattered in various attitudes of collapse, their large bodies slumped or sprawled, depending on how they had fallen. David Le Garou lay on a tangle of furs, his head back, his eyes closed as if in gentle sleep. Jean was stretched, face down at his feet, an arm flung outwards as if he had been reaching for his leader when he fell. Gérard was slumped as he had obviously been sitting, his back against a pile of saddlery, a deck of cards scattered all about him. Pierre had tumbled onto his side, the guitar still in his hand. His glossy, blond curls covered his face, gleaming in the guttering light.

Sól grinned at Christopher, his eyes bright with bitter satisfaction. He went to speak, then he saw Wynter step into the moonlight by the door and his face fell. He rose slowly to his feet. Christopher turned to her, and Wynter saw it in his eyes: he was just as stunned as she. He had not been party to this plan.

Sól's expression hardened. He dipped his chin. "You not rob this from him," he warned.

Wynter stepped across the slaves and dropped the tent flap behind her, cutting out the clear moonlight. Sól regarded her anxiously as she drew her sword. The fire-basin flared, sending orange light and dark shadows leaping across the Wolves' unconscious faces.

"What do you intend to do after they are dead?" she asked quietly.

Sólmundr grinned, slow and dark, taking her question as approval of his plans. "Good woman," he whispered.

Christopher turned from her and moved slowly around the

tent. He nudged Pierre with his toe, rolling him onto his back. The guitar slipped from the Wolf's limp fingers, hitting the ground with a faint melodic resonance. Christopher stepped over it and stood gazing down at Gérard.

"You dosed their water?" he asked softly.

"Hally, she gives to me the slow poison. She say to me, it maybe not kill the Loups-Garous because of what they is. It maybe to just put them under. She worry over this, but I glad it not kill them. I glad they alive for you, though I sad they not be awake to know it when you at last take your vengeance."

Christopher crossed the tent and sank to a crouch by David Le Garou's sleeping body. The Wolf's long brown hair was fanned untidily across his face. Instinctively, Christopher reached to push it back, but at the last moment he hesitated and withdrew his hand.

"I will to leave after," said Sólmundr, "and all can be my fault."

"Oh no, Sól," said Wynter. "No. You can't leave. We can find another way to deal with this."

Sól smiled at her. "There not be another way," he said. "But it good. I proud to do this. After everything that Coinín has risk for me and for Ash, to avenge him and his first father is my honour."

"We'll find another way," said Wynter firmly.

She glanced at Christopher, who, seemingly oblivious to the conversation, continued to crouch by David Le Garou, staring into his face. She was amazed at how calm he was. After everything that he had suffered at the hands of this man and his pack, she had expected more than this peculiar stillness. She went to speak again, but Christopher drew the long black dagger from his boot, and Wynter and Sól became very still and quiet.

With no discernible emotion, Christopher used his knife to flick the hair from David Le Garou's face, then slowly, almost caressingly, he ran the tip of the dark blade along the Wolf's brow and down his temple. David Le Garou's eyelid twitched, and Christopher paused. His knife slid across to press lightly against the corner of Le Garou's eye. Wynter readied herself to look away, but instead of pressing harder, Christopher simply sighed and ran the tip of the knife down the Wolf's cheek.

The blade scraped audibly against the light stubble on Le Garou's jaw, traced the vulnerable swell of his Adam's apple and came to rest against the lightly beating pulse at his throat.

"I could," whispered Christopher.

He pressed down, dimpling the flesh beneath his blade. The smallest bead of red welled up at the sharp tip of his knife, and Christopher's lips parted. He tilted his head, watching intently as David's blood trickled a thin red path to the Wolf's collar. Christopher lifted his eyes to David's face. Whatever he saw there seemed to break Christopher's strange detachment, and he snarled in sudden anger. Snatching the Wolf by his hair, Christopher dragged David's head up until their faces were within inches of each other. With a hiss that might have been a word, he once again pressed his knife against the pale arch of David's neck.

"I could!" he said.

He snapped the knife away from David's throat and plunged it between David's legs, jerking the blade up into his groin. "I could," he said again, staring into the Wolf's slack face. "I could take you apart, little by little."

The Wolf remained impassive, his eyes lightly shut, his mouth open. He was completely at peace, blissfully unaware of Christopher's rage. With a desperate noise, Christopher dragged him closer still and, once again, pressed the knife to his eye. The sharp tip trembled against the Wolf's dark eyelashes and Christopher desperately scanned his face for a reaction—but there was none.

"Curse you," he whispered. "Curse you. You goddamned *pox*."

Then, to Wynter's amazement, Christopher flung the Wolf back onto the furs, and with a shaking hand slipped his knife back into his boot.

"Coinín," said Sólmundr, "it not matter he not feel it. You need do it now! You might not ever again get the chance."

Christopher shook his head and stood up.

"We can burn the tent afterwards," murmured Wynter. The two men turned to look at her in shock, and she hefted her sword uncertainly. "If you must kill them," she said, "we could burn the tent with the Wolves' bodies inside. You can finally take your revenge, Christopher. They would be out of your life for ever. Sól would not have to leave. It would be very neat." She waited, thrown by their silence and the way they were staring at her in the crawling firelight. "I'm not sure I could stay to watch, though," she admitted softly. "I thought I could...but I don't think I could bear it."

"God help me, Iseult," whispered Christopher. "I love you more every day."

Wynter's eyes filled with tears and Christopher's dark outline was suddenly haloed in orange stars as the firelight split itself into pinpoints of brilliance around him. "I love you too," she said. Then she wiped her eyes, sheathed her sword, and turned for the door. "I shall wait outside."

"Stay," said Christopher.

"I can't, Chris. I'm sorry. I understand what you need to do. But I can't stay."

"No. Stay. It's all right. I ain't about to do aught."

Both Sólmundr and Wynter frowned in disbelief.

"But you might never get other chance!" cried Sól.

Christopher tilted his head fondly. "I will," he said. "Razi has promised me. He always keeps his promises. I ain't going to let him down."

"But..." Sól gazed around at the unconscious Wolves, unable to comprehend Christopher's decision to spare them.

Christopher left David Le Garou and crossed the tent. Crouching at Sól's feet, he gently lifted the fallen guitar and turned it to show the back. The polished wood glowed like honey in the warm light, the silver frets and the silver snake's-head pegs gleaming. On the back, inlaid in dark wood, a representation of two snakes twined around itself, each biting the other's tail. Wynter hunkered down by Christopher and gazed at it. It was very fine work.

"This is beautiful," she whispered.

"Aye. Hawk-worked. Dad had it made at the Hollis *aonach*, the year I was adopted. The same man made it as made the trunk." Christopher smiled and ran his fingers along the segmented back of the snake emblem. He went to speak, then the sight of his mutilated hand seemed to halt him in his tracks. His breath caught in his throat and he frowned, staring at his fingers. He clenched his hand and stood abruptly, looping the guitar strap across his shoulder. "Come on," he snapped. "Let's go." And he strode to the door, dragging it aside and darting out as if afraid to stay any longer.

Wynter got slowly to her feet. Sól was glaring at the prostrate bodies stretched all around him, his face twitching with rage. Wynter knew exactly how he felt. *Well*, she thought, eyeing the vicious rings of scar tissue on his neck and wrists. *Perhaps not quite exactly.*

"This is not your vengeance to take, Sól," she said softly.

"How can he to walk away?" he ground out. "How can...?"

"He's not walking away for ever."

Sólmundr huffed and shook his head, his anger and disappointment palpable.

"You think he is foolish to trust Razi?"

He did not answer and Wynter wondered if he was as much hurt by Christopher's rejection of his gift as he was angered by the Wolves' close escape.

Christopher called for them to *come on*. He was crouched in the shadow of the awning, dragging his father's bracelets from the slaves' limp arms. "Get out of there," he hissed, glancing in at them. "We need to get back before Razi returns from his brother."

Wynter picked her way out to him. Behind her, Sól snuffed the fire-basin, plunging the tent into pitch darkness. He came to her side, watching in silence as Christopher took his own bracelets from the second slave.

"Will they die, Sól?" asked Wynter, gazing down at the unconscious young men at her feet.

"I hope," he said coldly.

"Much as they aspire to be, they ain't Wolves," said Christopher, standing and kicking the slave's hand away from his foot. "So it's likely the poison will do them in."

"Will it be bad?" she whispered. "Sólmundr called it *slow poison*. That sounds bad."

"It just mean it sneak up slow," said Sólmundr. "It not..." he made a spasming motion, reminding Wynter of Razi when Christopher had drugged him in Embla's tent. "This one, it just pull you gently under. You almost not notice it until it too late, and then you die."

Christopher huffed dryly. "It's still too bloody good for them," he said.

Sól nodded in understanding. Wynter found their lack of compassion very strange. After all, did her friends feel no kinship to these two young men? As slaves, had they not all suffered the same things? Glancing at her, Christopher must have caught some of this in her face and he looked away, uncomfortably shifting the bracelets in his hand.

"You don't understand what they're like," he whispered. "You couldn't imagine. These are two of the Wolves' *boys*. The Wolves have raised them from little children and... they ain't normal," he said. "They're savage. They're horribly cruel."

"Some people," said Sólmundr, his eyes wide with unwanted memory, "they end up with not just bodies in slavery. Some people, their souls be slaves also."

Christopher shuddered, then shook himself free of his memories. "Come on!" he hissed, slapping Sólmundr on his strong arm. "Let's go."

Grimly, the warrior stepped over the slaves, heading for the gap in the army tents. Wynter moved to follow him, but hesitated as Christopher came to an abrupt halt in front of her.

"Sól!" he cried.

Sólmundr glanced back over his shoulder, frowning. "What?"

Christopher just shook his head, his eyes bright. He wordlessly lifted the fistful of bracelets, shaking them as if to say, *I can never repay you for these.*

Sólmundr's face softened. "Oh," he whispered. "Oh, aye." He cleared his throat. "*Ná bac, lucha.* Let's... let's go, before Tabiyb, he find you gone and we all in trouble." Glancing briefly at Wynter, the warrior turned and led the way back between the tents.

*   *   *

"Ah, shit," whispered Christopher. "Could he not have bloody waited, the awkward bollix?"

Razi was standing by the supply tent, his shadow and those of the soldiers accompanying him stretched long and black in the lowering moonlight. He was quietly dismissing the men.

"You may go," he said. "I shall be fine from here."

"His Highness's orders were to bring you to your tent, my Lord."

"Thank you, lieutenant, but there's nothing except shadows between me and my bed. Your presence should only serve to disturb the dogs, and they would wreak their vengeance by ruining everyone's sleep."

Wynter heard the lieutenant chuckle, and Razi sent him on his way with a nod of his head. The soldiers walked off and Razi made his way into the black canyon between the tents. Wynter sighed in frustration. There was no hope of sneaking back before him now. They may as well come clean. Sólmundr popped his head out, glanced at the retreating soldiers, then gestured that the way was clear. They slunk furtively across the road and reached the other side without anyone raising an alarm.

Razi was just ducking back out from their empty tent as they exited the alley, and he regarded them with alarm. "Where *were* you?" he whispered, but almost immediately he saw the bracelets in Christopher's hands, and he groaned and closed his eyes in despair. "Oh, Chris," he said. "No."

Wynter went to explain, but Christopher spoke before her. "Your brother's plans will be unhinged, I suppose."

Sól glanced curiously at Wynter and they shut their mouths.

Razi groaned again and tiredly ran his hand across his face. "God, he will be apoplectic," he said. Then to Wynter's utter astonishment he threw his hands out in resignation and sighed. "Oh," he said, "do not worry. Certainly I can find a way around it, though it would have been so much better if—oh, never mind. Do not worry, friend." He glanced at Christopher, genuine apology in his face. "It was unbearably cruel to stretch your tolerance any further. I am glad for you, Christopher. I only wish—" He shook his head. "No! I am *glad* for you," he said firmly. "I am glad it is over for you."

"You only wish what?"

Razi grimaced ruefully. "It matters not, friend. In the end, that was *my* plan and had nothing to do with your wishes or desires. In the end it is better that, having for so long deferred to my needs, you got to do things as you wanted."

"You only wish *what*?" insisted Christopher. "Tell me what you *wanted*, you damned fool, and stop always holding things back!"

Razi stepped abruptly into the moonlight and the weary acceptance on his face gave way to something harder. He held his fists before him, his eyes bright with desperate zeal. "I had wanted *more*, Christopher," he hissed. "I had wanted it to *mean* something."

Christopher gazed at him, waiting, and Razi, seeing that he did not understand, spread his hands, trying to find the right words.

"I had wanted that this should be more than a private, personal revenge. Something more powerful than a throat slit quietly in the dark. I had hoped that, when it came, your vengeance would symbolise something. I had wanted it to sing out, '*Behold. Here are the wages of evil. See what befalls those who live at the expense of those weaker than themselves.*' I had wanted the Loups-Garous' deaths to say, '*We shall not be tolerated. Our kind shall not prevail.'*" Razi stared ahead of him for a moment as if witnessing his plan blossom before him. Then he dropped his hands and sighed.

Christopher smiled. He glanced at Wynter and she took his arm. Wryly he jangled his father's bracelets in his hand and grinned at Razi.

"Lucky for you the Wolves ain't dead, then, ain't it?" he said.

Razi gaped at him.

"Nah," said Christopher with studied negligence. "Didn't feel right. Thought I might leave it for another day."

"Chris," said Razi quietly, "I have a plan."

"Thought you might." Christopher grinned across at Sól, a loving, affectionate grin at which the older man had to smile. Wynter's heart filled with pride. Christopher had been right. Thank God.

"You must put the bracelets back," said Razi.

Sólmundr's rueful good humour fell away, and Wynter cried out, "Oh *no*, Razi! That is unfair!"

Christopher froze for a moment, clutching the bracelets, his eyes wide with shock.

"But . . . why?" he managed eventually.

"Because they are evidence of a crime. Come on, friend. Show me what you have done, and I shall explain my plan as we walk."

There was no slinking through the shadows this time. Razi simply strode through the camp as if it was perfectly natural to be wandering about at night, and the others trailed along behind him like uncertain ducklings. They met a patrol on the road and Razi sighed with lordly impatience as the sergeant eyed the strange little entourage and explained that he would need to report them to the Prince.

"You do just that, sergeant, and I commend you for your diligence. Now I bid you go about your duty and leave me go about mine."

The sergeant hesitated, and Razi leaned in. "I should like you to give his Highness a message," he said. "You must repeat it exactly as I say, understand?" The sergeant nodded. "Tell him that I am simply taking advance payment for damages due, and his immediate business will not be disrupted. Please repeat that for me... Good. Now go ahead. I am certain the Prince will be most content with your attention to duty."

The soldiers left them.

Amazed, Sólmundr watched them go. Then he turned to look Razi up and down. "I think I take you home with me, Tabiyb," he mused. "You *very* impressive man."

There was not a trace of humour in the warrior's expression, and Wynter had to grin at the discomfort this brought to Razi's dark face. "Um," he said. "Um... right." With a nervous cough, he led the way into the shadows again.

Sólmundr winked at her. "Sometimes it too easy," he said, and led the way after their retreating friend.

The Wolves slept on. Razi ignored them, but he helped Sólmundr and Christopher drag the slaves out into the moonlight and propped them up against furs taken from the Wolves' tent. Wynter crouched by his side, gazing anxiously at them. It was difficult to tell in this strange light, but their colour seemed odd, their breathing fast and shallow.

"Will they die, Razi?"

"These are sevenths?" he asked, glancing up at Christopher, his fingers pressed to a slave's neck. Christopher nodded grimly. "So," murmured Razi, reaching to feel the other slave's pulse, "they are the sons of Wolves? Sired by them on one of their slaving raids and then kept as their own?"

"They ain't Wolves, though," said Christopher. Razi met his eye. "I'm certain of it," said Christopher. "For all that André has them convinced they could change if they want it badly enough, that just ain't the way it goes. It's like having red hair or blue eyes. You're either born a Wolf or you ain't. There's naught you can do about it."

He made this last statement very quietly, glancing at Wynter. She smiled reassuringly at him. It made no difference to her. Christopher was a good person, that was all, a good person who happened to be a Wolf.

"Still," said Razi, "they have Loup-Garou blood in them. They might be slightly different, perhaps, to normal men? There might be some physical differences that would make them more tolerant to the poison?"

Christopher shrugged, his eyes cold. He genuinely did not care.

Razi sighed. "In any case, there is nothing I can do for them, I have never heard of the plants Sólmundr has detailed, and I shall not risk a treatment when I do not know the tincture involved. They will live or die as the fates would have it." He stood and wiped his hands. "Would you like me to place the bracelets back on their arms?" he asked gently.

Christopher shook his head. "I'll do it."

"You are certain of this plan?" rasped Sólmundr.

Razi nodded. "Even if I cannot secure the testimony of the innkeeper's elder daughter, Christopher and Wynter can testify that it was the Loups-Garous who killed that poor child at the Wherry Inn. I shall see these curs tried in court, Sólmundr, using my father's new rule of law. I shall make an example of them that none will forget. My brother will build them up and their fall will be all the harder for it, and all the more public." He looked at Christopher. "But you must return your bracelets, friend, that we may prove they stole them from you on the night."

Christopher sighed. "It would be so much simpler to cut their throats," he groused, but he crouched nonetheless, and slipped the silver spirals up the arms of the slaves. Then he turned and went back into the tent, taking the guitar from his shoulder as he did.

Wynter followed him. "Don't give that back," she whispered, watching as he bent to place it by Pierre's side. "Please, love. I cannot bear the thought of him playing it again."

Sólmundr came up behind her, his long shadow blotting much of the light from the tent. "We can to keep it and hide it," he said.

Christopher shook his head. "They would look. They would find it, and then we would have to admit that we had been the ones who poisoned them. It's all right. I can..." He laid the guitar on the ground and stood. "I've already..." Suddenly he took a sharp breath. "No," he said. "I can't either." And to Wynter's horror he lifted his foot, ready to stamp down onto the fragile wood of his father's guitar.

"Don't!" she cried, already hearing the splintering of the beloved instrument beneath his boot.

But Christopher could not bring himself to do it, and he slammed his foot into the ground instead, crying out as he did so. Wynter put her hand to her mouth and closed her eyes in relief. Around them, the Wolves slept on. Outside, Razi crouched by the slaves, watching from the cold moonlight.

"Wait, Coinín" said Sólmundr. "*Fan nóiméad...*" and he

turned abruptly, heading to the remains of the Wolves' camp fire.

Wynter watched in silence as Sólmundr stirred the ashes, found an ember and carefully blew it to flame. He fed the fire from the Wolves' wood pile until a hearty blaze spread its warm light on himself and Razi and the unconscious slaves. Christopher edged past Wynter, his father's guitar in his hand, and went and stood on the opposite side of the fire from Sól, his face grave.

"You not ever get the chance to give your father proper ritual?" asked Sól.

Christopher shook his head. He sank slowly to his knees, his eyes on the fire, and Wynter moved from the shadows and came to his side. Sólmundr nodded in approval as she put her hand on her young man's shoulder.

"You want I should fetch Aoire?" he asked Christopher gently.

Christopher shook his head.

"You want me do it?"

Christopher nodded. He offered the guitar and Sólmundr took it from him with formal solemnity. The warrior kissed the smooth wood, then held it out across the flames. The light flickered warmly on his strong arms and his bracelets; it glowed in the depths of the polished wood. Sól began to speak in Merron, but Christopher murmured, "In Hadrish, Sólmundr, my family are here," and Sólmundr switched languages in mid sentence, saying, "...and peace with you, Aidan *an filid, mac* Oisín *an filid, as Tír na* Garron. A million thanks to you, for granting to me the son of your heart and now mine, Coinín *mac* Aidan *'gus mac* Sólmundr. See he walk in freedom now, as one of the Tribes. We have faith this make you happy as you walk in peace at the heart of the World, and we ask you reclaim your property which your son and mine has liberate for you and now returns as is right."

He kissed the guitar again and once more held it over the flames until Christopher took it. For a moment, the young man held the instrument poised across the hungry fire, his face determined. But then his strength seemed to desert him, and he snatched it back, curling himself around it as if incapable of letting go. His shoulder quaked beneath Wynter's hand, and she squeezed gently, her vision blurred with tears. Sólmundr tilted his head in sympathy as Christopher silently keened, his body rocking, his forehead pressed to the snake emblem on the back of the guitar. Then Christopher abruptly raised his head and, without further hesitation, placed his father's guitar into the heart of the flames.

" 'Bye, Dad," he said.

It caught immediately, the fire roaring to life around it, the strings snapping with sudden, sharp pops. Wynter sank to her knees by Christopher's side. He slid his arm around her waist. Razi came to stand behind them, and the three of them watched as the flames turned blue and green around the varnished wood.

They watched until there was nothing but ash and ember, until the silver fittings were nothing but meaningless blobs of metal. Then they rose together, as the sun began to cast its first faint light across the treetops, and walked in weary silence back to their tents.

Allies to the Prince

"What wrong with you lot? You look like you drink too much mead. Sól? You been sneaking brew?"

Sólmundr didn't bother to open his eyes, just waved a lazy hand in the Aoire's direction. The warrior was sprawled on a blanket, baking gently in the sun, Boro snoozing by his side. The other Merron were picking their way around him with tolerant amusement as they went about their chores. Úlfnaor directed a questioning look to Wynter and she shrugged noncommittally; better he think they had been at the wine than know what they had really been up to.

It had been almost midday when the sounds of camp and the airless fug of the tent had finally roused her. She had pushed herself from her bed, bleary-eyed and swollen-headed from lack of sleep, only to find that both Razi and Christopher were still snoring lightly into their blankets, dead to the world. She had roused them as best she could. Since then, all three of them had sat slumped outside the Merron tents, as listless and fragile as soldiers after the feast of St Barbara.

We should have stayed abed, thought Wynter as Razi cracked his jaw with an enormous yawn.

"I should get going," he murmured. "I have things to arrange."

Christopher's head drooped and his beaker began to slip slowly from his fingers. Wynter was eyeing this with weary glee—anticipating his no doubt colourful reaction to a lap full of tea—when the warhounds distracted her by growling and climbing to their feet. The hackles rose on their great necks and they lowered their heads, eyeing the alley between the tents. Sólmundr sat forward, the rest of the warriors tensed, and all the lazy relaxation left the air as David Le Garou came to the mouth of the alley.

He was alone, leaning at the corner of the tents like a derelict drunk, looking across the Merron to where Razi sat. "I would speak with you, al-Sayyid."

Razi, his face impassive, did not bother getting up.

Christopher carefully placed his beaker on the ground. "Good morning, David," he said. "Ain't you pretty today? Weren't no one around to brush your hair for you?"

Le Garou regarded him with loathing, and Christopher grinned, hard, bright and defiant. Wynter had to stop herself from crying out, "*Stop that, Christopher!*" She wanted nothing more than to throw a cloak over his head, so that he would be hidden and wouldn't aggravate this dangerous creature any further. There was something in Le Garou's dishevelled condition that made him seem even worse than before, as though the loss of some of his veneer had brought his evil closer to the surface. Wynter's sword, still sheathed, was lying on the ground behind her. She shifted her hand until she felt the hard reassurance of its hilt beneath her palm.

Le Garou tore his eyes from Christopher and back to Razi. "I would speak with you," he said again.

Razi crossed his ankles, leaned back on his elbow and laced his fingers. He shrugged lazily. "I'm a little busy," he said. "But I could spare a brief moment. Are you unwell, David? You're a touch pasty."

The Wolf was slightly worse than "a touch pasty." His eyes were red and sore looking, his hair a dull tangle around his grey face. With a scowl of discomfort, he pushed himself from the tent and stepped, squinting, into the sunshine. The hounds immediately blocked his way, their fur bristling into stiff ruffs, their bared teeth dripping. The Merron hummed to themselves and went about their business, doing nothing to clear David's path.

"Call them off," he said. Then again, with impatience. "Call them off, curse you! I have no tolerance for games this morning."

At Úlfnaor's nod, Hallvor called the dogs and she and Wari took them down to where the others were tending the horses.

"Merron scum," hissed David, staggering across the clearing and easing himself down onto Hallvor's abandoned seat. Sólmundr and Úlfnaor exchanged a look, but remained silent. David sat swaying for a moment, his eyes shut, then he reached into his belt-purse, fetched out both sets of snake bracelets and laid them onto the fire-stones.

"Here," he said, "I've been told that these belong to your boy."

There was a moment of frozen shock, during which time Úlfnaor got to his feet, his eyes fixed on the glittering jewellery. Sól murmured something, and the Aoire turned his head on a stiff neck to look at him. Sól said something again and Úlfnaor sat back down, his face dark with rage.

"Take them," said Le Garou, pushing the bracelets to Razi. "They are your property once more."

Christopher's hands knotted in his lap, but neither he nor Razi moved to touch the bracelets. It was all Wynter could do not to reach for Christopher's hand and clench it in her own. She could not bring herself to look into the Wolf's face, and so kept her attention focused on the toes of his expensive boots.

"It was Jean who stole them," he said. "At the Wherry Tavern, I believe? In the process I understand he attempted to harm your boy. He is, of course, yours to do with as you wish. None of us will intervene."

Wynter could not help it; she raised her eyes to see Le Garou's expression. It was blandly patient, as if Razi's reply were a simple formality. She could not believe the Wolf's audacity. It had certainly *not* been Jean who had done those terrible things at the inn. It had been the shadow-riders, the lower ranking Wolves, those men who now lurked in the forest, hidden and out of reach—and they had done it with David's permission, as reward for their patience on the long trek from the Moroccos. But Jean was an unruly whelp, foisted upon David at André's insistence and, according to Christopher, David could not wait to be rid of him. So now he presumed to use Razi for the task?

"I do not understand, David," said Razi politely. "Have you mistaken me for someone else?"

Le Garou's certainty slipped a little and he frowned.

"You have taken me for a trash haulier, perhaps?" asked Razi, "and so see fit to request that I divest you of your rubbish. Or do you simply wish to insult my intelligence by offering me your dirty work in the guise of favours?"

Le Garou blinked. When he next spoke, it was with carefully contained anger. "In my new life we are to be more than just neighbours, al-Sayyid. You must accept that I am now a trusted ally of his Royal Highness and soon shall prove myself the same to his Majesty the King. With my contacts here and in the court of the Sultan, I should be a useful friend to you, if you but have the sense to receive me as such. I have come to you this morning, with no accusations made about the events of last night, and have offered a token of peace and reconciliation. One simple act on your behalf will be enough to benefit me and restore your honour. Do not make the mistake of rejecting my kindness."

"I wish you the joy of your new life, David. May it grant you all the prosperity that you deserve, but I must ask you to take yourself and your *kindness* from under my nose. The stink of you is enough to make me retch."

"So be it," snarled David as he snatched the bracelets from the fire-stones and pushed himself unsteadily to his feet. "You'll find pride is a threadbare cloak when you've fallen from favour, *my Lord*. You will feel the cold soon enough, and will regret turning aside a genuine alliance." He weighed the silver bracelets in his hand and looked Christopher up and down. "They're not half as pretty without bells attached," he said, "but I suppose you are a man of simple taste. You must regret the loss of your trinkets, boy. It must sting that your master cares not to get them back for you. Still, my own boys will be glad to have them returned; they get such pleasure from wearing them. Adieu, al-Sayyid. I shall give your best to the Prince when next I speak with him."

There was a short, tense silence after he left. Then Christopher put his head into his hands and groaned, "Good Frith, Razi, if this doesn't work, I swear I'll skin you alive."

Sólmundr nodded in agreement. "Oh aye," he said. Wynter eyed his grim face and tried to convince herself that he didn't mean it literally.

Instead of listening, Razi was leaning to the side, looking down the alley. "David must be very certain of his position," he murmured, "if he felt he could lead me about like a pup on a string... ah!" He had spied something in the alley and it sent him to his feet. Straightening his shirt, he reached for the scarlet long-coat which he had shaken out earlier and hung upon the awning poles. "Come along, Wyn. Up, up!"

She must have looked entertainingly confused, squinting up at him, because he smiled and nudged her with his boot. "Up!" he said, shrugging into his coat. "You too, Christopher. Look lively, brush yourselves off and put on your cloaks, will you? Try and look a little dressed up."

They climbed uncertainly to their feet and made a desultory effort to straighten their hopelessly crumpled clothes. Razi sighed and shook his head. "Ah, well," he said, "you will have to do."

He turned to Alberon's lieutenant who was just at that moment coming to the mouth of the alley with three of Alberon's personal guard.

The lieutenant bowed uncommonly low. "My Lord," he said, "his Royal Highness would see you now, if you have a moment."

Razi nodded grimly and adjusted his collar. "Come along," he said. "If we hurry, we will be just in time for David Le Garou to witness this." He followed the lieutenant out into the dust and noise of the camp. The soldiers fell protectively into place at his back, and Wynter and Christopher trailed behind.

"Did he mean me to come along?" whispered Christopher anxiously.

Wynter shrugged, frowning. It seemed unlikely that Razi would take Christopher into Alberon's presence. Perhaps he meant to leave him on guard outside the tent? It would be a wonderful honour, but even so, a little presumptuous on Razi's part, especially in light of his recent shaky relations with the Prince. She tugged nervously at her cloak and trotted along, struggling to keep pace with Razi's long stride.

Christopher peered around the lofty entourage, trying to catch a glimpse of Alberon's tent. "The Prince is watching from the top of the hill," he murmured. Then he straightened in alarm and ducked back in behind the soldiers. "Good Frith! He's coming down!"

Wynter dodged swiftly to the left, glanced up the slope and dodged back again. Alberon was indeed striding down the steep path, blatantly heading towards his brother. Oliver followed calmly in his wake, his eyes scanning the crowd.

"I shouldn't be here," hissed Christopher. "We misunderstood." He scrubbed his hands anxiously on his trousers. "Look at me," he moaned. "I'm like a God-cursed gypsy. I ain't washed myself nor brushed my teeth. I don't even have my sleeves rolled up! I'll shame our lad!"

He began furtively trying to push his sleeves to the tops of his arms. Wynter gripped his hand to make him stop. "Stay easy," she whispered. "We're just here for show, the Prince will pay no heed to—"

"Brother!" bellowed Alberon, loud enough to shake the birds from the trees. "I am delighted that you could attend!"

Razi answered, almost as loud, "You have but to think it, your Highness, and I am there!" The soldiers on the road turned in curiosity and Wynter understood at once that she was part of a display. The loud, public, irrefutable resumption of communication between the Royal Prince and his bastard brother. She glanced over her shoulder and saw David Le Garou leaning weakly at the corner of the supply tents. He was glowering at the proceedings with undisguised frustration and rage.

The brothers met near the middle of the hill, close enough that the men on the road could hear their exaggerated conversation, elevated enough that they could be seen by all. With practised diplomacy, Alberon's lieutenant gestured his men aside so that all could witness the Prince clasp his brother's forearm and, in a thoroughly courtly gesture of filial accord, clutch Razi to him in a brief embrace. They stepped apart and Razi bowed low. Then, to Wynter's immense surprise, he turned to indicate her.

"Your Highness," he said. "The Protector Lady Wynter Moorehawke has come in the name of the King to offer her affection and support. Despite her recent terrible loss, our beloved sister could not rest easy until she found you and confirmed your Highness's health with her own eyes."

Alberon turned to her.

"Protector Lady," he said loudly, "we join you in mourning the loss of your great father. I am deeply moved that, despite the depths of your grief, you have journeyed here to find me. You are a credit to your sex, lady, and an example to all."

Gravely, Alberon took Wynter's hand and kissed it, bowing slightly from his hip. There was a sighing murmur from the surrounding men, and Alberon gently squeezed Wynter's fingers as he rose from his bow. She closed her hand tight against his, overcome with gratitude for this public recognition of her loss, and for Alberon's acknowledgement of her as an ally and a woman worthy of respect. She had no doubt that the dusty faces on the road were now suffused with sentimental protectiveness and sympathy; for there was nothing a soldier loved more than a tragically brave noblewoman. *God help us*, she thought, *but Albi certainly knows his men.* In this one greeting he had transformed her from suspected murderess and harlot to a shining icon of feminine worth.

"And your husband, Protector Lady? The man whose bravery

and knowledge of the wilds has ensured your safety and that of
the Lord Razi? Are we ever to be introduced, do you think?"

At the word *husband* the gathered men fell utterly silent. Wynter was amazed that a hundred burning holes did not appear in
Christopher's rigid back as all eyes turned on him. She did not
make the mistake of introducing Christopher herself, as if he
were some ragged sailor picked from the street by a common
jade. Instead she waited for Razi, her acknowledged male guardian, to step forward and do his duty.

Razi bowed, indicated his friend with a little gesture of his
hand and said, "Your Highness, as you wish, allow me to introduce to you my most trusted second and bodyguard, the Freeman Christopher Garron. A worthy person, your Highness, and
that most valuable of rarities, an honest man."

Christopher bowed very low and did not presume to speak.
Alberon regarded him with regal coolness. "I have heard much
about you, Freeman Garron," he said quietly. "My brother feels
he owes you much."

Christopher's eyes flickered to Razi, who nodded almost
imperceptibly.

"Thank you, your Highness," he said, "but the Lord Razi
owes me nothing. My debts to him, however, can never be
repaid, though I shall spend the rest of my life attempting to do
just that."

Alberon's face softened a little, as if Christopher's words had
thrown him, and he faltered a moment before nodding. When
next he spoke his voice was once more loud enough for the
crowds to hear. "You would not be the first commoner to have
proved himself worthy of the company of royals. All here know
how steadfast a friend the Protector Lord Moorehawke was to

my father the King. Welcome to my service, Freeman Garron. May you prosper in it."

Wynter tightened her jaw at the wry irony in this last line, but Christopher, all unawares, straightened from his bow, relief evident in his face. Alberon leaned close, and in the guise of shaking Christopher's hand, murmured low and private, "If you hurt my sister, Garron, you die a traitor's death. Understand?"

The men met each other's eyes. Christopher nodded and Alberon spun from him. "Behold my brother," he cried, slinging his arm across Razi's shoulders and turning him to face the camp. "He has journeyed here at peril of his life in order to aid us in our task of strengthening my father's kingdom. No prince could wish a more steadfast supporter. No man could have a brother more loyal."

The gathered men muttered uncertainly to themselves. Frowning, their eyes slid to Oliver who stood at Alberon's right, his hands folded blandly on his sword.

"Let all my allies know this face," cried Alberon, grabbing Razi's chin and wagging it. "It should not be hard to recall it, after all!" He looked around the assembled ranks of his men, and though his smile did not slip, the warning in his voice was clear to all when he said, "Make it known that this is a face beloved to me. Make it known that no harm shall come to this man, by my allies' hands or the hands of any other. He who harms my brother, harms me. Is this not so, Sir Oliver?"

"Aye, your Highness," said Oliver. "There's no man here who does not recognise the Lord Razi's devotion to you. There is no man here who would not die in his defence. My sword is yours, my Lord!" he cried, bowing his head to Razi. "My strength, my blood, my life, all pledged to your service."

It was the standard pledge of allegiance from a knight to his lord, but the men looked from Oliver to Razi with wide eyes, the knowledge of the rift between the two men apparent in their wary, sunburnt faces. Personally, Wynter had difficulty not spitting on the ground at Oliver's feet, but of course, there was not a trace of sarcasm in Razi's voice, nor even a hint of bitterness when he said, "My brother is blessed to have such fealty in his commanders and such fierce loyalty in his men. No knight could ever be truer, Sir Oliver. We work in common, and I am honoured to accept your protection and loyalty."

How he did not choke upon the words Wynter did not know, but she saw their effect as the soldiers' wariness turned to grudging acceptance. She knew that these men would follow Oliver's lead now, and would lay their lives down for Razi as surely as yesterday they would have slit his throat. Such was a soldier's life, after all. In the space of one moment, the very man they were engaging in battle could become the man to whom they must bow, and the why and wherefore of such changing fortunes would always remain beyond their grasp. These soldiers' only constant was in their loyalty to the Prince, and in the end all they could do was what the Prince asked of them and hope for the best.

Oliver straightened without meeting Razi's eye and Wynter turned from him, her face smooth and expressionless. Alberon squeezed Razi's shoulder and let go. He stepped forward and raised his hand for attention. At the back of the crowd, Wynter saw Gérard stagger up behind Le Garou, his face drawn, his proud bearing buckled under the effects of Sól's poison. Gérard went to speak and Le Garou snapped his hand up, silencing him, his eyes on the Prince.

"You may soon commence to packing," said Alberon, gravely addressing his men. "You will be on the road within the month."

Wynter saw shocked delight blossom in the men's faces. Still, they regarded the Prince in silence, as if doubting his meaning.

"Home!" bellowed Alberon, thrusting his fists to heaven, and his soldiers cheered in suddenly boisterous joy. Alberon raised his voice over theirs and cried, "My brother will go ahead as my envoy! He will prepare our way. You will be heading home within the month, men! The palace gates will be flung wide, your families that have, from necessity, disowned you, will fling their arms about you and we will be feted as the men who risked all to strengthen this kingdom!"

The men roared and jostled, and Alberon let them caper about for a moment, his expression tender. Then he slowly raised his arms over his head again, and gradually the men stilled, looking up at him in smiling anticipation.

"We have risked our lives for this," he said. "We have risked our fortunes, our good names, the love of our families. We have always known that the final step would be hardest. Now, thanks to my brother, it is as simple as packing our bags and strolling home. We are *done*," he yelled. "We have prevailed."

The men seemed to sigh as one. Wynter saw some of them close their eyes. Some turned their faces to the sky.

"We are done," repeated Alberon quietly. Then he raised his arms a little higher, and though his voice carried far across the silently gathered men, his next words had all the intimacy of a prayer uttered in the private company of friends.

"Long live my father," he said. "Long live the King."

And his men, like a congregation in solemn communion with God, answered low and heartfelt, "Long live his Majesty. Long live the King."

One Step Forward

Alberon broke from Razi as soon as they entered his tent. "There you have it, brother," he sighed, wearily taking a seat at the map table. "That should keep your head on your shoulders a while longer."

Christopher and Wynter hesitated at the door, and Razi impatiently gestured them inside. Oliver was about to make his way past them and into the tent when Razi directed the knight's attention down the hill. Wynter followed his meaningful glance. David Le Garou and Gérard were approaching the sentries at the base of the hill, David's face set in determination.

"Deal with that, would you, Sir Knight?" murmured Razi.

Oliver pointedly looked past Razi to Alberon, seeking the Prince's orders. "The Loups-Garous desire access, your Highness," he said.

Alberon sat back, regarding Wynter and Christopher with irritation. "In your nocturnal wanderings did you perhaps cause mayhem of which I should be aware?" At the young couple's blushing silence, the Prince turned cool eyes to Razi.

Razi shrugged. "There was some petty vandalism," he said. "Nothing of import."

Alberon sighed again, drummed his fingers, then waved Oliver away. "Try and fob them off, Sir Knight. Use your judgement. Be soothing."

"Aye, Highness."

Wynter peered past Razi, watching as Oliver descended towards the Wolves. Sólmundr, Hallvor and Úlfnaor were watching from the edge of the road, and Razi grimaced at the sight of them.

"Damn fools," he whispered, his eyes on Sól.

Alberon spoke coldly behind them and Wynter turned to find him staring at Christopher. "I have no patience for mopping up your messes, Freeman. This is not the time for personal vengeances. No matter how great the justification, I cannot have you and your people trampling their way over my negotiations and harming men who have come here in trust of my protection. This shall not happen again. Are we in accord?"

"Perfectly, your Highness."

There was nothing in Christopher's tone that could have been taken as offensive, but Wynter wished he could manage to bow a little lower and stare a little less. Alberon glared at him for just a fraction longer, then ordered Razi to *come away from the door, and leave Oliver to it!*

Razi pulled the insect netting across and came to sit at the table opposite his brother. Wynter remained at the door, unwilling to leave Christopher's side without knowing what was expected of him or where he should go. Razi glanced pointedly back at them, but it was not his place to offer an invitation and Alberon did not seem to notice their awkwardness, his attention being focused entirely on his brother.

"So," he said softly, "I have persuaded my men that we shall get them safely home. They seem convinced, poor fools. Their trust is a heavy burden."

Razi looked down at his hands, the knowledge of the men's peril evident in his face. "Albi, at the risk of angering you, I'm going to ask you, once more, to keep Lorcan's designs to yourself." Alberon tutted impatiently and Razi quickly went on. "Just until I have spoken to Father. Give yourself some ground to manoeuvre. If you do not send the designs home with Jared and the Combermen, then I can approach Father with a far greater hope of tolerance and—"

"If I do not send the designs home with Jared and the Combermen, they will lose the support of their allies. Everything must be timed just so. You *know* this, Razi. We've spent all last night discussing it. Everything I have planned, *everything*, is balanced on the most delicate of timings. If there is one single delay, then my entire network of resistances will fall apart. Without Lorcan's machines, the Midlander reformists will lose their courage, their Combermen supporters will slink into hiding and the Midlander rebellion will be over before it begins. Marguerite will go ahead regardless and usurp her father, but her kingdom will be exposed and weak and all is at risk of being lost. This has taken too much planning for me to falter at the last moment. It is now or it is never. I have come too far and risked too much to stop now."

Razi sat back, and Alberon watched him closely.

How young they look, thought Wynter. *How young, and how tired.*

"You do not have to pretend that you believe in me, Razi," said Alberon softly. "I do not ask that kind of falsity from you. I understand that you have no faith in my vision . . . simply tell me that you will do your best. Please? Tell me that you will do your absolute best to ensure that my men return to their lives, and that I shall at least get the chance to present my plans to our father. It is all I ask of you."

"I will do my best."

"Thank you," sighed Alberon, leaning his head onto his

hands. "Thank you...do try and get home without anyone slitting your throat, won't you?"

"I'll do my best."

Both brothers chuckled, and Alberon looked up at Razi from between his fists, his eyes smiling. "And then, perhaps, try and persuade Father not to kill me as soon as I come riding in the gates?"

Razi made a little sign at his throat. "Do not even joke," he warned softly.

Alberon nodded, sat back in a businesslike manner and slapped his hand on the table. "So, Freeman," he said, then frowned and motioned impatiently. "Why are you two loitering by the damned door? Get over here. Sit. Good. Freeman, I am taking my brother at his word and trusting that you will hold your tongue about anything discussed here."

Christopher nodded silently.

"I am running low on supplies," said Alberon. "As it stands, we have barely enough for the next two days, and the Lord Razi will need a good portion of that in order to see him through his ten days' journey home."

"Seventeen," said Wynter. "If one pushes one's horse and takes no diversion it should take a minimum of *seventeen* days to get from the palace to here."

Alberon looked at her with fond admiration, and she felt like smacking him. Was it really such an accomplishment that she could count?

"Razi will take use of my maps, sis. They will guide him through the summer passes to the north of the palace and get him home in just under ten days. However, there is barely enough scrub up there to keep a rabbit alive, and I will need to provision him and his party for the full ten days' travel. I myself will take my personal guard and follow him. We are too poorly provisioned to travel the same route, so we will ride in parallel, lower down the slopes. The going is slower there, but the hunting better and I will have a chance of feeding my men on the trail. Razi will arrive home about five days in advance of us. That should give him ample time to ease my father's fears and ensure my safe reception. After that," Alberon spread his hands and grinned, "it is in the hands of God."

"I would say it is in the hands of your *father*," commented Christopher, "and he's a mite more formidable than God, if you ask me."

The Prince was not accustomed to commoners chiming in with witticisms, and he regarded Christopher as if he were some amazing talking dog. Razi ducked his head, smiling. Christopher's dimples creased the corners of his mouth, and Wynter sighed. Alberon would get used to him eventually—or hit him—it all depended on the depths of his royal patience.

"Your supplies have been cut off, I presume?" she asked.

Alberon nodded. "Until recently we have been in regular receipt of small shipments. No one came to us, of course, but my provisioners would go down into the valleys and meet with my supporters. The men from the last trip have not yet returned."

"The poor fellow we found dying by the river: you suspect he was one of these provisioners?"

"I can think of nothing more likely."

"You fear the others have been taken?"

"Yes, Wyn, I do."

Wynter's belly knotted at the thought. Those poor men. "They will betray you, Albi," she said softly. "They may not want to, but they will. The King has employed inquisitors. No one can withstand their torture for long."

"That fellow Isaac did," murmured Christopher. "He endured an inhuman degree of torment." Wynter shut her eyes at the terrible memory of it. *He had been protecting Mary*, she thought.

Alberon cleared his throat. "My provisioners are already three days overdue," he said.

Three days!

"You must move camp!" cried Wynter. "You must do so *now*! They may already have given you away!"

"I could not relocate till now, sis. I needed the Loups-Garous to find me. But yes," he drummed his fingers and gazed out the door, "I must move."

"And you must feed your men," observed Christopher.

"Aye," breathed Alberon. "I must feed those men who accompany me back to the palace, as well as those I shall leave behind. I will order the majority of my men to remain in camp. I cannot allow them to return to their homes before I have secured my father's approval. They would be strung up and dead before the words 'long live the King' had left their lips. I need to keep them fed and watered for the time it takes for all of us to get home and ensure their safety."

"How many in all?"

"The Combermen and Midlanders are leaving tomorrow, so I reckon it at—"

"The Lady Mary is not fit to travel," interrupted Razi sharply.

"Well, neither is she fit to stay!" said Alberon. "Would you have her break her waters here? With a bevy of soldiers as her midwives?" He snorted in amusement at the thought. "My men would die of flusterment; they wouldn't have an idea what to do. No, there is naught I can do for the poor thing. Her fate is out of my hands; she will have to go back with her priest."

Razi subsided into frowning silence, and Christopher impatiently tapped the table to regain Alberon's attention. "How many men are you trying to provision?" he asked again.

"Eighty."

Christopher huffed and shook his head at the impossibly large number.

"But your people are *used* to providing for themselves!" cried Alberon. "I had supposed—"

"Eighty full-grown men are a bloody big clan," said Christopher bluntly. "A clan that size would have to spend the entire summer stocking up for winter. They'd trade a bit, farm a bit, be living off their horses. They certainly wouldn't just turn up in the forest with naught but their arses in hand and expect *An Domhan* to provide! That ain't the way nature works, your Highness."

"I am not a fool, Garron! You think I don't *understand* that? But my supplies are *gone*!"

Beneath the table, Wynter placed her hand on Christopher's thigh. "Freeman Garron," she said, "his Royal Highness finds himself in need. I am certain he would be grateful for whatever aid your people may have in their power to offer."

Christopher went to retort, then stopped. The importance of the situation seemed suddenly to make itself known to him, and she saw his irritation with Alberon gave way to an understanding of the opportunity being presented. Wynter, her expression bland, held his eye, squeezed his leg, then sat back.

"There...there ain't no magic wand that can be waved," he said, turning once more to Alberon. "Even for people as skilled as the Merron, the secret provisioning of eighty men and their horses is a monstrous task."

"I understand that."

"You need to send men into the valleys, bulk up the camp larder with at least some sacks of grain."

"We shall steal them if necessary, and make reparation later."

"It will be lean pickings . . . if there's any pickings at all."

"Understood."

Christopher was silent.

"Your people can do it?" prompted Alberon.

"If anyone can, they can."

Alberon ran his fingertips along the edge of the table. He plucked invisible fluff from his sleeve. "You understand," he said softly, "I would need be very delicate with my men about this? They take great pride in their capabilities. There can be no hint that they have been in any way . . . um . . ."

Christopher smiled bitterly. "The Merron lords are the most diplomatic of folk," he said. "Certainly they ain't about to ruin your men's appetite by crowing over who provided the meal."

Alberon regarded him very closely.

"I swear it," said Christopher.

"They are remarkably subtle when it comes to politics," murmured Wynter. "Take it from me, if it is diplomacy you need, these folk will oblige."

"If you wish to make use of the Merron, it might be wise to open talks with them soon," said Razi. "I will be taking Freeman Garron back to the palace with me and he will not be around to act as your liaison." He smiled in innocence at Alberon's hard look. "I need Christopher," he said blandly. "Without him I may well get eaten by a bear. After all, I don't know one end of a tree from the other."

Wynter hid a smirk. Alberon went to reply, but Oliver interrupted by ducking into the tent and jerking the door shut behind him. He did not look happy. "The Wolves are asking for a doctor," he snapped. "They are ill. One of their slaves is near dead, the other severely afflicted."

"Oh, Good *Christ*!" cried Alberon. "Have they brought the damned plague in on top of us, along with everything else?"

Oliver flickered his eyes to Razi, then away. "They hint at poison, Highness."

Alberon's face darkened. "Razi?" he growled.

Razi spread his hands in denial of involvement. Christopher gazed steadily at the table. Wynter examined her nails.

"Razi!" demanded Alberon. "You were prowling about in the night! You actually sent me *word* that you intended to interfere with the Wolves!"

"As I said, brother, petty vandalism, nothing more. The Wolves' illness is nothing to do with me."

"Le Garou is most insistent in his calls for a doctor," said Oliver. He looked significantly at Razi. "We have none but you in camp, my Lord."

"There is nothing I can do for them."

"*Razi*," growled Alberon.

"But there is nothing I can *do*," repeated Razi. "They were fool enough to eat something disagreeable and that is that."

"This is your opinion?" asked Oliver. "They ate something disagreeable?"

"Most disagreeable," murmured Christopher.

Razi gave him a warning look. "That is my opinion," he assured Alberon.

"And you know this how, brother?" asked Alberon tightly. "You simply sense it? You're that wonderful a physician? You can diagnose a patient's condition as if by magic through acres of tent canvas?"

"The Wolves ate something disagreeable," repeated Razi. "Your men have no need to fear the plague. I bet my life on it."

"I have no doubt you do," murmured Alberon, his eyes flitting to Christopher. Wynter glanced slyly at him and he caught her eye. "*Jesu Christi*," hissed the Prince, "you're like a trio of well-oiled snakes sitting there, with your shifty eyes and blank looks. Oliver, tell David that we are not fortunate enough to have a doctor in camp. Give him my sympathies, keep him appeased and keep me apprised. Do not let this escalate."

Oliver nodded unhappily and left.

"This will not escalate, will it, Freeman Garron? I shall not find myself stuck in a spiral of spite and counter-spite?"

"It may be wise," said Christopher, his scarred fingers drawing spirals on the tabletop, "to request that Úlfnaor's second join my Lord Razi on the trail."

"Certainly," said Wynter, "Freeman Garron could do with some assistance guarding us in the wilds. The lord and I being such sorry hands at forest-craft."

"Hmmm," mused Razi, "that is an excellent suggestion. If Sólmundr could be spared, of course."

"We're discussing that thin, sandy-haired fellow?" asked Alberon. "The one with those appalling shackle scars?"

Christopher nodded.

"I see," said Alberon quietly. His eyes dropped to Christopher's mutilated hands, and Wynter saw some measure of deeper understanding cross his face. "I'll assume that the appointment of this fellow to Razi's service will miraculously bring a halt to the Wolves' stomach problems?"

Christopher nodded again.

"I see." Alberon slapped the table with a decisive bang. "Very well," he said. "Razi! You have yourself the protection of the savage. I wish you joy of him. In your place, I should keep him far from my cooking pot, but that's just me."

Razi chuckled. "I shall bear that in mind," he murmured.

Wynter glanced at Christopher, smiling. He closed his eyes and she briefly took his hand.

"Now," said Alberon, rising to his feet. "Your maps..."

Consequences

"You insist on taking Wyn?" murmured Alberon, his eyes on the map. Wynter tutted, but the Prince paid her no heed and continued to discuss her as though she were not there. "Those mountain tracks are hardly fit for a woman."

"I am taking her, and that's an end to it," said Razi, peering at the thin thread of mountain pass which he was currently examining. "I will not leave our sister in camp without your protection, Albi, and I certainly will not send her travelling with you when Father's entire army is after your head." He pointed at the map. "This river, here," he said, "it is deep?"

"It is both deep and rapid. However, if you were to cross here..." He twisted the map so that Razi could see, and they bent low, murmuring, their equally tousled heads close together as they discussed the best way to ford the river.

Wynter sighed and pushed back from the table, stretching broadly and wincing at the stiffness in her back. They had been over the route three times already and were merely re-examining the alternatives. There was nothing left for her to learn.

Christopher had wandered to the door and was gazing through the insect netting, watching the camp. He was pensive and withdrawn, and Wynter assumed he was worrying about the Merron and their future. He had brought them into the conversation several times, and Alberon had been remarkably patient with him. But in the end there was little that could be done, and Christopher knew it.

The lords had not fallen prey to Marguerite Shirken's plan of entrapment, but that was about the only good thing that could be said for their situation. There was no room in this kingdom for their nomadic way of life, and there was little Alberon could do to avert the Shirkens' war of attrition against them. Even were the Prince willing to offer sanctuary—and there was no indication that he was—it was unlikely that Úlfnaor's party would accept his protection and leave their tribesmen in the North to struggle on alone. Eventually, the Merron lords would have to return home to deliver the bad news to their people, and to face whatever it was that life had in store for the tribes.

Wynter crossed to Christopher's side and took his hand. She leant against him, looking down into camp.

"This plan is madness," he said softly. "The King ain't ever going to allow this all to just slip by. What king would? His heir threatening the throne, toppling his allies, restructuring his carefully established relationships? If Jonathon allows all that to go unpunished, he may as well just hand the boy his crown and have done with it." He shook his head grimly. "They ain't going to succeed."

Wynter glanced back at the brothers. They had taken one of Razi's maps and were comparing it with Alberon's, measuring the distances and frowning. "Razi is a remarkable diplomat," she whispered. "He simply has to persuade Jonathon to meet with Alberon and—"

"He won't *succeed*!" hissed Christopher, turning to her. She squeezed his hand and glared at him in warning to keep his voice down.

He turned his face to the insect netting again, and they

listened for some sign that the brothers had noticed. But the low conversation carried on behind them and, after a moment, Christopher tilted his head to her once more.

"As soon as the King finds out that Razi lives, he'll take up arms and he'll kill the Prince, and that will be an end to it all. Razi will be forced to the throne, and we'll be attending his funeral by Christmastide because there ain't no way Jonathon's beloved subjects will let his brown bastard live as heir."

The cold possibility of this clenched itself around Wynter's heart. Christopher held her eye for a moment before turning his face back to the camp. Behind them, there was the rustle of another map being unfolded. Alberon murmured something and Razi huffed in amusement. He made some dry remark and the two brothers chuckled.

Christopher's hand tightened against Wynter's and she drew his fist up to her heart. She stared blindly through the mist of the insect netting as all the desperate possibilities of what might come to pass wormed their way through her mind.

At the beginning of all this, Alberon had no doubt believed that his father would back down. It must have seemed so unlikely that Jonathon would simply sweep his heir from him and begin afresh with Razi on the throne. Regardless of anything else, the consequences for the kingdom of such an act would have been apparent even then. By now, though, Alberon had to be aware of the hopelessness of his position. In his guilt over the Bloody Machines and his violent desire that they not continue in use, Jonathon had made the rift with his heir too public. He had taken things too far. Now, no matter what Razi did or said, how could the King ever permit Alberon return to the throne?

Neither Razi nor Alberon were fools. Wynter knew that they both understood the unlikelihood of turning back this tide. Still,

they seemed determined to forge ahead—Alberon in his steadfast belief that he could strengthen his father's wonderful kingdom, Razi in the hope that he could reconcile all.

"There is nothing else they can do," she whispered.

"I know."

"This is their only chance."

"I know."

"I will not abandon Razi to do this alone, Chris."

"Oh God, lass! I know! Neither will I."

She smiled. "I never suspected you would."

Down in the camp, a muted trumpet called muster to dinner,
and the two of them paused to listen to the distant clatter of men
falling into line.

At the map table, Alberon sighed. "I am clemmed," he said.
"Will we tidy up in the hopes that someone may present us with
a meal?"

Wynter listened, with her back turned, as the brothers folded
maps and cleared away pens and folios. Christopher sighed and
shook his head. He squeezed the bridge of his nose with his free
hand, hopelessness and misery clear in every line of his face.

Wynter kissed his scarred fingers in sympathy. "Would you
like to meet an old friend of mine?" she whispered. At his surprised nod, she led him past the table to Alberon's cot.

"He's asleep," she said, pulling back the insect netting and
sitting on the bed. "He's not terribly well."

Christopher hesitated at the sight of the cat. "Oh," he said.
"Uh..." he glanced back at Alberon, then turned to face her and
widened his eyes in secret warning. "I don't tend to get on with
cats," he said. "They tend to be...umm...*alarmed* by me. Seeing as how your Southern cats are a touch more vocal than most,
is it wise that I...?"

He contorted his face in a ridiculous attempt at non-verbal communication, obviously concerned that Coriolanus might leap from his nest, screeching, "Wolf!" at the top of his lungs.

Wynter smiled. "Don't worry, Christopher," she whispered. "Cori knows all there is to know about you. He will not be alarmed. Come here." She patted the cot and Christopher sat down. Without hesitation, he slipped his arms around her and put his chin on her shoulder, watching the sleeping cat. Wynter saw Alberon frown at this most uncourtly display of affection. She looked away from his disapproval and pulled Christopher's arm a little tighter around her waist.

"Poor wee thing," he murmured. "He's naught but skin and bone."

"I should like to offer the Lady Mary my protection," said Razi suddenly, and they all turned to look at him in surprise.

"Oh, Razi," said Wynter sadly. That was a hopelessly impossible kindness.

"Don't be a fool, brother," said Alberon, "she's a Midlander." At Razi's unreadable silence, Alberon sighed. "She is a *devout Midlander lady of court*. She will no more accept your help than she would sail to the Moroccos and take up service in the harem of the Sultan."

"I intend merely to offer my protection, Albi. I expect nothing in return."

"I do not imply that you wish to make the poor thing your concubine," said Alberon with surprising gentleness. "I am simply pointing out the unlikelihood of her accepting even the most courtly of advances from a man of your colour, creed and... um... birth. That is all."

"She has *nothing*, Albi," said Wynter softly. "Her husband's destruction has left her bereft of family and of fortune. She must be desperate for help."

"You would not think it to look at her," said Christopher, his voice warm in Wynter's ear. "She's a formidable little person."

"She has remarkable character," agreed Razi. "I should hate to think of her trekking home in that condition. And then, arriving to what?"

"She would be returning home to nothing," observed Wynter. "Worse than nothing if the purge against her family still rolls on."

"And so I would like to offer her my protection, Albi. If you would only agree to shelter her here while I am away, I should—"

"I thought I had made myself clear on this," said Alberon sharply. "This is not the place for a woman in her state. You cannot simply offer her your protection, then hand her over into my care without a thought. Either she is your responsibility or she is not! Do not foist the consequences of your magnanimity onto me."

"I cannot take her with me over the mountains!" exclaimed Razi. "Do not be ridiculous!"

"Then why offer your protection at all! That's nothing but words! If you're—"

"The Merron may protect her," suggested Wynter, "while they are here, at least."

"Oh, aye," murmured Christopher, reaching to stroke Coriolanus's back. "There's no way Úlfnaor would turn her aside, and should it come to it, Hally's sat birth vigil more times than we could can count, I'd say. The lady would be safe in their keeping until the Lord Razi returns, and your soldiers needn't fret over the possibility of having to help a baby come into the world. God knows, it ain't what soldiers are useful for, is it?"

At the ensuing silence, Christopher and Wynter looked up. Razi and Alberon were regarding them with strangely startled expressions. Christopher faltered uncertainly. "Uh...that is, if the lady agrees, of course," he said. "It's merely a suggestion."

"Of course she'll agree," said Wynter. She leant back, settling comfortably against Christopher's chest, and smiled. "Don't mind the brothers, love, they're just surprised, that is all. The Kingssons are not used to seeing things so straightforwardly."

Anthony announced himself at the door, and Alberon grinned in anticipation as the servant carried in a tray of dishes. "Food!" cried the Prince. "Get off my bed, you two, and come sit for your meal."

"Anthony," murmured Razi as the little fellow set the table, "would it be possible for me to wash first?"

Anthony nodded tightly. He was far more subdued than Wynter was used to, and she thought he seemed a little pale. She watched him from the corner of her eye as he placed the bowls, but refrained from asking if he was all right.

He set a basin and pitcher on Alberon's bedside locker and Razi came across to wash his hands. Wynter smiled as Anthony sidled past, but he didn't seem to notice her. Christopher, awaiting his turn at the wash basin, followed the little boy's progress with a concerned frown.

"Have we bread?" asked Alberon, rubbing his hands and looking around hopefully. "No, we don't. You've forgot the bread, mankin," he said. "Go get it."

Anthony was in the process of hoisting a jug of water to the table. He poured an unsteady beakerful for Alberon, and Wynter realised that his little hands were trembling.

"Anthony," repeated Alberon, already tucking into his porridge. "Didn't you hear me? Run down to the supply tent and get some bread."

At the words *supply tent* Anthony made a desperate little noise and lost his grip on the pitcher. Razi watched in dismay as his dinner bowl overflowed with the water meant for his beaker. Wynter rose to her feet, her hands out to steady the jug, but Christopher was already there and he lifted the pitcher from the child's shaking hands. Anthony stepped back, his face crumbling, and his eyes filled with tears.

"Hey, it's all right, mouse," assured Christopher, setting the pitcher down. "It's naught but water." He stirred Razi's bowl with his finger. "Look! You made soup. You *love* soup, don't you, my Lord?"

"I generally prefer it with a spoon," muttered Razi darkly. Blushing, Christopher took his finger from the bowl. Razi looked to Anthony. "What the devil is the matter with you, child? Have you the palsy?"

Anthony took a big deep breath and straightened his narrow shoulders in an attempt to gain his equilibrium. Wynter felt sure he intended to speak, but his mouth just squirmed about instead and his tears overflowed down his cheeks to drip onto his apron.

"Good Christ," protested Alberon, "all I wanted was some bread."

"I'm *your* servant!" cried the child suddenly. "I'm *yours*!" Everyone gaped at him, startled, and he flung his skinny little arm out, pointing insistently downhill and crying again. "I have nothing to do with Wolves, have I, Highness? They can't make me do anything! Just because the soldiers won't serve them! I'm just your servant, aren't I! *Aren't* I, Highness? I'm just *yours*!"

Christopher's face went hard and cold, and he straightened slowly from where he had been crouched by the boy. Anthony wrung his apron between his fists and looked pleadingly up at him, mistaking his rage, perhaps, for disapproval.

"But I don't want to," he whispered.

"You don't have to," hissed Christopher. "You don't have to do *aught*!"

"Christopher," said Razi gently, "they only wanted him to serve their food. I'm sure that is all."

"But I don't want to," whispered Anthony again. "Please. I'm *your* servant, Highness. I'm—"

"Yes," said Alberon. "Yes, Anthony. Shush now. It is all right. I don't need any bread, and you *are* my servant, no one else's. So hush."

Just then the strangest sound drifted up from camp—a low, keening moan.

Christopher's eyes narrowed as he listened to it, his shoulders hunched. The first moan was joined by another and the two voices rose slightly, not quite becoming a howl before dying down. Immediately, the sound rose up again, three voices this time, like ghost dogs mourning in their sleep.

"Why are they *doing* that?" whispered Anthony desperately, his eyes huge.

Razi met Christopher's eyes across the water-slopped table.

"The slaves are dead," said Christopher. "The Wolves are lamenting their loss."

"I don't want to be their boy!" cried Anthony. "That man said I must! But I don't want to! He said I must, but—"

Wynter snagged his tunic, pulling him in. "Shush now," she said softly. "It's nothing at all to do with you. The Prince is your master. That is an end to it."

"Will these deaths be a problem?" snapped Alberon. "Will they seek revenge?"

Razi shook his head. "David has too much at stake to run amok over this," he said. "He feels secure in your protection and will not be foolish enough to jeopardise his future." His eyes flickered to Christopher's livid face, then back to Alberon. "It is over," he said, picking nervously at his cuff. "I am certain of it."

Christopher just stared at the terrified little boy and said nothing.

The Defiant Gesture

"You very quiet," said Sólmundr, eyeing Christopher across the neck of his horse.

Christopher shrugged, tightened the girth on his saddle and snapped his stirrups into place.

"You feel not good?"

"I'm fine," he grunted, swinging into the saddle and pulling his horse around. "Stop acting the old biddy and saddle up."

Sólmundr met Wynter's eye. Christopher had been silent and prickly since the night before, and Sól, usually so easygoing, had nagged at the young man's ill-humour like an anxious hen. He was making Christopher worse.

The sooner Razi and I get them from camp the better, thought Wynter.

She tugged her saddlebags into place and glanced across to where Razi stood in conversation with Jared. The Lady Mary had refused Razi's protection, as Alberon had known she would. To Wynter's surprise, however, the priest had been remarkably open to the idea. Wynter tried hard to be gracious about his intentions, but it was easy to suspect that this had less to do with Mary's welfare, and more with the hassles of trailing a pregnant woman all the way home.

"I shall speak with her again," said Jared. "Try and convince her of the sense of it."

"Please do," said Razi. "And do your best to convey my sincerity, won't you? There will be nothing of the beggar's taint involved. No unsavoury implications. The Lady D'Arden will have every dignity, and her child the best of care. You *do* believe me, Presbyter? You *will* press my case?"

Jared sighed and ran his hand across the gleaming whiteness of his scalp. "I'll try," he said, "but I must leave soon. I should have left yesterday, if the truth be known. If I cannot convince her to stay, I must take her with me. There's naught else for it." He tutted. "If only the Blessed Virgin had not made that damned journey on an ass, my lady might feel less inclined to risk the same...oh, God forgive me for saying so!" he said and blessed himself quickly, three times in a row. "She *is* an exasperating woman, though," he muttered. "I'm not so certain you're wise in taking her on."

Razi extended his hand. "Do your best," he said quietly.

Wynter paused in the act of tying her blanket roll, and stared as the priest gripped Razi's dark hand and shook it. She did not know why, after all the things she had witnessed in the last few months, but this sight arrested her—a Midlander priest shaking an Arab's hand, their faces set in solemn accord.

The two men were caught in a slanting shaft of early light, and it rimmed them in gold, throwing their shadows long and misshapen against the sloping sides of the Merron quarters. As Jared released Razi's hand and turned away, Hallvor emerged from the darkness of the tent behind them. She carried Sólmundr's bright wool cloak in her arms, and as she slipped past Razi, the sun glanced hotly from her bracelets and glowed in the fluid blackness of her hair before she crossed back into shadow.

It was a moment so vivid and so inexplicably sad that it stole Wynter's breath.

Úlfnaor ducked from the other tent and waited while Razi watched the priest leave. Then the big Aoire smiled and bowed, offering his hand to Razi in farewell. The Merron gathered in a silent row behind them, their faces grave as the two men shook hands.

"We shall see each other again," said Razi, "when I am reunited with my brother."

"I want tell you thanks, Tabiyb, but there not ever to be enough words for it."

Razi nodded silently and turned away, heading for his horse. Úlfnaor's attention lifted to Sólmundr who was just taking to his saddle. The Aoire met his friend's eye and his face creased in wordless emotion. Sólmundr grimaced ruefully and shrugged. By his horse, Hallvor stood with his cloak in her hand, her dark eyes sad.

"*Sól, mo mhuirnín,*" she whispered, "*tar ar ais gan mhoill.*"

Taking his cloak, Sólmundr leant perilously low and pressed his forehead to hers, squeezing his eyes shut. "*Slán, a stór,*" he whispered.

"You to stay alive!" shouted Wari suddenly, and Sól laughed, his forehead still pressed to Hallvor's. He straightened and pulled his horse into line.

"Don't go hunting any Wolfs without me!" he said. "It is for my son and I their heads are keeping."

Úlfnaor and Wari nodded in dark understanding. Úlfnaor murmured a translation, and the other warriors grinned knowingly. Surtr made a cutting motion at his throat. Wynter frowned as she took to the saddle, glancing at Razi who was pretending not to notice or understand. Christopher, hard-faced and silent, just waited expressionlessly to pull away.

"Iseult?" Wynter glanced down to find Hallvor smiling gravely up at her. "You take care of yourself, *luchín*, yes? You and your odd little tribe." Wynter nodded. "And do not forget," Hallvor tapped her temple, a wicked twinkle in her eye, "if Coinín ever gives you any trouble, hit him in the head, preferably with your boot."

Wynter couldn't quite bring herself to smile. "You will take care of the Lady Mary?" she asked. "For as long as she remains in your care?"

Hallvor nodded. "I will protect her," she said. "I swear it."

She squeezed Wynter's hand, then stepped back as Razi clucked his mare past them, heading for the thoroughfare. Christopher pulled his horse into line behind him. He seemed lost in his own thoughts, and it was clear that he intended leaving without saying goodbye to his Merron friends.

"Coinín," called Úlfnaor. The young man paused. "*Fear óg thú, a Choinín. Tá neart ama agat.*"

Christopher nodded without looking back, and went to kick on.

"I will mind the little boy!" called Úlfnaor. "You not needs to worry."

Christopher reined his horse around, his eyes wide, and with a surge of painful understanding, Wynter realised that Úlfnaor had hit upon the source of his distress.

"He's so small," said Christopher urgently. "He ain't got a chance against them."

Úlfnaor shook his head. "They not get him."

"You need to watch them all the time, though. Watch Jean! Make him understand that if he does aught, we'll remember it. Let them know that we are *strong*."

"I swears it," soothed the Aoire. "You not to worry."

Christopher blushed suddenly, as if embarrassed by his outburst, and he straightened. Nodding curtly, he pulled his horse back around and glanced at Razi, who turned without further word and led the way between the tents. Wynter fell into place behind them, Sól, Boro and a cranky little pack mule trailing after. They followed Razi up the alley and out onto the road, where they fanned out behind him in unplanned unison, an unlikely squad of mismatched knights backing their lord.

There had been no plans for ceremony, but of course the soldiers had gathered to witness the departure of the man upon whom they were all dependent. Alberon and Oliver were standing at the head of the slope, and they watched as Razi led his little entourage to the base of the hill. It was not possible that a crown prince would come to stand by a lord's horse, squinting up at him like some common groom, so Alberon waited, his face bland, as Razi slid from his mount and trudged his way up the slope to kneel at his feet. Wynter scanned the crowd as Alberon gave Razi his blessing. She was appeased by the hopeful expectancy in the men's faces. They had truly taken Albi's words to heart, it seemed, and she could see no trace of sullenness or the repressed aggression of before.

It brought a mingling of unease and relief that the Loups-Garous were nowhere to be seen. Perhaps they were simply too ill to be bothered. *Let them stay abed*, she thought, discreetly scanning the tents behind her. *Let them keep their damned faces away and allow us depart in peace.* But it was a futile wish and her heart twisted with bleak anger as she saw Jean, his clothes crumpled, his pale hair tossed, stagger to the edge of the road and sneer at the proceedings on the hill.

Neither Sól nor Christopher noticed the Wolf's presence and Wynter faced front so that she would not draw their attention to him. The Wolves would not be a problem in any case. Razi was right. Alberon's promises had tamed them and they would do nothing now but posture. They knew that their future depended on Razi's survival. Even they would not be foolish enough to risk their fortunes in avenging the death of a slave.

At the royal tent, Razi rose to his feet. The Royal Prince took a letter from his coat, looked at it for a moment, then handed it over. Razi took it with a bow. Then Alberon, ever impulsive, broke the air of solemn formality and pulled his brother in for a hug. His voice drifted faintly down the brightening air as he tousled Razi's curls and, like a man years senior to his brother, said, "Take care of yourself, you damned pup."

Wynter smiled at the exasperation on Razi's face as he raked his hair into order and came striding down the hill.

As Razi took to his horse, Alberon met Wynter's eyes and smiled. He lifted his hand in fond farewell. Wynter nodded a bow. *Adieu, brother. We shall meet soon.*

"Come along," said Razi, turning to face into the morning light. "Let us fly. Our time is gold."

The soldiers had already begun to turn away, their minds drifting to the many chores that made up the military day. As the entourage urged their horses down through the dusty camp, Wynter saw Razi's head turn to the silent darkness of the Midlander quarters. He was, perhaps, hoping that the Lady Mary would show her face in farewell, but she remained decently secluded.

The supply tent was a hive of work as the cooks and rationeers began the complex process of feeding a camp of hungry men. From habit, Wynter let her eyes drift across the surface of the activity, watching for danger. At her side, Christopher did the same, his vigilance disguised by his usual careless slouch. She noticed something catch his eye, and he straightened slightly, following a movement in the crowd.

Anthony was making his careful way between the busy men, his little arms stretched out, his attention absorbed in not spilling the kettle of water he held poised before him.

Later—when things were over and nothing could ever be changed—Wynter would ask herself, *What if I had never reacted? What if Christopher had never turned his head?* But that kind of speculation is useless in such situations and, as so often happens, things simply unfolded without any plan or forethought. As soon as Wynter saw the little servant weaving through the heedless crowd, she startled and swung around to check for Jean. Her only thought was, *I hope Anthony is on the hill before that cur sees him*, but of course, Christopher was alerted by her sudden turn in the saddle and he followed her gaze directly to the Wolf.

Jean was dull and listless, his energy obviously sapped by the lingering effects of the poison, and he was simply leaning at the corner of the tents, watching Razi's progress through the crowd. He had no notion of the child, who was hidden from view amongst the men on the far side of the road, and Wynter realised at once that he'd had no intention of causing trouble. But Christopher's angry face caught Jean's eye, and the Wolf couldn't seem to resist the challenge in the young man's expression.

Grinning, Jean pushed himself straighter and called something in Arabic. Whatever he said must have been wickedly crude, because Razi swung around to look at him, his face raw with shock. Jean laughed knowingly, that horrible cackle, and his eyes flitted from Razi's scarlet face to Christopher's. He winked lewdly. Razi snarled and immediately turned away, furious that he had allowed himself to respond.

"*Tóin caca*," hissed Sólmundr and he, too, turned front, dismissing the Wolf with cool disdain.

Christopher, however, held the Wolf's eyes, and as his horse came level to where Jean was standing, Christopher ducked his chin and ran his fingers under his collar, pulling something bright from the neck of his shirt. Wynter knew what it would be before the silver teeth cleared Christopher's collar, and her heart fell as he tugged Razi's necklace out into the open and arranged it so that it lay gleaming against the dark fabric of his tunic.

Jean frowned, squinting, and Wynter saw understanding slacken the Wolf's face as he recognised the warm amber stones and the glittering silver fangs that now decorated his former slave's throat. He lifted his eyes to Christopher's, his smile gone. Christopher grinned. He pressed his scarred finger to the gleaming tip of a silver fang, then slowly extended his arm to point at Jean.

All the implications of this gesture crawled bright and clear across Jean's face, and he stumbled backwards, horrified. Wynter knew he now understood exactly where the Wolves' fortunes lay, and she understood, too, that this changed everything.

Christopher had just told Jean, *You have no future.* He had just told him, *This is your fate. One day you too shall be an ornament hung around a slave's neck.*

Jean turned and stumbled away between the tents, and Wynter suspected that Christopher had just undone the only knot that had been holding the Wolves in place. The muzzle of their restraint had come loose and nothing now remained to hold them in check.

An Unlikely Event

As soon as they left camp, Wynter pulled Razi aside and anxiously told him about the necklace and its possible effect on the Wolves. He swung to Christopher, appalled, and Christopher, shameless and defiant, simply sucked his teeth, pulled his horse onto the trail and kept going. Razi was left staring after him, speechless. After a moment, Sólmundr edged his horse past, fell into place by his young friend's side and they forged on.

Razi and Christopher barely spoke to each other for the next three days.

The trail brought them higher and then higher still; up beyond the majestic pines into hard country woodland, above that again into wind-twisted scrub, and then, finally, up into the shale-strewn wastelands and rock that would be their landscape until they reached the other side.

This high into the mountains the wind was tremendously strong. Slicing across loose beds of shale and rubble, and blasting down the black faces of cliffs, it cut through Wynter's many layers of clothes and ripped the heat from her body. She took to travelling with her cloak and blankets wrapped around her, her head ducked against the incessant gale. For the first time since she'd met him, Sólmundr covered his arms. Eventually he gave in completely and shrugged his wiry body into a heavy, felt-lined jacket and wrapped his head in a scarf. Only Boro didn't seem to feel the cold, and he ranged the barren landscape with cheerful, snuffling enthusiasm, his tongue lolling, his fur flattened in the wind.

On the third night, they plundered a copse of straggling furze bushes for wood and lit a guttering fire in the shelter of a rock. Sólmundr drew his covers around him and lay back, his eyes shut. He was quiet, as usual, content to let the others set the tone. Wynter huddled by his side, Boro stretched between them, his head resting warm in her lap. She scratched the hound's bristly ears and watched her men as they stewed in their silence.

Christopher, swaddled in his cloak and blanket, sat cross-legged by the fire, gnawing a strip of dried venison. His blanket was pulled, cowl-like, over his head and only his mouth and chin were visible as he doggedly chewed the last of the meat. Razi sat with his shoulders hunched against the cold, his eyes fixed on the flames. The wind gusted through a narrow gap in the rocks, flinging his curls across his face, and he shoved them back, pulling his scarf tight and binding it hard under his chin.

Behind them, the mountains rose black and featureless against the dusky sky. It would be dark soon. There would be no moon. Wynter scanned the sharp outline of the cliff edges for movement. The wind shushed slyly in the rocks around her and skittered through the loose shale.

"What can you possibly have been thinking?" cried Razi suddenly.

Christopher's jaw stopped moving for a fraction of a second, then he recommenced chewing.

"Úlfnaor *told* you he would protect the boy! Did you honestly think you'd help matters by exposing my intentions to the Wolves?"

Christopher swallowed his chunk of meat. He said nothing.

"You are an unruly *chard*, Garron!" said Razi, kicking a stone into the fire. "You have no more sense than a child!" He tucked his hands into his armpits and huddled deep into his cloak, his eyes roaming the uneasy shadows. "You are enough to kill me with exasperation."

"What done is done," murmured Sólmundr. "If they come for us, we fight. That all it is."

"I cannot help but feel that, had the Wolves been intent on harming us, they would have attacked by now," ventured Wynter. "No doubt David was loath to risk everything Alberon has offered him on so vague a threat as a finger pointed to a necklace." She glanced at Christopher, hoping he would agree, but he stayed silent, his face still obscured by his hood of blankets. "I should think that after all this time we are safe," she said.

Sólmundr slit his eyes and looked at her. "They sick anyways," he reassured her. "I not see them able to follow us. Even as Wolfs, they be too ill to journey this trail."

Razi huffed. "Well," he said, "David is certainly no fool. And I suppose Wyn is right: he would be unlikely to jeopardise his future based on a story brought to him by Jean." He settled back against his saddle. "Perhaps you are both right," he murmured. "Perhaps all will be well. But I still should have you pilloried, Christopher Garron. I am beyond words with anger."

Wynter smiled. She found it unlikely that any emotion could put Razi beyond words for long, and, to tell the truth, he didn't sound particularly angry now that he'd actually had his say. She looked to Christopher again, glad it was out in the open, hoping for a smile.

"The truth is," said Christopher softly, "I didn't even think about it. If I had, even just for a second, I wouldn't have done it." He looked up at Razi, the firelight finally illuminating his face. "I'm sorry."

There was something in the way Christopher said *I'm sorry* that sent a blade of fear slicing up Wynter's back. Sólmundr raised himself onto his elbow and waited solemnly.

"David may not act," said Christopher, "but if Jean thinks we threaten his life, he'll find a way to send the lower pack. They'll travel as Wolves and attack as pleases them. We can't outrun them, not even on horses, so when they come, we'll have to fight. There's six of them, and there's four of us, plus Boro. If we're lucky, the animals will smell them before they sneak up on us and we may get the chance to shoot."

If we're lucky, thought Wynter.

"How fast can they travel?" asked Razi. "Will they be here soon?"

Christopher glanced at Wynter and lowered his head without answering. Razi sat back again, his face grave. "Shit," he said.

The Wolves attacked on the fifth day, in broad daylight, out of nowhere. The wind was gusting steadily in from the top of the pass, howling into their faces, and there was no advance warning from dog or horse. Wynter wasn't even thinking about the possibility of an attack. It was too cold, the wind too wicked and the trail too narrow for her to be thinking of anything other than just getting by. She was looking up at the scudding grey sky, hoping that it wouldn't rain, when something darted across the top of the bluff above her. It flew down the slope so fast that she thought it nothing but a cloud shadow. Then it leapt past her, momentarily cutting off the breeze, and Wynter felt heat and smelled a Wolf's musty scent as the shadow hit Razi and carried him over the edge of the path.

She registered sky and rock where only moments before there had been man and horse. Then the screams of Razi's mare cut into her shock and Wynter twisted in the saddle, staring downwards while Razi, Wolf and mare tumbled away from her. Razi was tangled helplessly in his tack, and he appeared and disappeared from view as his horse rolled over and over, all the way down the steep slope to the bottom of the hill.

Christopher yelled, "They're on the ridge! They're on the ridge!"

Wynter looked up to see a Wolf launch for her, its jaws gaping. A crossbow *thwacked*. The bolt whined past her ear and the Wolf jerked in mid flight, as though yanked on a chain. It fell to the ground at Ozkar's feet, Christopher's arrow jutting from its chest. But it was not dead and it writhed an agonised circle on the rocky path, screeching and struggling, neither animal nor man in its distress.

Ozkar reared in panic. Wynter almost came unseated as he tried to back away from the creature thrashing at his feet.

"Corral your horse!" yelled Christopher. Then he, too, screamed. His cry was cut abruptly short, and there was a heavy thump and the rattle of something big hitting the gravel behind Wynter's horse.

Sólmundr bellowed in Merron, fury clear in his voice.

Wynter twisted in the saddle, trying to see Christopher. But Ozkar chose that time to turn on the too narrow path. His hooves slipped on the shale, and Wynter was sent lurching forward as his front legs slid over the edge of the bluff. She grabbed his mane to keep from sliding head first down his neck and into the chasm below. For a moment she swung dizzyingly over the drop. There was a brief, distressing glimpse of Razi, his red coat a vivid splash of colour on the rocks below, then Wynter pulled herself upright and leaned back in the saddle, giving Ozkar a chance to gain his feet.

Once turned, the horse dropped his head and lashed out with both hind legs. With a solid *whump* and a brief howl, the wounded Loup-Garou was kicked from the path. It sailed far out into the air before plummeting into the gully below.

Christopher's riderless horse reared and lunged on the perilous track between Sól and Wynter. Between its trampling hooves, Christopher was locked in furious combat with a second Loup-Garou. Wynter drew her sword. She heaved Ozkar into line, intent on stabbing the Wolf's back. But before she could act, Christopher and the Wolf rolled to the edge of the path and plunged down the slope. Wynter caught a glimpse of Christopher, his eyes yellow, his teeth bared, and then he and the Wolf slithered from sight in a rattle of stones and debris.

Sólmundr yelled hoarsely and Wynter spun just in time to see a Loup-Garou land on him. Sólmundr was hidden beneath the Wolf's massive body. His mare threw her head, her eyes wild as the Wolf's hind claws scrabbled great, bloody tracks into her shoulders and neck. The poor horse slid and slipped about on the loose gravel, almost brought to its knees with the weight of its struggling burden of rider and Wolf.

Wynter urged Ozkar forward, trying to pass Christopher's maddened horse and get to Sól. She saw the warrior's fist jerk back, and Sól punched the Wolf's head away from his throat. His knife flashed and there was a spray of scarlet as he stabbed at the creature's neck. Boro leapt, snarling, and caught the Loup-Garou's hind leg in his huge jaws. There was a bright *snap* of bone and the Wolf arched, screaming. Wolf and hound fell away from Sól. Tumbling to the ground in a growling frenzy of teeth and fur, they engaged each other in battle.

Sólmundr was dazed, and painted with blood. He slid sideways in his saddle. Wynter cried out to him, certain that he would slip to the ground. But at the last minute he righted himself and clung blearily to his horse's blood-drenched neck as Boro and the Wolf tore into each other on the ground at its feet.

In an effort to escape the savagery of Wolf and dog, Christopher's horse launched itself off the edge of the path. It slid down the loose surface of the hill in a barely controlled panic of flying stones and grit, then tumbled head over heels on the unmanageable slope. Ozkar mindlessly tried to follow, and Wynter yanked him round and yelled, "Stay easy!"

The fifth Wolf breasted the hill, heading for Sólmundr. Wynter opened her mouth to shout a warning. A shadow crossed her, then something fell on her from above.

Her sword flew from her hand as a Wolf's weight flung her back, and she sprawled, helpless, under the creature's hot and reeking body. She twisted. The Wolf's teeth missed her throat by a fraction, snapping the air by her cheek. Ozkar went down on his haunches under their weight.

Still in the saddle, Wynter felt the Wolf's hind claws rake her belly as he tried to gut her. Her many layers of clothes saved her from immediate evisceration, but her jacket fell open with a gasp of torn fabric and she knew that the next raking pass of his feet would expose her guts to the air. She fumbled for her knife with one hand and shoved frantically with the other, trying to push him off. He reared back, half-Wolf, half-man, and glared down at her with his not-quite-human eyes. He opened his distorted mouth for the killing bite. Then Ozkar began to struggle to his feet, and Wynter felt herself and the Wolf slide off his rounded backside in one sudden uncontrollable rush.

Wynter clung to the Wolf and the Wolf clung to her. Their eyes met for the briefest of moments, then Wynter was upside down and dangling, one foot caught in the stirrup, trailing head first down the treacherous slope.

The Wolf shot past her with a howl. He grabbed Wynter's cloak to stop his fall, and swung to the end of it, dragging it tight. Wynter gagged. The fabric cinched closed around her neck, and she found herself completely incapable of drawing another breath. She turned bulging eyes to look back at the Loup-Garou, and he grinned up at her. He rolled in the gravel to twist the cloak tighter on her throat. Ozkar surged to his feet and Wynter was dragged up, her foot still caught in the stirrup. The world grew dark as she was stretched between Wolf and horse.

Wynter kicked and thrashed and scrabbled at her neck. She was horrified to feel her hands grow numb. Her arms grew weak. She was being strangled to death with her own cloak! Then the Wolf's weight lifted. The fabric loosened. Her lungs filled with cold air and she was jerked violently onto the rough path as Ozkar heaved her up.

Wynter's foot fell free of the stirrup. She rolled to her side and lay gasping at the edge of the path. There was a storm of angry snarling on the slope below her, then a flurry of stinging shale blasted her in the face as the Loup-Garou flung himself over the edge. Wynter groped blindly for her knife. The Wolf's weight squashed the air from her as he rolled across her body. Lashing out, she sliced him on his thigh. His weight left her. Then another Wolf scrabbled its way up the slope and lunged after the first.

Wynter swung at this second Loup-Garou, aiming for its eyes. But it dodged her, and to her amazement, it threw itself at its companion, locking its jaws against the other Wolf's throat. The creatures twisted away, rolled beneath Ozkar's plunging feet and slammed against the base of the bluff wall. Confused, Wynter jerked to her knees as the second Wolf—small, sleek and jet black—took on the grizzled might of the first.

On the path behind her, Sólmundr staggered to his feet. Boro was still battling the huge Wolf that had dragged Sól from his horse, and the two animals collided over the headless body of the first Loup-Garou, their feet skittering and slipping about in its pooled blood. Sólmundr yelled a command to his dog. The wind whipped ribbons of gore from his arms as he lifted his sword high above his head. Boro leapt back, and the warrior brought his sword slicing down, cleaving the Wolf's head from its body. The corpse fell at Sólmundr's feet with two separate thuds.

"Stay still, Iseult!" cried Sólmundr. "We with you now!"

He attempted to slap Ozkar aside, and Boro, his hackles raised, crowded impatiently at his heels. Wynter rose to her feet, her dagger in her hand, her eyes on the smaller, black Wolf who still had his teeth locked around the throat of the Loup-Garou.

The black Wolf's lips pulled back from bloody fangs, and his eyes met Wynter's as he dug in and held firm. Wynter nodded, and the black Wolf shook his head, his teeth digging deep. Blood sprayed up. The Loup-Garou howled in pain. Its fierce claws gouged at the black Wolf's belly. Its teeth snapped at his shoulders in an effort to break free.

Wynter advanced in a crouch, her dagger out. Sól, still struggling to pass Ozkar, shouted at her to stay back. At the sound of his voice, the Loup-Garou twisted, and Wynter saw terror rise in its eyes as it took in the blood-soaked warrior and his gigantic warhound.

Desperate, the Loup-Garou slammed the black Wolf against the bluff wall and tried to shake him from its throat. The black

Wolf clung tenaciously on, but the Loup-Garou was bigger and stronger, and it slammed the black Wolf hard against the bluff again, blood scattering in big drops against the rocky walls. The black Wolf's frightened eyes met Wynter's as the Loup-Garou shook him like a rag, and Wynter knew he could not last much longer.

With a yell, she reared up and plunged her knife between the Loup-Garou's shoulders. It surged abruptly to its hind legs and shook its entire body, dragging the black Wolf and Wynter with it as it rose. The black Wolf fell away, taking a great chunk of his opponent's throat with him. Wynter, her hands still clenched around the handle of her knife, felt the Loup-Garou's muscles ripple beneath her. Then she was clinging to a man, tall and broad-shouldered and unbelievably strong. He flung himself backwards and slammed Wynter against the rocks, knocking the air from her. But it was the last desperate act of a dying man. The strength left his legs almost immediately, and he slid to the ground with a sigh, his throat gaping, his torso scarlet with blood.

Dodging past the horses, Boro flew for the black Wolf, his teeth bared, and the Wolf sped past Wynter, yelping and crying in fear. Wynter lurched from the rock and flung herself after them. Catching a handful of Boro's fur, she clung on, trying to slow him down, but her weight made not one whit of difference. The warhound swerved beneath her, trying to get a grip on the black Wolf as it dodged and twisted to avoid his snapping teeth.

Behind her, there was a sing of metal on stone as Sólmundr separated the Loup-Garou from his head. Boro swerved beneath her again, doubling back on himself as the black Wolf made another attempt to bolt. Wynter screamed, "Sól! Call him off!

Call him off!" Boro's huge jaws closed on flesh and fur, ripping a scarlet gash in the black Wolf's leg.

"Sól!" screeched Wynter. "It's Christopher! Call Boro off! Call him *off*!"

"*Frith an Domhain!*" Sól yelled. He called urgently to Boro. "*Tar anseo!*"

The hound broke off immediately and Wynter fell to her hands and knees, face to face with the black Wolf who was cowering by the base of the cliff wall. His hackles were raised in a spiky ruff around his snarling face, and his teeth and fur were red with blood. For one moment, staring into his slanting yellow eyes, Wynter was certain that she had made a mistake. Then the Wolf dropped to his belly with a whine, his eyes filled with pain, and he blinked around him in confusion and despair.

"It's all right, Christopher," she whispered, shuffling forward on her knees. "It's all right." She put her arms around him, pulling him in. He trembled against her, and as if in echo to his trembling, Wynter's entire body started to shake. Sólmundr staggered over, his bloody sword trailing in the dirt, and he sank to his knees by her side, all his strength gone.

Wynter felt the numbing blanket of shock settle down around her as she scanned the headless bodies, the gore-spattered path, the quaking horses. In her arms the black Wolf whined and she felt his body shudder as his human nature struggled to the fore. As the changes began to take their toll, Sólmundr drew off his bloodstained cloak and laid it across their friend's shivering body. Wynter held on while Christopher came back to them, and as she waited, her eyes were fixed on the slope and the motionless patch of red at its base.

Vigil

"I not be long," rasped Sól. "The mule will not to have gone far, then I ride to end of pass, try find good way down for to bring the horses."

"Yes, yes," said Wynter, her eyes on Razi's body far below.

Sólmundr glanced at Christopher, who was just finished buttoning his jacket. "You all right for slope, *luichín*?"

Christopher nodded and pulled his cloak around him, tying the stays with shaking hands.

Sól grunted uncertainly. "I be with you soon," he said. "You not do nothing till I with you, *tá go maith*? You not move him or nothing till I get there?"

Satisfied with their compliance, the warrior heaved himself painfully into the saddle and clucked Ozkar on. His own horse limped behind at the end of a lead line, and Boro ranged ahead, following the scattered trail of goods left by the fleeing pack mule.

Christopher pushed himself to unsteady feet. Wynter glanced back, then put her foot over the edge. "I'm going ahead," she said. "You take your time."

She started down without waiting for him to join her, dropping almost immediately to her arse and angling her descent to try and maintain some control. It was hellishly unstable. She scrabbled crab-wise down the slope, digging her heels and hands into the harsh ground in an effort to control her speed. Rocks and loose pebbles showered down on her from above as Christopher began his own descent. Wynter forced her attention from Razi and scanned the narrow gully, looking for the horses and the Loup-Garou that Christopher had felt certain he'd left wounded but still alive amongst the rocks.

The Wolf that had carried Razi over the edge lay sprawled and unmoving on the opposite side of the gully floor, its neck twisted unnaturally, its long, dark hair covering its face. Even dead, even naked and vulnerably human, it frightened Wynter by its presence. She wished that Sól had gone down ahead of her with his sword and taken this Wolf's head from its shoulders, the way he had all the others. Her eyes kept switching anxiously between it and Razi.

Halfway down, there was an abrupt increase in the hail of rocks from above, and Christopher yelled as he lost control of his speed. He hurtled down the hill towards her, and Wynter turned her face away as he sped past in a stinging spray of stones, trailing dust and a fluid litany of curses behind him. He tumbled once, star-fished frantically onto his belly, and spun a slow, lazy circle as he reached the lower slopes. Wynter scrambled after him, only slightly more in control of her descent, and they both slid to a halt in a drizzle of stones and dislodged soil.

They got to their feet, sand and small rocks dribbling from every fold of their clothes, their bloodstained faces now white with dust. They stood stock still for a moment, gazing at their friend's motionless body. Then Wynter bolted for Razi.

Christopher ran to the Loup-Garou, drawing his katar as he went. He swung the sword above his head, and Wynter turned her back as he brought it down. She had had enough of blood for today, even Loup-Garou blood, and though she wanted the creature disposed of, she could not witness the deciding blow. As Christopher's sword separated the Wolf's head from its shoulders, Wynter knelt at Razi's side. He was breathing, but her heart squeezed at his lack of movement. She hesitated, desperately wanting to help but not knowing where to start.

"Help me fix his cloak," she whispered as Christopher's scuffed boots came into view. "It's all twisted around his head."

"Is he alive?" he said, his voice curiously flat.

At her nod, Christopher fell to his knees as if his legs were unhinged. He flung his sword onto the gravel behind him and knelt over their friend, his hands poised. "What do we do?" he cried. "Sól said not to move him!"

Wynter tugged Razi's cloak from its uncomfortable tangle around his neck and pulled it down to cover his body, tucking it in around him as if he were a child at bed time. He was utterly limp, his dark face slack. Apart from some raw patches on his cheek and jaw, he seemed otherwise unharmed.

"What do we do?" cried Christopher again.

Wynter looked up at the empty path, praying for Sól's return. "I don't know," she whispered. Clenching her hands in the fabric at Razi's chest, she forced herself not to say the words that sprang most easily to mind in such a situation, *Get Razi. Call Razi. He'll know how to fix it.*

"He not wake at all?"

Wynter shook her head, watching while Sólmundr pushed his fingers into Razi's hair, palpated the back of Razi's head, pressed Razi's temples, squeezed his skull.

"He not bring up sick?" murmured the warrior. "He not move? He not make sound?"

Again, Wynter shook her head. Sólmundr ran his hands down

Razi's ribs, felt along his arms, squeezed the bones of Razi's legs. Then he sat back, gazing down into Razi's unresponsive face. "He not broken," he said quietly. "He seem good." He smiled reassuringly at Wynter. "You not to worry, *a luch*. We must just to wait. Soon Tabiyb will to wake."

"It's getting on to dark," said Christopher. "We need to take shelter. I can't find the other Loup-Garou body. I'm fair sure it's dead, but still, it means there could be two of them out there."

Sólmundr nodded gravely. "Come on," he said, rising to his feet. "You help for to carry him."

Sól insisted on a fire. He insisted on hot food. He made antiseptic tea and washed out their wounds. They huddled together in the cramped space between leaning boulders as the wind moaned and growled its way down the pass and the light seeped from the sky. Razi did not so much as stir. He seemed dead, lying there swaddled in his cloak, and Christopher sat with his hand on his chest, staring out past the tiny circle of fragile light as the gritty dusk turned to night. Wynter sewed her jacket. Sólmundr bound the terrible bites on Boro's legs.

"Tomorrow you help me tie up the mare," he said softly, his face intent as he tended the hound. "I must try burn shut tear in her shoulder."

"It will abscess," murmured Christopher. "I'll sew it up for you and we can pack it in mud to keep the flies off."

Out in the restless night, something big came clattering down the rocky path, and the three of them froze, their hands reaching for their swords. The sound of hooves echoed from the gully walls and they heard Ozkar whinny in greeting as horses approached the camp. Wynter crawled to the edge of the firelight and peered around the rocks. Razi's big mare came trotting from the shadows, Christopher's sturdy little horse at her side.

Their saddles sat crooked on their backs, their tack and equipment trailing behind. Wearily, they joined their herd-mates at the highline, their shapes merging in the semi-dark.

"*Jesu Christi*," she whispered and crept out to check their condition.

Christopher came out to guard her, his eyes on the shadows, his sword in his hand.

"They are in rude health," breathed Wynter in awe, releasing the poor creatures from their tangled burdens. "They have hardly a scratch!"

Christopher nodded tightly and gestured that she hurry up. The wind had died to a gusting breeze and a narrow moon cast inkwell shadows from rock and crevasse. His eyes roamed this darkness constantly, his bruised face grim.

As Wynter hoisted the saddles from the horse's tired shoulders, a howl rose up from the rocks above them. Long, protracted, filled with loss; it was the lonely call of the remaining Loup-Garou. There was no threat in the sound, only sorrow, only pain, and as Wynter laid the saddles on the ground and backed carefully to Christopher's side, the Wolf's voice fell to a sobbing moan and died away. The horses trembled and huddled a little closer but showed no greater signs of fear than that. Boro did not even growl.

Christopher took Wynter's arm, tugging her backwards, and they edged their way slowly to the fire. The howl rose up again, moaning its hurt to the moon.

"It's wounded," whispered Christopher. "It won't attack." And he pulled her back down between the leaning rocks and into the warm radiance of the firelight.

The night turned to morning. The morning spun towards noon.

*   *   *

Sólmundr hunkered in the opening between the rocks and laid his sword across his knees. He squinted against the midday sun as he scanned the bluff above, the breeze tousling at his loose hair and tugging his cloak. "We not find them," he rasped. "There is signs of at least one, moving about in the rocks, but I not find body of other. It might to be still alive but I doubt it. It fall very far."

"It likely fell down between the rocks," said Wynter dully. "It's nothing but meat for crows by now."

Sólmundr ceased his restless scanning of the skyline and peered in at her. He didn't ask how Razi was; any fool could tell that the young man's condition hadn't changed. Sucking his teeth, the warrior met Wynter's eyes, the obvious question clear in his face. She sat beside her motionless friend and stared back at him.

"We wait," she said.

Sólmundr sighed, and his eyes dropped to the diplomatic folder lying across Wynter's knee. For a moment Wynter thought he would speak, that he would be the one to say the very thing she was thinking. But the warrior just nodded, rose to his feet and went to help Christopher tend to the horses. Wynter frowned in misery and squeezed her eyes shut, her hands closing around the leather covers of the folder.

This was day six of their ten-day journey. Alberon was at this very moment travelling the lower slopes somewhere with his entourage of men, already five days into his own trek home. Every moment that they delayed here was a moment stolen from Alberon. Regardless of their circumstances, the unheeding clock of their plan ticked relentlessly on. If Razi did not get to the castle in time to appease the King, if Alberon turned up in advance of his brother—the consequences would be catastrophic.

We can afford one or two days' delay, thought Wynter bleakly. *Certainly we can afford that!* Even if Razi took two full days to recover, they would still make it home three days ahead of Alberon. Three days would be plenty of time for a man like Razi to persuade the King. Wouldn't it?

Beside her, Razi breathed on, the steady rise and fall of his chest the only indication that he was alive. Wynter clutched the diplomatic folder to her chest and willed him to wake.

Noon passed. The sun set. Night crept in once again.

"It's just a suggestion," said Christopher softly. "I think you should consider it."

"No."

"But it makes perfect *sense*! Why must you be so damned exasperating?"

"In what way does it make sense, Christopher Garron? Tell me how, by any stretch of anyone's fertile imagination does it make sense for *you* to turn up at the castle bearing papers from the Rebel Prince?"

Presumably in some kind of effort to prevent his brain exploding, Christopher clutched his head between his hands and squeezed. "I will explain that the Lord Razi is wounded in the hills and that I am speaking on his behalf," he grated. "Sól and Boro will protect yourself and Raz until the soldiers come to find you. It's. Perfectly. *Reasonable*."

"The Wolves will kill you."

"Oh, don't be ridiculous!"

"The Wolves will kill you, and if *they* do not, the King's men will."

Christopher scrubbed his face with his hands and muttered darkly in Hadrish. Sól sighed and threw some dried horse dung onto the fire. The moon was dark, the sky heavy with clouds. Beyond their little ring of firelight the night pressed thick and impenetrable, the air made unbearably cold by the wind.

The Loup-Garou howled low and mournful in the rocks above, and Sólmundr grimaced out into the darkness. "I going to kill that *cac*!" he hissed.

The damnable creature had remained hidden all through the daylight hours, but as soon as darkness had fallen, it had resumed its melancholy song. Boro growled, but Sólmundr refused to let the big dog be drawn out into the rocks. He did not trust that the Loup-Garou really was alone.

"Iseult," persisted Christopher, "look at me. *Lass*, look at me!"

She looked at him, her face set.

"Iseult," he said gently, "we can't let him down. What will he say if those papers don't get through? What'll he think if we continue to just set here on our arses and let precious time dribble through our fists? At least if I go ahead there's a chance of setting things straight. At the very least it might make their dad think twice about shooting off arrows when Alberon rides into sight."

Christopher waited for her reply, his face earnest in the unsteady light. He was so utterly convinced that he could make it past the gate guards and into the King's presence that Wynter wanted to kiss him. Razi's chest rose and fell beneath her hand, their friend as still and as silent as the day before.

"If Razi has not woken by tomorrow," she said, "we will strap him to his horse and finish the journey together. None of us goes on without him."

Sólmundr glanced up at her, but said nothing. He didn't have to point out how risky that journey might be for Razi; they all knew it.

"It's the only way," she said. "Regardless of what the people may think of him, Razi is still his Royal Highness the Prince, heir to the Southland's throne. In his company, no one will prevent our access to the King. Without him, what are we? Nothing but a Northern savage, a gypsy thief and a disgraced murderess, carrying between them the incendiary papers of a rebel prince already declared *mortuus in vita*. Forgive me, but if any of us attempted entering the castle without Razi by our side, we would be dead before we set foot on the moat bridge. Even if Razi..." she paused, the words too hard to articulate. Then she forced herself to go on. "Even should he die, we shall still have to bring him with us. Without him we have no hope. With him, there is at least the slimmest of chances that our story will be heard."

She could not look into their faces, though she could imagine Christopher's expression well enough.

"That's what you want to do?" he said. "You want to strap Razi to his horse like a bundle of luggage, and offer him up to his dad as if he were goods being exchanged for favour?"

"Yes."

"You want to trek him across these mountains, regardless of what it does to his health?"

"Yes, Christopher."

There was a long, bitter silence and she finally glanced up. "Please don't look at me like that," she said softly. "Please, Christopher. Don't." He shook his head and tightened his jaw, and she set her face against his anger. "Tell me something," she said, her voice harder than she would ever have wished it to be, "if the choice were given to Razi himself, what would he do?"

She looked from Christopher to Sólmundr, challenging them to tell her anything but the truth. They dropped their eyes and she nodded. "We leave tomorrow," she said. "All of us. So get some sleep, it is my turn to watch him."

Day Seven: Both Sides of the Coin

"Come here and eat."

Wynter gave the pack mule's straps one last tug and followed Sólmundr to the fire. Christopher handed them a bowl of porridge and they ate in silence. On the path above them, buzzards squawked and scuffled, their huge wings rustling as they fought over the dead. More circled in the sky overhead, scanning for predators before spiralling down to join the grisly meal. Sólmundr had dragged the nearest Loup-Garou corpse up into the rocks, flinging its head after it like a shot put. There too, buzzards hopped and quarrelled as they ate their fill. Wynter tried not to listen; she would be happy to leave those sounds behind.

"I'm done." Christopher threw his bowl to the ground. "You clean that." He got to his feet, snagged a waterskin and headed for Razi who still lay within the shelter of the rocks. "I'll see if I can get him to drink. Call me when we're ready to go."

Wynter and Sólmundr exchanged a glance and went on with their breakfast. It was the most their friend had said all morning.

"Oh!" cried Christopher. They both turned to see him drop to his hands and knees and peer into the shadows of the rocks. He smiled broadly. "Hello," he said.

"Hello," answered Razi.

Wynter and Sól flung their bowls aside and ran to crouch at Christopher's side. Razi was sitting against the rocks, his covers tangled around his legs. He seemed so startled by their abrupt appearance that Wynter couldn't help a shaky laugh.

"Hello, Razi," she whispered. "How do you feel?"

"Fine," he said.

"Your head it not pain you?"

Razi turned his dark eyes to Sól. He thought for a moment. "My neck hurts," he said. "I feel stiff."

"Come out of there, man!" cried Christopher. "Have something to eat!"

Razi emerged, blinking, into the sunshine and they guided him to the fire, supporting him on either side as if he were an old man. Wynter sat him down on a rock.

"You want to drink?" asked Sól. "You thirsty?"

"I'm thirsty," said Razi.

Sólmundr offered him the waterskin. Razi took it, but then just sat with it in his hand, gazing at it. Sól flickered a glance at Wynter. "You not thirsty, then?" he asked.

Razi just kept looking at the waterskin, as if uncertain what it was.

"Um...are you hungry?" asked Christopher, snatching away the water and thrusting a bowl of porridge into Razi's hand. "You must be hungry."

"I'm hungry," agreed Razi, but he made no effort to touch the food.

"Then eat it," said Wynter, her heart beginning to flutter in her chest. Razi gazed up at her, his eyes wide with uncertainty. "*Eat* it, Razi," she cried.

Razi ate the porridge, scooping it mechanically into his

mouth. When he was finished, he left his fingers in the bowl and sat there, puzzled, food on his lips.

"Razi…" ventured Wynter, but his look of strained confusion stopped her from asking, *What is wrong?*

There was a moment of silence between them. Then Christopher took the waterskin, dampened the corner of his cloak with it and wiped Razi's face and fingers clean.

"Come on," he said hoarsely, helping Razi to his feet. "We're going."

When Razi saw the horses, saddled up and ready to go, his face lost all its puzzled vacancy and he broke away from his friend and went to his mare. She whinnied and stamped, happy to see him.

"Hello, darling," he said, stroking her noble face.

Wynter got slowly to her feet as Razi confidently went through his usual pre-ride check. Apparently oblivious to the terrible scratches and cuts on the poor animal's skin, he ran his strong hands down her legs and checked her hooves. He made a careful examination of her horribly scuffed tack, tightened the girth and checked the balance of the saddlebags. Satisfied, he patted the lovely animal on her bruised neck, murmured in Arabic that she was "a wonderful beast" then swung smoothly into the saddle.

Backing the mare from between the other horses, Razi drew her around and smiled at Christopher with the same politeness that he would give any groomsman in any tavern stables.

"Thank you, my man," he said. "She's in fine form."

"Yes," whispered Christopher.

"You took good care of her."

"Yes. Thank you."

At his friend's bleak stare, Razi lost his certainty for a moment, and his eyes hopped from Christopher to Wynter and back.

In the ensuing silence, Sólmundr gathered up the breakfast things and roughly scoured them clean. "Let us to go," he said, and crossed to stow the equipment and take to his horse.

"Are you joining us, young lady?" asked Razi. "This seems a bleak enough place to linger. It might be wise to stick with us for a while. At least until we're somewhere more hospitable."

"All right," she whispered.

Razi frowned in sympathy. "Don't cry," he said, "we shan't let anything happen to you." He smiled—Razi's warm, encouraging smile, now completely devoid of any trace of recognition—and gestured for Wynter to get onto her horse. "Come along, it will be all right now. We'll look after you. Pretty soon you'll be home and safe, and all this will seem like a bad dream."

Wynter took to the saddle. Everyone waited, as usual, for Razi to take the lead, but he simply sat there. After a moment, he glanced anxiously at Christopher, and there was some small hint in his expression that he knew something wasn't right.

"I am sorry," he said, "but I'm not too certain where we are headed."

Christopher's face creased for just a moment, then he nodded, cleared his throat and pulled ahead, leading the way up the gravel path to the head of the gully. Razi's expression cleared of all doubt and he fell unquestioningly in behind Christopher's little mare, absolutely content to allow someone else lead the way.

Christopher led them from the relative tranquillity of the gully back into the unrelenting gales of the mountain passes. The wind snatched all attempts at communication from them, and for hours they travelled with their heads down, their eyes squinted against the blasting air.

Fear and shame vied in equal measure for dominance within Wynter. Her reaction to Razi's condition was a gall in her heart. Battling the gale and her own anxious thoughts, she was appalled to find herself dwelling more on the effect that Razi's confusion would have on the kingdom rather than on Razi himself. Had her friend been limp and unconscious, it would have been easier to fret for him. But there he was, strong as ever, guiding his mare with his usual skill through the harsh mountain terrain. Yet he was completely useless.

Useless? My God! When had she ever judged Razi by his uses to her? Yet she was incapable of weighing her joy at his apparent health over the damage that his condition might do to Alberon's delicate negotiations. Even her hope that Razi would soon recover was overshadowed by fear that he may not recover *soon enough*.

They turned a corner—quite literally the path took a sharp branch left and down—and suddenly the wind was gone. It was as if someone had shut the door in a quiet room, blocking the storm outside, and for a moment the effect was almost stunning. Wynter straightened, blinking. Behind her, Sól's saddle creaked as he turned to regard the path behind them. The wind could still be heard there, moaning past the narrow mouth of the ravine, rushing like water through the pass they had just left.

"*Frith an Domhain*," murmured Sól, unwrapping his scarf.

It was much warmer without the breeze, and Wynter quickly divested herself of cloak and scarf. As they rode on, the men did the same, though it was not clement enough to do without jackets.

The further they ventured into the ravine, the quieter it grew. This sudden silence made Wynter feel vulnerable some- how, as if they were the only prey in a darkly shifting world of silent predators. Unease settled on the party and they rode with heads swivelling on tense necks, eyes scanning the loose gravel slopes and precipitous bluffs overhead. The horses' footsteps echoed from watchful cliffs and Boro's skittering expeditions onto the shale sounded horribly loud.

Christopher scanned the jumbled slope below them, his eyes hopping from rock to rock, while Razi's attention seemed focused on the rough landscape that loomed to their left. Boro repeatedly tried to run up into those same boulders, his hackles raised, but Sólmundr kept him firmly to heel. Wynter, however, kept her eyes on Razi, and as soon as the path widened she kicked forward to ride side by side with him.

"There is someone up there," he murmured. "My horse can sense them."

"It is a Loup-Garou," said Wynter, regarding him closely. "He is tracking us. I suspect there is another in the rocks below."

Razi seemed more surprised than disturbed. "Loup-Garou?" he said. "I have heard that they are vile creatures. Your friend is right to keep his crossbow strung."

He went back to scanning the rocks. His calm acceptance of the situation was terrifying; his lack of questions bizarre.

"Razi?" asked Wynter.

He smiled, and glanced kindly at her. "You should really call me 'my Lord'," he said. "My knights might take offence otherwise. Though in private you may call me, 'Razi', I shall not mind."

Who does he think I am? thought Wynter in despair. "Razi!" she cried, drawing his full attention again. "Where do you think we *are*?"

Wynter saw confusion rise up in Razi's face.

"What do you think we're doing here?"

Obviously, neither question had occurred to him, and he looked about him as if for the first time. "I..." he said. "We..." Not finding an answer readily to hand, Razi's confusion rapidly turned to panic. "I should know that," he said, the knowledge that something was wrong suddenly very clear in his face.

"I should *know* that!" he cried. "I *do* know that! It's *here*!" He clutched his forehead, as if to capture a black shadow there. "It's right *here*! OH!"

Razi slammed his fist into his temple, startling his mare and causing her to throw her head in fear. Razi hit his temple again, very hard, as if trying to dislodge something within his brain, and Wynter grabbed his arm, appalled.

"Don't!" she cried.

"But I should *know*!" he shouted, his horse pawing and dancing beneath him. "I should *know*."

"It doesn't matter," called Christopher.

Razi reined his panicked horse to a standstill and stared at his friend with anxious hope.

"It's all right," said Christopher.

"You are sure?"

"Yes. You know your name, do you not?"

Razi nodded. Christopher did not ask, as Wynter would have done, *Do you know what it means? Do you recall who your father is?* Instead he waited patiently while Razi turned to look at Sólmundr. The warrior smiled sadly and raised his chin in greeting.

"I...I am the Lord Razi Kingsson," murmured Razi, turning to scan Wynter's face, "al-Sayyid Razi ibn-Jon Malik al-fadl."

"There you have it," said Christopher, and he turned his horse without meeting Wynter's eye and set off up the trail again. "That is all that counts."

Razi relaxed instantly. "Ah," he said. "Good." He laughed ruefully. "Good. That's very good."

But it's not *all that counts!* thought Wynter. *It's not all that counts at all.*

Up in the rocks, something snickered. Wynter and Christopher crouched in their saddles, reaching for their swords. The sly, dirty sound skittered from rock to rock around them and slithered its way in echoes from the cliffs above. Boro tried to bolt after it, but Sólmundr snapped at him, "*Tar anseo*," and the warhound came reluctantly to heel.

Razi did not crouch. Instead he straightened indignantly and glared into the rocks with absolute disdain. "Loups-Garous vermin," he hissed. "Surely there's something that can be done about the damned things?" And with a tut of disapproval, he swung his horse around and nodded for Christopher to lead the way.

They journeyed until late into the evening, when the waning light made the uneven ground too treacherous and the danger of Wolves too dire to continue on. Still deep in the heart of that silent, echoing valley, they set up camp in a sheltering alcove of rock.

The horses tended to, the equipment checked, Wynter once more took Alberon's folder and sat with it across her knee. She ran her hands across its plain cover and contemplated the impact it would have upon the kingdom. Glancing at Razi, she wondered how he would have tackled presenting this to his father. Certainly he did not believe in Alberon's plans. In fact, they seemed to go against his very nature. But, despite his very great difficulty in seeing Alberon's point of view, Wynter was certain Razi would have done his best to represent his brother's argument. She could not fathom how he would go about defending a plan so contrary to his own personal beliefs, but if anyone could have managed the task, it would have been Razi.

Now, as her friend placidly watched the sun withdraw its dismal light from the valley, Wynter hugged the folder to her chest and fretted over what was going to happen. Razi had not recognised these documents when she had shown them to him, and he had simply gazed curiously at her when she had tried to explain his mission. The urge to grab him and shake him and scream, *What are we going to do?* had been almost too much to handle. But, despite her frustration, Wynter did not want to cause another of Razi's horrible panics, and so, faced with even this mildest of confusion, she had risen to her feet and walked away from him. Razi had been sitting, ever since, with his back to the cliff wall, completely still and passive. Wynter thought he had never looked so serene, and to her shame, that infuriated her.

Sólmundr hummed as he cooked the supper. Boro lay at his side, his chin on his paws. Now and again, the giant hound's ears would swivel upwards and he would growl at something unseen in the rocks above. But he was used, by now, to Sólmundr calling him back, and he made no attempt to run off to what Sól was convinced would be a fatal encounter with not one, but two Loups-Garous.

Christopher was fussing with the mule-packs. He too was driving Wynter mad, though it was hard for her to understand why. It was not really that she *blamed* him for the terrible encounter with the Wolves. It was more, oh God forgive her, that she wanted him to blame *himself.* At least a little. At least to the extent that she could then hug him and tell him, "This is not your fault." But Christopher's reaction to Razi's condition was so calm, so hard-faced and practical, that it left Wynter with no room for anything—not anger, not forgiveness, not even affection. Christopher had become remote and as brittle as ice. He cursed quietly to himself, tugging at the luggage, and Wynter was just about to ask him to stop fiddling and to sit down, when he strode past her, something in his hand.

"Here," he said crouching by the fire and plopping the doctor's bag at Razi's feet.

Sólmundr tensed. Razi frowned uncertainly, and Wynter sat straighter, clutching the folder to her chest. She waited for Christopher to demand, "Do you know what this is? Do you recognise it?" But instead, he snapped the catches on the bag and opened it.

Razi jerked forward, as if tempted to stop him.

"It fell off the mule," said Christopher, peering inside. "Some of the vials are broken."

"Be careful!" Razi shot out a hand and grabbed Christopher's wrist, stopping him from reaching into the bag. Gently he pushed the young man's hand aside. "If you cannot tell the contents of the broken vial, a cut could prove disastrous." He smiled reassuringly at his friend. "I should like to check it for myself."

Christopher watched as Razi took the bag and began an expert survey of its contents. As their friend sorted through the tools of his trade, Wynter saw Christopher working himself up to speak. As he struggled to articulate his question, Christopher's emotions seemed to worm their way to the surface of his composure so that when he finally spoke, his expression was achingly raw and vulnerable. It stabbed Wynter to see all the hurt and all the guilt that he had been hiding from her. She almost cried at the knowledge that Christopher had chosen not to share with her his pain and grief.

"Is anything important broken?" he finally managed.

How would he recall? thought Wynter bleakly. *He barely knows who he is.*

But Razi answered without hesitation. "There is not much damage. Just a few tonic vials and a crushed pill box." He glanced up, smiling, and it almost broke Wynter's heart when he said, "Everything is just as it is meant to be. Nothing of any importance is lost. What happened to it?"

"It fall when Wolfs attack," said Sólmundr.

Razi made no response to that, but his attention focused on Sólmundr's bruised face as if noticing the wounds for the first time. "That cut on your cheek is quite inflamed," he said. "I can treat it for you, if I may?" He must have mistaken Sól's silence for reluctance, because he smiled again. "I'm a doctor," he said. "Did you not realise that? Here, come over and I shall see what I can do."

As Sól submitted to Razi's care, Christopher gazed at Wynter. The knowledge of what had been retrieved was written large in his glittering eyes. Wynter tilted her head and smiled sadly, the knowledge of what remained lost written in her own.

Day Eight: Messages

Dawn did not break to birdsong in this particular valley, or even to rosy tinted skies. Instead, the light seemed to drizzle in, grey and uniform, as if seeping up from the rocks themselves.

Wynter pushed herself upright and groaned. *How do soldiers do this*, she wondered, *day after day on a campaign? Of all the tasks presented them, how do they ever manage to push their bruised bodies from bed?*

Alberon, she realised with a wince, would be the one to answer her that.

Carefully, she disentangled the covers and slipped from Christopher's side. Neither he nor Sólmundr stirred. Like all Merron, they trusted their warhound to guard them in the night, and Boro had been the camp's sole sentinel against the Loups-Garous.

"And a good job you did of it too," she whispered, crouching to fondle his ears. He gazed ruefully up at her, not lifting his chin from his paws. In order to prevent him from running after the Wolves, Sólmundr had tethered the warhound to his ankle, and Boro could not quite reconcile himself to the indignity. There was a palpable air of embarrassment about him. "Never mind, dog," murmured Wynter. "You're still a big, brave beastie."

The hound sighed and submitted to her caresses with stoicism. Once again, Wynter thought what an incredible creature he was. Sól could make his fortune from the breed. She had observed as much to him the night before, and Sól had commented dryly that he preferred his lungs inside his ribcage, if it were all the same to her.

"It is a capital offence amongst our people to trade the *Cúnna* to strangers," explained Christopher.

"Though," observed Sól, "Shirken once plan to take them for himself." At his friends' expectant silence, Sólmundr had flashed his gap-toothed grin. "When enough of his men lose their heads, he give up idea. Even the puppies take man's hand off at the wrist. *Nach ea, mo ghadhar?*" he said, scrubbing Boro's head. "Only the Merron can to handle *na Cúnna Faoil.*"

"In that case I should have gifted Shirken ten of them," muttered Wynter. "Five for him and five for his pestilent daughter." At the men's lack of comprehension, she grinned. "Though the poor hounds would have need of a purging after, I should think."

Sólmundr laughed.

"The poor things would need more than a purge," smirked Christopher. "Shirken being rotten to his core, they would as likely die of poison."

Then Razi, chuckling, had asked, "Who is Shirken?" and the mirth had quickly drained from the conversation.

Wynter groaned at the memory and wandered across to where Razi stood a little apart from camp, staring up into the rocks above.

He glanced at her as she approached. "Those creatures have gone," he said.

"How do you know?"

"I have been watching since first light. Only a few moments ago I saw them running along the base of that ridge and move off in that direction. Your warrior friend is right, there *are* two of them."

Wynter pulled her cloak tight and shivered. "Where are they going, I wonder?"

"Even the devil's spawn needs to eat. I suppose they have gone to hunt."

She shrugged her cloak high around her neck and Razi winced at the bruising on her throat. "Your neck is livid," he said. "Do you have any difficulty swallowing...um...?" he peered at her, once again struggling to recall her name. He couldn't seem to hang on to it at all.

Wynter refrained from yelling, *I'm Wynter! It's Wynter, Razi! Try and remember!* Instead she said, "I am the Protector Lady Wynter Moorehawke, my Lord."

Razi frowned uncertainly; the formality seemed to take him by surprise.

"Delighted to meet you, Protector Lady," he said, bowing slightly. "If your chaperones don't mind, I would be pleased to check your throat."

She allowed him guide her to a rock and sat down, raising her chin while he gently probed her neck with his fingers. He did not once ask how she managed to ring her throat with bruises.

"Do you enjoy being a doctor, my Lord?

He smiled. "It is all I ever wanted to be."

"It is unusual enough. A king's son would surely find himself with more urgent things at hand than lancing boils and dressing scurvy." His fingers paused at her throat. She pressed on. "As a pastime it is commendable, but surely your duties in court would present you with tasks infinitely more important?" He sat back, staring at her, and she knotted her hands together, almost afraid to continue.

"You consider the relief of suffering to be a task beneath us?" he asked softly. "The saving of lives is, to you, a pursuit unworthy of a king's son?"

"Not at all," she said. "But a man such as yourself must surely have bigger obligations?"

"Obligations," whispered Razi.

"Yes, my Lord!" she urged, thrilled to see recognition flare in his eyes. "Do you remember? Do you remember what your obligations are?"

"Mary," he said in amazement. "How could I have forgot her?"

"Mary," said Wynter flatly. "You remember *Mary*."

"She needs my help."

"*Jesu Christi!*" Wynter threw her hands up despair. "Razi! I swear to God, if I need to shove you down another hill, I shall! You are bound to drive me to—" Before she could say any more, a horse screamed in the pass above them and a stranger's harsh cries of fear had them surging to their feet.

Boro tried to run up the shingle slope, barking and straining against his chain, eager to get to the fray. Sólmundr was dragged several feet, his cursing muffled in the covers that had been drawn up over his head. Razi leapt across his kicking body and raced for the horses. As Wynter skirted the men, Christopher threw back his covers, grabbing his sword and shouted at her in hoarse Merron.

"*Cad é*, Iseult? What is it?"

"Get your weapons!" she yelled. "Something's happening on the ridge!"

She reached Ozkar just as Razi finished bridling his mare. Without waiting to saddle up, he grabbed the creature's mane and leapt on, urging her up the path. Wynter was no great lover of bare-backed riding, but she did the same. As she galloped past, Sólmundr released Boro and the warhound shot ahead of Razi's mare, streaking across the grey rocks like a shadow of the wind.

It did not take a moment for Sól and Christopher to catch up, and before Wynter was even halfway up the rocky path, the thunder of their horses was a reassurance at her back.

There was one rider, astride a tough little horse built for speed and endurance. The man was yelling and lashing out with his sword while a snarling Loup-Garou forced his mount to back towards the cliff-face. Unknown to the rider, the second Loup-Garou was slinking around behind him. Wynter was alarmed to see it making its way up the rocks to the shelf over the man's head, obviously planning to drop on him from above.

"Watch out!" yelled Razi, kicking his mare over the uneven ground. "Watch out! Above you!"

The rider did not hear and he kept valiantly lashing at the Loup-Garou, his terrified horse falling back with each of the Wolf's snarling leaps forward.

"Look up!" screamed Wynter.

Boro came into view then, shooting from between the rocks, and just as the first Loup-Garou leapt again for the horse's throat, the giant warhound flew through the air and tackled it. The two creatures rolled to the side in a savagery of teeth and fur, and the rider was left swiping at empty air for a moment. Thankfully, his horse shied sideways, away from the fighting creatures and out from under the ledge.

Behind Wynter came the familiar *thwack* of Christopher's crossbow. The bolt shot to the ledge above the rider and plunged itself into the ground next to the creeping Loup-Garou. Christopher spat a ripe curse as the creature leapt in fright and ran away, unharmed. At its companion's yipping retreat, the other Wolf broke free of Boro's clutches and raced, howling, into the jumbled rocks. Boro followed.

Wynter saw the man's relief turn to fear as he registered the four riders thundering towards him. He pulled his terrified horse around to face them, and she did not blame him that he crouched in his saddle and lifted his sword. She could not speak for herself, but her companions certainly made a wild spectacle. Dishevelled and fierce, they had their swords drawn and their unshaven faces were wicked with aggression. They were the very illustration of the word *bandits*. The poor fellow, his back literally to the wall, scanned their ranks for an opening through which to flee. As he readied himself, his intention obviously to barrel through their horses and take his chances, Wynter recognised him from King Jonathon's court.

"Andrew!" she yelled. "Andrew Pritchard! HOLD!"

At the unlikely calling of his name, Pritchard pulled his horse to, regarding them with wide-eyed amazement. Almost immediately, he recognised Razi's distinctive face. That seemed to terrify him even more than the thought of bandits, and, with a cry, he kicked his horse forward, hoping to shoot the gap between Christopher and Sól and escape down the path before they could turn.

"Stop him!" screeched Wynter, and in an act of quite astounding agility, Sólmundr threw himself from his horse's bare back and tackled Andrew Pritchard to the ground.

Pritchard fought and struggled, but Sól pinned him to the ground, his strong forearm pressed to his throat. "Be good, now!" Sól warned. "Be good!"

Christopher leapt from his horse, kicking the man's sword aside, and Wynter ran across to stand over him. At the looming ring of assailants, Pritchard yelled, trying in vain to push Sólmundr from him. Christopher grinned, wickedly amused at the poor man's panic.

"Calm down, friend," he said. "Pretty and all as you are, we ain't about to violate your chastity."

"*Jesu!*" screeched Pritchard and he kicked and writhed with extra ferocity.

"Lord Andrew!" snapped Wynter. "Be still! We shall not harm you!" She tapped Sól's shoulder with her sword and said in Hadrish, "Sól! Get off the poor man!"

Sólmundr leapt back, grinning, and he and Christopher levelled their swords at Pritchard's head.

"I will not talk," cried the lord, staggering to his feet. "You may save yourself the trouble of your barbarian tortures."

Razi came to Wynter's side, his face curious. Wynter leapt in before he could speak. "Lord Andrew," she began, but Pritchard's eyes were on Razi, and he spoke across her as though she were not there.

"We might have known it wasn't your head in that sack," he spat. "What poor black bastard did you have *that* done to? All that you might skulk about in safety and continue your plan to undo your brother!"

Christopher's fist came from nowhere, and Pritchard was back on the ground before Wynter registered the blow.

"That was the Lord Razi's *friend*!" hissed Christopher, leaning over Pritchard, his face like poison. "And he were brought down by the likes of *you*. So don't you lay that poor lad's death at the Lord Razi's feet, or so help me God, I'll skin you alive!"

This exchange was conducted in Southlandast and Sólmundr

could not possibly have understood it. Still, he responded to Christopher's anger by pressing his sword to Pritchard's throat, no trace of wicked humour left in his weathered face.

Pritchard, his hand to his nose, regarded Sól's blade through narrowed eyes, then glared up at Razi. "I will not betray the Prince to you," he said.

Razi looked at him with horrified confusion. He opened his mouth to speak and Wynter dropped to a crouch by Pritchard's feet, purposely drawing the man's attention before her friend could betray himself.

"Lord Andrew," she said, "you have mistaken the Lord Razi's intentions. You both work to a common purpose. My Lord Razi has only just left his brother's camp in the Indirie Valley. He travels now bearing papers from the Prince. He travels in the Prince's name, his task being to press the Royal Prince Alberon's case and to reconcile the true heir with his father the King."

Pritchard regarded her with court-wary eyes. Slowly his attention returned to Razi.

"We..." said Razi. Wynter's hands knotted. Razi cleared his throat, his voice strengthened. "We can show you the Prince's documents. If that would ease your mind?" Wynter briefly closed her eyes in relief. Even addled out of his wits, Razi was smooth as butter.

Pritchard sat slowly forward, and Wynter saw a strong desire to believe dawn in the man's face.

"My Lord Razi has been sent ahead of his Royal Highness," she assured him. "The Prince has bid him to smooth the way with their father. He intends to assure the King that there is no threat to his throne. To let the King know that his Royal Highness has no intention of staging a coup."

"I fear you are too late, my Lord," whispered Pritchard. "I fear

we may both be too late. I think the King may already have
lured your brother out, and I suspect he may already be set to
strike."

Razi gravely extended his hand. "Get up. Tell us everything
you know."

"I must hurry, my Lord," said Pritchard, accepting Razi's
assistance in climbing to his feet.

Sólmundr made a show of swatting the dust from Pritchard's
back and shoulders, and Pritchard shrugged him off with an
irritated snarl. Grinning, Sól began mockingly to fix the man's
dishevelled hair.

"Sólmundr!" snapped Wynter.

The warrior demurely spread his hands, displaying the two
little knives he had removed from Pritchard's person. Wynter
smiled.

Andrew Pritchard eyed Sól with murderous disdain. He
pushed his hair back off his face with no more discomposure
than if Sól had produced an iced bun from the folds of his cloak.
"I'll have those back, please," he said.

"When we're done talking," murmured Christopher.

Pritchard curled his lip and turned to Razi. "I must hurry, my
Lord. The King's plans have been in effect for much longer than
I can tell. I must try and reach the Royal Prince before he accepts
his father's invitation to parley."

Wynter exchanged a glance with Razi. He was doing his best
to play along, but expecting him to bluff his way through this
was like asking a blind man to guess a colour by touch. Andrew
Pritchard took their silence as mistrust. "Good Christ!" he cried,
flinging his hands out. "Do we have an accord or not? We could
dance around ourselves for days here, or we can commence to
deciding a course of action. What shall it be, my Lord?"

"What is it you suspect the King of planning?" asked Razi in a commendably neutral attempt to move the situation along.

Andrew Pritchard's eyes skittered from Razi's dark face to Sól and Christopher.

"You can trust the Lord Razi's men," said Wynter.

Pritchard made no secret of his scepticism, but he went on nonetheless. "Some members of council were providing his Royal Highness with supplies and information. The King rooted them out. They were ... they were persuaded to talk." Pritchard's usual sneer turned nauseous and he frowned miserably.

"I am sure they were," muttered Christopher, sheathing his sword.

"From what little I understand, they gave up the meeting point for Prince Alberon's provisioners. When next the Prince's men arrived to collect supplies, the King's soldiers took them."

"Those poor men," whispered Wynter. "They were already two days overdue when we arrived in Alberon's camp."

"I doubt they were tortured, Protector Lady. The King's men had orders to send them back to the Prince carrying a message from his Majesty offering forgiveness and a chance to parley."

"It is a trap?" asked Razi.

Pritchard nodded. "I suspect so, my Lord. But I am days late finding these things out. The King has already left for his rendezvous, and though I race to warn the Prince, I fear he may already have departed his camp and moved beyond my reach."

"Alberon ..." breathed Wynter.

"It's possible the Prince did not receive the King's message," said Christopher. "He certainly hadn't by the time we left camp, and he was due to leave the very next day. It's possible that he's right at this moment travelling the slopes below us as we planned, heading home to the palace."

"If that is the case, my Lord Razi must get to the palace before him," said Pritchard. "Otherwise it will look as though the Prince is attempting a coup while the King is away. You must return and convince all parties involved to hold fire until legitimate parley has been established."

"It is useless us returning to the palace if the Prince is blithely heading to a rendezvous elsewhere!" cried Wynter.

"Perhaps we should all return to the camp," said Christopher.

"Where is the King planning on meeting the Prince?" asked Razi.

Pritchard shook his head. "His Majesty took off with a tiny entourage of men, but told no one of his destination. There have been reports of a camp settled by the Chér Ford. But I do not know for certain. I had to leave before I could confirm the sightings. Though a royal pennant was reported, I can't confirm that it is the King; it could be just rumours."

The Chér Ford. Wynter knew of it. Silted over with treacherous mud, its ferry house a ruin, the ford had not been used by travellers for generations. It was deep in the remote woods, and was three days' journey from the palace. If Alberon had received the King's message and had decided to act on it, rather than follow their plan to return home, he would almost be there by now. She had no doubt he would be riding into a trap.

"You must go, Lord Andrew!" she cried, pushing Pritchard to his horse. "You must continue to Alberon's camp and try and convey your message to him! You must *fly*!"

Christopher and Sól handed Pritchard his weapons and he leapt onto his horse.

"What will you do?" he shouted, holding the animal in place. They had no answer for him. "Get yourselves back to the palace! Keep the Lord Razi safe and wait for news." And with a brief, frowning look of despair he pulled his horse around and galloped back onto the trail.

Christopher watched Pritchard rapidly disappear from view. "I suppose it's useless offering my opinion," he said.

"Unless it differs from your usual suggestion that we leave this mess behind and head to the Moroccos," said Wynter.

"It doesn't have to be the Moroccos," he said. "Anywhere would do."

Wynter smiled sadly at him, and he sighed. "Come on, Sól. Let's get the horses, and call Boro in from his hunt."

"Huh," grunted Sólmundr as they turned to go. "You better explain to me that man or it danger that I get cranky."

The men began to walk away.

"Thank you, Christopher," called Wynter, not really wanting him to leave.

Christopher paused. He turned back. His eyes flitted briefly to Razi. "This is his chance, you know," he said. "It don't matter what they want, they can't make use of him now. He could be free, if you let him walk away. He could be free of the lot of them and we could all start afresh."

He stood for a moment, waiting for her reply, and when she couldn't give him one he nodded and turned away again. Wynter had the horrible feeling he was turning away for good.

"Christopher!" she cried.

He glanced back. "Hold your peace, woman," he said softly. "I'm only off to get the horses."

They smiled, each understanding the other, then, with a last glance at Razi, Christopher headed off to do his job.

"They delivered a man's head in a sack?" whispered Razi.

Wynter turned to him without answering.

"A friend of mine? They delivered his head in a sack?"

"Razi," she asked gently, "do you recall nothing at all?"

He put his hand to his head. "It does not bother me until I am prompted. Then I realise...I seem to have no thoughts!"

"That sounds peaceful," she said.

"It *is*!" he admitted. "It's really quite peaceful—until I realise that it is not normal." Razi glanced at her, almost ashamed and said, "I must confess, it does not sound like I have much worth remembering."

Is that what this is? she thought. *Have you surrendered?* "My Lord," she said carefully, "much as you might wish to, you are not a man who can afford to forget."

His face fell in horror and Wynter immediately regretted her suspicion. "You think I *feign* this?" he cried. "That I somehow *desire* to be this way? You think this is cowardice! That I shirk, and dissemble this affliction!"

"No, Razi!" She grabbed his arm. "No! Not at all!" But he had seen it in her face and he went to shake her off. "I'm sorry!" she said. "I'm sorry! Truly!"

His anger transformed to despair and he clutched her hand and squeezed it, looking around him in utter confusion. "I do not know what to do," he whispered.

"Well, we must do something, Razi. Even if it is to simply pick one action and stick with it to the last. We must do *something*. And we must do it *now*."

Day Ten: Irrevocably Committed

In the end it was Wynter who made the decision, and to her surprise the others fell in with it. It was a strange feeling, laying out the maps and plotting their route while three men nodded and listened intently to her opinions. She was unaccustomed to that. She was unaccustomed to the undiluted responsibility. It was terrifying.

Three days later, deep in the heart of a stately pine forest, she lay next to a tiny fire and watched as the last light of day drained from the tops of the trees. The knowledge of how randomly she had chosen this course of action burned in the pit of her belly; it lay like lead in her chest. Everything, *everything*, rested on her having taken a flip of a mental coin. There had been nothing logical about it. She had simply played an internal game of eeny-meeny-miny-mo and chosen a course of action by chance.

Each time she shut her eyes she saw Razi and Sól and Christopher as they had been when she persuaded them to do this. Brown eyes, blue eyes and grey, staring gravely at her and trusting her. *Jesu*. And tomorrow would reveal the truth. Tomorrow morning they would finally reach the Chér Ford, there to discover...what?

"You'll stick like that."

She startled and looked up into Christopher's smiling face. "Pardon?"

"You're lying there with your face knotted like a handkerchief... it'll stick like that if the wind changes." He plopped down beside her and shrugged his blankets around him. "I wouldn't be able to love you anymore if that happened, you know. You'd be much too ugly."

She laughed.

"Stop fretting," he whispered gently.

"I can't, Christopher. I really can't. What if I've made the wrong choice? What if we get there and all we find is the remains of some bandits' meet-up or the litter of a hunters' camp. We'll have wasted so much time. I'll have thrown all Albi's chances away."

"Lass," he took her hand, rubbed her knuckles with his thumb, "what's done is done. Truth is, you were the only one of us with balls enough to make a decision. Had you left us to it, we'd *still* be on that mountainside dithering to and fro while the Wolves snickered at us from the rocks."

"No, you wouldn't."

"Yes, we *would*. You quite ruined things for poor Sól, you know. He had lovely dreams of setting up home there with Razi. He'd picked a nice little spot for a hut and everything."

Sólmundr grimaced at him from across the flames and went back to checking Boro for ticks. "Razi should to be that lucky," he murmured.

"I still do not understand what purpose I shall serve you," said Razi softly. He tapped his temple. "I am as blank as a clean slate."

"You are our access to the King, Razi," said Wynter. "After that," she held up Alberon's folder, "these will have to speak for themselves."

He regarded the folder with uncertainty, sighed, and rubbed his forehead. "If you say so," he said and lay back, wrapping himself in his covers. His head was aching again, Wynter could tell by the tension in his eyes and mouth. She had hoped these headaches were signal to a change in Razi's condition, but so far they had been nothing but pain, mild, slightly nauseating, and totally free of the burden of memory.

Out in the darkness, the Loups-Garous began their low moaning, and Christopher threw his hands up in frustration and despair. "Good Frith," he said. "Bloody..." He jumped to his feet. "Shut up!" he yelled.

The Wolves chuckled and snickered. "Make us," they growled. "Come and make us, sly-boy." They drew the word "boy" out until it was something low and wicked and dirty. Wynter hissed in disgust.

Christopher kicked a stone into the darkness. "You come here," he muttered. "You slithering *caic*. I'll feed you to the dog."

"You calm down," said Sólmundr, "or I chain *you* to my ankle, and it be Boro that wriggle up beside your woman tonight."

"Why are they still here, anyway?" hissed Christopher prowling the edges of the shadows. "Why don't they go back to their master? WHY DON'T YOU GO BACK TO YOUR MASTER?" he shouted.

Sólmundr looked up at him, his face serious. "Because you giving them too much amusement, Coinín. Look at you! They play with you like a toy."

Christopher flung him a withering look and continued to prowl.

Razi, still lying back against his saddle, watched him pace, his dark eyes thoughtful. "David Le Garou," he said suddenly, and everyone turned to look at him. He nodded at the question in their faces. "I remember him. David Le Garou." He gazed at Christopher. "We owe him," he said darkly. "I remember that too."

Christopher stood very still, as if frightened to disrupt Razi's newly emergent thoughts. Wynter sat slowly forwards. Razi, his hands folded casually on his chest, looked from one to the other of them with the same mildly curious frown on his face. "You are both very good friends of mine, aren't you?" he said. "We've known each other a terribly long time."

Wynter nodded.

"I owe you both," said Razi. "I owe you much." Then he shook his head, sighed and shut his eyes. "Yet I still cannot recall your names."

"Do you remember your brother, Razi?"

"A small boy? Full of life? He loves his hounds... Oh," he cried, his eyes flying open in surprise. "I have remembered my father! He was a *wonderful* man! Gentle. Kind. He taught me much."

Christopher exchanged a glance with Wynter. "What did he look like?" he asked.

"But you knew him surely, Chris?"

At Razi's use of his name, Christopher's face crumbled in pain. Razi seemed to mistake this for confusion and he went on trying to describe his father. "He was a smallish man? With dark hair cropped close to his head? Slim, sallow face, big nose." Razi smiled in fond remembrance. " 'Bigger nose than head,' he used to say. He was a lovely person... I am fair sure you knew him."

"Oh, aye," whispered Christopher. "I knew him for a while, but..."

"But what?" Razi raised himself onto his elbow. "But *what*, friend?"

Christopher frowned desolately at Wynter and she shook her

head in dismay. "You are describing Victor St James, Razi—your tutor. Your father is the *King*. St James was certainly no king."

"But he was a doctor," whispered Razi. "He was a *wonderful* man."

Wynter nodded sadly. "But he was not your father," she said.

Razi lay back against his saddle again, lost in confusion.

Out in the darkness, the Wolves once more began to laugh. Christopher flung a stone in impotent rage. "Go *home!*" he yelled. "Go home! You poxy whoreson curs!"

Sólmundr sighed. "Your father may not be no doctor, Tabiyb, but he at least rid his kingdom of that vermin."

"Aye," muttered Christopher, "he did that."

"Then . . . then why are they here?" asked Razi.

"That was your damned brother," sneered Christopher, glaring out into the snickering darkness. "He invited the poxy things back." He glanced across, and the look on Razi's face made him laugh despite himself. "I know," he said in sympathy. "It's all just a mite too perplexing, ain't it?"

Late into the night, Wynter woke from a dream in which her father stood staring down into a valley of silent ghosts, his hands red with blood. She had been shouting across to him from the other side, *Dad? Dad! I don't know where I am.* But even as she called to him, Lorcan had turned and walked into the misty rain, and she had understood that she was all alone. She woke with the diplomatic folder clutched to her chest. She'd fallen asleep with it in her arms.

Christopher lay warm beside her, his strong arm looped around her waist. She slid carefully down under their covers until she could rest her chin against the top of his dark head, and she put her arm around him, pulling him closer.

"Y'all right?" he murmured, and she nodded. "Go asleep," he said. "They won't come near the dog."

She lay staring out into the impenetrable trees, holding Christopher close and listening to the Wolves as they whispered in the darkness beyond the light. She could think of nothing to say when she met the King. She could think of nothing to do. Across the fire, Razi's dark eyes reflected the light as he too lay awake, thinking. Sólmundr sighed and rolled over, grousing at his blankets.

"Lass," whispered Christopher, "go back to sleep."

But she didn't, and neither did he, and when dawn finally broke, it found them still lying there, staring pensively into the forest as the trees emerged slowly from the dark.

Day Eleven: Chér Ford

Well, it is still here, she thought, scanning the small group of plain tents, the one smoking camp fire. *But this is no royal party. There are too few men, no supply wagons, no military presence.* Her heart sank at the growing likelihood that she'd made the wrong decision. She had wasted so much time.

Enough of that! she told herself. *Christopher is right. What is done is done! We are but three days from the palace. If we hurry, we may arrive back on the same day as Alberon. Perhaps even hours ahead of him. It is possible that we still have some time.*

She looked back at her companions. She had insisted that they take the old cart road through the forest, approaching the ruined ford house from the east. This abandoned track was detailed on her map with the orange broken line of a "disused trail" and had been labelled "unpassable to cart and wagon." Certainly it was horribly overgrown, filled with light saplings, waist high in grass and snarled with trailing clots of bramble. But it was still relatively open ground when compared to the shadowy depths of the surrounding woods, and it made their approach easier and gave them a good view of the camp. More importantly, it allowed the camp to see them and reduced the all too likely danger of them being shot as spies.

Boro, bristling with hostility, tried to dash ahead through the high grass, but Sólmundr called him to heel. The warhound returned with great reluctance, barking and snarling into the trees and at the camp. Sólmundr snapped at him, obviously telling him to behave.

"It's difficult to tell from here," murmured Christopher, eyeing the small group of men who now stood shading their eyes and watching their approach. "But they don't look to be soldiers. I don't see no uniforms or pennants, nor any other fancy royal things."

"We were wrong," sighed Razi.

"We will pass on through," said Wynter. "It will be easier to follow the track around and back onto the main road. Then we must fly like the wind to the palace. *Jesu*, I cannot believe that I have made such a grave—"

"Go no further, travellers! You must needs turn back here."

Wynter jerked her horse to a dancing standstill as men emerged from the surrounding trees like shadows made flesh. They filled the path ahead and behind. Boro snarled and prowled, glaring up at Sól as if to say, *I tried to tell you.* The warrior sighed, lifted his hands from his sides, and told the hound, "*Tarraing siar!*"

Though they were dressed in ordinary clothes, the surrounding men levelled their crossbows at the travellers with all the dispassionate intent of professional soldiers, and Wynter's heart soared. She had never thought to see the day when she would be quite happy to have an arrow so coldly aimed for her heart. She lifted her hands above her head and grinned at the puzzled man whom she recognised as the lieutenant of the King's guard. Squinting up from the bushes, he was obviously thrown by her apparent delight.

"You must turn back now," he said slowly, convinced perhaps that she'd escaped from some bedlam and could not understand. "You cannot make use of this road."

"Thank you, lieutenant," she said. "I commend you for your vigilance. However, we come bearing papers for the King. I would be grateful if you would convey my greetings to him, and request please that his loyal servant, the Protector Lady Wynter Moorehawke, in the company of his son, the Lord Razi, might be granted access to his presence."

They were divested of their weapons and brought on foot down through the long grass and into the King's camp. This was a tiny entourage indeed, no more than ten men, with only four tents between them, one of which would obviously be reserved for the King himself. Wynter, scanning about her, was gratified to see no sign of heavy artillery or even the deep wheel tracks that would signify its passage through camp. This meant that no cannonry had been through here. The ground bore no trace of any foot traffic, or horses other than those evidenced at the camp's highlines, so no great numbers of archers either, waiting in hiding to rain death on Alberon and his accompanying men.

Wynter could not prevent the surge of hope this evidence brought to her heart. She could see no sign at all that the King intended an ambush. Could it be that he had relented? Had Razi's supposed death brought Jonathon to his knees at last, and had he been sincere in his offer of parley to his one remaining heir? Hard as it might be to believe, it seemed as if the impossible had come to pass. Wynter glanced up at Razi, nervous and wary by her side, and thought to herself, *Perhaps we can manage this after all.*

The lieutenant led them from the pollen-laden grass, and the rest of the King's men gathered silently around. The soldiers eyed Sól and Christopher with disbelief—and kept their distance from Boro.

"If that creature so much as cocks its leg, shoot it," said the lieutenant, and his men levelled their crossbows and followed the warhound's progress with their fingers on the triggers.

Wynter watched the soldiers from the corner of her eye. She was impressed at their stone-faced lack of reaction to Razi's sudden return from the dead. For the most part, their responses were confined to furtive glances and only the occasional nudged and whispering comment. These were obviously well-seasoned men but, aside from the King's lieutenant, Wynter recognised none of them, and there was no sign of any of the other tall and broad-shouldered longbow men who comprised the King's personal guard.

Where are Jonathon's men? thought Wynter, risking a glance behind her. Certainly they could not all be crammed within one of these small tents. Had there been turmoil within the ranks? Had the King's own men fallen victim to a purge? Surely not. Jonathon had gone to pains to tell her father how much he trusted his guard. The men themselves were undyingly faithful to the crown. What could have happened to them?

"Wait here," said the lieutenant, and, leaving them under the watchful eye of the others, he approached what Wynter presumed to be the King's tent.

To Wynter's great shock, the lieutenant did not stand to attention outside the awning, announce himself loud and clear, and wait for the order to approach. Instead, he went right up to the closed door of the tent, murmured, "It's me" through the canvas, and waited there, leaning across the entrance like some forward peddler at a hovel.

Wynter glanced at Razi. Even in his present state, her courtly friend regarded this lack of decorum with frowning disbelief. "Is...?" he asked. "Is that fellow announcing himself to a *king*?"

A man came to the door, and Wynter recognised him as being the captain of Jonathon's personal guard. Another huge man, he stooped to listen as the lieutenant murmured in his ear. Then he raised startled eyes to Razi, unable to hide his shock.

Wynter heard the lieutenant whisper, "Is he in any condition?" The officers' eyes met, and instead of replying, the captain glanced furtively into the tent behind him.

Wynter straightened in alarm. What on earth were these men up to? Why did they not simply announce Razi's arrival to the King? And what could the King possibly be doing in there? Surely he wasn't standing calmly aside as two of his own men whispered at his door?

She stepped forward, and in a high, clear court-voice, demanded, "Why do you not announce us?"

The guards flinched, and Wynter purposely raised her voice so that whoever lurked within the tent could not fail to hear. "Do your duty this instant!" she said. "And announce the Protector Lady Moorehawke and the Lord Razi to his Majesty the King!"

There was a sound within the tent of something clattering to the ground, and the captain ducked inside, leaving the lieutenant to stare anxiously at Wynter's angry face. Within the tent, Jonathon's voice said, "It is him? *It is him?*"

"Announce us," she hissed, "or suffer the consequences."

"I suggest you do as the lady commands," said Razi darkly.

The lieutenant opened his mouth, but the door was pulled back before he could reply, and the captain stepped out again, his face tight with anxiety. "My Lord Razi," he said formally, "Protector Lady Moorehawke. The King bids you enter."

He stood aside, leaving the door clear, and Wynter hesitated.

Razi, her noble friend, looked solemnly down on her from his great height. He radiated all his usual kindness, an indomitable source of strength; but Wynter knew he was depending on her. She knew *everything* was depending on her. Alberon, the King, the very kingdom itself: it all rested on her shoulders. Without thinking, she turned to Christopher. Wordless, her heart fluttering in her chest, she gazed at him. He gazed silently back.

I can't do this, love. What do I say?

"Protector Lady?" said the captain.

What do I say?

"The King awaits, Protector Lady!"

"In the end you can only tell him the truth," murmured Christopher. "How he reacts is up to him."

He was right, of course. Anxiously, she clutched Alberon's folder and stepped back. She felt on the point of being overwhelmed, still her voice was steady when she said, "Wait here, Freeman Garron, Lord Sólmundr. Please keep the dog in check." They bowed, and Wynter turned to go.

Christopher said, "Protector Lady." She turned back. He leant in to speak warmly in her ear. "We'll be all right, lass, you and me, no matter what. Just do your best, it's all anyone can do."

She tilted her head just for a moment, so that her cheek touched his, then pulled back. He smiled at her—that shamelessly blatant, lopsided smile—and Wynter felt the familiar warm surge of affection for him. "This will be done soon," she said. "And then we shall decide where it is we most want to go, and what it is we shall do with our lives."

"That would be nice," he said. He glanced up at Razi. "Don't worry, doctor." He tapped his temple. "You don't need anything more than what you've got up there already."

Razi squeezed Christopher's hand for a moment. The captain coughed pointedly. Wynter nodded. And she and Razi turned and headed for the door.

*   *   *

The King had just begun to rise when they ducked into the tent, but at the sight of Razi, he paused in mid action, his face slack with shock. The captain made as if to follow them inside, and the King whispered for him to get out. For the briefest moment, the captain hesitated in the doorway, then he nodded, stepped outside and pulled the tent flap shut behind him.

The King stayed where he was, staring at his son.

Razi moved cautiously into the tent. He looked the King up and down, and Wynter could see him trying to reconcile his memory of the small, dark Victor St James with the hugely imposing, blond man who was actually his father.

"Your Majesty?" he asked.

"Razi?" whispered the King. "Son."

Jonathon pushed himself upright and Wynter's heart sank as she realised that he was, once again, quite drunk. "Son!" he cried and shoved out from behind his table, toppling a folding chair in his haste.

The King descended upon them. Razi flinched, lifting his hands as if to ward off a blow. But Jonathon just grabbed him and pulled him into a rough embrace, causing Razi to stagger under his unsteady weight. Clenching his fist in Razi's dark curls, the King buried his face in his son's shoulder.

"You live," he said. "You live."

Razi, his hands held out from his sides, submitted with alarmed confusion. His eyes met Wynter's across the top of his father's head, and she lifted Alberon's folder, nodding encouragingly that he should speak. "We have..." he said uncertainly. "That is, the lady and I, have..."

At Razi's mention of her, the King turned to Wynter. "Child," he said, "I am sorry. Poor Lorcan. There was nothing I could do."

Wynter made a tiny sound of grief, but that was all she could manage. Her throat was suddenly too small to allow words. She had not realised that she had been clinging to a last slim fragment of hope; that she had cherished, secret even to herself, the belief that there had been a mistake. But that last slim hope was gone. There had been no mistake. Lorcan was dead.

Why was she still standing, when the world had stopped? How was it that she did not fall down? How was it she did not scream? All the terrible questions rose up inside her: *did he die alone? Did he suffer at the end? Did he call for me in vain?* And she was drowned by them. She was struck motionless and senseless and dumb.

Seeing her distress, Jonathon's eyes filled with tears, and he stretched out his hand as if to pull her into an embrace. His sympathy threatened to undo her entirely and, to save herself, Wynter thrust Alberon's folder out like a shield and cried, "We have brought these, your Majesty. They are from the Royal Prince."

Jonathon dropped his eyes to the folder, then raised them again to her face. He did not seem to understand.

"From the Royal Prince Alberon, your Majesty. For you."

The King stepped back as though she had threatened him. Still clinging to Razi, he looked from Wynter to his son's dark face and back. "What treachery is this?" he whispered.

"No treachery. Just messages from your heir, begging that you understand him. There is no coup, your Majesty. There never has been. The Prince plans no treason. He—"

But the King had spun from her and turned on Razi. Gripping his son's shoulders, he scanned his face and whispered. *"He* has sent you?" At Razi's carefully neutral expression, the King's horror turned to rage. "Where have you *been?*" he screamed, shaking Razi hard. "You poisonous child! While I mourned you and thought you dead, where have you been? What have you *done*?"

Startled at this abrupt turn to violence, Razi flung his arms up and broke easily from his father's grasp. Stepping back, he lifted his fists in silent warning. The King's face darkened in that frightening, lethal way of his and he hunched his shoulders.

"You would fight me, boy?" he said. "You think to best me?"

His fists still raised, Razi watched the King and said nothing.

"Your Majesty," cried Wynter "If you would but listen..."

She tried to step between them, anticipating a return of the King's terrible, violent treatment of his son. But Jonathon deflated suddenly. Right before her eyes, he seemed to crumble in defeat. He seemed to shrink and age. He turned from Razi as if in a daze and wandered across to sit heavily into his chair.

"So, he has sent you," he said, "and I am undone. How cruel is it, Razi, to have mourned your death only to find betrayal in your longed-for resurrection. It is God's punishment, I suppose, and well I deserve it. What, after all, did I expect? God help you, despite all my dreams for you both, how could I have hoped that you would escape your God-cursed heritage. As I took my kingdom, so shall it be taken." He trailed into silence for a moment. Wynter opened her mouth, but Jonathon went on in a whisper, speaking to himself. "At least my sons are not their father's type of coward. At least they thwart me like men, and do not slither about as poisoning, devious... Oh God." He clutched his head suddenly and moaned. It was such a deep, heartfelt expression of pain that Wynter, despite her own distress, felt pity for him. "Oh God," he whispered again. "I have shaped my kingdom's fall."

"Majesty?" she ventured. "Will you please hear me?"

Jonathon glared up at her from between his fists and snarled,

"It is the worst kind of mistress that lays herself down for a Prince and expects his power in return. If the Lord Razi has messages to convey, then don't have him convey them through *you*, woman. However poisonous their content, let him not do me the discourtesy, nor himself the dishonour, of transferring them through his whore."

Razi's sudden roar made them both leap. "How dare you!" he cried. "How *dare* you speak to her like that? Retract your slander immediately! It is the lowest thing in the world to dismiss a woman on terms of her virtue! How simple for you! How neat!"

"Razi," hissed Wynter, "this is the *King*."

"He is a *nobleman*," snapped Razi. "He should act like one!"

The King frowned at him, his usually circumspect, hitherto unfailingly political son, now scarlet and raging at nothing more serious than a petty slight to a woman. Wynter saw Jonathon register the strangeness of this, and she saw that sharpness in him that her father had so loved; that famous Kingsson intelligence, not yet completely destroyed by distress and wine.

"What is wrong with you, boy?" he said. "Do you take offence because of your mother?"

"Majesty," she said, "my Lord Razi is not himself. Please. I beg you. Let me explain?"

Jonathon glared and did not give his permission to speak. Still Wynter approached, and placed the folder on the table by his clenched fist. "Your Majesty, these are from your heir. The Royal Prince bid his brother take them to you. He bid him explain that his intention was never to usurp you as King. The Royal Prince's only wish is to present to you his plans for the future."

The King regarded the folio with a kind of numbness. His big hand slid a little on the surface of the table as if he wished to touch the leather folder, but he did not. Wynter took a chance on leaning in a little and softening slightly the courtly tone of her voice. "Your Majesty," she said, "whatever your differences, the Royal Prince does not wish to grasp the throne. With respect, your Majesty, he wishes only to strengthen your kingdom."

The King met her eye. "He has done a poor job of that," he said.

He was close enough for Wynter to smell the wine from his breath. She could smell camp fire from his clothes. "May I suggest that there were two of you involved in that particular misadventure, your Majesty."

Rage flared again in the King's face. "Do not mistake yourself for your father, girl. Lorcan was the one person in this life who ever talked thus to me. No one shall take his place, whether they carry his name or not."

Despite the prickle of fear in her belly, Wynter held the King's eye and whispered, "I cannot help but feel that had you allowed your heir speak thus to you, much of this kingdom's recent problems may have been forestalled. It seems that a little more talk and a little less rage may well have calmed this storm before it even began."

"My *heir* has stolen and broadcast that which I wished suppressed. He has machinated behind my back, twisting deals with my enemies. His actions have poisoned court against his brother and divided my men. What is it you would like me to do about that, girl? Shrug in defeat and hand him my crown?"

The stark truth of this twisted like a knife in Wynter's heart, the enormity of Jonathon's problem suddenly horribly clear. In the face of Alberon's very public defiance, what choice did Jonathon really have? Either he was King or he was not. Either his heir bowed to his will or he did not. It was how kingdoms worked. It was the way of the world. Alberon wished the country run one way, Jonathon wished it run another. Their visions were irreconcilable, and one of them must bow or one of them must die. That was the black and white of it. Wynter drew back, lost for words, and Jonathon nodded.

"So I am undone," he said.

"But you will speak with your heir now?" asked Razi.

"Have I a choice?" muttered the King, "now that he has sniffed me out."

Razi frowned across at Wynter. *What could that mean?*

The King tutted at him. "Stop hovering like a God-cursed chambermaid, boy." He gestured bitterly to the folder. "Come here and summarise your brother's terms. I assume he's only hours behind you, and I shan't sit here reading this pap while his men advance upon me."

"But, your Majesty," said Wynter, "the Prince's men do not advance, Alberon travels with only—"

"Oh, *enough,* girl! *Jesu Christi,* you are like a crow cawing incessantly in my ear! I asked the *boy,* dammit! Razi, get over here and detail me your brother's terms before I lose my patience entirely and greet him with your head on a pike."

At Razi's hesitation, the King glared up from under his brows. Razi swallowed hard at the warning in his face. "I . . . I cannot detail the documents, Majesty. I do not know what they contain."

"You pledged your support to your brother without discussing his aims?" growled the King. "*You?*" Razi flickered a glance at Wynter and the King turned his head to stare at her in disbelief. "Once again, I am directed to you, Protector Lady?"

Wynter thought her lips might crack from fear when she opened them to speak. "My Lord Razi is unwell, your Majesty," she said. "We were attacked on our way here. His horse tumbled down a hill, taking him with her. He awoke with little memory of who he is, or what has passed between him and his brother."

There was a stark, crackling silence.

"I remember that I am a doctor," ventured Razi.

The King's face so darkened that Wynter only barely restrained herself from stepping back.

"This is the lowest of tricks," hissed the King. "The cheapest of manipulations! You hope to distil my hopes into one heir, do you? With this ridiculous fabrication you hope to remove yourself from the picture? You think yourself so important, little man, that first you fake your own death and then feign madness, all to fling me into Alberon's arms? Are you such a *coward*, boy? Have you no spine?" Jonathon slammed his fist into the table, tears in his eyes. "I would rather you came at me with a halberd," he cried. "I would rather you drew your God-cursed *sword*, than insult me with this!"

"I do not recall you at all," cried Razi. "Certainly I cannot conceive of you being my *father*. I remember my father clearly! I loved him. I do not *know* you!"

"Oh, Razi," breathed Wynter, "no."

"I am a *doctor*!" cried Razi. "That is what my father made of me! I am a doctor! I do not know what it is I am expected to make of this," he gestured to the folder. "But I cannot help you with it! This is *your* poison! *You* take it!"

Wynter sank to a chair, weary to her bones of trying, and put her head in her hands. There was an abrupt scrape of the King's chair, and the table thudded beneath her elbows as he jerked clumsily to his feet, but she did not bother looking up. *All is lost*, she thought. *All is chaos*. The surrender was almost blissful.

The ensuing silence made her glance up. Razi and Jonathon

were gaping at her, and for a moment she did not know why. Then she realised she was slumped at the table, slouching like a beggar with a bowl in the very presence of the King. She blushed and went to rise, but Jonathon waved her down again and sank to his seat once more. It was perhaps this more than anything else—the very uncourtliness of Wynter's gesture, the complete and utter lack of art in her despair—that made him believe.

"I swear to you," whispered Razi, "I recall nothing of which you speak. I am a doctor, your Majesty, I am a scientist. Everything else," he gestured to his head, "is gone."

To Wynter's amazement the King huffed a laugh. "What a twisted joke . . . to give me what I always wanted, instead of what I find I need." He looked up to the heavens in bitter amusement. "You always claimed that God had a blackened sense of humour, Lorcan." He sighed. "We can but bloody laugh."

"Your Majesty," said Wynter, "whatever the future holds in store, Alberon does not come to you at arms. He comes with only the smallest entourage of men, his intentions nothing but peaceful."

The King huffed again. "What needs he of arms, when the damage is done?"

"Will you read the documents, your Majesty?" asked Razi.

"What for?"

Razi thought for a moment. "That you may know what is in store?" The King regarded him closely. "That . . . that you may do more than simply lash out in the dark?"

At the King's grimace, Razi stepped to the table, diffident and uncertain. "I have one other thing," he said. "I have never been certain if it is part of our journey, or if it is a personal possession of my own. I must confess, I have longed to open it, but the fear that it might be yours has swayed me to caution. Can you tell me...?" With a final hesitation he reached into his coat and withdrew a small document, folded to a square and sealed with wax. Wynter recognised it at once.

"Alberon gave that to you," she said, "just as we were leaving camp. I had assumed you would place it in the folder."

Razi shook his head. "For some reason I did not." He offered the letter to his father. "Your Majesty? Do you suppose he meant it for you?"

The King took the letter. He opened it. Alberon's writing was firm and neat, it took up barely a page. The King read it twice, then placed it on the table. He turned it, obviously intending Razi to read. Wynter leaned discreetly forward, reading from a distance.

Father,

I am a dull, knot-headed boy—did my tutors not always tell you thus? I have no power over words, unless I speak with soldiers, who seem to understand me well enough. You have always wished it were not so. I have wished so myself. Next to my clever brother I am a toad. But you and I found our common ground this last five years, did we not? In all that horror, you found a pride in me, and a use for my own peculiar strengths. Though I wish it had not been in such a manner as war, I was glad to be of service to you. That I could help protect your wonderful hopes for our people's future.

I am doing this still. I wish I had the power to persuade you of it, to convince you and make you understand. I have waited and waited for Razi's return, knowing he would be the one to put into words that which between us has only ended in screaming and blows.

If I could take all the curs who threaten this kingdom and pile their heads at your feet I would do it. I wish only to be your guardian. I wish only to be your strong right hand. I believe in this kingdom and that which you wish to do with it. Listen to Razi. He will assure you of it.

Wynter tells me you may have destroyed my things. I hope you preserved her letters (they are in my red leather trunk). It is their influence that has me sitting now, cramping my fingers and my brain in this clumsy effort to speak. It was easier than I thought it would be—perhaps you and I should only ever have written notes? Certainly it may have prevented a few black eyes.

I will leave off now. I pray we meet on friendly ground. Alberon.

Father, one last thing, perhaps we could allow Wyn keep her gypsy? He seems an unlikely fellow, but Razi is fond of him.

There was a long moment's silence. Wynter reached forward without thinking and placed her fingers on the parchment. *Oh, Albi.*

The King immediately slid the letter out from beneath her fingertips. She did not look up at him, could not look up at him, and so she did not see where he put it. His voice was very quiet when he said, "Sit down, boy." Razi sat. "Child," Jonathon turned to Wynter, "get the captain to brew some coffee. Tell him to bring us something to eat."

Wynter moved to the door, and as she ducked outside to get the King his food, Jonathon pulled Alberon's folder to him and unlaced the ties.

Day Eleven: An Understanding

Wynter sipped coffee and watched the King read. It was the first time she had ever seen the man working, and she was astonished at how quickly he processed the tightly packed manuscripts, how immersed he became in their contents. He had a very particular method which interested and intrigued her. First he would scan the document at incredible speed, reading from beginning to end, his brows furrowed. Then he would straighten the pages, tap them into alignment and work his way through again, pausing at relevant passages. He would take notes on a separate sheet. Sometimes he marked the original papers in some way, underlining sentences, ticking words, ringing whole paragraphs of the text. When he was happy that he had squeezed every jot of information from one document, Jonathon would pass it to Razi, bidding him read it and its notes, and then he would move on to the next.

During the course of this intense period of concentration, the King drank two or more pots of tar-black coffee and demolished a manchet loaf with olive oil and cheese. Razi read in frowning silence. He seemed to be absorbing information afresh, seeing all the various angles as if for the very first time, but he couldn't add much to Jonathon's deliberations. Indeed, the King seemed to offer the documents more for his son's benefit than for anything else.

Occasionally the men would ask Wynter to fetch ink or food. Occasionally they would ask for her recollections of Razi and Alberon's conversations, but mostly they ignored her, and she sat in silence observing them work. She watched as the sun moved across the canvas, she listened to the peaceful rustle of papers, she drank coffee, and she thought.

If Alberon had accepted the King's offer to parley, and the King seemed convinced that he had, then he would be here soon. He would arrive with only a small, non-threatening entourage, and he would find himself greeted by the same. Unless both parties resorted to daggers in the back or poisoned each other's wine, it seemed likely that father and son were finally about to sit down and talk. It seemed likely that this damaged kingdom was on the verge of some sort of repair. For the very first time Wynter might have an opportunity to think on what her future—her personal future—could hold.

She had to confess, all that she had previously expected from life seemed somehow inappropriate now or unpalatable to her. Her time in Albi's camp had, once again, brought home the stifling constrictions of court life. Her time on the trail with Christopher had made her long for more than an existence dedicated solely to her craft. She watched Razi work and she realised that, like him, she had been stripped of her past. All she had left was herself, the man she loved, and the skills that God and her father had given her.

What on earth was she to do with that? Where on earth could she go with it?

"His communications with the North," said the King, his quill scratching away even as he spoke, "how were they effected?"

Wynter dragged herself from her thoughts. She put down her coffee. "These most recent messages were sent via the Merron, your Majesty."

He paused in surprise. "That Hadrish thief?"

"Christopher Garron is not a thief," said Razi mildly, his attention focused on a sheaf of Jonathon's notes. "I have told you before."

The King and Wynter exchanged a look. Wynter went to comment, but the King stopped her with a shake of his head. "The Merron?" he prompted her.

"Noblemen of a Northland's tribe, your Majesty. One of their number has accompanied us, if you wish to question him. He waits outside with Freeman Garron. But the Merron seem to know little of the Royal Princess Shirken's intentions, your Majesty. They work for her in the hope that their efforts will save their kind from destruction . . . a futile hope, I fear."

The King raised an eyebrow. "Futile indeed," he said dryly. "I am intimately aware of Marguerite's attitude to her non-Christian subjects." He shuffled the papers once again, lifted a particular page. "This proposed marriage," he murmured, "it astounds me."

Wynter sighed. "It is madness," she said.

"It is genius," he replied. Her shock seemed to tickle him, and he smiled at her, a warmly amused smile, very like his youngest son's. "Should Marguerite succeed in pushing her father aside without causing revolt—and I suspect that if anyone can do it, she can—a marital alliance between these two kingdoms would be . . ." Jonathon shook his head. "It would be immense," he said. "There would need to be an agreement regarding heirs, of course. That should be easy enough to hammer out . . . perhaps a division on grounds of sex or age? Yes. Age, I think. One heir North, one South, with provision for separate succession in case of death...foreign education. Padua perhaps? Hmmm. Complete autonomy of rule, of course." He huffed in amazement. "It is an entirely new method. Who would have imagined the boy capable of its proposal?" He lost himself in thought, murmuring away to himself, making notes. "He would not be able to handle her, of course, poor child. He has no idea of what those people are capable but, perhaps..."

Razi met Wynter's eyes as the King, deep in thought, shuffled papers and muttered his tangled calculations. "This foolishness with the Midlander resistance," said the King eventually, "that *cannot* be allowed."

Wynter's heart sank for Jared and Mary and their desperate hopes for reform. "But the Midlander envoys have already been sent home, your Majesty," she ventured. "They are of the belief that they have your Majesty's support. They greatly depend on it. The Royal Prince...the Royal Prince has given them copies of my father's designs in the hopes that my father's machines will strengthen their position and help end the appalling conditions their people currently endure."

Jonathon's expression drew down into distress. He turned his face away as if Wynter had attempted to show him some disgusting thing. "No," he said. "No, no. We shall smother that one." He carefully set two of the documents aside.

"Mary," said Razi. The King and Wynter glanced expectantly at him. "*Mary*," he insisted. "The Lady Phillipe D'Arden and her child. They have sacrificed all for the Midlander reform. Are we to allow them to fail?"

Jonathon sat back. "Phillipe D'Arden, Razi? You have met him?"

"I..." said Razi, suddenly uncertain again. "I have met Mary," he said.

Jonathon looked to Wynter. His expression left little doubt that he thought Razi was wandering in his mind. Wynter smiled. "In fact, the Lady Mary *was* in Alberon's camp, your Majesty. From what I understand, the Lord D'Arden fell victim to the Midlands inquisition. The Lady Mary and a Presbyter named Jared came to negotiate in his place."

"Phillipe D'Arden is dead?" breathed Jonathon. "Oh no. Oh, what a blow to mankind. Phillipe was an intelligent and wonderful man. I have many of his theses in my library. You should read them, Protector Lady, when you have the chance. An intelligent, *wonderful* man, much in sympathy with your father." Jonathon hung his head. "*Jesu*. Such waste. I will never fail to despair at the destruction so often wrought by those who purport to act for God. One wonders why he simply does not sicken of us. Why he does not simply wipe the earth clean of us, and leave it to the honesty of the lower beasts."

"The Reformists need your help, Majesty. They need your strength."

He shook his head. "No," he whispered. "No. I cannot. I simply... this must end. We must... it must be made to go away."

Wynter leant in. She placed her hand carefully on his arm. "Majesty," she said, "my father was a great man—a *great* man. Who, I have come to understand, struggled with a horribly troubled conscience."

Jonathon's eyes widened with horror. Wynter did not look away.

"You and I both know," she whispered, "that this box, having been opened, cannot again be closed. No matter what memories it may contain."

The King withdrew his arm from beneath Wynter's grasp. He shook his head.

"Of what does the lady speak?" asked Razi. His father turned to him, searching his curious face with furious concentration. Wynter tentatively replaced her hand on Jonathon's tightly clenched fist.

"The Lord Razi has no longer any recollection of what we discuss," she said. When Jonathon once again met her eyes and did not withdraw from her touch, she continued gently on. "Your Majesty, I understand that a good man must fling those things from him that sully his soul. It is a commendable impulse to cast from us that which we wish not to have done and to bury it so it may never be done again. But perhaps it is the burden of a great king that he face those things which damn him. That he grasp the nettle of a troubled conscience, and think of the betterment of his people. Your Majesty, all your attempts to suppress my father's machines have only led to disaster. To deny their existence now is folly, for there was no turning back once you drew them once more into the open. You cannot allow your own past to destroy you, your Majesty. You cannot allow it to destroy this kingdom. You are a king, and you must steel yourself to carry the heavy burden of a king."

All the danger went from Jonathon's face. He was, for a brief moment, just a man. A desolate man, desperately haunted. "Nothing good has ever come of those machines, child. They have paved my way to hell."

"Whatever you have done, your Majesty, is done already. The future of your kingdom lies in what you choose to do next."

Jonathon slid his gaze to the documents pertaining to the Midlander reform. Reluctantly, he moved his hand to them. "Perhaps the mere sight of Lorcan's designs could be enough to strengthen the reformer's cause? Perhaps something may be done, without recourse to actually..." He placed the reform documents back with the others. His fingers lingered on them a moment. "Shall we see, Lorcan, what good might come of the evil we wrought?"

Wynter looked at his troubled, heavy face. *The evil we wrought.* The King closed his eyes and wearily ran his hand through his shining curls. Would she ever know the truth? *Now is not the time to ask*, she told herself.

Razi's deep voice cut into her thoughts. "You have reconsidered your heir's proposals?"

The King's lips twitched, he kept his head propped in his hand, and with one finger traced the neat rows of Alberon's rounded script. "With modifications," he said, "some portions of it may well be effected. This marriage, for example. An astounding innovation. He did not trust me with it, of course. The usurpation of a king, he felt would be too much. Indeed, he was probably right... coupled with the threat of Lorcan's machines. Had the boy only spoken more. Had I only listened..." he trailed again to thoughtful silence.

How little we know of what is in his head, thought Wynter. *How he must have missed my father all these years. The one friend to whom he could confide without fear of seeming weak.*

"You will speak to your heir?" she asked gently.

"Certainly, it is a better prospect than that which lay before me this morning," whispered Jonathon, gazing at the documents. His eyes wandered to Wynter. He regarded her for a moment, scanning her hair, her eyes. Then he sighed, sat back, scrubbed his face and seemed to shake himself free of his heavy melancholy. He cleared his throat and straightened in his chair, a king once more.

"How did he find me in the end?" he asked, briskly gathering the papers.

He mistook their silence for reluctance and looked at them from under his brows. "How did he know to send you *here?*" he asked, tapping the sheaves into order. "Come now!" he said. "I shall need to know. Who was it that betrayed me?"

Razi glanced at Wynter in utter confusion.

"Did your Majesty not arrange to meet the Royal Prince?" she asked.

The King's hands froze in the act of tying the folder. "You said he sent you," he said darkly.

"He *did,*" said Wynter, "with these. But... Majesty, did you not arrange to *meet* his Highness?"

"You said he *sent you here!*" roared the King, surging to his feet in panic.

"No, Majesty! We were headed for the *palace,* but on the trail, we met a messenger who told us you were camped here. We diverted our course and came to deliver his Highness's messages."

"A messenger? One of Alberon's men?"

"Yes, Majesty. He was in much haste to reach him. He seemed to believe you wished to ambush the Prince. Do not fear though, it is unlikely that he has managed to divert his Highness. I suspect the Prince will have left camp before the man arrived— whatever your arrangements are, I have no doubt they still stand."

"Then Alberon is...? NO!" The King pushed the table back.

Wynter and Razi leapt from their chairs and ran after him as he tore his way through the tent door.

"François!" he yelled. "François!" The captain came running. The soldiers all stood to attention. "My horse!" shouted the King. "Hurry! I must forestall him!"

The captain gestured to a man who ran to get the King's

horse. Then he stepped close to Jonathon, his voice low. "You have changed your mind, Majesty?"

The King grabbed him by his shoulders. "Most strongly, friend. Pray God for me that I am not too late."

Hope flared in the captain's eyes and he squeezed the top of the King's arm. "Thank God!" he cried. "I shall get my horse."

"No. Keep these innocents here. They must never see, you understand?"

The captain nodded. "I swear it."

A soldier led the King's horse through the milling crowd. Jonathon grabbed the reins from him and swung into the saddle, scattering men in all directions. "Stay here!" he cried as some of the soldiers ran for the highline. "You will *stay here!*"

"Christopher!" yelled Wynter. "Get the horses! We must accompany the King!"

Christopher and Sól began to push their way through the reluctant soldiers. The King turned in the saddle, staring down at Wynter, and she glared stubbornly back. He nodded.

"Release the Lord Razi's men," he called to the captain. "Give them their weapons and their mounts." At the captain's uncertainty the King's face drew down in sorrow. "They know all there is to know, François. God help them. They are already part of our poisoned circle. Give them their weapons, leave them join me. But keep these others here!" Jerking his horse around, the King thundered away through the long grass, his last order trailing behind him on pollen and dust.

Wynter, Razi, Christopher and Sól were soon hard upon his heels.

Day Eleven: The Machine

They tore through the forest, spurring their horses brutally onwards until the poor animals' flanks were lathered, their mouths streaming with foam. None of the other horses could match the two royal mounts, and while the King and Razi raced ahead, Wynter, Sól and Christopher made up a trailing rear guard, dodging and weaving to keep up as best they could on the increasingly dense forest paths. It was a horribly dangerous way to ride. They stayed low in the saddle to avoid overhanging branches and prayed to their various gods that their horses did not break a leg.

Wynter risked a look at Christopher. He glanced her way, questions and fear in his eyes. Razi travelled straight as an arrow on the path before them, his head low to his horse's neck, his eyes fixed on his father's back. Sól was slightly behind them, bringing up the rear. There had been no time for explanations, and though they all rode together, each was separated into their own frantic bubble of anxiety.

Boro tried to keep pace, but even his valiant determination could not match the horses' speed. Wynter heard him bay in horror as his master drew ahead, his howls quickly fading beneath the drumming hoof beats. She glanced back to see the poor hound, already far behind, still running frantically to catch up.

A branch swept perilously low, almost knocking Razi from his saddle. Christopher yelled, and Wynter ducked only just in time as it swooped past. She tore her attention from Boro and focused forward again, her eyes on the path and the figure of the King forging the way ahead.

Goddamn it. She should have known that Jonathon would never have given in. He had *not* been sitting in sullen acceptance, awaiting his heir's arrival. How could she ever have thought it? Rather he had been stewing in guilt and despair while his men waited elsewhere in ambush for his son. *It is a better prospect than that which lay before me this morning.* Wynter could only imagine what lurked in waiting for Alberon, but she was fairly certain, now, that it involved the King's small, highly trusted squad of personal guards; and she was fairly certain it involved her father's Bloody Machine.

The narrow path broadened and the watery forest light brightened. Daylight streamed through the thinning trees ahead, and the King was a broken silhouette against them as he charged up the widening path. They broke into the open on a slight rise as the King pulled to a halt, looking down. To their left, perhaps a hundred yards from them, the shambolic remains of an abandoned forge house; to their right, lower ground and another loop of the overgrown road cutting through the dense forest. They clustered together at the tree line, panting and breathless, their panicked horses stamping and breathing hard. Wynter's heart was thundering in her ears. The King stared anxiously to the road.

"There!" he said. "Oh God! There!"

And here they came! Alberon and Oliver, trotting warily from the darkness of the trees. Behind them, astride his own shaggy pony, followed the little servant, Anthony. His small face aglow with his own importance, his pots and pans a-jingle, the child looked all about him, full of glee. Four wary soldiers flanked the Prince, their crossbows drawn and ready, their eyes on the forge.

"Good Lord!" cried Razi. "Mary!"

Wynter snapped her attention to the last pair of riders emerging onto the road and gasped in disbelief at the sight of the Lady Mary riding from the shadows. Dusty and uncomfortable on a stately dappled horse, the lady looked exhausted, her tired face very pale. Grave as ever, Hallvor pulled her painted mare to the lady's side and looked keenly around.

"*Mo mhuirnín!*" whispered Sól, startled by his friend's unexpected presence.

"Why on earth—?" Wynter gaped at the lady in horror. Why? *Why* would Alberon have dragged that poor woman with him?

"That damned *pup!*" hissed Razi. "Did he think to hide behind her skirts?"

"He took the little boy, too," said Christopher, staring at Anthony. "Perhaps he could not stand to leave them with the Wolves."

Alberon was squinting up at the forge house, his eyes blinded by the sun. For a moment no one noticed the King's party, swaddled in shadow at the edge of the trees. Then Jonathon broke from his trance and trotted his horse into the sunlight.

Mary saw him immediately. Her face lit up at the sight of Razi by the King's side, and she said something, smiling. Alberon turned. His eyes hopped from Jonathon to Razi, to Wynter, and he relaxed.

You are all here, his grin said. *We have done it.*

Wynter straightened, intending to warn him, but Alberon had turned already to Oliver, who was still focused on the forge house. Alberon spoke and Oliver turned sharply, seeking. His eyes found the King, and his face softened into hope. He half-raised his hand, then dropped it again as if uncertain of his place.

"Cousin," whispered Jonathon. He lifted his hand in greeting.

An expression crossed Oliver's tired face, gratitude perhaps, or relief: some emotion too strong and too deep to register as anything other than pain. Then he broke into a hopeful smile and lifted his hand again. Wynter saw his mouth form the word *Jonathon*.

At the same moment, a metallic rattle broke the silence of the glowering ruins of the forge house. A loosely packed drystone wall fell, clattering to the grass, and the King's guard stepped into view as the lethal elegance of Lorcan Moorehawke's Bloody Machine was revealed to the riders on the road.

"NO!" bellowed the King.

Even if his soldiers heard him, even if they witnessed his raised arm—and Wynter was never certain that they had—what could they have interpreted from it? Only that the man who had sent them here was ordering them to strike as planned. The huge men at the side of the machine began to crank an iron handle.

Wynter cried out and spurred Ozkar forwards, screaming at Alberon to *get down*. At her voice, two of Alberon's soldiers turned towards her, raising their bows in alarm. The other two stared helplessly at the sleek iron monster now levelling its gaze upon them from the ruined wall.

Cogs turned. Barrels rotated. There was a *kak kak kak* of huge ratcheted pieces moving together, and then, one after another, a series of deafening bangs rent the evening air. The machine and its crew were quickly obscured as streams of smoke poured from the revolving barrels. Harsh flashes of light blinked through the sudden gloom.

Oliver, his face appalled, stood in his stirrups and spread his arms as if to shield the Prince. Alberon spun, screaming at Anthony to *ride*! The little servant gaped at him, boy and pony frozen in horror. Wynter thundered down the slope towards them. Behind her, Christopher yelled her name, then all sound was lost under the rapid percussion of the machine's fire as she descended into the shallow, smoke-filled valley.

The soldier on Alberon's right flew from his horse, his head bursting apart in a fine mist of blood and brain. Alberon's gelding reared in terror and a row of scarlet wounds erupted across its massive chest. Blood instantly drenched its belly, and it took three dancing steps back, still reared on its hind legs like a circus horse. The soldier on Alberon's left jerked back in his saddle, his crossbow discharging into the air with a heavy *thwock*. His throat was shredded and Anthony was instantly coated in an abrupt wash of the poor man's blood. The little boy cried out once as the blood hit him, then he went absolutely still, his eyes white and round in his dripping face, his horse quivering beneath him.

Alberon's horse slammed down onto all four legs, and stood for a moment, wide-eyed and rigid, blood streaming from its nose. Then it keeled over, carrying the Prince with it. Alberon rolled free before he could be crushed in the horse's spasming death throes.

Oliver yelled and spun in his saddle, reaching for Alberon. "Your Highness!" he cried, "Here!"

"Just *run*!" screamed Wynter, spurring Ozkar on. "Albi! Just RUN!"

The machine continued to bark out death. Smoke rolled across the field of grass.

The ground by Mary and Hallvor spewed up four successive puffs of dirt as the gun spat into the earth at their horses' feet. Mary's mount reared and the lady screamed, clinging to its mane in terror. Hallvor grabbed for its bridle.

The men at the machine tilted the barrels and, still cranking, swung the gun back the way it had come. The trees beside Hallvor splintered. The leaves by her shoulder tore. Her painted mare staggered as a shot punctured its neck. In the moments left to her, the healer spread her arms and twisted her body to cover Mary. Hallvor's shoulders disappeared beneath a shocking fountain of blood. She was thrown violently into Mary's arms, and the two women went down behind the falling horses.

Wynter's scream was echoed by Sól's. Even as she galloped towards the place where Alberon had fallen, she twisted her head, trying to catch a glimpse of the women. Sól was galloping towards them. Still screaming in horror, her face hot with tears, Wynter was engulfed in a choking billow of acrid smoke.

Up ahead, one of Alberon's remaining soldiers took aim at the machine. It spat its mindless fire and he toppled back onto his horse's rump, his eyes wide and staring to the sky. Behind him, Alberon climbed unsteadily to his feet. He looked about for Anthony who still sat, frozen in horror, on his little horse. Oliver was pulling his own frenzied mount around, trying to put himself between the boys and the machine. He was yelling at them, his voice drowned by the barking gun. He lifted his eyes to see Wynter thundering towards him and swung his arm in dismay, shouting soundlessly for her to get back.

The machine barked.

Oliver jerked a rattling puppet dance as a series of shots caught him. He fell momentarily from view, and Wynter screamed his name, her voice a painful scratch in her abused throat. Then

Oliver rose into sight again as he dragged himself back into the saddle. Slowly, he pulled his horse around to stand between Alberon and the gun. Wynter stood in her stirrups. She screamed Oliver's name once more. Alarmed by her bellowing, thunderous advance, Alberon's last soldier raised his bow and took shaky aim at her.

"No!" she cried. "No! We're on your side."

The machine swung back for another sweep. The soldier lurched as a shot caught him under his arm. He loosed his arrow as he fell.

Wynter ducked. The arrow shot past. She glanced behind to see Jonathon fly from his horse. He hit the ground, the bolt jutting from his shoulder, and rolled just in time to miss being trampled by Christopher's little mare. Razi jerked his own horse to a skidding halt and galloped back to his father.

Ozkar stumbled and Wynter was thrown without warning. She flew through the unresisting air and hit the ground with a violent smack. There were stars and blackness. She rolled head over heels on the rough ground, staggered to her feet and kept running—heading blindly through the smoke and the fear, heading for Alberon.

The harsh sound of the gun ceased without warning. In the sudden, unexpected silence, Ozkar thundered past, trailing smoke as he headed for the trees. Wynter flinched but kept running. Her ears rang with the aftershock of the gun; she only dimly registered the sound of horses and men screaming in pain around her. Her own heart was the loudest sound, that and the name *Alberon* repeated constantly in her head.

A stray horse loomed, its shoulders black with gore, and Wynter slapped it aside.

Above the chest-high pall of smoke, Anthony sat atop his little horse—a small boy drenched in blood. He was gazing at the men in the forge house as they released the spent barrel-ring and hoisted a fresh-loaded one into its place. Their crew mates carried the first away to be reloaded. The gun crew heaved the lever to engage the new barrels, and Anthony watched with no emotion as they swung the gun around to face him.

Alberon rose from the river of smoke and reached for the child. Shoving his hands beneath the boy's armpits, he dragged him from the saddle, and Anthony slid like a sack of loose grain into the Prince's arms.

Spinning with the limp child cradled to his chest, Alberon looked for somewhere to go. Anthony's little head lolled to his shoulder, his eyes wide and blank and staring. Desperate, the Prince glanced up at Oliver, who still swayed protectively in the saddle above him. Alberon's expression fell as he registered the knight's chalky face. Oliver's tunic was scarlet from shoulder to hip. A sheet of blood coated his horse's side and dribbled in a steady stream to darken the ground at its feet.

Alberon roared in wordless horror. Oliver, still gazing down upon him, slid slowly sideways from the saddle.

"Albi!" screamed Wynter, still running. "Albi! Run! Run before they can fire!"

Razi's deep voice cut above the residual whine in her ears. A muffled bellowing somewhere behind her. "STOP, YOU CRETINS, IN THE NAME OF THE KING! IN THE NAME OF THE KING!"

Deaf from the gunshots and blinded by the smoke, the men at the forge took careful aim and once again began to crank the handle. The machine coughed its brutal roar. Great gouts of earth sprayed from the ground, arcing a curved path towards the Prince.

"Get DOWN!" screamed Wynter.

Alberon twisted his body to shield the little boy, and ran. Oliver's horse staggered under another rain of fire. Oliver spilled lifelessly to the ground. The horse fell.

Shots followed the Prince's hunched retreat, biting the ground at his heels. Wynter reached for him, as if to pluck him from death's relentless path. The smoke bit her eyes and throat as she drew breath again to scream. Alberon jerked. Blood erupted from his shoulder. He jerked again. Blood sprayed from his hip. Anthony's small hands flew up as the two of them spun. Blood flew from Alberon's mouth and he hit the ground, Anthony still clutched to him like a doll.

Alberon rolled, once, twice, three times, then came to a stop, still shielding Anthony with his body. For a moment, rigid tremors shook him. Then, to Wynter's horror, her friend seemed to deflate and both he and his little servant lay corpse-still on the smoky ground.

The machine cranked on. The earth puffed up in a series of lethal explosions as the shots arced a path from Alberon to Wynter. She ran towards them, her mind filled only with Alberon's lifeless sprawling body, the horrible way the ground was darkening where he lay. Something hit her, shoving her sideways, and the ground spat up by her foot as the arc of the machine passed by.

She was tumbled over and over, a band of iron clamped around her waist. Then a slim weight pressed upon her, holding her down. A lilting voice in her ear, shouted above the noise. "Stay easy, you bloody fool!"

Christopher was lying across her, pressing her into the ground as he jerked his crossbow up and took aim. She struggled against him, trying to reach Alberon, and Christopher elbowed her hard in the ribs. "*Stay still!*" He took aim, fired, and Wynter looked up to witness one of the machine crew lurch back, Christopher's arrow jutting from his brow. There was a brief pause in the firing as the machine crew regrouped, and Christopher rolled onto his back, trying to reload.

Wynter began slithering beneath the smoke to Alberon.

"RAZI!" bellowed Christopher. "STOP!"

Wynter twisted, gaping back over her shoulder.

Running from the curled body of the King, Razi had leapt onto his horse. With a cry, he pulled the terrified animal around, and just as the machine began to shoot again, galloped straight for it.

Wynter lurched to her feet in horror. Christopher, still lying on his back, took aim and fired. Another of the machine crew fell and the machine temporarily dipped its nose, shooting aimlessly into the earth. Men who had been working in the background ran forward with the fresh-loaded barrel-ring, heaved it into the ready position, then took their fallen comrades' place. They pulled the muzzle around to aim at Razi and fired.

Razi kept going. Wynter saw shots tug his tunic. Saw one shred the corner of his doctor's bag. Razi leaned forward in the saddle. He settled against the horse's neck, and Wynter realised he was going to try and jump the wall.

She began to run, waving her arms. "Stop firing!" she screamed. "Stop firing!"

Behind her, Christopher leapt to his feet and took aim again. His bolt clattered harmlessly against the metal carriage of the machine, and the men swung the weapon in response and drew down. Wynter skid to a halt as the gun's multiple eyes turned to stare at her.

The machine fired *BAM BAM BAM*, the shots running

towards her in a straight line. She leapt aside. The ground puffed by her foot. Shots cut a path from her to Christopher.

"GET DOWN!" she screamed.

He did not get down. Instead he stood, legs akimbo, slapped the bow to his shoulder and fired once more. A gunner sprouted an arrow from his chest and fell from sight. Christopher went to reload. The last round hit him. He dropped, and the machine fell silent as it ran out of shots.

In the ringing silence, Christopher curled on the ground, his eyes bulging, his hands clenched around his thigh. Blood poured from between his fingers. Wynter skid to his side, snatching her scarf from her neck, and wrapped it tightly around his wound.

"You fool!" she cried, knotting the scarf. "You fool!"

"Razi!" he yelled, struggling to see over her shoulder. "Stop!"

The men at the machine were scrabbling to reload. Frantically they hauled the lever to release the spent barrel-ring and allowed the next one to clang into place. All the time, Razi was thundering towards them. He shouted, "*Hup*" and his huge mare launched from the ground. There was silence as she tucked her legs and sailed across the tumbled remains of the wall. Rider and horse trailed ribbons of smoke behind them as if they were made of cloud, descended from the sky.

At the sight of all that great weight of horseflesh bearing down on them, the terrified men lifted the muzzle of the reloaded gun. But it was too late, and as they released their first shots, Razi and his beautiful horse crashed down on top of them. Wynter howled in despair as gun, men and horse toppled sideways in a horrible screaming tangle and fell behind the wall.

"Razi!" yelled Christopher.

Wynter staggered to her feet and stumbled forwards through the smoke. Within the ruins, Razi's big mare was kicking and neighing, trying hard to gain her feet. There was a man screaming in there somewhere, and Wynter was sure he was caught beneath machine and horse, that massive weight grinding him against the ground. Suddenly, and with a huge surging effort, the mare lurched upright. Clumsy, staggering, the big animal managed to haul herself from the wreckage of the machine and over the wall. Clattering her way across the uneven scatter of rocks, she sank to her knees on the grass and toppled to her side, shuddering in agony and fear. She was a terrible mess, her lovely body torn, her legs ruined. Wynter staggered past her, blinking against the tears and the smoke. That poor man's screaming ceased abruptly. Without his voice it was very quiet. Out of sight behind the wall, someone began a piteous moaning.

Wynter dropped to her hands and knees and began an awkward clamber across the fallen stones, wanting and not wanting to see what lay on the other side.

It took a moment for her to register a man's hoarse voice, calling over and over on the battlefield behind her. "Alberon! Alberon!"

She paused and looked back. Jonathon, the arrow still jutting from his shoulder, was staggering towards his son's body.

As the King lurched past, Christopher pulled himself to his elbows and twisted anxiously to look over his shoulder. Sólmundr was carrying Hallvor's body across the field towards them, his face streaming with tears. The warrior strode through knee deep smoke, his blood-soaked friend held out before him like an offering. Hallvor's head lolled in the crook of his arm, her long hair hanging to the ground. Mary stumbled along behind, her hand knotted in Sól's tunic, her eyes fixed on the healer's lifeless face. "*Tá sí marbh!*" cried Sól. "*Tá Hally marbh!*" and Wynter had no doubt in her mind that Hallvor was dead.

Padua: Five Years Later

The little boy ran, fear and excitement spurring him on. It was the first time he had been allowed to travel this journey alone and the city had never seemed so big or so crowded. He clutched the crackling parchment note to his chest as he dodged through the heedless citizens, his small feet flying in their green leather boots.

Breaking from the gloom of a crowded arcade, he emerged into the harsh light and sun-blasted stillness of the big piazza. It was midday and the open spaces were relatively deserted. Even the shadows stayed close to the feet of the buildings, waiting for the heat to pass.

Pigeons scattered from the uneven ground as the boy skirted the bronze statue of the Man On His Horse. *Honeycat*, his mama called him. That always made the little boy smile; he loved the taste of the word in his mouth. *Honeycat*. It seemed such an odd name for so imposing a man.

As he jogged past, the little boy glanced up at the statue. He loved the man's horse, he loved its wide, strong neck, he loved its knotted tail. Though, like his father, the little boy disapproved of the rider's spurs. He never failed to wince at the sight of them, and shake his little head. A good rider should have no need of such a brutal tool.

The sun tyrannised the open air, hot as a furnace, and the little boy hurried across the piazza and into the protective shadows thrown by Il Santo. He raced along the smooth stone walls of the Basilica—past the first little door, past the great big door, past the second little door—and then out into the sunshine again before ducking into the shelter of another *sottoportego* and down a dim and quiet arcade street. It was time for siesta, and work on the new city walls had paused for an hour or so. In the absence of the usual dust and noise, the entire world seemed to be napping.

The little boy heard the end of lessons bell just as he turned the corner and began to run down the sunny little lane that led to the compound and the site of the new hospital. Free from their classes, the bigger children began to trickle from the arched gateway, and the little boy slowed his progress, pretending to be preoccupied. It was not that he was afraid of the bigger children. Of course he wasn't. But there was something about this *particular* group—a certain pride, a certain lack of courtliness—that made him uncomfortable. It was unfair to them, he knew; they had never done him harm. But still, he hung back.

The bigger children walked together, talking softly in their own strange language, their slates clutched at their chests, their satchels on their backs. The little boy was just about to crouch and pretend to tie his lace, when a familiar figure came strolling out amongst them, and the little boy straightened with a grin and ran on.

"Good afternoon, Anthony!" he called in his clear little voice. "Are you done your alphabets for today?"

The young servant turned and the little boy took great delight at the surprise and concern in his face, "My Lord!" he cried. "Hast thou come here all alone?"

The little boy tutted. "I am well able to cross the city alone, Anthony. I am not a baby, you know."

Anthony hefted his satchel onto his shoulder and scanned the arcaded streets behind the boy. "Does thy father know thou hast…?" Something caught his eye and he smiled. "Of course, my Lord," he said, looking back to the child and bowing. "I do keep forgetting how big thou art."

The child glanced suspiciously behind him, but there was no one there.

Anthony's friends stopped to wait for him at the corner of the street. An equal mixture of boys and girls, they paused in a bright splash of sunshine, and it gleamed on their silver bracelets and shone in their long hair. They smiled, but did not bow. The little boy had long ago given up taking offence at this. After all, as his mama always said, a nod was as good as a bow where these folks were concerned.

"I have a message," he said importantly, holding the parchment out to show them. "Papa entrusted it to me!" Anthony's friends raised their eyebrows and made impressed noises, and the little boy turned back to his servant. "You may go with your companions if you wish, Anthony," he allowed. "I shall not need you till much, *much* later. I am well able to return home alone, once my work is done."

"Thank you very much, my Lord," said Anthony, his lips tugging at the corners.

Bowing with a rather amused solemnity, the young servant strolled off to join his friends. They glanced back at the small child with undisguised fondness, waving and smiling with quite an appalling lack of propriety. The child watched them go with a patient shake of his little head. Anthony was a very good servant—indeed he could almost be called a friend—but on occasion he did keep rather dubious company.

Glancing behind him once more—there was most definitely

no one there—the little boy ran beneath the sandstone gate arch and down the lane that led to the compound's stable yards. The sound of hooves on cobbles came to him as he rounded the corner, and he paused at the sight of the chief of horses leading one of the Arabians across the yard. The little boy faltered for a moment in the shadows.

It was not that the little boy disliked the chief of horses. In fact, he liked him very much, but there was something about him that made the boy shy. It was hard to define. There were those terrible scars, of course, and his horribly accented Italian. But it had more to do with a strange feeling of *loss* that the little boy felt around this man. There was a sense of hidden grief to him that made the little boy feel sad. He was often filled with the desire to clamber up the man's wiry body and hug his scarred neck, but the man's noble reserve made such a gesture seem inappropriate.

A familiar, nudging presence at the child's back made him turn and he was greeted with a blast of musty dog breath and a face full of slobbering kisses.

"Dog!" spluttered the little boy. "Stop at once! Or I shall be drowned!"

The hound, of course, declined to stop and the little boy abandoned the pretence at annoyance and embraced his shaggy neck, laughing. The huge creature snuffled down the collar of the child's tunic with great enthusiasm and the child giggled at his tickling whiskers.

"Boro," called the chief of horses. "Leave the lord be."

The great hound broke off his slavering attack and trotted over to his master. Nudging the man's hands and licking his scarred wrists, the dog rolled his eyes in adoration and whined like some ridiculously huge puppy.

"Bloody fool," growled his master. "I take back of my sword to you if you not behave." The dog grinned and yawned and flopped down into the dust, showing his belly for a scratching. The chief of horses sighed and shook his head, but crouched down to oblige nonetheless. "My Lord," he said, squinting across at the little boy, "you come for to take out your horse? It a little hot for riding yet, *nach ea*? Maybe you wait for evening and then I bring you down along the river?"

"I am on business, Freeman! I have come all the way here with a message for the Protector Lady!" He held out the note with great pride.

The chief of horses' face drew down in concern. "You come alone?" he said. "Across the city? Your father knows this?"

"Papa *sent* me, Freeman. I am quite old enough, you know, to deliver a message."

As the child spoke, the man's eyes drifted to the corner. Whatever he saw there wiped away his grim concern and his weathered face softened into amusement. The child snapped his head around just in time to glimpse his father's aide duck back behind the wall.

"Marcello!" cried the little boy. "I *see* you!" He stamped his foot in rage. "OH!" he cried, "Papa sent you to follow me! After he promised I was to do this *alone*!"

The dapper little man stepped out into the sunlight. He smiled, and tilted his head. "I assure you, my Lord, your father did not send me. The Lord Razi has absolute faith in you, and trusts entirely that you shall deliver his message. I am here on separate business and it is but a coincidence that we have arrived together."

The little boy glared at him. Marcello Tutti spread his hands in all innocence. "I swear by the Holy Mother of Jesus, my Lord,

I am here for my own ends." His dark brown eyes lifted and met those of the chief of horses. "Is that not so, Sólmundr?" he said softly.

The chief of horses ducked his head, and the small boy frowned curiously up at him. "You have gone very pink, Freeman," he observed. "You really should not go about without your hat, you know. Papa says the midday sun can quite fry a man's brains."

For some reason, this made Marcello Tutti chuckle, and the chief of horses went even pinker.

The child looked from one to the other of them in confusion. "Um," he said, waving the paper, "I must deliver Papa's message. Now you *must* not follow me on the way home, Signor Tutti! I am very able to travel alone, you know!"

The Italian bowed his agreement, and the child turned in haughty pride and walked off, heading for the schoolhouse and the building site beyond. A soft conversation rose up behind him as he trotted across the yard. Marcello Tutti's cultured voice, and the chief of horses' quite awful but warmly rasped Italian.

"You owe me a game of chess, my friend."

"I not play no longer, not till you agree to be honest."

"I will be honest. From now on, I will be unflinchingly honest. If you win, it shall be upon your own merits and not because I allow it."

There was a brief silence. At the corner, the child glanced back at the two men. Marcello Tutti was squinting up at the chief of horses, a shy anxiety clear in his face.

"So...I may visit tonight?" he asked. "After I have seen the Lady Mary home from mass?"

The chief of horses gazed down at the dark little man, and something in his expression made the child wait. He wanted to hear the man's answer for some reason. For some reason it felt very important that he know it.

The Chief of Horses reached and plucked something from Marcello Tutti's shoulder. "You got a leaf there," he said gravely. Then he met Marcello's eyes and grinned his rare and charming gap-toothed grin. "I see you tonight," he rasped. "After you finish with your religions. You be honest, and we soon see who wins the game."

Marcello Tutti relaxed into a smile. "Tonight," he agreed, and the little boy ducked around the corner, satisfied that all was well between his two friends.

Down the flagstone path and into the shadow of the schoolhouse. All was still and quiet now that the Protector Lord had closed up for the day, and the little boy's footsteps echoed from the whitewashed schoolhouse wall, its blue painted snakes and bears watching as he ran past.

Then around into the resinous smell and sawdust of the hospital site, and he came to a halt.

The great timber frame of the building itself was almost complete and it soared above him, cutting the seamless blue sky into mathematical slices. All was colour—the red timber, the dusty golden sunshine, the purple shadows. All was stillness. The heady, living smell of fresh-sawn wood and shavings spiced the air.

The little boy gazed upwards, listening.

There was a light thud as something hit the ground behind him and a warm voice lilted in his ear. "How do, Isaac? Have you come to learn your ABCs?"

The child squealed with delight as he was swept up by strong arms. He was instantly engulfed in that familiar spicy scent as the Protector Lord swung him onto his slim back. "You want to go visit the lass?" he asked, smiling sideways over his shoulder as Isaac knotted his little hands beneath his chin.

"Yes, please."

"Don't choke me on the way up, mind. And don't let go! I'll never hear the end of it if you plummet to your doom!" Tucking his long hair into his collar so that it wouldn't get into the little boy's face, the Protector Lord grabbed a rung on the first ladder and began to clamber, hand over scarred hand, to the top of the scaffolding.

Secure in the absolute certainty that he wouldn't fall, Isaac clenched his legs around the Protector Lord's waist and rested his chin on his shoulder. The lord's necklace tickled the little boy's wrist as they climbed up and up, and Isaac shifted so that he could watch it glinting in the sun.

Isaac loved that necklace. Recently, he had succeeded in counting all the ornaments upon it. He had numbered them all—twenty-four warm, amber stones, sixteen fangs of silver, eight of gold. The Protector Lord had been delighted with him. He had proclaimed him *excellent good at the 'rithmatics* and asked when he could hire him as a teacher at the school. The Protector Lady had beamed with pride, but she had not allowed Isaac take a turn wearing the necklace. It was the Protector Lord's, she had said. He had waited too long for it. No one else must ever wear it.

Up they went, and up, until they were high above the sleepy towers and cupolas of the sun-baked city. The Protector Lord was not even slightly breathless when they finally breasted the rough planking of the uppermost tier and he stooped to let the little boy slither from his shoulders.

"Christopher Garron! You best not have brought that child up on your back!" The Protector Lady poked her head out from the

A-frame of the hospital roof and glared. Her crotchety old grey cat slipped carefully from her shoulder and slunk across the red timbers like smoke. He looked his human companions up and down with the usual disdain, settled himself in a patch of warm light, and closed his beautiful green eyes. His name was Coriolanus, and he was so old and threadbare that Isaac thought he resembled nothing more than a dusty grey rag curled carelessly onto the timbers.

"What did I tell you!" cried the Protector Lady, as she clambered from the timbers and jumped onto the scaffold. "The boy comes up in a basket or he doesn't come up at all! Isaac Kingsson? Do you want your good mother hunting the Protector Lord down and beheading him in a violent rage? Can I not at least depend that *you* shall keep a sensible head on your shoulders?"

The Protector Lord just grinned and leaned recklessly out from the scaffold, suspended above the sheer drop by his heels and one misshapen hand. His hair came loose from his collar and swung behind him, a dark raven's wing against the blue sky as he turned his face to the sun and shut his eyes.

"Oh hush, lass," he murmured. "Sure isn't the lad as nimble as a little green monkey."

At the sight of him hanging over the drop, the Protector Lady went a little pale. She placed her hand upon a strut as if by steadying herself she might also steady him. If Isaac had not known her better he would think she was afraid she might fall. But of course he *did* know better; the Protector Lady was famous for clambering the scaffolds, quick as any ship's boy. She was never afraid she would fall. The little boy grinned as the lady called softly to her husband.

"Christopher," she said, "come in." Her voice was so low that Isaac was surprised the Protector Lord heard her. But the lord's

clear grey eyes opened immediately, and he ducked his head to
look in at her. "Come in," she said.

The Protector Lord swung in under the bar and landed on the
wide scaffold boards with a bounce. He winked at Isaac.
"Women," he said.

"Huh," she said, releasing her hold on the strut and clearing
her throat. "If you fall and sully all my lovely wood, your ghost
will be mopping up the mess for all eternity."

"I have no doubt," murmured the Protector Lord. He crossed his
arms and lounged against the beams, smiling tenderly at his wife.

The Protector Lady came and crouched by Isaac. She grinned
at him and Isaac grinned back. He knew very few women who
would crouch down like that. It had to do with her clothes, he
supposed. "How do, little pud," she said, tapping his nose and
pushing back his sandy hair. As usual, her own hair had come
loose of its long plait and was tumbled around her shoulders in
messy auburn waves. Her face was a sunburst of ochre freckles
after the long hot summer. "Is your dad with you?"

"Papa was called to the university very early, Aunty Wyn.
They are to begin lessons again next week, you know! There is
much to do."

The Protector Lady smiled. "Your mama must be very happy
that she can resume her studies."

"Oh, yes, though she tires of always sitting behind the curtain, it quite obscures her view of the tutors!"

"She should bring a scissors and cut a damned big hole in it,"
grunted the Protector Lord. "She will continue to press for
recognition?"

"Oh yes," nodded Isaac.

"I despair of them ever granting her the blue robe," sighed the
Lady.

"That don't take her talents away," said the Protector Lord. "It don't make her any less learned, just because they refuse her a doctorate!"

"Papa says Mama is quite the best person he has ever met for cutting open and sewing shut a patient! He has crowned her the Lady Mary, Mistress of the Scalpel, Master of his Heart!"

The lord and lady laughed in delight, and Isaac, very pleased with himself, thrust the now crumpled message out before him. "I have brought this!" he said. "It is from Papa. He entrusted it to me!"

The Protector Lady eyed it dubiously. "Isaac," she said, "if your father continues to expand upon his plans, this hospital will never be built! Please tell me he has not sent you with yet another extension to the wards or more storage for the bleeding room or some manner of new dissection chamber."

The child laughed. "No, Protector Lady, it is news of the baby!"

The Protector Lord straightened. "What news?" he said.

"I do not know. Papa read it, handed it to Mama, kissed her and left for the university. He entrusted me to take it to you. He said he will see you soon."

"How did he seem?" asked the Protector Lady, taking the message and clutching it in her hands. "Was...was he sad?"

"No, lady!" cried the child in surprise. "Of course not! Sad! How silly! He was just...Papa! Busy. Smiling. Just Papa!"

The Protector Lady opened the message and scanned its contents. "It is from Alberon," she cried. "Oh, it is a boy! Born last month!" She looked up at the Protector Lord and quoted from the letter. "He says the child is *a fine, bawling manling. I cannot wait until I have done overseeing the new fleet and can get around to buying him a horse...*" She read on in silence and her smile faltered. "Oh," she whispered. "Oh." Her eyes filled with tears. "The babe is to be called Oliver."

There was a small moment of quiet. Then the Protector Lord said dryly, "An unusual enough choice." The lady met his eye.

Isaac frowned. The Protector Lord's bitter expression was as difficult to understand as the lady's tears.

"Ain't Jonathon afraid what people might think?" said the lord. "Naming his new boy after the man what almost brought his kingdom down?"

"Christopher," whispered the Protector Lady. "Don't. You know someone had to take the blame. Better someone already beyond pain than those left alive."

The Protector Lord tutted and turned to look out at the city. Behind Isaac, Coriolanus suddenly rose to his feet, muttered something about *the fickle fortunes of man*, and slunk away. The Protector Lady watched his stiff progress through the slats of sunlight and shade until he had moved out of sight behind the timbers, then she sat looking down at her hands, her face grave. The silence became itchy and uncomfortable.

Isaac squirmed. "Papa...Papa seems most *pleased* to have a new brother," he ventured.

The lady took a deep breath and sniffed. "Aye!" she said. She shook herself, then waved the letter cheerfully in his face. "And you have a new uncle, little pud! How wonderful for you! Certainly the Royal Prince Alberon is delighted...he says you shall both have to take the little chap fishing whenever you get around to visiting your grandfather's kingdom!"

"I should very much like that!"

The Protector Lady dragged Isaac onto her knee and tickled him until he shrieked.

"And what of Queen Marguerite?" asked the Protector Lord quietly.

The lady subsided against the scaffold bars, the little boy cradled fondly in her arms. "Gone back home already," she said. "She took but two weeks' rest after the birth, then headed North to finish her campaign against the Haun. Apparently she and Jonathon have decided this child shall be a Southland's Prince, by dint of his being first-born."

Christopher sighed, shook his head, then spread his hands and laughed. "Why not!" he said. "It's as good a way to choose as any, I guess."

"I doubt Jonathon will regret his darling wife's absence," said the lady dryly. "One could hardly call their union a love match." She rose to her feet, lifting Isaac on her strong shoulders. "Speaking of which, a certain husband of *mine* promised coffee and manchet once his students had gone! Perhaps there's something wrong with my nose, but I don't smell coffee! Where's my manchet, little man?" She pretended to root in Isaac's coat. "Have you hid it? Have you? Is it in your britches?"

Isaac squirmed and shrieked and wriggled. Finally the lady thrust him from her with a weary sigh. "Here," she said, "you will just have to cook this piglet. It's all I can find to eat, I'm afraid."

The Protector Lord swung the little boy onto his back with an order to *hold tight*, then launched himself over the edge. Isaac grinned at the lady's faint *Jesu!* He glanced up to see her looking over the edge, shaking her head at them as they descended the ladder. She was all lit up against the very bright blue of the sky, her untidy red hair ruffled and streaming out like ribbons on the hot breeze. As he watched her, she leant her elbows on the scaffold bar, laced her work-hardened hands and gazed out across the huge and troubled magnificence of the city. Her face fell into that grave kind of watchfulness so familiar to him, and he regarded her with all the love possible in his small and happy heart.

The Protector Lord climbed down and down. Just before he reached the final levels, where the roof would no longer be in their line of sight, Isaac saw the Protector Lady catch sight of something down by the stables and straighten. She smiled, raising her hand, and Isaac's heart leapt because he knew *that* look too—that beaming anticipatory grin. His father was coming! The lady must have seen him walking through the gate.

Just before the Protector Lord swung them both in and onto the ground, Isaac saw the Protector Lady swing herself out onto the ladder and begin to follow them down. The little boy laughed and slithered from the lord's shoulders. He hit the ground running, determined to beat them all to it and meet his father halfway.

Glossary

The language used by the Merron in this book is equivalent to modern day Irish. The most commonly used words and phrases are translated here.

Note: Apparent inconsistencies in the spelling of some words, like "Domhan" and "Domhain" relate to the rules of Irish grammar.

agus—and (often abbreviated to *'gus*)
agus é ag rith—and he's running
a luch—mouse (when addressing someone as "mouse") *luch* on its own just means "a mouse"
an Domhan—the World (the Merron's version of God)
aoire—shepherd
Aoire an Domhain—Shepherd of the World
aonach—a fair
cad a rinne tú?—what did you do?
cad é?—what is it? What? What's happening?
cac/caic—shit/s
cén fáth na saighdiúirí—why the soldiers? What are the soldiers doing here?
ciúnas!—silence!
cneasaí—healer

coimhthíoch—stranger

cosc ort nóiméad—stop (yourself) for a moment

croí-eile—other-heart

cúnna—hounds

fan—stay, wait

fan nóiméad—wait a moment

fear óg thú, a Choinín. Tá neart ama agat—you are a young man, Coinín. You have plenty of time.

filid—ancient noble and hereditary title. A filid would be responsible for preserving the history of his people in oral form and then teaching it to the next generation. The preservation of history in its oral form was very much the traditional role, and any moves to write history down would have been frowned upon. The modern version of the word, *file*, has come to mean simply "poet."

go h-álainn—beautiful

iníon—daughter

iníon Ingrid an Fada—daughter of Ingrid an Fada

is mé atá ann!—it's me (I'm the one who's here)

luichín—little mouse

mac—son, son of (*mac* Oisín *an filid*, *as Tír na* Garron—son of Oisín *the poet*, from the land of Garron)

"Maidin Ór"—"Golden Morning"

mo mhuirnín—my beloved/sweetheart/darling

ná bac faoi, a chú—don't take any notice of them, hounds

ná bac faoí—don't bother about it (in the sense of "you're welcome")

nach ea, mo ghadhar?—isn't that so, my (hunting) dog

na Cúnna Faoil—the wolfhounds

níl iontu ach amadáin—they are only fools

slán, a stór—goodbye, dear

tá go maith?—all right?

tá na Haun ag imeacht—the Haun are leaving

tarraingígí siar!—pull back (plural)

tar anseo!—come here!

tar ar ais gan mhoill—hurry back; come back without delay

tá sí marbh!—she is dead!

tóg go bog é—take it easy

tóin caca—shit arse

Acknowledgments

With huge thanks to Svetlana Pironko of Author Rights Agency for her protection and guidance. A wonderful agent and friend. Also to my first publishers The O'Brien Press, who took a chance on me and have supported and helped me, and held my hand all through this adventure. In particular, thanks to Michael O'Brien for his fearlessness. Many thanks and much love to Sorcha De Francesco (Ní Chuimín) and Phil ó Cuimín, who gifted me their beautiful conversational Irish. Thanks to Pat Mullan, whose kindness and generosity of spirit opened a door I had begun to think was locked for good. Pat, I'll never be able to thank you enough. And always, thank you, Catherine and Roddy.

extras

orbit

meet the author

Celine Kiernan

Born and raised in Dublin, Ireland, CELINE KIERNAN has spent the majority of her working life in the film business, and her career as a classical feature animator spanned over seventeen years. Celine wrote her first novel at the age of eleven, and hasn't stopped writing or drawing since. She also has a peculiar weakness for graphic novels as, like animation, they combine the two things she loves to do the most: drawing and storytelling. Now, having spent most of her time working between Germany, Ireland and the USA, Celine is married and the bemused mother of two entertaining teens. She lives a peaceful life in the blissful countryside of Cavan, Ireland. Find out more about the author at www.celinekiernan.com.

introducing

If you enjoyed
THE REBEL PRINCE,
look out for

COLD MAGIC

Book 1 of The Spiritwalker Trilogy

by Kate Elliott

The history of the world begins in ice, and it will end in ice.

Or at least, that's how the dawn chill felt in the bedchamber as I shrugged out from beneath the cozy feather comforter under which my cousin and I slept. I winced as I set my feet on the brutally cold wood floor. Any warmth from last evening's fire was long gone. At this early hour, Cook would just be getting the kitchen's stove going again, two floors below. But last night I had slipped a book out of my uncle's parlor and brought it to read in my bedchamber by candlelight, even though we were expressly forbidden from doing so. He had even made us sign a little contract stating that we had permission to read my father's journals and the other books in the parlor as long as we stayed in the parlor and did not waste expensive candlelight to do so. I had to put the book back before he noticed it was gone, or the cold would be the least of my troubles.

After all the years sharing a bed with my cousin Beatrice, I knew Bee was such a heavy sleeper that I could have jumped up and down on the bed without waking her. I had tried it more than once. So I left her behind and picked out suitable clothing from the wardrobe: fresh drawers, two layers of stockings, and a knee-length chemise over which I bound a fitted wool bodice. I fumblingly laced on two petticoats and a cutaway overskirt, blowing on my fingers to warm them, and over it buttoned a tight-fitting, hip-length jacket cut in last year's fashionable style.

With my walking boots and the purloined book in hand, I cracked the door and ventured out onto the second-floor landing to listen. No noise came from my aunt and uncle's chamber, and the little girls, in the nursery on the third floor above, were almost certainly still asleep. But the governess who slept upstairs with them would be rousing soon, and my uncle and his factotum were usually up before dawn. They were the ones I absolutely had to avoid.

I crept down to the first-floor landing and paused there, peering over the railing to survey the empty foyer on the ground floor below. Next to me, a rack of swords, the badge of the Hassi Barahal family tradition, lined the wall. Alongside the rack stood our house mirror, in whose reflection I could see both myself and the threads of magic knit through the house. Uncle and Aunt were important people in their own way. As local representatives of the far-flung Hassi Barahal clan, they discreetly bought and sold information, and in return might receive such luxuries as a cawl—a protective spell bound over the house by a drua—or door and window locks sealed by a blacksmith to keep out unwanted visitors.

I closed my eyes and listened down those threads of magic to trace the stirring of activity in the house: our man-of-all-work, Pompey, priming the pump in the garden; Cook and Aunt Tilly in the kitchen cracking eggs and wielding spoons as they began the day's baking. A whiff of smoke tickled my nose. The tread of feet marked the approach of the maidservant, Callie, from the back. By the front door, she began sweeping the foyer. I stood perfectly still, as if I were part of the railing, and she did not look up as she swept back the way she had come until she was out of my sight.

Abruptly, my uncle coughed behind me.

I whirled, but there was no one there, just the empty passage and the stairs leading up to the bedchambers and attic beyond. Two closed doors led off the first-floor landing: one to the parlor and one to my uncle's private office, where we girls were never allowed to set foot. I pressed my ear against the office door to make sure he was in his office and not in the parlor. My hand was beginning to ache from clutching my boots and the book so tightly.

"You have no appointment," he said in his gruff voice, pitched low because of the early hour. "My factotum says he did not let you in by the back door."

"I came in through the window, maester." The voice was husky, as if scraped raw from illness. "My apologies for the intrusion, but my business is a delicate one. I am come from overseas. Indeed, I just arrived, on the airship from Expedition."

"The airship! From Expedition!"

"You find it incredible, I'm sure. Ours is only the second successful transoceanic flight."

"Incredible," murmured Uncle.

Incredible? I thought. *It was astounding.* I shifted so as to hear better as Uncle went on.

"But you'll find a mixed reception for such innovations here in Adurnam."

"We know the risks. But that is not my personal business. I was given your name before I left Expedition. I was told we have a mutual interest in certain Iberian merchandise."

Uncle's voice got sharper without getting louder. "The war is over."

"The war is never over."

"Are you behind the current restlessness infecting the city's populace? Poets declaim radical ideas on the street, and the prince dares not silence them. The common folk are like maddened wasps, buzzing, eager to sting."

"I've nothing to do with any of that," insisted the mysterious visitor. *Too bad!* I thought. "I was told you would be able to help me write a letter, in code."

My heart raced, and I held my breath so as not to miss a word. Was I about to tumble onto a family secret that Bee and I were not yet old enough to be trusted with? But Uncle's voice was clipped and disapproving, and his answer sadly prosaic.

"I do not write letters in code. Your sources are out of date. Also, I am legally obligated to stay well away from any Iberian merchandise of the kind you may wish to discuss."

"Will you close your eyes when the rising light marks the dawn of a new world?"

Uncle's exasperation was as sharp as a fire being extinguished by a blast of damp wind, but my curiosity was aflame. "Aren't those the words being said by the radicals' poet, the one who declaims every evening on Northgate Road? I say, we should fear the end of the orderly world we know. We should fear being swallowed by storm and flood until we are drowned in a watery abyss of our own making."

"Spoken like a Phoenician," said the visitor with a low laugh that made me pinch my lips together in anger.

"We are called Kena'ani, not Phoenician," retorted my uncle stiffly.

"I will call you whatever you wish, if you will only aid me with what I need, as I was assured you could do."

"I cannot. That is the end of it."

The visitor sighed. "If you will not aid our cause out of loyalty, perhaps I can offer you money. I observe your threadbare furnishings and the lack of a fire in your hearth on this bitter-cold dawn. A man of your importance ought to be using fine beeswax rather than cheap tallow candles. Better yet, he ought to have a better design of oil lamp or even the new indoor gaslight to burn away the shadows of night. I have gold. I suspect you could use it to sweeten the trials of your daily life, in exchange for the information I need."

I expected Uncle to lose his temper—he so often did—but he did not raise his voice. "I and my kin are bound by hands stronger than my own, by an unbreakable contract. *I cannot help you.* Please go, before you bring trouble to this house, where it is not wanted."

"So be it. I'll take my leave."

The latch scraped on the back window that overlooked the narrow garden behind our house. Hinges creaked, for this time of year the window was never oiled or opened. An agile person could climb from the window out onto a stout limb to the wall; Bee and I had done it often enough. I heard the window thump closed.

Uncle said, "We'll need those locks looked at by a blacksmith. I can't imagine how anyone could have gotten that window open when we were promised no one but a cold mage could break the seal. Ei! Another expense, when we have little enough money for heat and light with winter blowing in. He spoke truly enough."

I had not heard Factotum Evved until he spoke from the office, somewhere near Uncle. "Do you regret not being able to aid him, Jonatan?"

"What use are regrets? We do what we must."

"So we do," agreed Evved. "Best if I go make sure he actually leaves and doesn't lurk around to break in and steal something later."

His tread approached the door on which I had forgotten I was leaning. I bolted to the parlor door, opened it, and slipped inside, shutting the door quietly just as I heard the other door being opened. He walked on. He hadn't heard or seen me.

It was one of my chief pleasures to contemplate the mysterious visitors who came and went and make up stories about them. Uncle's business was the business of the Hassi Barahal clan. Still being underage, Bee and I were not privy to their secrets, although all adult Hassi Barahals who possessed a sound mind and body owed the family their service. All people are bound by ties and obligations, and the most binding ties of all are those between kin. That was why I kept stealing books out of the parlor and returning them. For the only books I ever took were my father's journals. Didn't I have some right to them, being that they, and I, were all that remained of him?

Feeling my way by touch, I set my boots by a chair and placed the journal on the big table. Then I crept to the bow window to haul aside the heavy winter curtains so I would have light. All eight mending baskets were set neatly in a row on the narrow side table, for the women of the house—Aunt Tilly, me, Beatrice, her little sisters, our governess, Cook, and Callie—would sit in the parlor in the evening and sew while Uncle or Evved read aloud from a book and Pompey trimmed the candle wicks. But it was the bound book of slate tablets resting beneath my mending basket that drew my horrified gaze. How had I forgotten that? I had an essay due today for my academy college seminar on history, and I hadn't yet finished it.

Last night, I had tucked fingerless writing gloves and a slate pencil on top of my mending basket. I drew on the gloves and pulled the bound tablets out from under the basket. With a sigh, I sat down at the big table with the slate pencil in my left hand. But as I began reading back through the words to find my place, my mind leaped back to the conversation I had just overheard. *The rising light marks the dawn of a new world,* the visitor had said; *or the end of the orderly world we know,* my uncle had retorted.

I shivered in the cold room. *The war is never over.* That had sounded ominous, but such words did not surprise me: Europa had fractured into multiple principalities, territories, lordships, and city-states after the collapse of the Roman Empire in the year 1000 and had stayed that way for the last eight hundred years and more; there was always a little war or border incident *somewhere.* But worlds do not begin and end in the steady mud of daily life, even if that mud involves too many petty wars, cattle raids, duels, feuds, legal suits, and shaky alliances for even a scholar to remember. I could not help but think the two men were speaking in a deeper code, wreathed in secrets. I was sure that somewhere out there lay hidden the story of what we are not meant to know.

The history of the world begins in ice, and it will end in ice. So sing the Celtic bards and Mande djeliw of the north whose songs tell us where we came from and what ties and obligations bind us. The Roman historians, on the other hand, claimed that fire erupting from beneath the bones of the earth formed us and will consume us in the end, but who can trust what the Romans say? Everything they said was used to justify their desire to make war and conquer other people who were doing nothing but minding their own business. The scribes of my own Kena'ani people, named Phoenicians by the lying Romans, wrote that in the beginning existed water without limit, boundless and still. When currents stirred the waters, they birthed conflict and out of conflict the world was created. What will come at the end, the ancient sages added, cannot be known even by the gods.

The rising light marks the dawn of a new world. I'd heard those words before. The Northgate Poet used the phrase as part of his nightly declamation when he railed against princes and lords and rich men who misused their rank and wealth for selfish purposes. But I had recently read a similar phrase in my father's journals. Not the one I'd taken out last night. I'd sneaked that one upstairs because I had wanted to reread an amusing story he'd told about encountering a saber-toothed cat in a hat shop. Somewhere in his journals, my father had recounted a story about the world's beginning, or about something that had happened "at the dawn of the world." And there was light. Or was it lightning?

I rose and went to the bookshelves that filled one wall of the parlor: my uncle's precious collection. My father's journals held pride of place at the center. I drew my fingers along the numbered volumes until I reached the one I wanted. The big bow window had a window seat furnished with a long plush seat cushion, and I settled there with my back padded by the thick winter curtain I'd opened. No fire crackled in the circulating stove set into the hearth, as it did after supper when we sewed. The chill air breathed through the paned windows. I pulled the curtains around my body for warmth and angled the book so the page caught what there was of cloud-shrouded light on an October morning promising yet another freezing day.

In the end I always came back to my father's journals. Except for the locket I wore around my neck, they were all I had left of him and my mother. When I read the words he had written long ago, it was as if he were speaking to me, in his cheerful voice that was now only a faint memory from my earliest years.

Here, little cat, I've found a story for you, he would say as I snuggled into his lap, squirming with anticipation. *Keep your lips sealed. Keep your ears open. Sit very, very still so no one will see you. It will be like you're not here but in another place, a place very far away that's a secret between you and me and your mama. Here we go!*